# VECTOR ZERO

# VECTOR ZERO

BRYAN McBEE

*atmosphere press*

Published by Atmosphere Press

Cover design by Matthew Fielder



atmospherepress.com

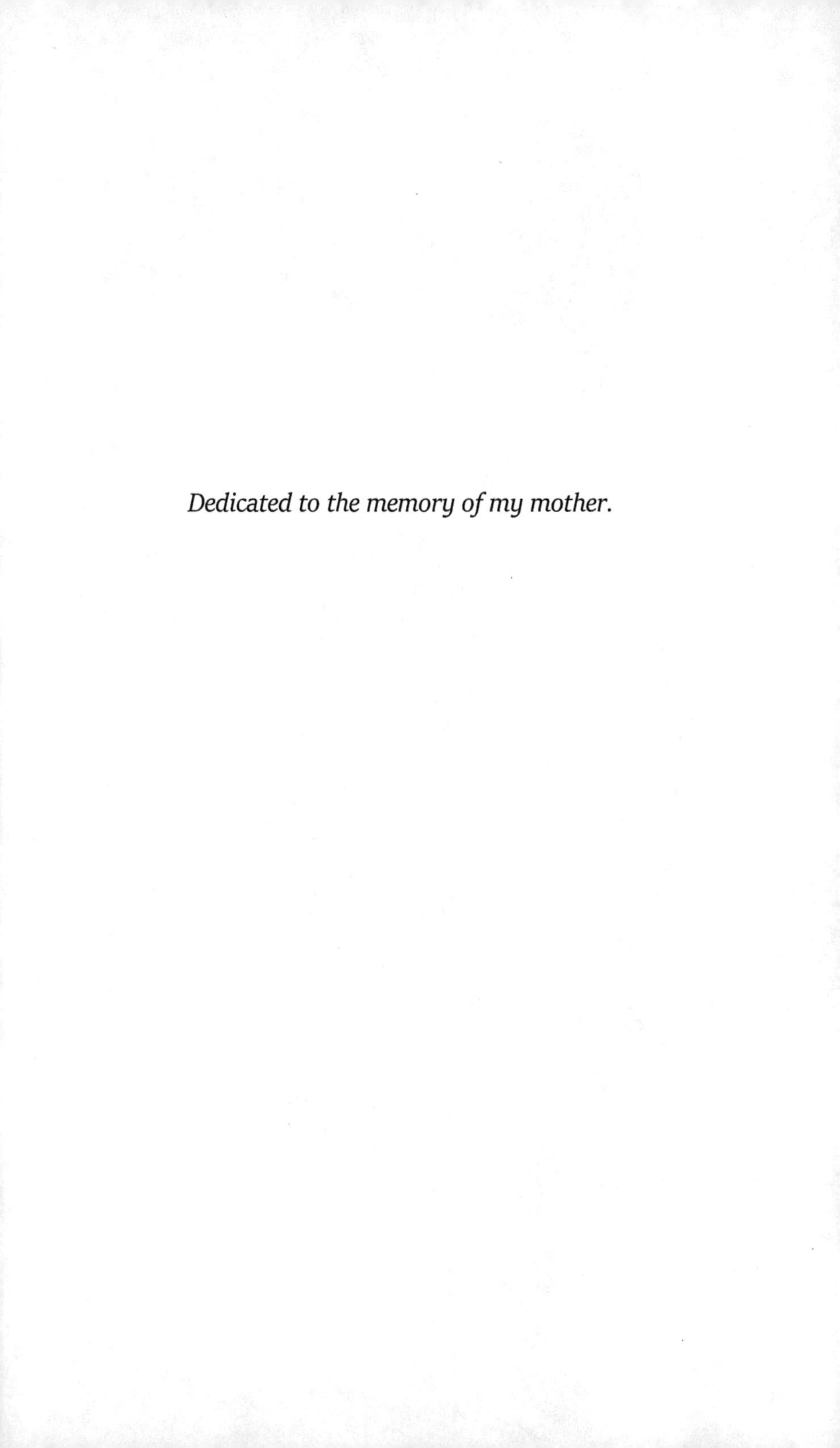

*Dedicated to the memory of my mother.*

# Prologue

The storm promised to be particularly brutal, as it advanced like a wave over the countryside. Hovering at just over six thousand feet, the dark gray mass of accumulated clouds looked ominous, blotting out the wan winter sunlight with its bulk. The first in a series of heavy winter storms since the start of the new year, the heavy cloud layer delivered torrential snowfall beneath its shoals. The temperature dropped quickly, almost bottoming out some of the cheaper garden thermometers.

Shelly Christianson noted the clouds fast approaching while she was leaving for work. As she closed and locked her front door, she glanced up at the darkening sky, blinked once and nodded to herself, thankful she'd had the forethought to stock up on ice melt for the driveway and chains for her Bronco. Without giving the storm another thought, she got in her truck and drove to the hospital to start her shift. The ground beneath the roiling clouds was covered in white, as though from a giant's paint brush. Another stormfront advanced beneath the heavy winter weather. This one travelled fast along the highway towards Shelly's hometown,

Harper's Glenn. When it hit the little town, this storm promised to push Shelly, and all the other residents, to the limits of their physical and emotional endurance and beyond.

For now, however, things were peaceful. People were getting up for work and going about their day like normal, blissfully ignorant of the hell headed their way.

# January 7th

The wind blew hard and cold, gusting in the storm-sodden night. Flurries formed an impenetrable wall of white against the glare of the headlights. Thick, heavy flakes reduced visibility to scant yards ahead. The road was covered in a thick carpet of new snow. It was the first heavy snowfall of the year and it was already shaping up to be a small blizzard. Nevertheless, Martin Fallon pressed the accelerator as close to the floor as he dared, coaxing as much speed from the ten-year-old beige Volvo as he could. Every so often the tires slipped and went squirrely, forcing him to cut his speed to retrieve control. Unaccustomed to driving in such conditions, it took every ounce of his concentration just to keep his car on the road.

*Perfect*, Fallon thought, when the first fat flakes touched his windshield an hour prior as he raced down the narrow, two-lane blacktop. *Just what I need right now. Do you hate me, God? Is there something I've done to upset you lately?*

Of course, there were probably many things Fallon had done to piss off the Almighty. In placing this blizzard in his path, God was indicating that he was either angry with him or testing him. Fallon thought it was a test. That he was being forced to prove he was worthy of doing God's work. This snow was but one test of many. He also had to prove he was craftier and could outwit those who chased after him.

It was simple, if he could escape them, he passed the test. If not...

The consequences were dire enough; he put them out of his mind. "I won't go back," he muttered to the dim dashboard lights. "I can't. I won't. I won't!" He tightened his grip on the steering wheel and again pressed the accelerator a little closer to the floorboard.

He had to be bold if he wanted to shake his pursuers. Those who would stop at nothing, exhaust every means at their disposal, to see him captured and back in their clutches. Especially the colonel, that fucking Preston Aldridge. He was cunning and ruthless and hot on Fallon's trail. Fallon had to be quick to stay ahead of Colonel Aldridge and keep his freedom. If they caught up to him, all would be lost.

Shaking his head against these negative thoughts, Fallon continued speeding through the thick falling snow on chainless, balding tires. The speedometer needle hovered between fifty and fifty-five miles per hour. He pushed his luck through the bends, trusting fate to guide him safely through high-piled drifts. The nearly worthless tires on his stolen car slipped and skidded constantly as they crunched through the thickening layer of snow. The windshield wipers barely kept up against the flakes accumulating on the glass and Fallon worried that they might get stuck on the lump of snow growing at the bottom of the windshield. The radio didn't work, so the only music he had was the patter of snow hitting the roof as he drove.

A huge gust rocked the car sideways. Fallon overcorrected and nearly spun out. His breath caught, every muscle in his body clenched as he watched the Volvo's nose slew towards the guardrail. Just when Fallon thought he was going over the side, the tires found their grip and he straightened out of the slide. Once he had the Volvo moving in a straight line again, the tension drained from him, and he unclenched his teeth to take a deep, calming breath.

His heart hammered against his chest and stinging sweat trickled into his eyes, chilling him despite the blasting heater. If he continued at this insane speed, he would eventually end up a frozen smear down the highway shoulder. On the other hand, if he slowed down, his pursuers would close the distance between them. He could only assume they were already gaining on him. They would certainly be better equipped than he for this weather. The army had all sorts of vehicles and gear for moving quickly through all types of terrain and weather conditions. Fallon's only advantage lay in his head start. He could not afford to lose any time. Everything depended on his ability to stay as far away from them as possible.

Fallon consciously increased pressure on the gas pedal, forcing a few more miles per hour from the poor old car.

*Need to move faster*, he thought.

"Probably not a good idea in this," he said aloud.

Coming around a gentle right-hand curve, he drove into a thick drift, and the steering went soft in his hands. Before he could react, the tail end swung left, and he slid sideways towards a deep irrigation ditch paralleling the road. He let up off the gas, pumped the brakes, wrenched the wheel. As if in a dream, Fallon watched in helpless fear. As the car spun out of control, he saw the edge of the road and the deep culvert just beyond and nothing he did could prevent it.

The side of the car hit the guardrail and slammed him into his seatbelt hard enough to knock the wind out of him. With a shriek of metal scraping against metal, the Volvo thundered down the breakdown lane, kicking up dirty wakes of snow. Nothing but a thin barrier of sheet metal and wood separated him from the short, steep embankment on the other side. When he had traction again, he tramped down hard on the gas pedal. The tachometer and screaming engine told him he was taxing the old car too hard, but he didn't stop. He powered through the remainder of the slide and pulled away from the shoulder. Under control again, Fallon started to relax a little. That was too close for his comfort.

Feeling the pressure, he again pressed down on the accelerator. There was no other choice. Panting, he knew in his heart that God would see him through to the end, guiding him to freedom. He glanced down. The needle wavered dangerously around sixty.

He returned his attention to the road just as the tires lost their grip for the final time.

The rear end skittered left, right, left again. Fallon turned into the skid but couldn't correct quickly enough. Before he could react, he was through the guardrail, over the embankment and off the road.

The front bumper and most of the grill were torn away when he hit the bottom of the ditch going forty-five. The noise was incredible. Every seam and joint in the vehicle screamed in protest over the abuse. The car shuddered and rattled as it slammed up out of the irrigation culvert and then bounced from rut to rut over ice-crusted shrubs before finally hitting a waist-high snowdrift. Flying snow whitewashed the windshield, completely blocking his vision. Still going, he drove through what must have been every furrow and gopher hole in front him. Thinking it was the brake pedal, he floored the gas. The tires spun wildly for a moment with the added power, found traction and powered the battered Volvo straight on through a snow-blanketed field. He finally came to a stop when the old car slammed into a rock pile, going thirty-eight miles per hour.

The world in front of him went dark. The shriek of rending metal, shattering glass, and splintering plastic filled his ears. The impact threw him nearly out of his seat and his head hit the doorframe, dazing him. Momentum pushed the car further on, tipping it sideways. The Volvo slid on its right side for another ten feet before tipping over completely, coming to a rest on its roof. There, the dying car lay like a turtle turned on its back, wheels spinning ineffectively, with cold snow howling all around.

Fallon came to a moment later, and found himself hanging upside down, held in place by the lap belt. For an instant, he didn't know where he was. Sheer terror coursed through him as he tore at the harness and imitation leather of the dash and door panels. Searing pain racked his head, cutting through his panic, sobering him like a bucket of ice water. He pressed his eyes shut, willing the pain away.

After a few minutes of staying stone-still, his head still pounding and freezing cold, Fallon moved. When he opened his eyes, his vision had cleared up and he was in a better frame of mind to assess his situation. The car was a mess. The passenger side window was shattered, letting in the cold and the snow. The frame was twisted and covered with icy mud and brambles. Snowflakes and irregular cubes of shattered safety glass covered everything. It took a few minutes of careful struggle to free himself from the seatbelt. Being upside down completely disoriented him. The car door screeched open from its warped frame.

Outside the wrecked car, Fallon started shivering immediately. He was off the highway but couldn't see how far he was away from the road. The cold bit into him, sending razors of pain through his skin, past his muscles and straight to the nerves. The night was a noisy and windy frozen hell. He had no gloves, no coat and wore only a pair of thin cotton work pants. His shoes were designed for standing all day long in a sterile, man-made environment, not trudging through the cold in the out-of-doors. On top of his long-sleeved button-up shirt he wore a thin windbreaker. The left sleeve had caught and torn almost completely off while he was crawling through the broken door and the wind hissed through, freezing his barely insulated shoulder.

He thought he'd traveled no further than a dozen or so yards and hoped he could follow the trail of destruction back to the highway. He fumbled the keys out and nearly dropped twice them trying to unlock the trunk. Lines of cold agony traced from the pads of his fingertips along the tops of each finger, connecting on the top of his palms, before traveling up his arms. He managed to get the trunk open finally and took stock of what spilled onto the snowy ground. There wasn't much. Well-used spare tire, rusted scissor jack and tire iron, and a flashlight with dead batteries. No blanket or anything else that could keep him warm. There were road flares, however. That was some consolation. He shivered and sighed before heading up the embankment towards the road.

*Someone will be along soon*, he hoped. *Someone will find me and help me. I just hope they do it before the army gets here.*

Flares in hand, he trudged through the field, back toward the highway.

Harold Cunningham puttered along at a steady thirty-five miles per hour. Not too fast, not too slow. Outside the wind howled, slightly rocking his truck cab with each gust; the snow blew, sounding like sand as it pelted his windows. But none of it rattled good old Harold as he cruised along, warm and comfortable. He had no fear of the white blanketed blacktop in his ten-ton snowplow. Once or twice, he hit a slick patch, that gave him a moment of pause, but each time the massive blade on the front of his monster big rig cut a way through. Diffusers mounted on the back sprinkled coarse-grain sand mixed with salt, to melt the ice and snow and provide better traction.

He had been driving plows for the county for going on eleven years. He knew these roads like he knew his own neighborhood. Each time he encountered a heavy drift or a slick spot in the road, he calmly powered through, his hands loose on the wheel. His only complaint, despite the heater going full blast and his extra thick wool socks: Harold's toes were cold in his boots. Though the wind was still going full gale, the snow had let up a bit. It was a good thing, too, as Harold came around a bend and saw a line of red sparks sputtering in the road ahead. One of the flares was circling and bobbing about in the air above the roadway, as if dancing for him. Harold was nearly on top of the flares and had to stand on his breaks. The huge vehicle shuddered to a stop several yards past the figure waving the road flares.

He swore softly as he zipped up his heavy winter parka and climbed down to investigate.

"Just what I need right now. Be lucky if I don't catch my death out there."

On the ground, he found a tall, skinny man shuffling towards him, clutching himself tightly. The fellow looked to be in pretty bad shape. Saying that the guy was underdressed for the weather would have been an understatement. Blowing snow had plastered him, and he was soaked through and shivering. There must have been an accident and now this guy was stranded.

"You okay? What're you doing out here with no coat?" Harold asked, once the man was within earshot. The man groaned through clenched jaws. Harold waved him nearer. He was chalk-white, verging on blue. He needed to get warm, fast. "You'd better get up in the cab quick, before you freeze to death." He helped the stranger into the truck and buckled him in before hurrying around to the driver's side.

"T-t-thanks for stopping," the man said, after several seconds of stuttering, then leaned his head against the seat and closed his eyes.

Harold decided that he was going to have to leave the rest of his route unplowed for the time being. The stranger in his cab desperately needed medical attention. He got rolling again and radioed Saint John's, the closest hospital hereabouts.

"Shelly," he said into the hand mic. "Shelly, this is Harold, you there, girl?"

"I'm here Harold. What do you need?" a voice answered after a brief burst of static.

"I found a stranded motorist out here on the highway. He's got no coat or hat and he looks half froze. I'm bringing him in right now. You copy?"

"Ten-four, Harold. We'll warm up a bed for him."

"Thanks, darlin. Over and out."

Next, he called into dispatch and told them what had happened and where he was going. They said they wouldn't be able to get a wrecker or any highway cops out there till the storm broke, but they noted the location and acknowledged that he would be a little behind plowing the rest of his route.

Clipping the hand-mic back in place, Harold looked over at his unexpected passenger and shook his head. *Stupid people*, he thought. *Why is it nobody thinks to plan for weather like this? It's January, for Christ's sweet sake and this guy doesn't even have a decent coat on. If I hadn't come along, he would have froze to death.*

The man was ashen gray. With the heat cranked full blast, he wasn't shivering so much anymore, but he still didn't look too good. Harold reached beneath his seat and brought out his coffee thermos, thought a moment, then put it back and grabbed the other one.

"Here you go, mister," he said giving his passenger a little shake. "There's hot tomato soup in there. You're welcome to as much of it as you like." The stranger opened his eyes and accepted the thermos with a nod of thanks and unscrewed the cap with trembling fingers.

Aromatic steam wafted from the carafe as the stranger poured himself a cupful and drank it down. A few minutes and more soup later, the stranger was able to tell Harold his story. He was a salesman, returning from a conference. He'd thought he could beat the storm when he set out, which explained his poor clothing choices. The stranger also hadn't planned on losing control of his car and running it off the road back there. Then he emphatically thanked Harold for stopping to rescue him.

"My only thought after that was to flag somebody down and get help. So, I got into the trunk, looking for anything that might help keep me warm, but couldn't find anything useful, except for the flares."

"Jesus-God, mister!" Harold said. "How long had you been standing out there?"

The stranger shrugged and shivered. "I don't know. My watch was broken in the crash. I think probably at least half-an-hour or so. Without the flares, I doubt you would have seen me."

"Almost didn't even with 'em," Harold said. "These trucks don't got a great view to the ground ahead."

The stranger looked through the windshield and nodded. "I can see that. It's providence really that you saw me at all. Thank you again for stopping." Harold's passenger passed him the half-empty thermos.

Harold smiled. "Think nothing of it, mister." He took the thermos and drank deeply.

They drove the rest of the way in silence. Still shivering, the stranger fell asleep in the cab beside him. He was still gray, and his fingers and lips looked blue. Frostbite was serious. Hypothermia was even more so. If he had been out in that blizzard for thirty minutes like he said, dressed as he was, then there was no telling how much damage was done. Even now, Harold figured his body could be going into shock and shutting down. They were only a couple miles away from Harper's Glen and it would only take them ten minutes to reach Saint John's. Harold concentrated on the icy road ahead and prayed he could get to the hospital in time.

After that, Harold would get back on the clock and plow

out the rest of his section of the highway. He still had a lot of miles to go before he could clock out. His shift was supposed to end at dawn, but during big storms like this, the county didn't fuss much over a little overtime, as long as the roads were cleared and safe for travelers.

Colonel Aldridge examined the crash. He had only arrived a few minutes ago, but his troops had already combed it over and found everything there was to find. The old Volvo had gone off the road, traveling between forty and fifty miles per hour, slammed into a rock and slid on its side for a few yards, before resting on its roof. On the ground beneath the open trunk lid lay a scattered emergency kit: a packet of bandages, frozen drinking water, a broken flashlight, and soggy matches, all covered with snow.

Aldridge limped carefully back up to the line of military four-by-fours waiting on the roadway. The snow made walking more difficult than it already was and he was panting when he reached his command truck. His leg twanged with the promise of greater discomfort to come. He leaned against the side of the truck and wished for his pain killers, then straightened up as he heard boots crunching through the snow towards him.

Captain West appeared around the side of the vehicle. "Sir, we've checked the area in and around the car. There's no sign of the subject."

"I gathered. What else have you found?"

"There are signs that a large vehicle stopped about an hour ago, sir. We think it may have been a highway snowplow. There are depressions in the snowbank on the right side of the road, a few feet away from where we found the burnt-out flares. We think the plow was flagged down by the subject and stopped to render assistance."

Aldridge frowned. "Please, stop referring to him as 'the subject', Captain. His name is Fallon. It's a man we're hunting, not a deer or a bear or a little lost kitty cat. So, let's stop underestimating him. Understood?" Colonel Aldridge looked at the cleared road ahead of him and swore under his breath. "Some good Samaritan has made our lives harder. That dumb son of a bitch is dead, and he doesn't even know it." He swore again. This wasn't going to be easy. But what did he expect? Nothing had been easy so far, so why should it change now?

They returned to their separate vehicles and the caravan started rolling again. Seated again, Aldridge sighed with relief. Walking hurt. He had done a lot of walking and running in the last month. He tried not to let his discomfort show in front of his men, but that was becoming more difficult. His entire existence these days, it seemed, was an exercise in pain.

Capturing Fallon would be difficult, but not impossible. Fallon had managed his escape brilliantly. It was only luck that a lone surveillance camera had recorded the direction in which he'd left. And luck again which brought that footage to Aldridge's attention. Aldridge had taken as many men as he could and set out immediately in pursuit, barely three hours behind Fallon. The rest of his troops were on the road behind him; they were hauling all the equipment, vehicles, and weapons they needed to contain the situation. As well as nearly the full roster of the project's technicians and doctors. Aldridge felt confident that if he could locate Fallon and detain him long enough for the rest of his people to arrive, then they could put a stop to this situation before it got further out of hand.

He would not allow himself think about failure. There was no other option in his mind but to succeed. No matter what it cost. There was too much at stake.

Coming around the bend and finding the wreck of Fallon's car had sparked excitement in him. For an instant, he thought their search would be over that easily. That they would find him dead or pinned in the wreckage. Those hopes were dashed once his men climbed down to the car and found it empty. Not quick. Not easy. Now hundreds would die. Casualties of the struggle between Aldridge and Fallon.

Aldridge was lost in thought and didn't notice the caravan stop. Captain West came running back from the lead Humvee and tapped on his window. The radio was out in his truck, so he had to relay messages in person.

"Sir," he said, his breath steaming in the freezing night air. "The road ahead isn't plowed."

Aldridge opened his door and, gripping the frame tightly, stepped onto the slippery blacktop, careful to slowly ease the pressure onto his right knee, to have a look for himself. The snow had eased up, but the wind still blew furiously. The road ahead of the lead Humvee was indeed unplowed. A seven-inch thick layer of powdery white lay over the highway surface. Aldridge shivered inside his gray thermal smock. Even army-issue extreme cold-weather gear couldn't keep the chill out. He circled around to the right side of the truck, examining the road and woods around them. It was then that he noticed the freshly plowed interchange.

The plow had turned off here, instead of continuing. The Good Samaritan left the highway to deliver someone to the local hospital. Aldridge pounded his fist into his side in frustration. Fallon had reached a city.

"Captain West!"

"Yes, sir?"

"I want roadblocks set up on all the freeway ramps into this town. Make sure that no one else enters or leaves until further notice. Then join me at the hospital with the remainder of your men."

"Yes, sir. Do you think the subject, er, Fallon is in the city?"

"I don't know for sure. But I believe he is and if I'm right, then we must trap him here. This is damage control. We must capture him quickly and quietly, or else it will spread out of control again. Speed is of the essence, Captain. I want this concluded quickly. Tonight, if possible."

West ran back to his vehicle, and a moment later the five trucks carrying his platoon peeled off, heading for the highway on/off ramps. For a moment, Colonel Aldridge just stared off into the trees, envisioning what was coming, what he would have to do. The remaining five trucks sat in the middle of the highway a moment longer, while Aldridge delivered orders over the radio. Then they turned and climbed the upward grade of the off-ramp and started for the city.

They passed a sign welcoming them proclaimed Harper's Glen, population 25,138, to be the friendliest city in America.

Fallon couldn't keep his eyes open. He felt himself drifting off. Slipping away. Even with the truck heater going full blast, he just could not get warm. With every beat of his heart, he felt himself growing colder, as if the blood in his veins had been replaced with ice water. He couldn't focus on anything for more than a second or two. His head hurt and he couldn't feel his fingers, toes, lips, or nose. His jaw was sore from clenching it shut to stop his teeth chattering. All he wanted was to lay down somewhere and be warm.

"Don't you worry, fella," the truck driver said. "We're almost there now. Just a few more minutes and we'll be at the hospital."

*A few more minutes*, Fallon thought. *I don't care anymore. I don't want any of this anymore. I'm so tired. I just want to sleep. Let someone else do it. Someone lift this burden from me.*

Fallon regretted the thought immediately. A single tear leaked from his eye and he resolved never again to question God's intentions and plans. It wasn't his place. He was only the messenger. It was the message that was important. As soon as he got the message out and among the people, he could rest. He could even die if need be. Once the message was delivered, he was no longer important.

Until then, however, he had to keep going.

For the first time since he started this crazy chase, he was truly scared. He thought he had been scared before, with the Colonel snapping at his heels and time running out. His escape had almost failed and his mission had very nearly ended before it could even begin. He thought he'd been scared then; but those were just tests, preparing the way for this moment, when he lay in the grips of hypothermia and at death's doorstep.

It wasn't just his own life he feared for. He had forfeited his life long ago. He feared that Colonel Aldridge would find him and detain him. He feared his crusade going incomplete.

All his life, what he truly feared was failure.

His eyes drifted closed and he went to sleep.

Shelly Christianson was also having trouble keeping her eyes open. She was entering the final stretch of her fourteen-hour shift and she was ready to go home. She had been awake and on her feet so long that coffee no longer had any effect, and she was operating on willpower alone. Her back ached, the arches in her feet were sore and her knees had been loudly complaining for the past two hours. She had been meaning to replace her worn-out shoes—needed to last month, in fact. But she just hadn't gotten around to it yet. Shelly resolved to do it when she got back. After she clocked off, she was taking a rare four-day weekend, almost a mini-vacation, and she fully intended to relax as much as possible before returning to the hospital. At first, she had resisted taking the time off, but now that the weekend was here, she found herself looking forward to it, and there was no way she was going to let anything stand between her and the break she deserved.

Her last real time off had been almost a year ago. But there had been no rest or relaxation then. Only jail, the trial and Brad.

Her boss, Doctor Francis, knew she needed a break and had called her into his office on Monday to insist that she take some time away. Shelly reluctantly agreed. He wanted her to take a week, but she insisted that she was fine with a long weekend. She had a lot of things to sort out and needed time to do it. But she also didn't like to be alone with her own thoughts for too long. Staying busy allowed her to temporarily forget, or at least to ignore, the heavy weight her conscience bore. So, she stayed busy, working twelve and fifteen-hour days, picking up shifts from the other nurses whenever she could. This worked to keep her mind occupied but had nearly burned out her body.

Picking up the pieces of a broken life is hard enough without the constant intrusion of work, but Shelly wasn't sure she was ready to clear away the mess just yet. For the time being, she was simply happy to be alive and living somewhere where nobody judged her.

It had been a quiet night so far, but most nights were quiet in the Glen, just a few accidents due to the sudden snowstorm and the usual spatter of Thursday night patients and calls. The only excitement came when a snowplow driver named Harold called on the radio to tell her he was on the way in, bringing in a possible hypothermia case. With quiet patience, born from her years spent as a nurse, Shelly prepared the ER to receive the patient. Then Shelly made her final rounds, checking charts and medications, ensuring that her charges were in their proper places and finishing her paperwork. Shelly was about to sign off for the night, once everything was made ready for her replacement, Anne Littlewolf, when the automatic doors opened. She looked up to see a balding, barrel-chested man in shabby coveralls running up to her.

Her first panicked instinct was to slam her palm down on the alarm button beside the computer, which summoned hospital security and the police. But the concern written on the man's face stopped her. Then she remembered the dispatch call and relaxed.

*This must be the plow driver who called in*, she thought. She had hoped the driver would take a little more time to get here, so her replacement would have to deal with the case, and she could simply go home.

No such luck.

Not tonight.

Not ever.

"I need help!" he called out, halfway to her desk. "Please, I need help."

Shelly picked up her stethoscope. "What is the problem, Harold?"

"I have a guy in my truck, near froze to death." The heavy man paused to catch his breath. "We gotta get him inside. He's passed out and I don't know if he's still breathing or not."

Shelly called for an orderly and the three of them went out to the massive plow truck to collect the unconscious man inside.

Fallon came around slowly, blind and confused. Bright-white light seared his eyes when he tried opening them. Keeping them closed was better, but only a little. He could still see the baleful glare through his eyelids, which were backlit pink and veiny. Next, he tried moving. Another difficult task. His joints and limbs ached and popped. His whole body felt like one big, exposed nerve. Little by little, he became aware of the room around him and immediately identified where he was. Fallon knew that bleached, antiseptic smell anywhere; the easy-on-the-eyes taupe and tan colored walls; the well-worn and easy-to-clean vinyl furniture; the television hanging from a swivel arm bolted to the wall.

He was in a hospital.

He had spent enough time in them to know it automatically. With that realization dawned sudden terror. His breath caught and a cold perspiration broke on his forehead. Had they caught him? Had they taken him back? Heedless of the protests from his agonized body, he sat straight up and looked around.

Nothing was familiar.

It was a hospital all right. But it was not his hospital. He hadn't been caught. Not yet.

His breathing slowed and he calmly laid back. He was still ahead of them. But how much time was lost? How close were Aldridge and his minions? Fallon had no way of knowing. His distress receded and he murmured a brief prayer of thanks. He then began assessing the situation. It was too dangerous to stay in a place like this. His mind was slow to formulate ideas and plan his next actions. He needed to get moving, but it would do him no good if he did not have an idea where to go.

Fallon forced himself to relax and concentrate. He had almost fallen back to sleep when a nurse appeared at his bedside to take his vitals.

"Oh, good," she said. "You're awake, Mr. Fallon."

He looked up at the speaker. "I'm Nurse Christianson. You're my last stop for the night, but you'll be in good hands with Nurse Littlewolf. We'll get you well and back on your feet in no time."

Moving with practiced efficiency, she stuck a thermometer under his tongue and ejected the plastic covering into the trash after recording the reading. She checked his blood pressure and made another note on his chart. No motion expended any more effort than absolutely necessary to complete each task. "If it weren't for you, I'd be home right now, soaking in a hot bath." She gave him a stern look, then winked and smiled. It was a wonderful smile. Her bedside manner was compassionate and well-practiced.

"Where..." Fallon tried to speak, but his voice was weak, barely more than a whisper. He swallowed, took a deep breath, and tried again. "Where am I?"

"Saint John's hospital in Harper's Glen."

"How... long... have I been here?"

"It's been about two hours since you were brought in. Mr. Cunningham, the plow driver, said he had to run a few stop signs to get you here quickly. Good thing he did, too. You were already going into shock when he pulled up."

"You've been here the whole time?" She nodded. "Thank you. Thank God for you." *Christianson*, he thought. *Christian. Surely that's no coincidence.* He took it as a sign that God meant for him to live and carry on.

She gave him that sweet, business-like smile again as she finished marking his chart. "Doctor Meric will be here to see you in a few minutes. In the meantime, just get some rest." He watched her leave. At the door she turned back. "Sleep well, Mr. Fallon."

He muttered a good night and lay back. He was just starting to relax again when he snapped up, fully awake.

Two hours.

His lead had been squandered. There was little chance now that he was still ahead of them. Aldridge was coming. Likely, he was already here. Dread coursed through him like an electric current. His heart pounded and he winced as he sat up and threw his feet off the bed. His first attempt failed, but his second try got him out of bed, on his feet and moving. He pulled the IV from is arm, then crossed the room on wooden legs to the dressing cubby, where he found his clothes and quickly dressed. He checked for the lockbox and found it beneath the folded pile with his wallet. It was a hardened steel case, the size of a cigarette pack. Six small dials on the top could be spun to input the combination, which unlocked the case. He didn't open it. The dials were still in the same position he had left them in when he escaped. The case and its contents were the only things he cared about. He made sure it was safe in his front pants pocket, then finished dressing.

Cold wind bit at her as Shelly stepped through the automatic doors to the parking lot, tugging her coat and whipping her dark hair. Large wet snowflakes blew past, as she trudged into the early-morning dark to her truck parked on the far end of the hospital staff lot. She took a deep, cold breath and let it out slowly, feeling the tension of her shift drain away. She planned to draw a hot bath, light some candles, put on her forest sounds CD, and relax. Years of therapy had taught her a thing or two about controlling and adjusting her moods. After the bath, she would pack a few things and get ready for the trip. She planned to stop at the store for food and other camping necessities. Then she would be on her way. She thought she might try to catch a short nap before leaving. Falling asleep behind the wheel was not a great way to start a long weekend.

First, however, she had to negotiate the treacherous vastness of the hospital parking lot. The concrete surface was covered by thick, crunchy snow, which covered a layer of ice. The pitfalls were plentiful, and Shelly was careful where she placed each step until she reached her Bronco. Relieved she hadn't slipped and fallen on her ass, Shelly bid the hospital farewell, started the engine, put the Bronco in gear and pulled out of the lot.

She was passing through the first traffic light when she glanced at her rearview mirror and saw a trio of large olive drab painted trucks pulling in. She gave them no further thought, turned left and slowly made her way home. The cabin waited and she did not want to waste a single moment of her precious time off.

He cracked the door and peeked through, then recoiled, biting back a gasp.

A soldier stood in the hallway by the nurses' station, talking to the nurse on duty there. They were arguing. Although their voices were kept low for the sake of the patients asleep in the ward, Fallon could easily hear what the nurse was saying, though the soldier was harder to understand through his protective breathing mask. She was refusing to allow him access to the ward. By the motions he was making with his hands, Fallon assumed the soldier was insisting he be granted admittance.

They were here.

They had found him.

But they didn't yet know exactly where he was, or else they would have pounced already. They must have only just arrived and were securing the building. Nurse Christianson had called him by his name, which meant they had taken his driver's license and entered him into the hospital computer system. A system easily accessed by the army. They hadn't clapped irons on him yet. He was still free and intended to stay that way. If he moved fast, he might be able to slip away before they could lock the building down completely. It would be close, but he thought he could make it. There was no other choice but to try.

He was about to move when he saw the nurse throw up her hands in frustration and point in his direction. The soldier nodded thanks, turned, and began walking towards his room, his weapon held ready. The nurse, looking frightened, picked up the phone, probably to call her superiors. Frantic, Fallon stumbled back. There wasn't much time. He couldn't hide. He couldn't run. The soldier would be upon him in seconds.

He could not let them take him again. He had to do something. He had to think. Think, damn it! Time was running out.

Fallon looked quickly around his room, desperate for anything that could be used as a weapon. There was no time left. He could hear the soldier's boots clacking against the linoleum floor, growing louder and closer. His eyes rested upon the tray next to the bed and the object on the lower shelf. He dashed to the cart, grabbed the empty aluminum bedpan, and rushed back to the door. He stepped out of sight, just as the soldier pushed open the door and entered the room.

Before the man could react or look around, Fallon swung the pan at the back of his knees. Caught by surprise, the soldier buckled with a yelp. Fallon dropped onto the man's back, ripped off his helmet and began hitting him repeatedly with the bedpan, until the soldier was unconscious. Panting, he stripped the body, pulled the cold weather uniform on over his clothes, picked up the rifle and left. Dressed in the gray pixel-patterned uniform and hidden behind the ill-fitting biohazard mask, Fallon walked without fear down the corridor. He waved to the nurse as he stalked towards the exit. He reached the double doors just as they opened, admitting Colonel Aldridge.

Fallon froze.

Wide-eyed with new fright, he nearly gave himself away. Then he recovered, and remembering what he had seen the lowly enlisted personnel do every time they crossed paths with Aldridge, he snapped to attention and saluted. Colonel Aldridge returned the salute automatically, without stopping, or even noticing him. He was just a soldier like any other, one of thousands of identical background fixtures: a thing, not a person.

Outside, Fallon turned right and nearly slipped on the ice. Quickly catching his balance, Fallon briskly walked away from the hospital. He had gotten away. He was free.

He had taken no more than a dozen steps away when he heard a shout behind him. "Hey! Where the hell do you think you're going?"

Fallon turned and found three soldiers striding towards him. This time he didn't hesitate or panic. He unslung the soldier's carbine and fired.

Colonel Aldridge was speaking with the duty nurse when he heard the shots outside. He joined West and four soldiers as they ran back the way they'd come and into the parking lot. Aldridge followed as close as he could, but because of his limp he was unable to keep pace. Ducking behind a short concrete divider, West beside him, Aldridge drew his pistol while the rest spread out along the low wall.

They moved out cautiously to investigate. Dashing from car to car, the six of them quickly and quietly crossed the parking lot. Aldridge himself had not done this sort of thing since Afghanistan. Though he was in excellent shape, he found himself panting after a few bounds. The exertions took their toll on his leg, which pulsed uncomfortably. He knew he was going to be in agony later, but he put it aside for now and focused on the situation in front of him.

On the far side of the lot, he heard screaming. Then more shots. He threw himself into a slushy mound of snow, soaking him instantly and chilling him to the bone. He landed hard on his leg and bit down hard to keep the scream from escaping. Intense pain shot through his left leg. For an instant he couldn't see or hear, couldn't even breathe. All the world was anguish. With great effort, he willed himself to draw a breath. After a moment, he managed to raise his head out of the dirty parking lot slush. Glancing around, he saw the rest of his boys had found cover where they could.

A moment passed and he was sure that the shots were not aimed at him or his men. Once more he got to his feet and signaled them up and moving.

At the far side of the lot, he found three more men. Sergeant Murphy lay on his back, staring at the overcast night sky. His skull was opened to the chilly night air and his brains sprayed on the ground above him. Another man, Private Wilkins, was gut-shot and screaming. Private Martinez had propped himself up against a small red economy car. His shoulder was bleeding, a hit from a ricochet.

Three soldiers had started administering first aid to the wounded, while the fourth ran back to the hospital for help.

Aldridge crouched beside Martinez. "What happened, soldier?"

Martinez took a moment before answering; he winced when the soldier bandaging him moved his arm in a delicate way.

"Sir," he said through gritted teeth. "We were patrolling outside the hospital, making sure no one left the premises. We had just pulled in and dismounted the truck, when Sarn't Murphy noticed another soldier leaving, all in a hurry. He, Sarn't Murphy that is, grabs me and Wilkins there and tells us to come with him. Once we're in shouting distance of the guy, Sarn't Murphy gets his attention and demands to know where he's going. The guy turns and fires on us. Sarn't Murphy was hit first, shot his helmet right off, along with most of his head. Wilkins was hit next. He was standing in front of me. I got behind cover here and the fucker still managed to hit me. I returned fire, but I don't think I hit shit, sir. I waited for a couple seconds, listening for him. But I couldn't hear shit over Wilkins' screaming. So, I popped up, fired off a few more, then I grabbed Wilkins and dragged him behind cover with me."

"What about the soldier who fired on you? Did you get a good look at him?"

"No, sir, he was wearing a pro-mask."

"Thank you, son. You did a good job here." Aldridge stood up, slow dread filling his belly. Just then, two medical teams and a squad of soldiers arrived. He turned to Captain West. "Take this squad and track down the man who did this. I believe these men here were attacked by Fallon. If possible, I want him taken alive. If that's not possible, just make sure he doesn't get away. Understood?"

"Roger that, sir." West was already turning away to take his men and go.

"Keep in radio contact, and I'll get you more men soon."

West nodded. "Yes, sir."

"And Charley, put on your masks."

Everyone in the battalion had been vaccinated, but they also knew what they were dealing with, what they were chasing and were all scared to death by it.

"Yes, sir," West said. He rounded up his men. They donned

their protective masks and chased after Fallon through the gloomy frost. The medics had the wounded men on gurneys by then and were trundling them inside.

Upon reentering the building, Aldridge learned that another soldier had been found in Fallon's room, beaten unconscious. This confirmed to him that Fallon had indeed attacked his soldiers while escaping. He ordered a room-by-room search be conducted of the whole hospital. Fallon was no longer there, but his men needed something to do and the search would effectively lock the building down, preventing anyone else from entering or leaving. Everybody inside had already been exposed. They would all need to be quarantined. There was a little time yet before they became symptomatic. Hopefully, Aldridge's techs could get the lab up and running quickly. In the meantime, his medics could take care of the hospital staff.

The lab and the rest of his men should be arriving soon.

Would they be enough? Would anything he was doing be enough? He was authorized to take any measure necessary to contain the situation. But how far would he have to go? What was the limit?

He did not know. But all too soon, he knew he would find out.

Fallon only fell a couple of times while he ran. The thick-piled snow provided surprisingly good traction for his boots. He lost the rifle the first time he fell. No great loss there, he had fired it empty. Discarded also were the helmet and protective face mask. He certainly didn't need them. The frigid night air immediately froze the perspiration on his face as he ran. He still hadn't fully recovered from standing in the blizzard unprotected. His cheeks burned, he could barely keep his eyes open and couldn't feel his nose at all. All he could do was ignore the pain and discomfort and keep going.

At an intersection, Fallon paused. The neighborhood he

was running through was mostly residential. Darkened houses surrounded him. To his right he could see lights and roadside signs for businesses. He turned that way and followed the street to a small strip mall. At the next intersection, he turned left. He took two more lefts and a right at random. There was a clear trail behind him in the snow, but there was nothing he could do about that. Though it was snowing furiously, his tracks would still be visible for anyone to follow. Again, his safety lay in gaining as much of a lead as possible. He had no idea how much time it would take before more soldiers came to track him down. But he knew it was not long. Once they were out, he was done for. There were hundreds of them, and they had trucks and dogs and guns. He had only this small town to hide him.

This was his greatest challenge yet. God's path had been laid before him. He needed only to find the way.

A couple blocks later, he came across the brightly lit parking lot of a twenty-four-hour Walmart. Darting between the cars, he went inside. The warmth inside was almost painful. His nose, ears and fingertips were shocked and burning. Involuntary tears blurred his vision as he ducked quickly into the bathrooms after being greeted at the front door by an elderly woman with blue hair. There he took a moment to inventory the soldier's pockets. In the wallet he found two fifties and a few singles. Enough, he hoped, to buy him a new pair of snow boots. The coat he would keep, but his feet were freezing and the tracks from the boots were giving him away, like little neon arrows pointing out which way he had run. He wandered past the produce and grocery aisles and made for the shoe section in the back of the store.

He bought the first pair of insulated snow boats he found in his size, giving him close contact with the cashier in the process, and changed into them in the restroom. He had a few dollars left and thought about buying something to eat. It had been hours since his last meal and he was famished. Painfully aware that time was slipping away, he decided against it. He would eat later. Hopefully.

Sitting in the stall on the toilet, he quickly thanked God for the warning that nurse had unintentionally given him. Without her, he would almost certainly have been captured back at the hospital. The more he thought about it, the more he came to realize just how fortunate that was. Divine intervention again.

*God must have put her in my path,* he thought, *to help me. To show me the way. Meeting her was no mere coincidence. She's meant to guide me away from here. To safety.*

"Maybe she will be able to help me again," he said to himself. "Maybe she is my salvation."

Fallon remembered seeing a phone booth outside the front doors, a rare sight in this day and age. If he hurried, he could find her address and be on his way before his pursuers were any wiser. Smiling, he left the stall and carefully exited the restroom, looking around first to make sure no one was looking for him. Standing beside the tiled restroom entrance, he spotted the soldiers as they entered the store and quickly ducked back in. Peeking around the corner at them gave him a sense of déjà vu. He watched as they huddled together at the entrance for a moment, then split up and began searching the store for him.

They left no one to watch the front.

Their mistake was his good fortune.

Smiling at this turn of good luck, Fallon quickly left, pausing only long enough to tear the phone book from the pay phone with one quick and violent tug. Then he was off again. Fallon paused beneath a streetlamp to search the book. He dreaded every heart-pounding second, he stood there exposed. But doing the Lord's work meant risks. Fallon accepted that and read quickly. He needed to find her house. He was stretched to the very limit of his endurance and needed to rest. Cold, tired, and hungry, he needed to stop someplace safe. That someplace, he had decided, was with Nurse Christianson. His guiding light.

God smiled upon him again. There was only one Christianson listed. According to the map in the front of the book, her address was only a few blocks away. Soon, he would be under a roof, warm and safe again.

Then he would figure out what to do next.

Steam fogged the mirror opaque. The sage-colored bathroom walls were damp with condensation. It was dark, but-for the light from the candles spread around the tub. They were arrayed in clusters; short and fat, slender and tall, tea candles like the ones placed in Jack-o-Lanterns at Halloween, and even a matched set of scented aromatherapy candles designed to soothe as they burned. Shelly had lighted them before stepping into the bath. She wanted to soak and scrub away the pains of the day, so she could start the weekend off right and enjoy her mandatory mini vacation to the fullest. Sitting on the edge of the tub beside her head was her favorite blend of oolong tea, mixed with honey and mint. She had been in the tub for about an hour by this point. The near-boiling water felt so good, she seriously considered spending the rest of her weekend there. Pruned skin be damned.

She didn't relish the idea of the tepid air outside the tub, but knew she needed to get started if she was going to keep to her schedule. In the end, she gave herself another ten minutes, then got out to pack for the cabin.

She had been back in Harper's Glen for less than a year and was still reacquainting herself with how the place had changed during her absence. A new store front here, a formerly vacant lot now filled with houses there. It was disturbing at first, seeing her childhood home so different from her memories. But slowly she adjusted and began to enjoy her return. Last week, she had even accepted an invitation from Anne Littlewolf to join her and some of the other nurses at a Jimmy's Tavern for drinks. Shelly showed up on time, drank two drinks, made some small talk, laughed when it was appropriate, then gave an excuse and left. Her shrink would have told her it was a bold step in the right direction, if Shelly had still been seeing her shrink, that is.

Shelly left all that behind in L.A. Her last months there were miserable. When she learned that the hospital in Harper's Glen had an opening on their nursing staff, she jumped at the job. She was vastly over-qualified for the position and even took a drastic pay cut, but she didn't care. She simply couldn't stay in L.A. one more minute. So, she put her condo up for sale, left her job, packed a rented moving van, and moved back home.

The journey had been terrifying. Every time she stopped for gas, she imagined she saw Brad. That he was following her, lurking in every restroom, in line behind her at every restaurant counter, ready to grab her every time she got out of the van. The pepper spray and forty-five Uncle Rory had loaned her and taught her to use, were no comfort. Somehow, she felt they would have no effect on him if he came after her again. Each time she stopped, she spent nearly ten minutes with her eyes closed, going through the calming exercises her therapist had taught her. Once she felt brave enough, she left the moving truck, ready to face the world full of Brad.

Out of the tub, she quickly toweled off. Earlier, she had laid out some of the things she intended to take with her to the cabin. Clothes, a flashlight and batteries, extra blanket, sleeping bag. She had to go to the store in the morning for food and other provisions. The cabin was closed this time of year and there was very little up there. Maybe a few cans of soup and some of those military MREs Uncle Rory had loved so much. There wasn't much in her own cupboards either, so anything she wanted she'd have to buy and bring with her.

She bought groceries on a week-by-week basis. When she went to the store, she got mostly junk. Cheap TV dinners, frozen pizzas, and sweet snack food. She'd had enough overpriced gourmet food and healthy salad sprigs to last a lifetime. Nothing in her kitchen was organic or natural, nothing was name-brand, and most especially, nothing was healthy. She realized it was all an unconscious effort to distance herself from her life with Brad. But she didn't let that stop her from buying the crap food anyway. She relished it. She had even stopped working out every day. Her toned stomach was starting to sag, the muscles in her arms were shrinking slightly and her butt was starting to grow. She noticed her first varicose vein a few weeks ago and cheered. She came close to ecstasy when she found a smattering of pimples on her cheeks. She was starting to look like a normal woman, instead of one man's perfect ten centerfold fantasy. For the first time in years, she was happy with her appearance. She looked the way she looked because she wanted it, not because she was forced to by someone else. She thought she might start going back to the gym soon, maybe in the spring. But for now, she was happier not worrying about it.

While throwing clothes into an old gym bag, she stopped before the full-length mirror hanging inside her closet. Since leaving L.A. she had purposely disregarded her looks. She usually just tied her hair back in a quick ponytail to keep it from her eyes. Whenever she went out, she would wear any combination of T-shirts, jeans, sweaters, or sweatpants and she avoided putting on a single bit of makeup as though it carried some form of noxious communicable disease. Despite her blatant crusade to be who she wanted, at times, what she was doing to herself made her sad.

*I was so pretty*, she thought, whenever she caught herself in a mirror. *Why am I doing this? It isn't to disgust Brad. He doesn't care anymore. He can't.*

Without answering her own question, she would usually look away from the mirror in shame.

This time, she did not look away. This time, she confronted

what she saw without flinching. Her thick, black hair fell to just below her jaw. Her fashionable cut was fraying away with split ends. Her tan was fading. Without makeup, she noticed a few wrinkles around her narrow, ice-blue eyes. The last collagen treatment was wearing away and her lips were shrinking; her upper lip had a natural cupid's-bow shape, and her bottom lip was simply a pink line under it. She was turning thirty in a couple of months but looked like she was twenty-five. She was five feet ten inches, with a medium build. She was a small C-cup, and her breasts were among the few victories she had ever won against Brad. He had loved huge double Ds and demanded she get the required implants. She refused and weathered the storm of his fury for days afterward. She thought she was basically average-looking, in nearly every way, and had no idea what he'd ever seen in her.

She had even asked him about it once after they had dated for a couple months. "You have a magic charm," he said, flashing her a grin full of perfectly straight, white-capped teeth. "You're a chameleon. One day, you can be Plain Jane, the next, you can rival super models. That's a rare thing. And I love you for it." Later she found out it was just about the *only* thing he loved about her, and that she wasn't the only one he felt that way about. But by then, it was already too late.

A sound broke her reverie. She frowned, quickly dressed in a sweater and pajama bottoms and grabbed the baseball bat from her closet. She initially felt a little silly for taking such a precaution, for being so jumpy. Noises caused by the storm had startled her at least a dozen times since she arrived home. Shelly tried to ignore them, telling herself they were simply background noise, nothing threatening. This time was different. The noise she heard sounded like it had come from *inside* the house. Careful to stay near the walls, Shelly ventured from her room to investigate.

*It's probably nothing. Just the wind knocking against the house again, that's all,* she thought. She was halfway down the short hallway when she realized her cell phone was on the bedside table next to her alarm clock. She had been planning on taking a nap and had left it to charge.

Silently cursing her carelessness, she continued down the hall. The two spare bedrooms were on the right side of the hall. Both doors were shut. She never had visitors, and no family to speak of, so the unfurnished rooms remained closed. The first doorway on the left led into the kitchen. Past that, the hall opened into the living room on the left and the dining area on the right. Feeling cold air wash over her bare feet Shelly peered into the kitchen and saw her backdoor had been forced open. She could see into her white-washed backyard and hear the wind blowing gently through the kitchen.

For a moment, she stood stupefied, unable to believe the reality of what she was seeing.

She couldn't move. Couldn't run. Could even barely think.

*Brad's here!* Her panicked brain screamed. *He's found me! Get the phone. Call the cops. Get out. Run. Damnit, run!*

But that was impossible. It couldn't be Brad. There was absolutely no way he had broken and entered her house.

Brad Duncan had been dead for two years.

She needed to get to her phone, lock the door and wait for the police to come and rescue her. Turning to run back down the hallway, she ran into the man who had snuck up behind her. He grabbed her and pinning her arms to her sides. Shelly tried to pull away, but he held her fast.

"I don't want to hurt you," a hoarse voice whispered into her ear. "But I need your help. I need to get away from here. If you don't give me away, I promise to let you go unharmed."

Once again, she was a victim. The familiar submissiveness settled over her, as though she was with Brad all over again. She felt like crying. It wasn't fair. This should not happen all over again. She had suffered enough. Why was the world conspiring to make her suffer more?

"Please let me go. You don't need me. You can have my

car. Take it and go, please." She hated the pleading tone she heard in her voice.

She felt the man hesitate. "No," he said. "I can't drive in my condition and I can't wait until I'm better. I must leave right now. So, you have to help me."

The man slowly drew her back down the hall, towards her bedroom. Her mind screamed for her to act, to do something and fight back. But the years spent docile and subservient had conditioned her against taking such action. Tears streaked her cheeks as they entered her bedroom.

Emily Dollard was having the worst day of her young life. Four hours ago, as pulled into the lot at the start of her shift, she thought, *I fucking hate Mondays*. She was twenty years old, slightly pudgy, but liked to think that there was "a little more of her to love." She had hair the color and consistency of hay and suffered constantly from a light spattering of acne. She hated working for Walmart and planned on finding a new job just as soon as she could get away from this dead-end, one-horse, shit-hole town. She had been stuck working the graveyard shift—which she hated—because no one had been willing to switch shifts with her. She arrived late to work, again, which brought on the usual litany of lectures from her dipshit boss, Robb.

Her day had begun badly and had only gotten worse as it went along. To start with, she was three weeks late for her period. For every regular kind of girl, this was not a good sign under any circumstances. When she told her boyfriend, Chet, earlier that morning, his measured response had been to break up with her.

His parting words were, "You promised me you were on the pill. This is your fault. So, it's your problem. You fix it. Then maybe we'll talk." Then he was gone.

Emily felt that was completely unfair of him. He was the one who didn't have a condom but insisted on having sex anyway. Granted, she had wanted to as much as he had, so she trusted him when he promised to pull out. At the last second, his promise apparently slipped his mind. She had felt his hot seed dripping out of her for the next few minutes, all the while loudly cursing him and his stupidity. She demanded that he take her to a clinic and buy her the morning after pill, but he only shrugged and said he didn't have any money until next Friday when he got paid.

Payday came and went, with no clinic visit. Now she was probably pregnant and without a man to share the burden.

To top it all off, now she was trapped in Walmart and could not leave.

It was after six in the morning. She was locked in the back office, pondering life's unfairness. A couple of hours ago, just before her first break, some tweaker-looking guy in an oversized army jacket bought a pair of the cheapest boots the store sold. Emily remembered thinking at the time that the guy must have been on meth and out for a midnight stroll around the store. His eyes were bloodshot and sunken, his hair was greasy and pasted to his head, he was pale as hell and he kept glancing around nervously, anxious about something. She knew a few people who had tried meth and that was how they had acted when they were high. Besides, she'd thought, only a tweaker would decide he needed new boots in the middle of the night.

She figured the guy must have been turned on by her, because he leaned in close to pay. Only he didn't say anything or try to pick up on her. Thank God. He only breathed heavily. Almost like he was panting. His breath smelled slightly of old fruit.

It was really weird. And really, really creepy.

Just as the tweaker left, a bunch of real-life army men stormed the store, wearing scary-looking masks, waving their guns around and scaring the shit out of her. After racing up and down the aisles, they got the night manager—fat, sexist

Robb—to gather all the stockers and clerks by the registers. One of them, their leader, she guessed, passed around a picture and asked if anyone had seen the man in it. When the photo came to Emily, she recognized tweaker. He looked better in the picture for sure; healthier, not haggard and strung out.

"I saw this guy a few minutes ago," she said. Then she told them what he bought and her impression about his drug addiction. No sooner had she finished recounting the entire transaction, she was immediately hauled away, separated from the others. The army men wouldn't let her talk to anyone, or call home, or even leave to go to the bathroom. They took her cell phone and unplugged the computer and office phone, so she was completely cut off. She pounded on the office door. "I have to pee," she told the guard outside. "I need to take a pregnancy test." He only stared at her through the eye holes in his mask and said nothing.

Emily threw herself onto the couch and cried for a while. *What have I done wrong? What's going on here? Why won't they let me pee?*

She sprang from the couch, grabbed a lamp from the desk and hurled it at the closed door. "Why won't you let me pee? Why are you doing this to me? You can't just keep me locked up in here like this. I didn't do anything. I didn't do anything!"

There was no response from the other side. Cold terror set in as she paced the room.

The office was upstairs, with windows in one wall, facing into the store, so that Robb and the other asshole managers could watch the store and make note of who they thought wasn't working hard enough. To pass the time, Emily stared through them and what she saw wasn't encouraging. More army guys swarmed the store. They had blocked off the front doors and were actively turning people away.

*What's going on here?* she wondered for the hundredth time and then she cursed the unfairness of life. None of this would be happening to her if she had just called in sick. She wouldn't be trapped feeling sorry for herself over her missed period and Chet leaving her.

She had just about made up her mind to pee in the wastepaper basket by the desk when the office door slammed open and the army leader stamped in. At least she thought it was him; they all looked the same with those freaky masks on. He was carrying a cotton surgical mask in his left hand. "Put this on," he ordered. Through the mask his voice was muffled and hard to understand.

She meekly accepted the mask and tied it over her mouth and nose. Then she was escorted from the office. Down in the store, Emily saw everyone wearing masks like hers. The soldiers had rounded everyone up and were herding them onto trucks.

*Just what the holy fuck is going on here?*

She turned to the soldier striding next to her, and asked, "Where are you taking us?" Her mind conjured up black and white images of Jews marching into death camps to be slaughtered, like she had seen in some old movie. She shivered.

She had not really expected the faceless soldier to answer her. Why should he? After all, Emily was just something she had to move. All he cared about was keeping Emily going in the same direction as the others. Keep her in line and not making trouble for him. The soldier had his job, and he was accomplishing it with as little difficulty as possible.

Suddenly, Emily was very afraid. She wanted to call her mother. Tears filled her eyes. She was being marched off to die, she was certain of it, surrounded by strangers who wouldn't talk and didn't give a flipping shit about her. Her fear mixed with a fresh feeling of anger. She wanted to lash out at the army men kidnapping her and her coworkers. She wanted to hurt them. She hated them for their stony indifference. What gave them the right to do this to her? She wanted to run away and hide, but she was sure they would shoot her in the back if she bolted. Everywhere she looked, death seemed to look back at her. It was unreal. This was the kind of thing that happened to other people, in other towns. Nothing like this could happen in Harper's Glen, the world's most boring shit hole.

She was about to scream when the soldier surprised her by answering her question: "We're taking you and your friends to the hospital. Don't worry. You'll be taken care of there." He said nothing more, simply marched her and the others along. The empathy in his voice reassured her, but his answer mystified her.

*Why are we being taken to the hospital? Do they think we're sick?*

No explanation was given. She was simply marched along. Silently, she thanked him. It was nice to know there was a human being under that frightening mask.

# January 8th

The dark and heavy low hanging clouds over Harper's Glen threatened to choke the town off with another snowfall. It was early and Aldridge had just finished the first of many meetings with the local leadership.

Tom Henderson, the mayor, had been particularly outspoken in his displeasure over the military presence in his town. As well he should have been; when he had gone to bed the night before, everything was fine. Then he was woken by soldiers at his door in the wee hours of the morning, whereupon he learned that a deadly disease had taken up residence during the night and the army had instituted a quarantine. It was enough to make anyone uneasy before breakfast.

"I don't care what authorization you say you have!" he shouted. "There is no way in hell that your presence here is legal!"

Aldridge remained calm. He had dealt with hotheaded politicians before. "Mayor Henderson, you don't seem to fully appreciate the gravity of the situation."

"I understand it plenty, Colonel. You and your people are

conducting illegal domestic operations in my town. I demand that you remove your forces and restore all communication and highway access immediately."

Aldridge frowned slightly and shook his head. "You are mistaken, sir. My presence here is completely legal." He removed a sheet of paper from the folder on the conference table in front of him and slid it across to the irate public official. The text of the memorandum was thick with obtuse language and legalese, but Aldridge knew the mayor, who had been a lawyer before being elected to office, would have no trouble at all reading and comprehending it. In plain terms, the paper was an executive order, granting Colonel Preston Aldridge full power and authority to conduct his mission, as he saw fit, to its successful conclusion, by any means necessary.

Henderson reread the document twice. He slapped the order onto the tabletop and swore, loudly and colorfully. Then he said, "It appears as though we are at your mercy, Colonel."

Aldridge nodded, as if that fact were never in dispute. "Mercy is the reason we're here, Mayor Henderson. I will locate and apprehend the man I am seeking as quickly as possible, to minimize the impact on your town."

Henderson huffed at that, but Aldridge continued as though he hadn't been interrupted. "What I need from you, in order to bring this situation to a quick and satisfactory conclusion, is the full control and cooperation of your police and emergency services. I've already set up my command post in the hospital, so my men can assist in the care and vaccination of any sick and injured. I'm also going to need you to make a public statement, insisting that your people here cooperate and do nothing to interfere with us in any way."

Henderson was silent for a moment, envisioning the ramifications of such a statement. *If I do that*, he thought, *there's no way in hell I'll be able to run for office next election. I'll be finished here.* Seeing no other choice, he said, "Very well,

Colonel. I'll make your statement and you'll have the full cooperation of all town services." He held up the executive order. "I want a copy of this. It may be my only defense when this catastrophe is over."

Aldridge nodded and took the paper back and his clerk stamped COPY in big red letters across it. "You may have this one, sir. Thank you for seeing reason so quickly. This could have been a lot more painful if you hadn't."

"Oh, it's plenty painful, Colonel. You've pretty much destroyed my political career. Hell, once this is all over and done with, I'll be lucky if I don't have to move away. My constituents may just demand my head on a platter."

"I'm truly deeply sorry about that. But there really is no other way."

"I know." They agreed to more terms and drew up a document recognizing Aldridge's authority in town. Then Henderson gathered up his papers and his entourage and left.

Once he was gone, Aldridge sighed and did the same. "That could've gone better, eh, Walters?"

His clerk, Specialist Walters, was the only other soldier in the room with him during the meeting. Everyone else was occupied with locking down the town or hunting Fallon, so that Aldridge left to conduct the meet and greets without a security detachment or entourage. "Yes, sir. It could also have gone a lot worse. As you said, he listened to reason."

"You're right. It just doesn't get any easier. Where are we going next?"

Walters consulted some notes. "The sheriff's office is next on the list, sir."

"Ah, yes. What's his name again?"

"Peter Landon, sir."

Aldridge nodded and rubbed his eyes. "Let's hope he doesn't give me as much trouble as the last one."

The first days of a new quarantine were always the hardest. Establishing control and ensuring compliance from the people he was protecting by imprisonment was a tall order. Aldridge was tired, but there was still so much to do and no time for rest.

After meeting with Sheriff Landon and ensuring his cooperation, Aldridge returned to his command post inside the hospital, where he waited, anxiously tapping out the desk in front of him with a pen and listened to the reports coming back to him from outside the hospital. There was little else he could do until the rest of his men and equipment arrived. Around him, chaos was already beginning to take hold, as people discovered the army had come to town. He stared calmly at the computer screen, scrolling through personnel files of the hospital staff. On the desk at his right hand lay the current hospital shift roster. He had people out right now gathering up all the nurses, orderlies and doctors, everyone who had worked the prior shift and gone home. The list wasn't long. Only ten names. But each one of those names meant at least ten more people were at risk.

Ten more disease vectors. Ten more victims.

*Thank God it was the middle of the night,* he thought. *And in the middle of a blizzard.* Only these people's direct friends and families were in danger. He wasn't used to such strokes of good fortune and was immediately suspicious of it. He shuddered to think of the mess he'd have to deal with if Fallon had arrived on a clear, sunny day.

Just then a radio report came in from West's team, requesting more people at the local Walmart. Apparently, Fallon had gone there and purchased new footwear and infected some of the on-duty clerks.

Captain West had quarantined the store and was bringing the entire workforce to the hospital. Aldridge sighed; that was at least forty or more people. Who knew how many people had been inside the store between Fallon's visit and West's arrival? Dozens more could be infected.

"This is only the beginning," he told the computer screen.

The hospital had already been locked down and most of the staff detained and inoculated. He needed them hail and hardy and helping him if he was going to contain this situation. Aldridge only had a few prepared vaccines on hand. They had nearly run through their supply in the previous quarantines. They had no ammo against the virus, at least not until the refrigerated truck arrived. Until then, only a select few would receive the lifesaving injections.

It was a stroke of bad luck that Fallon had been brought here. Most of the trained medical personnel had encountered either him, or coworkers who had. The vaccine would make them useless with flu-like symptoms for at least a day. After that, they would still feel terrible, but they would be able to help. Until then, he and his men were on their own. The hospital itself was being scrubbed down and made ready to accept the patients soon to flood its halls. Unless there was a medical student or a part time EMT among the group coming from Walmart, none of them would get any. Until he had the ability to provide for everyone, only the most valuable people would be saved. Heartless reasoning, but that was how things had to be. There was a twelve-hour window from the time of infection for the patient to be vaccinated; after that, it was a crap shoot. Two days after the initial infection, it wouldn't matter if the victim bathed in vaccine. The virus would have multiplied and spread too far in the host's body. Aldridge knew he was sentencing those people to death. Unless the next shipment of vaccine arrived soon, there was no hope for them.

Pragmatic by nature, Aldridge decided to make the hospital his command post. Located as it was near the center of town, he could monitor the crisis and direct his troops easily, waging war against the silent terror that had invaded the community.

The snow was badly hampering his efforts. His support teams and reinforcements were late in arriving. They should have been in place already. The troops he had brought with him were stretched perilously thin. Only help from Sherriff Landon's people had allowed him to successfully shut down highway access. Without those twenty cops, he would not have been able to segregate Harper's Glen. Even now, Aldridge worried about the people who could have slipped through the cracks while he was getting set up and he prayed earnestly that Fallon was not one of those people. If Fallon was still here, then in a few hours he wouldn't be able to escape. All streets, highways, backroads, and farm lanes were being mapped and sealed off. The cops were ideal for that. In two hours, three satellites would be moved into geosynchronous orbit above and he would have a real-time, top-down view of the city and surrounding region. He had two hundred men with him, less three casualties and another thousand on the way, not including the medical personnel.

His best and only chance to stop it and reverse it was finding Fallon. The team out gathering up the off-duty doctors and nurses was almost finished. Only three more people to detain, all nurses: Higgins, Bradshaw, and Christianson. Hopefully, they would come along without a fuss. Doctor Francis had given his men trouble when they showed up at his doorstep and had arrived slightly bruised for his trouble. Aldridge's teams were authorized to use deadly force if necessary, but fortunately, the sergeant in charge had responded to the shotgun aimed at his men by jamming a rifle butt into the good doctor's stomach. Aldridge was glad of that. He would need every doctor and nurse he could get his hands on.

As fast as they had moved, Fallon had been faster. He was already in the wind. And the clock was ticking.

They would have to root him out, and if that meant tearing this little town apart, Aldridge was prepared to do that. When Fallon walked out of the hospital, he ended any chance of minimizing collateral damage. Now hundreds would suffer and die.

*Messy*, Aldridge thought, trying not to grimace. There was no way around it. His career was finished. He would never be able to recover from a disaster of this magnitude. Even before Fallon's little adventure, his career had been winding down. He'd been assigned to the research facility to keep him out of the way until his retirement could be processed. The army was not forgiving of war-time mistakes.

He sighed, his breath loud in his ears. The filtered air tasted stale and old and seemed to sting, slightly, the back of his throat. The protective mask he wore constricted a little. He had never liked wearing the damn things. Even though he and all his men were inoculated, they felt better with the masks on, and seeing him wearing his reassured them as well. They knew they would be all right if Colonel Aldridge was with them, taking the same risks as them. He had acquired a favorable reputation among his people. That reputation hadn't been tarnished by the judgment of the court martial, rather it had been strengthened by it. His men knew he would stand up and fight for them.

He shook his head and looked back at the computer screen. Cold data. Numbers. Dates. The personal medical history of every man, woman, and child in Harper's Glen. People with lives, families, histories.

All expendable.

In two hours, he intended to meet with the hospital's chief of medicine. The side effects of vaccination would not have set in yet and he should be lucid. Aldridge needed to win his support and assistance. He hoped the rest of his people would get here soon. Come sunrise, the townsfolk would learn they had been quarantined and were not likely to be happy about it. Two hundred men wouldn't be able to control them. Not without the additional riflemen, armored vehicles and helicopters that were on the way. And without the serum, there was no chance he'd be able to stop the spread.

He checked the last situation report from the convoy. They

were still spread out on the highway, dealing with icy conditions, slide-offs and deep snowdrifts. The whole group halted time and time again to fish some stricken vehicle from a snowbank. To call their speed a snail's pace would have been overestimating it.

Aldridge had had enough. He went to his radio operator, located just down the hall from his office. "Get me Major Panelli."

"Right away, sir." The specialist fiddled with a dial, spoke into the hand-mic, turned and passed it to Aldridge. "Major Panelli on the line for you, sir."

"Major, what's your ETA?"

"We've had a few more slowdowns, sir, but I'm pretty sure we should arrive by zero-nine-hundred."

That was four hours away.

Aldridge gritted his teeth and clenched his eyes shut for a second. Then he took a deep breath. "That's not good enough, Major. I want no more slowdowns. Get here as quickly as you can, with whatever you can. Leave the rest behind to self-recover and catch up at their own pace. Understood?"

There was a short pause on the other end. "Understood. Sir, I have to report that the last truck to go off the road was the refrigerated truck."

The silence was thick with Aldridge's worst fears. "What's the condition of the equipment inside?"

"The techs tell me nothing inside has been damaged as far as they can tell, sir. But they're stuck pretty deep and the tow trucks are busy on three other slide-offs."

"How quickly can you get here, if you self-recover the rest?"

"It'll scatter the convoy to hell and gone, sir, but I can be there inside of an hour with at least five hundred men."

That decided it. With nothing but bad choices before him, he chose the least unpalatable option. Right now, he needed troops more than anything else, including the vaccine.

"Best possible speed, Major. Out." Without waiting for a confirmation, he handed the hand-mic back to the radio operator. "I want regular reports on their progress."

"Yes, sir."

On the way to his office, Aldridge came across the Walmart employees, who were less than happy to be the army's guests, being led into the newly established isolation ward. Many of them were rowdy and yelling threats at the soldiers. Several sported fresh bruises. He could feel their rancor. One blonde girl glared at him ferociously as she filed down the hall towards the waiting rooms where they were going to be locked up. They were dead and it was his fault. Fallon had killed them, but Aldridge's decision to leave the serum behind had doomed them.

Fallon paced the marble length of counter from fridge to sink and back again, gripping the crumpled wrapper of the peanut butter fudge bar he'd eaten. It was practically the only food in the house. He was exhausted, famished, and scared. His fingertips were still tingling and slightly numb. His face burned as the cold melted away. He'd exerted so much effort reaching this point and now he wasn't sure what to do next. He didn't know where to go. He had counted on a sign to show him the way. But what he got instead was a woman nearly catatonic with shock and fear.

*Could I have been wrong about her? Have I misread the Lord's intentions and found a sign where none existed? By coming here, have I wasted valuable time and doomed myself?*

*I don't think so.*

If he was wrong about the Christianson woman, what else had he been wrong about? He didn't want to think like that. Along that line of thought lay a slippery slope of hindsight, threatening to unravel the very reasons he'd begun this pilgrimage.

Fallon closed his eyes and cleared his mind. Of course, God

was on his side. God wanted him to succeed and escape. God needed him to be free, just as much as Fallon needed it himself. He had not misread the signs. He was supposed to find this woman and she would help him. He was simply being a fool and expecting too much. God couldn't provide all the answers. His own fears and doubts plaguing him and making him second guess himself. The answer was here somewhere. He merely had to open his eyes and find it.

After entering her home and catching her by surprise, Fallon secured her in the bedroom. She was unresponsive now, but that could change in an instant. He didn't want her to do anything foolish. Not until she gave him the help which was promised. He needed her, badly, but feared she would turn on him the minute he gave her the opportunity.

*She needs to understand what's going on,* he decided. *She needs to.*

*Not everything, of course, but enough to make her want to help.*

He would have to give her the communion, but he had already decided to do that. She would need it if she were to help him continue in his work and escape Aldridge's clutches.

He nodded once to himself and then went through her cupboards until he found a glass. He removed the small steel case from his pocket, flipped the dials to the appropriate sequence and opened it. Inside were four slender vials containing clear, odorless liquid. Fallon filled the glass from the tap and topped it off with the contents from the first vial.

That settled, he left the kitchen and went down the hall towards the bedroom. He needed to move. They couldn't stay in her house much longer. Aldridge's men would be sweeping out across the city to find the hospital staff from the night shift, snatching them up and stealing them away to some dark place. They could not stay, but he had to make her understand a few things before they left. Then they had to decide on a destination. Where would they go? Where *could* they go? The army was certainly blocking off all access to the city, if they had not already done so, that is.

*A path will present itself,* he assured himself.

He paused after entering the bedroom. He felt bad about tying her to the bed and gagging her. He hadn't wanted to but couldn't think of any other option at the time. Now he had to release her and convince her of his righteous intent. Freeing her would be easy. Harder, would be persuading her to listen to what he had to say.

Dawn peeked in through the window, casting the east-facing bedroom in eerie gray. Fallon set the glass down on her nightstand and slowly untied the gag around her mouth. Then he undid the knots around her hands and feet. The whole time he had been in the house, she hadn't made a single sound. No shout of alarm when he surprised her from behind, no cry of protest when he led her into the bedroom, no struggle when he tied her to the bed. He couldn't fathom such docility in another person and briefly wondered what could have caused it.

He extended a hand to help her up. "I'm not going to harm you," he said. "I need to talk to you. To explain a few things to you."

No response from her.

"I need your help."

Nothing.

"Please."

She turned slightly and looked up at him. Maybe it was the pleading urgency in his voice. Maybe it was the word itself. Or maybe she'd had time to comprehend that he was speaking to her. Fallon didn't know, but she had responded. Slow and unsure, she accepted the proffered hand and let him help her sit up. Once upright, Nurse Christianson returned to staring into the middle of nowhere. Fallon's heart fell slightly. He had hoped her response was progress. Giving her space, he moved to the far wall of the room to make himself as nonthreatening as possible. Not that it counted for much. He was an intruder in her home, holding her hostage. He was a threat. There was nothing he could do to change that perception easily.

But he had to try.

"I'd like you to listen to me carefully. When I'm done speaking, if you still have nothing to say to me, I'll go. I don't want to, you understand, but I will. I need your help, Nurse Christianson. I need your help desperately."

Shelly couldn't believe what she was hearing. The man who had broken into her house and attacked her was begging her to help him. She almost felt like laughing in his face. That would be the wrong thing to do, of course. She'd made that mistake once, and Brad had put her in the hospital for it. So, she sat quietly. These kinds of men needed to talk, to justify their actions with words. They wanted to convince everyone, including themselves, that they had done nothing wrong. If you let them talk long enough, they would convince the devil of their innocence. Shelly decided to let him, she would pretend to listen, buying time to get help or find a way out.

"I'm on the run," he said. "There are people chasing me, who want very much to capture me and take me away with them. I can't allow that to happen."

"Who's chasing you?" Shelly asked, and immediately regretted it. She knew it was what he was hoping for, a chance to convince her he was one of the good guys. Silently, she berated herself and told herself not to play along, to just sit there and shut up.

"I'm on the run from the United States Army," he said.

Shelly almost asked why but stopped at the last second. He waited, as if hoping she would take part in the conversation. Silently, Shelly studied his face. Even in the gray, lightless room, she thought he looked familiar. She couldn't quite place where she'd seen him before. Then she had it. He was her last stop before leaving work, the exposure case Harold, the plow driver, brought in. She could see he was exhausted, on the ragged edge.

"You were in the hospital earlier, weren't you? You're Mr. Fallon," she said.

Fallon nodded. Shelly desperately tried to recall everything she could about him. He was forty-five years old, no wedding ring, tattoos, or other identifying marks. Few personal effects were taken off his body when he was admitted, just a wallet, car keys and a metal cigarette case. He had responded well to treatment and had already begun recovering before she left for the night. She had only spoken to him once. The rest of the time, he had been unconscious. Now he was in her house. He had accosted her and tied her to her own bed. Now he had the gall to ask her to help him.

Sudden anger flared within her. It must have shown on her face because Fallon retreated a couple paces.

"Who the fuck do you think you are?" she demanded. "What right do you think you have, to barge into my home, hold me hostage and then ask me for help? How does that make any sense in your warped little mind, you sick, twisted asshole? How can you honestly stand there and expect me to listen to anything you have to say after you've threatened my life? You locked me in my own goddamned bedroom. What makes you think that you have any right to ask me for anything?" Despite her anger, Shelly regretted the outburst, and immediately feared his reprisal

None came. Instead, Fallon held up his hands. "If you'll just let me explain, my actions will become clear and you'll see that I had no other choice."

She didn't say anything. Her anger had dissipated a little. She was calmer, more in control, less ready to provoke him. She didn't want to hear what he had to say but saw little point in fighting him. She would bide her time. Wait and watch for her opportunity to make a break for it. She only hoped he wouldn't become violent before then. At least he hadn't raped her. There was that, at least.

The silence between them was heavy and uncomfortable. Fallon seemed to be searching for a way to begin. His brow was furrowed, his eyes closed to slits. The look of concentration he wore made him seem angry, or in pain. It was nothing Shelly wanted to watch, so she let her eyes wander around the room, searching for anything that could possibly help her.

Finally, Fallon looked up, a resolute expression on his face. "Your town is in grave danger," he said.

Shelly had been expecting all sorts of fantastic stories, but this had not been on the list. "What kind of danger?" she asked, against her better judgment.

"The army has come here. They're going to tear your town apart, piece by piece." Her disbelief must have shown on her face because he moved to the radio on her bedside table. "First, they're going to cut off all means of communication." He flipped it on, and static filled the room. He pressed the auto-scan button, and the digital display began scrolling through radio frequencies, not stopping for more than a second before moving on. Each time the tuner halted only white noise issued from the speakers. The dial had gone all the way around and started scanning over the same frequencies again. Fallon toggled to the AM band, with the same results, before turning the radio off. Then he picked up her cell phone and handed it to her. "Try calling someone. Anyone. Call the police."

She stared, wide-eyed, at the phone in his outstretched hand. He was giving her a way out. He wanted her to call someone for help. It was a trap. It had to be. After a second's suspicious hesitation, she snatched the phone from his hand, unlocked the screen and immediately dialed nine-one-one. She bounced from her bed and stepped over to the far corner of her room. Like the stereo, there was nothing. No reception bars, dial tone, no ringing; her phone endlessly said, "Connecting..."

After two minutes, she ended the call, laid the phone gently on her dresser and turned back to Fallon, who had waited patiently before continuing. “There’s no way to contact anyone in or outside this city. The roads in and out will all be blocked off as well. With every passing minute, they are tightening their grip.”

Shelly shook her head. She drew a breath, held it and then asked, “Why would they do this? Has there been a terrorist attack or something?”

Fallon smirked. “That’s probably the story they’ll spread to cover it up. But no, there hasn’t been any kind of attack. The army’s purpose here is twofold; the first reason is me. They’re looking for me. I can’t let them catch up to me. Colonel Aldridge would love nothing more than to get me back in his clutches.”

“Was he your commanding officer? Are you AWOL?”

His answering laugh was one of the saddest, most pitiful things she had ever heard.

“In order to be AWOL, you have to have first enlisted. I was never a soldier; I was a lab geek.” She could feel the anguish in his words as he spoke. “Up until earlier tonight, I was a part of a project, an illegal, biological weapons project, headed by Colonel Aldridge. I don’t have the time now to give you any more details. All I can say is that I escaped and now they’re hunting me.”

“Why? What did you do to them?”

“Because of what I know. Because of what I’ve seen, I can ruin the lives of hundreds of very highly placed people and put them in prison for an exceptionally long time. Aldridge is a cold, ruthless man. He’ll stop at nothing to safeguard his career, and the careers of the people he answers to, against threats like me.”

“How are you a threat to him?”

“The research done at his facility was illegal and top secret. If the world were handed proof that the United States was mass-producing biological weapons, there would be hearings, investigations, and a public witch hunt on a massive scale. Everyone involved would be humiliated and destroyed. These men are power players, and they will stop at nothing to protect themselves, even if that means killing one little town no one's ever heard of. They'll do it without hesitation. No nation can withstand pressure from the global community, not even the United States. Action would be called for. And Aldridge would be among the first crucified. So, he has a vested interest in capturing me."

Shelly said nothing. It was a lot to take in at once. The idea that such a thing could happen was almost beyond comprehension.

"What's the second reason?" she asked.

"The second reason is to cover up the fact that the biological agent they were developing got loose."

After a moment of silence Fallon said, "You still don't believe me. You think I'm a lunatic." He grimaced and shook his head. "That's understandable, I suppose. But I need your help to get away from them. I have to keep moving, if I'm going to get away and blow the whistle and stop them."

"You can let me go," she said, feeling unexpected tears trickle down her cheeks. "I'll give you my car. You can take it anywhere you need. Just please let me go. I can't help you."

Fallon locked eyes with her and gestured with the kitchen knife. "I can't do that. I have nowhere else to turn. I'm desperate. You're the only one who can help me. Do you know of any place we can go, where we won't be disturbed for a few days, while I figure out a way out of here?"

She shook her head.

"Don't be so hasty. Surely there's somewhere you know of, secluded and private; somewhere out of the way."

She thought for a moment. Being somewhere secluded and private with him was the last thing she wanted to do. But she had little choice in the matter. "I have a cabin, up in the hills."

"Good. Take us there, please." The relief in his voice was profound.

She hated herself for telling him about the cabin. Maybe it was the pleading tone of his voice. Or maybe she had let herself be convinced by his story. She wasn't yet sure. But there was no backing away now. She had decided to help him.

For a moment, she considered making a break for it. Then she discarded the idea. Besides, there really was some weird stuff going on here. She wanted to be somewhere safe until she knew more about it. She thought about Uncle Rory's cabin and repressed a smile. She had a lot of good memories there. For years, Rory maintained it as a place where he and close family could escape. She'd stayed there after running away from Brad and lived there for nearly three months, piecing her life back together. In the end, when she returned to L.A. and her life there, Brad had found her and brought her back, forcibly.

There were other, better memories of the place as well. There was a desk in the room Uncle Rory used for an office and in the bottom left drawer was the forty-five automatic he had taught her how to shoot. Shelly wasn't sure how much she believed of Fallon's story, if she even believed any of it at all. But now she saw her way out. One way or another, she would get out of this mess. She would not wait to be rescued this time. Experience had taught her that the only reliable person she could count on for help was herself. If there was going to be any rescuing done tonight, she was going to have to do it herself. She survived Brad; she could survive Fallon.

She would never be a victim again.

She went to her nightstand, picked up the glass of water she didn't remember putting there and drank it down.

She did not see Fallon's grin as he watched her drink.

"Thank you," he said.

Aldridge looked at his watch. It wasn't quite time yet. He was tired. More than tired. He felt like weeping from exhaustion. His eyelids itched and burned. Every blink was a struggle to just to open them again. How long had it been since he'd slept, or even slowed down? Forty hours? Fifty? The clock gave him no answers. Simple math was beyond him now. Just meaningless numbers jumbled around in his head.

For the last month, he had only been allowing himself around six hours of sleep in every forty. He knew he couldn't continue like this for very much longer. The only things keeping him going were coffee, adrenaline, and army-approved speed. Soon he'd start making mistakes and he could not afford that. He didn't need to give General Collins any more rope to hang him with. The bastard had enough already.

Miserably, he shook his head. "I'll sleep," he told himself, "after I meet with the doctor."

He checked his watch. Thirty minutes to go. He sighed in exasperation. He didn't want to wait thirty minutes but knew he would. There were strict guidelines and regulations to follow, and he was going to follow them.

*It's not like I'm addicted, after all*, he told himself. *I just need to stay alert, stay awake and keep going.*

The pills had served him well in Afghanistan when he and his men were trapped in hostile territory, far from help and support. He had needed to stay awake then to ensure the safety of his men and get them out of that mess. Now he needed to stay awake to track and find Fallon. There was nobody else. It was his responsibility, his burden, and he would bear it alone.

Lately the pills weren't helping as much. He was past the point for anything but real, honest sleep to be of any help. He knew he needed to, but just could not tear himself away long enough to do it. A look at the wall calendar told him it was Thursday. No, it was morning now. Today was Friday. That meant he had been pushing hard for a month. A month of quarantines. A month of chasing Fallon around backwater towns. A month of failure. He had to handle the situation now. Any more delays or screwups and the operation would be taken from him by General Collins, who would run through the town like a steam roller, pulverizing everything in his path to find Fallon. Aldridge was attempting a more surgical approach, which took more time, but meant less risk to the civilian population. Those above him didn't approve of this. Many felt he was unfit for the task, that he was too emotionally wrapped up to effectively conduct it. At all costs, they wanted the whole ordeal concluded quickly and quietly.

Aldridge rubbed his eyes and instantly started drifting away. He snapped his head up and forced them open again. Not yet. Too soon. His vision doubled and blurred. He tried blinking it clear, but that did nothing to help. He could feel the nagging ache in the back of his head, like an itch that refused to go away even after being scratched. He looked at his watch again and decided it was close enough. His trembling fingers reached into his front jacket pocket and fished out a small black bottle. From it he shook out four pills: one white round tablet and three small blue ones. The white was Modafinil, which was what was currently keeping him awake and functioning. The three smaller blues were Lorcet. He needed them to numb the pain of the wounds he received in Afghanistan. He popped them into his mouth and dry-swallowed all four at once. Then, without fear of sleep, he closed his eyes and waited for the pills to take effect.

Already he felt a little better. Calmer. More in control. In ten hours, after the Modafinil wore off, he'd get some shut eye. Until then, there was work to do.

Aldridge had set up his office in a windowless conference room in the center of the hospital, just up the hall from his radio operators. He had total control over the local sheriff's office and the highway patrol. The major arterial roadways connecting Harper's Glen to the rest of the highway network were severed, and a perimeter had been established around the town. As soon as the weather cleared, helicopters would start patrolling the barricades and UAVs would be up and flying around the city perimeter. Meanwhile, he had his soldiers conducting patrols. Aldridge had ordered all hard phone lines disconnected and had his electronic warfare operators block the town from all incoming and outgoing radio and cellular traffic. With those connections severed, Harper's Glen was totally and completely cut off. The quarantine was nearly complete. Even though dawn was still a few hours away, people were awake and had noticed the soldiers in their town as they went about their morning routines. Later today, the mayor was scheduled to give a speech, explaining what was happening and what was expected of everyone during this crisis. Once the people realized they were cut off from the rest of the country, there was sure to be a panic. The hope was that the speech would curb that panic and ensure their cooperation. If everything went well, some upstanding citizen would recognize Fallon and report his location to the nearest soldier or police officer, and this long nightmare would be over. Aldridge hoped that would be the case this time. But he wasn't confident. Why should anything be easy now? It hadn't been thus far.

There was a knock at the door and Captain West entered. "Sir, Doctor Francis is here to speak with you. Also, Major Panelli arrived a few minutes ago, along with four more troop trucks."

Aldridge nodded. "Good. Bring the doctor in, please." He wanted to speak with the hospital's chief of medicine before the side effects of the vaccine hit him. "Show him in and have Major Panelli come in here as well."

"Yes, sir."

A few minutes later, just when Aldridge was beginning to feel comfortably numb, there was another knock and West led Major Panelli and Doctor Francis into the room. Then West excused himself and left.

Doctor Francis didn't wait for an invitation, as he crossed to a chair and sat down. He was fiftyish, small and overweight, with severe rosacea. He wore a thick salt and pepper beard that matched the fringe of hair ringing the sides of his balding head. For a moment he sat panting, as though the walk to Aldridge's office had exhausted him. Which it probably had. The flu-like symptoms had already begun. In a little while, he would be bedridden for a full day.

Aldridge smiled pleasantly. "Thank you for coming, Doctor."

Francis spent a moment regaining his composure, and after a short silence he fixed Aldridge with a glare that would have turned a first-year intern inside out.

Aldridge cleared his throat, glanced at Panelli standing in the corner by the door, then continued. "I really am sorry for the ordeal you and your staff have been forced to endure. It was necessary to commandeer your hospital and to detain and inoculate your personnel as quickly as possible, so that you may assist us in this crisis."

At this, Francis broke his silence, interrupting Aldridge. "The only crisis I see, Colonel, is that you've invaded our town and kidnapped every doctor and nurse in it. I don't know what kind of goddamned game you're playing here, but rest assured, you won't get away with it."

Aldridge smiled again and let the doctor's words hang in the air for a moment. It was always the same: the same threats, the same haughty attitude and denial that something like this could be happening. Aldridge had seen it too many times recently to be impressed by it. Francis was no different than anyone else he'd spoken to. Once he had the facts, the good doctor would do everything he could to help.

"Doctor, please allow me to introduce myself. I am Colonel Preston Aldridge. I am in command of a special project with USAMRID. I can understand your displeasure over your treatment thus far. Believe me, I can. But it was necessary for us to move fast to bring you here. This situation has the potential of escalating far beyond our ability to control it. The steps we've taken have been for the safety of all concerned. For the safety of the greater good."

"And what exactly is 'the Situation', as you put it, Colonel Preston Aldridge of USAMRID? Why have we been goddamned kidnapped?"

"That is what I've brought you here to explain. I am going to need cooperation from you and your staff. To do that, you need to know exactly what we're dealing with." He reached into a box on the floor by his desk, removed a quarter-inch thick folder and slid it across the desk to Francis. "This contains all the information you will need to help us combat this outbreak."

At the word *outbreak*, Francis froze while reaching for the folder, which was what Aldridge had been hoping for.

*I have your attention now, don't I?* "You don't have to read it all right this minute. I know you're a busy man. And things are going to get much more hectic around here in the coming days. But share that with your people. Bring them up to speed on what we're asking of them."

Francis accepted he folder without taking his eyes off Aldridge. By now he had recovered and was glaring again. "I'm not going to let you dismiss me without an answer. I'm a goddamn American citizen, goddamn it! I'm the administrator of this hospital. I've been a doctor for twenty-four years. You want my help? Unless you answer my questions, you can kiss my fat, pimpled ass!"

Aldridge frowned. He had expected this, but he had also hoped that Doctor Francis would be more cooperative. This exchange was wasting time he didn't have.

He sighed dramatically. "Doctor, we're trying to contain an outbreak of extreme virulence. The bug has entered your town, contaminated your hospital, and has by now moved out into the general population. I've been tracking the vector of this disease, attempting to halt it before it reaches a major population center and spreads to the rest of the country. My mission is to contain the spread of this disease, capture Patient Zero, and eliminate any other disease vectors we find." He paused and fixed Francis with a flat stare. "To that end, I've not only taken your hospital and, as *you* put it, kidnapped your staff, but I've also quarantined your entire town until this crisis is abated. I can stop the spread here, but I need your help and cooperation to do it."

Francis' eyes were wide. "When... how did this happen?"

"Earlier this morning, a patient was admitted to your emergency room. He is the primary carrier of this disease: the patient zero. We are still trying to ascertain how he contracted the disease and why he hasn't succumbed to it yet. But first and foremost, we're trying to save lives. To do this, we need to halt the spread by finding patient zero and giving him the medical attention he needs before he spreads it any farther. Can I count on your help?" Aldridge paused for a second, but Francis was still reeling from what he'd just learned and didn't answer. "Please, Doctor, we haven't got much time. Will you help me?"

Francis nodded. He spoke slowly, as if weighing what he wanted to say. "I'll tell my people. You'll have our full cooperation. Colonel, I'm sorry for my hostility. I didn't know... I thought maybe—"

"That's all right. There is no need to apologize. Your reaction is perfectly understandable. Go and let your people know what they're going to be dealing with."

Francis got up to inform his staff what was going on and prepare, but stopped at the door. "What about our families?"

"Your families have all received the same vaccinations you have. They were most likely contaminated. We need to reduce as many vectors for this disease as possible. Don't worry, doctor. Your family will be fine."

Francis nodded and left.

Major Panelli stayed.

"You're getting good at that speech, sir," he said. The sarcasm in his voice was subtle, but Aldridge heard it loud and clear.

Aldridge sighed. "Practice seems to make perfect after all." This was the third time Aldridge had made that speech, or some variation of it to a hospital administrator. Everyone's reactions had been much the same as Francis' had been. The same concerns, the same arguments, the same fears. Aldridge told them all just enough to stoke their fear and bring them over to his side. Of course, he had not told Doctor Francis everything, any more than he had told the mayor, or the sheriff, or the previous hospital chiefs everything. The file he had given to the doctor was almost identical to the ones he had passed out to the others. The doctor's contained more medical data, however, enough information to give an idea about what was happening and how to deal with it. But it did not tell the whole story. Not by a long shot. There were even a few outright lies in it.

For one thing, Aldridge knew exactly how Martin Fallon had become Patient Zero.

His work for the army had infected him.

Aldridge nodded. "Hopefully, that will be the last time. We're on track here, Major. I think we'll catch him this time."

"Yes, sir," Panelli didn't mention that this was the third town they had cornered Fallon in. He also didn't mention how each time Fallon had managed to slip away before they could fully close the quarantine. Each time before, Aldridge had focused on helping the people infected and creating a liaison with the hospitals and law enforcement. As a result, fewer people died, but Fallon escaped.

This time, they had moved faster. For all intents and purposes, the town was already sealed off. Aldridge had learned from his mistakes and decided to complete the quarantine first, ensuring the capture of their quarry at the expense of the people he was hiding amongst. It was likely that more people would die this time around, but now they had a good chance of succeeding.

Practice indeed made perfect.

Aldridge rubbed his eyes. “How’s the rest of the convoy coming along?”

“Most of the trucks have arrived by now, sir. The cold truck is still on the road, but Lieutenant Parsons thinks they’ll arrive, without further mishap, in about half an hour. I got here, as per your orders, as quickly as I could with as many men as I could.”

“Good. Get them set up and running as soon as they arrive here. We need to start distribution as soon as possible. We’ve had too many mishaps already, Major. Let’s keep it smooth and simple. I want this to end here.”

Snow crunched loudly beneath the tires as they drove without headlights through the gray dawn. Shelly maneuvered the Bronco slowly and cautiously down the white-carpeted street. She kept her breathing slow and regular, trying not to give in to the panic she felt clenching at her chest.

*It wouldn’t be good,* she thought, *to wrap us around a telephone pole. Though I might be able to make a getaway if I do.*

Shelly glanced into the rearview as they pulled onto the street and saw lights had appeared behind them. Fallon craned around to look. “It’s an army truck,” he said. “Make that three of them. And they’re stopping at your house.”

Shelly didn’t reply right away. She was apprehensive about Fallon and his fantastic story. He had convinced her they were in danger; however, she was still leery and refused to completely trust him. “What are we going to do if they’ve blocked the roads out of town, like you said?”

"In that case, you'll have to find us another way out there."

Shelly frowned in the dark. A couple blocks later, she switched on her headlamps and increased speed. There was a twenty-four-hour convenience store and gas station less than two blocks away. She planned on fueling up there and buying what they needed for the cabin. Fallon sat silently in the back seat, lying across the seats to make himself as invisible as possible. When Shelly pressed him for more information, Fallon wouldn't answer her directly. "Now's not the time for this discussion, Nurse Christianson. Once we're at your cabin and safe, I'll share with you everything I know."

*Which should give you plenty of time for you to come up with a few good lies*, she thought. She didn't ask anything further and drove in silence.

They pulled up to the station. She pumped the gas, while Fallon went inside to start their shopping. The storm had passed. Even though the snow and wind had stopped, outside the Bronco it was freezing. Shelly watched her breath beneath the gas station's neon road sign. She looked up and down the snow-encrusted street. There was not another soul to be seen. The night was surprisingly calm, almost serene. Everyone was in bed, bundled up and warm. Peacefully unaware of the changes during the night.

*This must be what it would feel like to be the last person on earth: alone and cold.* She looked up and saw the clouds were gone and the stars were out, shining bright and strong through the clear air. Not for too much longer, however. Later, Shelly would remember this as the turning point. She could have gotten back into her car, and gone straight to the authorities to turn Fallon in. She could have saved herself. She could have done that, but the thought to do so didn't occur to her until later, when it was too late.

Right then, however, she was still too nervous and more than a little frightened. For all her self-proclaimed independence, she was still easily cowed by men. Brad had done his work well.

The pump clicked. She replaced the nozzle and went inside to pay.

They left the store twenty minutes later, laden with two heavy bags each, as well as a road and terrain map of the town and countryside.

The clerk, Randy Mills, was annoyed at having to ring out such a large order in the middle of the night, when he would rather be kicked back reading one of the titty magazines kept behind the counter, and would remember them later. Especially since the chick was a fox and the dude was a skinny creep who kept trying to lean in close while he rang up their order, like he was trying to kiss him or something. When they left, he noted they turned right out of the parking lot, headed away north. Then he promptly put them out of his mind as he reached for the latest issue of *Perfect 10*.

“That chick belongs in this magazine,” he said to himself, as he leafed through the pages of naked women.

Shelly kept to the side streets. She turned on the heater full blast, to regain some feeling in her fingers. Her eyes darted from the road to the rearview, stealing furtive glances at Fallon, who was again lying across the back seat, out of sight of any passing cars. The air grew lighter with the rising sun, and she almost didn’t need her headlights anymore. In the emerging light of the new day, she could see evidence supporting Fallon’s wild story about army occupation. Every few blocks she saw an army truck on a cross street, often heading away from them, for which she was thankful. Overhead, she heard the rotors of a helicopter, circling. They passed the Walmart on Mission Street, and she was stunned by the mass of soldiers she saw there, turning away the few early-morning shoppers.

Just to reconfirm the fact in her own mind, Shelly turned on the radio. Static. The army really had taken over Harper’s Glen.

"Now do you see?" Fallon said from the back. "The armies of Legion have come. Ready to do battle and lay waste to your little town. We must move quickly, Nurse Christianson, before they trap us. There is no time for delay."

She met his dark and bloodshot eyes in the rearview. Under the inconsistent streetlights, she noted how thin and pale he was.

*How long has he been running?*

Shelly returned her eyes to the road and increased speed. They were heading north, passing through older residential neighborhoods. She turned right, then left a few blocks later, turned down a narrow alleyway. Fifty feet farther on, they passed the final line of houses and turned onto a sunken farm road between two pastures. The path was marked only by barbed wire, strung to mark the boundaries of each field. Shelly paused to engage four-wheel drive. Wooded hills loomed ahead of them. They were nearly free. Twenty yards later, they were safe under the canopy. Shelly slowed and started threading her way through the trees in a northeasterly direction.

At Uncle Rory's insistence, there was no real path or road leading to his cabin. It was his retreat. His refuge from the world. He had shown her how to get there and assured her it was hers whenever she needed it. That was years before. With Uncle Rory gone, the place really was hers.

Thinking of Rory brought tears to her eyes. She missed him terribly.

The going was slow. The trees close to town were sparse. There were good-sized gaps in the stands of blackjack pine. As they traveled deeper into the woods, Shelly had to slowly maneuver her Bronco around dense growths of Engelmann and Ponderosas broken up by the occasional clumps of Douglas Firs. Snow had collected in deep drifts beneath openings in the canopy. The white carpet was thin where the trees were thick and treacherous everywhere else. Navigating the forest floor took every ounce of Shelly's concentration. Several times she was forced to backtrack and go around heavy deadfalls and thickets and even one impassable ravine. After a little over an hour of bouncing along rutted, rough ground, Shelly stopped the Bronco on the concrete slab next to the cabin.

The sun was out, trying unsuccessfully to warm the frozen earth. Shafts of sunlight poured through the branches, providing some light to the early-morning gloom. Shelly unlocked the door and went inside.

Uncle Rory's cabin was a small, simple structure, built like a rustic mountain-man log home. It was low, almost squatting, next to the little creek a few yards away and surrounded by trees. Uncle Rory always said he didn't want anyone to know where the cabin was, lest the world be given the opportunity to find him. He was like that sometimes. Whenever he was stuck on a story, he would come out here to clear his head and avoid distractions so he could finish his novels. Sometimes, whenever the urge took him, he would just take a month or two off and hide out. Only a few people knew where the cabin was. Not his agent, publisher, either of his ex-wives or his brother Travis—her dad. Shelly was one of the privileged few.

Two years ago, Uncle Rory picked her up from the hospital and took her home. During the drive, he spoke to her directly and frankly about everything that had happened, about the inquest and the investigation. Rory told her he had hired the best attorney his money could buy and there was no chance she'd have to do time.

"Just let me take care of it, honey. You'll never see the inside of a jail cell. Not if I can help it."

She loved Uncle Rory more in that moment, than she ever had before. He was her knight in shining armor. He was the one who always arrived at just the right moment to rescue her. She wished, for the millionth time, that he had been her father, rather than the worthless drunk who had tried and failed to raise her.

Uncle Rory died a year later, and she was crushed. When she found out he had left her everything, she told the lawyer overseeing the will, through a heavy bout of sobbing, that she did not want anything, she just wanted her uncle back. Standing outside his cabin that wet Wednesday afternoon with keys and deed in hand, Shelly decided that Uncle Rory had been the father she deserved, but never had.

Grief and remorse twanged within her. She still missed him terribly. She paused on the front step for a moment, looking the place over, then unlocked the door and let Fallon inside.

She was struck by how strangely she was acting. Here she was, bringing a complete stranger to her hideaway, her refuge, the only place in the world she truly felt safe. Her need for security was outshined by her desire for answers. She didn't completely trust Fallon, but he was right about the military presence in town. Something terrible was happening. Fallon was the only one who could answer her questions. She was, therefore, stuck with him for the time being. She shook her head and went around the back of the car to unload their groceries. Fallon had already opened the back hatch and had three bags in hand. She took the last and led the way to the front door.

The folder on his desk contained several more folders, numerous photographs and nearly a ream of paper in typed reports and summaries, making it absurdly thick. It was a nearly complete look at Fallon's history. Aldridge almost had it memorized. Without looking, he could quickly and accurately quote the facts of Fallon's life: birthplace, schools, even the name of his senior prom date—Carey Marie Halverstead. But as detailed as the file was, it didn't bring him any closer to Fallon. Elusive as always, the bastard continued to slip away.

Aldridge closed his eyes. The nagging ache in his leg was growing into real agony. The Modafinil—which he had developed a significant tolerance to—was wearing off, as was his pain medication, and he was starting to drift into exhaustion. He didn't want to take another handful of pills. Not yet. But he felt his willpower slowly eroding before the onslaught of exhaustion and pain.

In an attempt to distract himself from his woes, he tried to recall facts about Fallon's childhood. His mother, a woman by the name of Audrey Fallon, was a devoutly religious woman and a strict disciplinarian, who believed the modern age, with its easy conveniences and loose morals, was rife with sin. She did everything in her power to protect her young son from the wicked world outside her door. She was unwed, and there was speculation that she became pregnant due to an unreported rape. The house he grew up in was adorned with religious iconography. On every available wall or surface was placed an effigy to Christ our Lord and Savior, the Virgin, His mother and all the saints and angels in Christendom. So cluttered and packed, everywhere the eye turned, it encountered one idol after another. There was no computer, no stereo sound system and certainly no tool-of-Satan videogames. A simple radio was always tuned to the church-sponsored AM band stations and the only television was a ten-year-old, twenty-four-inch cathode ray tube set, which was always set to the evangelical channels.

In this house Fallon was home schooled and lived alone with his mother until the age of eight. He suffered his mother's love, care and attention as she educated her son about the evils of the world, often with a belt or electric cord, regularly resulting in him being locked into the hall closet without food or water for days at a time. These were dealt to him as penances for some sinful act or other.

When Child Protective Services took him away, Audrey went insane with rage and grief, and little Fallon had to be moved to three different foster homes during the next two years. She mailed death threats to the first family and set their dog on fire. During Fallon's time with his second foster family, she showed up at his school, signed him out of class and attempted to flee the state with him. She had gotten two counties away before she was pulled over for impeding traffic. Never having learned to drive, she was fearful of maintaining any speed above a reckless thirty-five miles per hour on the highway. When they placed Fallon with his third family, the state took extra precautions against his mother finding him again.

Fallon never saw his mother again. Audrey killed herself three months after being let out of jail.

By all accounts, Fallon spent the rest of his childhood healthy and happy in his new home. His foster parents were decent, hard-working people, who couldn't have children of their own and lavished attention on him. Being a highly intelligent young man, he quickly caught up with the other students his own age. Then, just as quickly, he surpassed them. His foster parents worried about the effects his abuse and the loss of his mother, who had been a dominant force in his life, would have on him. Once he was free of her, Fallon turned away from religion and devoted himself wholeheartedly to study and learning. He wasn't a social outcast, but neither was he the most popular kid in class. His teachers remembered him as a polite and quiet pupil, who turned in his A-plus assignments on time. Due to the tragic home life of his early years and his outstanding test scores, Fallon was awarded a full ride scholarship to college once he graduated at the early age of sixteen.

None of this was of any use to Aldridge. He had memorized these facts long ago. He felt that by knowing, he would be able to find him. While the theory hadn't panned out so far, it gave him an understanding of Fallon, why he ran and why he was hiding. Aldridge knew Fallon better than any of his closest friends, men he had served in combat with, even better than his ex-wife.

Keep your enemies close, as the old saying went.

He was confident they would catch him this time. Fallon had to be tired. It had been a long, desperate chase, and he had to be as worn out as Aldridge was. He couldn't keep going forever. There was no question in his mind that Fallon would slip up. When he did, Aldridge would be there to catch him.

The pain in his leg and the itch in his bones were palpable, nearly unbearable. He could abide the discomfort no longer. From the top, right-hand drawer of his little metal desk, he pulled out his pill bottle. It was time for sweet relief. At the last second, pills in hand, he decided not to take the Modafinil. Staying awake wasn't doing him, his mission or anyone else any good.

It was time to sleep.

He popped the pain pills, laid down in the cot that had been set up for him, and was swept away into sweet oblivion.

Stepping inside, even after only a few seconds of bitter cold, was a relief. The cabin's interior wasn't very warm, but it was near tropical compared to the icy world beyond the doorstep.

Fallon set down the bags and unzipped his parka. He looked around and smiled. The cabin was just as rustic inside as it was out. Most of it was taken up by a single large room. To the left, at the back of the house was the small, but well-equipped kitchen. To the right of the kitchen was a small bedroom. There was a large granite fireplace in the north wall. The south wall was lined with packed bookshelves, and there was a cluttered writing desk in the corner. There were few windows, but they were large, high up and well placed to let in the most light possible. There were a few paintings on the wall, and the cabin's original owner at least had the good taste not to have a bear skin rug slung beneath the fireplace, or a moose head on the wall.

Fallon instantly felt at home and comfortable and safe.

"This is a nice place," he said. "Have you owned it long?"

"It was my uncle's. He used it as a writer's escape."

Fallon nodded appreciatively. "What kinds of books did your uncle write?"

"Fiction. Thrillers and mysteries, mainly."

Fallon nodded again but didn't say anything. He only read serious books and had no time for fake stories about people who never existed doing impossible things in faraway make-believe places. He liked his reading to be grounded sternly in fact. Although lately he had been consumed with reading the Bible and reabsorbing the messages therein.

After spending a few minutes unpacking the food, Shelly disappeared through a narrow door into a small back room, which was solely occupied by the cabin's diesel generator. There was no central heating or air conditioning, but they at least had lights. Once the generator was running, Shelly motioned towards the door. "Go around back to the woodbin and get us some wood for a fire." She then removed a tissue from her pocket and violently blew her nose.

He zipped up his parka and went outside. The dark, ominous clouds had returned, and it had started snowing again. Just a light flurry of lazy flakes, but it was enough to make him shiver. His earlier close call with hypothermia had given him a dislike for the wintertime and everything to do with it.

Despite this, he smiled. *This will cover up our tire tracks,* he thought and gave a little laugh. The Lord had provided yet again. He was safe and one step ahead of his enemies. Now he had time to think and plan his next move.

He couldn't help but marvel over how far he'd been allowed to come. When he had started, Fallon hadn't imagined he'd make it three days before Aldridge and the army caught up with him. Then three days had gone by, then five, then a month and he was still free.

*Aldridge will never catch me. Soon I'll be free to spread the word of God, and expose their crimes to the whole world,* he thought. There weren't enough armies in the world to stop him from completing his righteous mission. He merely had to stay alert and stay ahead of them.

Piling stove-lengths in his arms, he pondered what to do about Nurse Christianson.

*She doesn't yet trust me or believe me, not completely, anyway.*

Must work on that, bring her around.

He had thought about the problem she presented him during the ride up and hadn't come up with any good solutions. Without her, he almost certainly would have been captured. She was his savior, but she was a liability too. God may have put her in his path, but he certainly hadn't left instructions for how best to use her.

Briefly, he'd thought about telling her everything...

*No, it's still too early for that,* he thought.

Eventually, yes, he would have to tell her everything. By now, the army had to know—or at least suspect—she was helping him and would hunt for her as mercilessly as he. Most of all, Fallon thought about how nice it was not to be alone anymore. Even mistrustful company was better than none at all. He thought he might even enjoy some conversation with her. Maybe even a little more. After all, now she was the Eve to his Adam.

He turned, careful not to slip in the snow, cradling the wood close to his chest and nearly ran face-first into the muzzle of a large automatic pistol aimed at his forehead. He stood dumb, unable to process what he was seeing. His eyes followed the handgun as it raised overhead and came swinging back down. He barely had time to flinch before the heavy steel contacted with his temple and everything when dark.

The narrow hallway stretched on endlessly. The walls were close and poorly lit. Vast spaces were unlit, while others strobed with an inconsistent florescent flickering. The air in the hallway, heavy with smoke, was hard to breathe and stung the eyes and nose.

*There's a fire,* he thought, before continuing into the haze. Leaden smoke came from everywhere and nowhere, filling the confined corridor, adding to the already claustrophobic atmosphere. The heat pressed oppressively. Urgency compelled him faster; he quickened his pace until he was flat-out running.

*Just a little bit farther. Just a little bit. I can make it this time. I know I can.*

The hallway didn't end. In the light or in the dark, the same plain, cream-colored walls surrounded him, their blandness threatening to consume him. It was like he was running underwater. Suddenly, the hallway branched right and left. He went left, as he always did, sprinting through the flickering haze. The wall with the door appeared so suddenly he could not stop in time and slammed headlong into it. Thick, gray tendrils poured through the cracks in the doorjamb in pulses, like heaving breaths. One moment spilling through, the next being drawn back in, like a dragon breathing a tired pant. He ignored the smoke and reached for the knob. The second his hand grasped the iron, he gasped and quickly drew back, expecting a burn. But there was none. As always, the knob was cool to the touch.

He threw open the door and stepped boldly through. Before him was not a dragon or fire of any sort. Instead, before him lay a sunbaked landscape, pockmarked, blasted and hellish. Jagged mountains rose tall and formidable in the distance, with waves of rolling hills and deep ravine valleys at their feet, which leveled out into poppy fields as far as the eye could see. He saw the burnt-out husks of hundreds of vehicles and thousands of corpses. From somewhere to his left came the harsh staccato of automatic weapons fire, yelling and the boom of an exploding grenade.

He looked down at himself and found he was suddenly wearing full battle kit, before he ducked behind the rusted, flame-scarred hulk of an old truck and dove into a small bomb crater for cover. Quickly scanning the area for threats, he adjusted his helmet and ducked back down.

"They're coming around the left, sir," someone spoke from behind him. He turned and found a young soldier. He recognized the boy's face but was at a loss for the name. "Where the fuck's our air support? What do we do now, sir?" There was fear in the boy's eyes. He clutched his rifle in a death grip and was nearly hyperventilating, his fear edging close to panic.

Instead of answering the young soldier, he shifted his pack, looked around again and left the crater, abandoning the young soldier to fate. He searched for the doorway, but it was nowhere to be seen. Tracers sliced through the air around him as he ran, cutting first one way, then another.

Where was the door? He had to find it, had to go back through. Adrenaline coursed through him as his fight-or-flight instincts took over.

In the distance he could see silhouettes moving in his peripheral vision, soldiers fighting for their lives. His consciousness seemed to separate, floating up and away from his body. He saw himself then, fighting and killing, struggling to survive. He knew what was coming, but he couldn't stop looking. From the sidelines, he watched himself tackle two men in turbans and long, black dress-like garments head on; he smashed one of them in the face with his rifle butt and shot the other in the stomach and chest, all in one fluid motion. He dropped down to one knee and took aim at a third, as a grenade landed in a small hole a few feet from where his other self knelt.

He wanted to warn himself, to tell himself to get away. He screamed in silence. But it was no use.

It never was.

The explosion was louder than all the others combined; a concussive pop rang through his whole body. Preston saw himself thrown flat, saw the blood and torn flesh of his leg and his paralysis was broken. He turned and fled away from the carnage, dragging his mangled leg behind him.

He could not stop. Could not wait. He had to keep moving. He had to find the door again. All around him he saw bodies falling. Cut down by bullets. Blasted apart by explosions. Pummeled to death by enemy hands. Screams surrounded him, following as he ran. He couldn't outrun them. Each new cry spelled out the misery endured until death's final reward released it. The enemy was everywhere. His people were being overrun. He knew it. And there was nothing he could do to help. Nothing he wanted to do. He had more important matters to see to.

He turned right and, still sprinting, climbed into the hills below the mountains. His progress slowed as he clambered over boulders the size of suburban houses and slid down into deep, thorn-filled ravines. He tossed aside his rifle and helmet, dropped his assault pack and pulled the quick-release ring to slough off his body armor. His clothing torn and bloody. The skin on his face and hands covered with bleeding cuts and sooty dirt. The sun glared menacingly upon him. The heat of it threatened to bowl him over. Several times, he tripped and fell as he limped. Each time, getting back to his feet again was a struggle. Still, he trudged on.

He was almost there. He was sure of it.

Topping another small rise, he saw it. The entrance to one of the caves the Afghan fighters used as bases. He half-slid, half-tumbled down to reach the cave mouth.

Littered about the entrance were the bodies of dead Tunnel Rats. The soldiers had been stripped clean of everything useful and lay naked in the sun, being picked apart by birds and bugs. He didn't spare them a second look as he rushed headlong into the darkness before him.

He burst out the other side in the middle of the compound parking lot. Four-story, slate-gray buildings ringed the lot on three sides. The whole area was surrounded by electrified razor wire. The heat was almost unbearable. Everywhere he looked, people were running. More screams, more misery filled his head. The flames licking out of the compound windows seemed to beckon him still closer.

Out of breath and exhausted. Bleeding and limping. Filthy and tattered. He continued searching. There in front of him was the door. He had to get inside. He had to find them and get them out of there.

He started for the collapsing pyre in the center. More screams filled the air, and he recognized his own voice among them. He had hobbled barely a dozen steps when something, some immovable force of nature, slammed into him, throwing him to the rough concrete. He looked up, into the face of his assailant, and Fallon smiled down at him knowingly. His snake's eyes locked with his. It was too late. There was nothing he could do. The next instant, Fallon was gone, leaving only a wisp of smoke in his wake.

Aldridge snapped awake, the scream in his mouth barely contained by his sweat-beaded lips. For several long seconds, he didn't know where he was. He searched frantically for attackers in the corners of the room. The shadows in the room threatened him from the corner of his eye. Aldridge reached for his pistol and had disengaged the safety before sense returned to him. Finally, with deep, panicked breaths, he calmed enough to recall where he was and what he was doing.

His watch told him he'd gotten four hours of sleep.

He sighed and shook his groggy head. Four hours was more than he had been able to manage ever since this chase began. Every night, ever since he came back from Afghanistan, he was plagued by dreams. The same dreams, thundering through his head like a storm. Tragedy piled upon tragedy. He was afraid to sleep. Afraid of what his own mind would do to him. Without looking, he reached for the bottle of pills on the desk. Once they were down, he put on his boots and got out of the cot. There was work which needed doing. The Modafinil would keep sleep at bay and with it the dreams. All he had to do was keep hold of himself in the meantime.

"I've almost got him," he told the sweat-soaked bedspread. "This time, he's mine. Nothing's going to stand in my way. Not this time. I'm going to make the bastard pay."

The cabin was no longer cold. The fire Shelly built heated the front room and there was plenty of wood cut for an extended stay. Outside the wind had picked up, blowing high drifts of snow about the small clearing. She momentarily forgot about the communication blackout and turned on the radio to check the weather. Nothing but dead silence from the speakers. Her concern over the weather was just a distraction, something to take her mind off deciding what to do next. She paced the room, wringing her hands, thinking hard about her situation. She had been taken hostage by a total stranger telling wild conspiracy stories. That his story fit the facts before her only made things worse, not better. If the army really was chasing him, then Shelly wasn't so sure she wanted to be around him.

She stopped pacing and looked at the couch where Fallon lay. In the hour since she'd hit him, the red spot on his head had darkened into an ugly bruise. She had wasted no time dragging him into the cabin. After tying him to the couch, she'd conducted a thorough examination of his injury and didn't think he was hurt too badly. Fallon at first pulled away from her, afraid she might strike him again. But he quickly seemed to realize that wasn't her intention and let her examine him. The bruise on his head was ugly and there was a tiny cut in the middle of it where the pistol sight broke the skin, but otherwise there seemed to be no serious trauma.

Finding nothing wrong, and satisfied he wouldn't be able to escape, she left him and went into the bedroom to think. Shelly lay down on the bed and stared at the ceiling. Though it felt like forever, when she checked the clock on the wall, she found only a few minutes had passed. Feeling restless and trapped, she got up again and began her nervous circuit of the front room. She wanted to be rid of Fallon, however, the way to do so eluded her. She had already helped him escape. She was sure the army wouldn't believe she'd been coerced. Besides, she didn't trust them. Authority figures had never helped her in the past, and she couldn't see that changing now.

Deep down, though she didn't want to admit it just yet—not even to herself—she believed Fallon's story. She saw the army trucks swarming the streets and the TV and radio blackout. This combination could not be mere coincidence. She trusted her eyes and her instincts, and both told her the army was there to hunt down and destroy Fallon, along with anyone who got in their way. Handing him over would probably doom her as well. There was no way out.

Frustrated, she felt like screaming and crying at the same time.

Shelly sat down hard in the rocking chair, put her face in her hands and started quietly sobbing. Things seemed desperately hopeless. The bleakest since her last day with Brad: the day of the knife. She had found deep reserves of strength that day. Strength she hadn't been aware of. Brad had been sure that he had beaten the fight completely out of her. When she'd lashed out, the look of surprise in his eyes was almost comical. He had been in control of her for so long, he did not know how to take it when she fought back. He was completely and totally shocked when he collapsed with the knife sticking out of his chest, his life emptying slowly onto the floor with each erratic pump of his heart. More quickly than she had expected, Brad was dead, ending her nightmare.

Shelly ceased sobbing and looked up to find a bleary-eyed Fallon watching her. There were some questions she wanted answered. There would be no more evasions or cryptic replies. She would learn what she wanted to know, or else she would turn him over to the army, consequences be damned. She wasn't about to let another man use her.

Not again.

Not ever.

She stared at him for a time and he stared right back, though somewhat groggily and unfocused. Having had no sleep for almost twenty-four hours, Shelly was tired, but didn't feel like sleeping just yet.

Finally, Fallon broke the stalemated silence. "Are you going to kill me?"

The question stopped her cold. He was obviously afraid of her. That much was clear. She was at a loss. She had not thought about killing him—not once—while he had been unconscious on the couch. But now that he had said it, even as ridiculous as it was, she couldn't shake the idea.

For a long moment, Fallon waited for her answer. She imagined how easy it would be. No one knew where he was, and only a few of the hospital staff even knew he was in town. There was nothing at all which would connect him to her. She could easily just shoot him, blow his head clean off and dispose of his body in the woods. She knew of a couple of deep ravines where he wasn't likely to be found. Then she would be free and clear to return home.

Shelly shook her head and in her most reassuring nurse's voice said, "No, I'm not going to kill you."

Fallon seemed little relieved by this, but said, "Okay. Then if it's all the same to you, I'm going to get some sleep. My head hurts." He wriggled about until he was comfortable, closed his eyes and dropped away.

"Don't—You can't sleep yet—I have questions..." Shelly

started. But it was too late. She could already hear the rhythm of his light snoring. “God damn it!” Shaking her head, she turned away and went back into the bedroom. She coughed into the back of her hand.

*Just what I need right now,* she thought. *What a great time to get sick. I don’t need this right now.*

What was she going to do?

She was no closer to an answer now than she was ten minutes ago. Should she kill him? It would certainly simplify things for her. She would be a tragic hero. A victim of circumstances beyond her control, but strong enough to rise above them and conquer. It would be easy. She still had the gun, and he was still tied to the couch. She had wrapped his wrists and ankles with heavy packing twine, then bound them together around his waist and to the couch itself. She was sure he could not get loose. It would not take much. She could do it while he was asleep.

Shelly shook the thought away. She was not going to kill anybody. Not again. There was another solution, a better one. She was sure of it. She simply had to keep looking until she found it.

Shelly paced the room. More and more, she found her gaze straying to the bed, imagining how heavenly it would be to slip beneath the covers and just float away. After a few more times around the room, she still hadn’t thought of anything helpful. She decided she wanted answers and would get them from Fallon now. Suddenly thirsty, she went to the kitchen for a glass of water.

Fallon waited until the sounds of Shelly’s pacing ceased before opening his eyes. He looked around him at the empty room and sighed heavily. Anything that might free him was far out of reach. The knots securing his hands and feet were tight and inaccessible. For the first time since his adventure began, Fallon was really scared and didn’t know what to do next.

*Why has the Lord delivered me into the hands of this madwoman?* he wondered.

*It must be another test,* he answered himself.

All he had done to reach this point, every step he had taken, was wasted. She had blindsided him, voiding all his careful planning and preparation. Instead of escaping, he had trapped himself. Now he had to figure out how to get out of this new mess.

He could see that the communion he'd given her was already working on her. He had to get her to free him while she was still able. Before illness completely incapacitated her.

*There is no time for doubt,* he thought. He was following the path laid out for him. His destiny was set and clear. Fallon was as sure of it today as he was when he had discovered the Lord's Beauty. *All will be well. Just keep faith.*

He decided then to share most of what he knew with her, answer her questions and win her over to his side. He had to win her over, and if the truth was what it took to convince her, then he would give it to her. Or at least enough to do the job. He wouldn't fail. He couldn't. There was too much at stake. Success was within his grasp, he merely had to reach out and take it. Thus decided, he got as comfortable as he could. It was going to be a long day.

Behind him, he heard the kitchen tap turn on and quickly closed his eyes again. A moment later he gasped as cold water poured slowly over his head. Fallon gave his head a little shake to flick the water from his eyes. The shock made him jerk hard against the cords binding him.

Taking deep breaths, he forced himself to relax. Shelly Christianson sat calmly in a chair before him, her knees folded against her chest, her arms clasped around them. She seemed totally relaxed. Looking into her eyes, he saw nothing but cool, clinical detachment. It was the same look he had seen in countless other doctors' eyes over the years. She wasn't viciously, or maliciously attacking him. She merely thought he was asleep and selected the quickest, most efficient means to wake him. When he looked at it that way, Fallon could even understand it. However, being soaked with cold water wasn't something he enjoyed.

"I want some answers," she said. "I'm not going to sit here in the dark while you take a nap. You're going to tell me what I want to know, or I'm going to pack you up and deliver you to the army with a big bow on your head. Got me?"

After a moment, he regained enough composure to speak. "You're absolutely right. I think it's time I was honest with you." She said nothing. "I didn't tell you more before because I didn't think we had the time to waste on full explanations. I needed us to move quickly. And we did, for which I'm grateful. I should have told you more while we were in the car, given you more reason to believe me. I didn't, and I was wrong. I'm sorry. It's unreasonable to ask you to trust me if I don't first trust you. Ask me anything. I'll tell you everything I know."

After a moment more of silence, he said, "Go on, ask."

She let go of her knees and leaned forward, but was careful to remain out of his reach, her eyes intent upon his. "Tell me exactly why the army is chasing you."

He thought for a moment. "I was a research assistant in a secret army project. The goal of the project was to create a new weapon for the military. The weapon was viral in nature. Don't look so shocked. The military's been involved in this sort of research since the fifties. There is no moral high ground to hide behind. Just because there are laws against such a thing, doesn't mean that it isn't done. The nation's enemies aren't resting, and our government isn't either. The American public has this view that we're always the good guys. So, to maintain that illusion, research into biological weaponry must be conducted in secret, to maintain the public trust that the government and the military are doing everything to safeguard them. If they don't know about it, they don't care what happens. Until it infringes upon their rights and freedoms, then the hammer of the righteous falls.

"Anyway, I was involved in some extremely illegal research. My team was tasked with creating a new weapon, one which could change the face of warfare as we know it. We tweaked it and twisted it until we created the stuff of nightmares. A bug so virulent, the army was afraid to test it for fear it would escape into the population. The project director assured them he had a test plan which was completely safe and foolproof. A few test subjects were brought in to test it: prisoners, sentenced to death, with no chance of reentering society again—people on the fringe, vagrants, and runaways. We tested the virus on them. It worked beyond all their expectations: ninety-four point seven percent contagious, short incubation period and completely incurable without immediate vaccination. It could wipe out an entire region in a week. A city the size of New York could be completely dead within a month. Then the army could move in and assume control of the area without a single shot fired. No American casualties, which is all the people of this country care about. It doesn't matter how many others die, if there are as few American boys dead as possible."

Shelly frowned. She had never been the most patriotic of people, but the thought of her government conducting such illegal research made her uncomfortable.

Fallon continued. "But the only thing the American public dislikes more than the death of American youths, is the appearance of impropriety. We've all grown up believing the civil war was fought to free the slaves, the Revolutionary War was to free us from English oppression and the Iraq wars were to free others from the crush of tyranny. We've grown accustomed to thinking we have the moral high ground, that we're the good guys, no matter how wrong we are. That we'll never be as bad as the Nazis, or any of history's other great villains. We can't be. We are America, after all. It's an article of faith which people must believe in. No matter how much we distrust the government, or what conspiracies we choose believe, we almost unanimously believe we are a good people, a beacon of hope for the rest of the world. The truth, however, is much scarier; too scary for the average citizen to accept. We are no different from any empire in the past, using force and abusing power to achieve whatever ends we see fit. No better, no worse, and we will do anything to protect our gains, even if that means sacrificing a few for the greater good."

Shelly was lost at this point and growing annoyed. She didn't know where Fallon was going with this crazy political diatribe, but she was sure he was using all this talk of grand politics and conspiracy to misdirect her and throw her off guard. She had heard such grandiose speeches before, and they were always either a distraction, or precursor to some kind of reconciliation. This time she wasn't having it. She wanted the truth, and she wasn't going to stop until she had it.

"What does any of this have to do with you kidnapping me?" she demanded. "Or why the army's after you? You're just using all this talk of moral high ground and politics to confuse the point and evade the question. Answer me now, or I swear to God I'll hand you over to them."

Fallon closed his eyes and leaned back. "I'm trying to give you some background, which you'll need to understand what I have to tell you. There are reasons for everything that happens. Cause and effect. What I've told you so far explains why the military is so anxious to see me recaptured. I suppose you're right, though. I was avoiding answering your question directly. I guess I feel the need to justify my actions to someone."

He sighed. "Here goes. We performed every imaginable test on this virus, to investigate its lethality. We couldn't keep snatching prisoners. That would have called attention to us sooner or later. So, we started grabbing people off the street, vagrants mostly and drug addicts, people who wouldn't be missed, because society was already ignoring them, all totally unaware of what we were doing to them. A few of them were even happy during the early part of the trials. We were feeding them and providing them with shelter and a comfortable bed to sleep in. Meet just a few of a person's basic needs and they will forget their discomfort for a time.

"The project director, now he was a real son of a bitch. He felt the human trials were lacking an 'all-inclusive test base.' The snatch teams were ordered to bring in more people from a wider area and in greater varieties. He wanted to find out how the virus reacted to every probable variation of the human species, so there would be no surprises when the bug was used in the field, if such a day ever came. He felt the virus could behave in unexpected ways. The cold-hearted bastard was right in the end. By accident, we found out pregnant women live longer than every other demographic of test subjects. Initially, the virus attacks the fetus completely, leaving the rest of the woman's biological systems essentially untouched.

"I remember one subject. She was about fourteen. Addicted to methamphetamines, though when we picked her up there was a smorgasbord of drugs in her system. This girl was about sixteen weeks along when we took her in. She didn't even know it. She was the first pregnant subject we'd ever tested. If the teams had known, they probably would've just left her on the street to live out her fate. By the time the rest of the group she'd been brought in with were dead or dying, she was only just becoming symptomatic. She lasted a full six days longer than anyone else had, ever. Those first few days after becoming sick, she sat huddled in the corner of her cell, clutching her knees, rocking back and forth, her uterus slowly bleeding out the remains of the fetus inside her. After that, she crashed and bled out in the expected seven days."

"That's horrifying." Shelly suddenly didn't want to hear

any more. What the man tied to her couch was saying terrified her. Shelly steeled her nerves and forced herself to listen to the rest of his story.

“It was. It is. But the Director was ecstatic. This was exactly the sort of thing he’d been hoping for. He used this new development as an excuse to expand the program. Colonel Aldridge disagreed with him. He wanted to slow down and assess the results of this wrinkle. The Colonel wasn’t concerned with the loss of life so much as the need for accurate documentation. So, the snatches stopped for a while and the project was put on hiatus. The Director worked feverishly, cutting his way through bureaucratic red tape as fast as he could, to have pregnant women included in every test run from then on. He claimed that this unexpected development needed further study.”

Fallon paused. He was staring at the floor, a look of anguish on his face. It was as though he didn’t want to think about what he was remembering. Shelly let him be for a moment, but she knew that if she gave him time, he would think of a way to talk himself free. So, still probing for information, she switched subjects. “Tell me about this project director. You’ve insulted him twice now. Why don’t you like him?”

Fallon fixed her with a stony look. His mouth downturned in a look of distaste, as though he had swallowed something sour. “I have never met a more godless, amoral, heartless bastard in all my life. The Director was a man motivated solely by his work and the power and prestige granted him by virtue of his position. He was also a lunatic, responsible for the deaths of dozens of people.”

“You keep referring to him in the past tense.”

“He’s dead,” Fallon said quickly. “He died the night I made my break from the facility. I killed him. A man such as him couldn’t be allowed to live. When I decided to run, he tried to stop me, and I decided to make him pay for all the suffering that he'd inflicted upon others in the name of science. Having decided to leave, it was just a question of what I could do to bring that place down. I stole files, set fire to the labs, and ended the project director. Now the army is chasing me down to keep me from telling the whole world about the atrocities I witnessed... that I helped to commit. I'm trying to make the world a better, safer place. His only goal was to secure his own prosperity within the corrupt status quo."

"Do you still have these files?" she asked.

Fallon shook his head. "I lost them. It's been a long and desperate chase. I wish I still had them. Then you'd be convinced I'm telling the truth."

It was obvious Fallon was troubled by everything he'd described. But she could not bring herself to trust him. Not yet anyway. "Tell me about this virus."

"It can be transmitted through the air like a common cold; however, direct contact spreads the contagion more effectively. The victim will feel the rapid onset of fever, malaise, muscle pain, headache, as well as severe joint inflammation and pain. Once inside, it instantly attacks the lymphatic system and begins breaking down the host's white blood cells. It settles in the liver and kidneys, where it multiplies rapidly, converting those organs into virus factories. It rewires the victim's immune system and turns it against them. From there, it begins breaking down blood vessels and causing coagulopathy and hypovolemic shock, and the patient bleeds out. The incubation period lasts one or two days, with terminal crash occurring between seven and nine days after.

"The virus spreads so quickly through the body it could potentially burn itself out without spreading to any neighboring cities or regions. This ability to control and contain it once it is unleashed into a target population is what makes it desirable as a weapon. It is almost one hundred percent contagious. If you're within twenty feet of someone sick with this thing, then you've got it. The facility was simultaneously developing a vaccine to counter the virus. They wanted to be able to ensure that only the right people were killed off by it, without creating any collateral damage, or having it backfire on us. The vaccine must be administered within the first twenty-four hours of infection for a one hundred percent chance of recovery. Vaccination any time after that has a drastically reduced chance for success. If the victim isn't vaccinated at least forty-eight hours after infection, there's almost no chance for recovery."

Shelly couldn't believe it. As a nurse, she had dealt with illness and contagious outbreaks before, so she knew the dangers microbes presented. But to hear that a government institution was actively committed to creating the microscopic monster Fallon had just described was overwhelming. She had misgivings about politicians and authority figures, the same as anyone else, but she had a tough time believing that the government could be involved with something so evil.

"I can't imagine," she said, "that there would be people out there who could justify creating something so horrible."

She stopped herself. She was being naïve and knew it. She had seen the kinds of horror and indifference people were capable of first-hand. She knew, as anyone who had suffered through abuse knew, just how easy it was for some people to wear a smile while inflicting pain and torment. Some people enjoyed it, loved it, even thrived on the pain they caused others.

"You can play the skeptic all you like, Nurse Christianson. But what I'm telling you is the truth. I ran because I realized what we were doing was wrong and an affront to God. I only desire the means to make good my escape and spread the word of what's happening to the world. They lost control of the virus, which has by now reached your little town. They are hunting me and actively engaged in damage control and cover-up for their mistake. This is also why I administered the vaccine to you."

Shelly blinked. It took a second before the full meaning of his words registered. "What did you just say?" Fallon had drugged her? How was that possible? When could he have done it?

"You drank the vaccine this morning before we left your home."

Shelly stood and slowly stepped away from him. Looking into his eyes, she saw the truth there. Fallon had drugged her. Her stomach clenched in knots and her heart pounded, sending ice through her veins.

*Not again*, she thought.

She had not been drugged since Brad, though he had used Rohypnol to make her more submissive during a rough part in their relationship, when she was trying to get away from him. Unwanted memories lashed at her. Her helpless paralysis, watching as Brad picked her up and carried her to the bedroom, incapable of doing anything to stop him. The fuzzy, dreamlike trance that followed, where she could almost imagine everything he did to her was happening to someone else. He had only drugged her twice. Both times had preceded a severe beating and domestic rape. Towards the end of their marriage, she had turned so submissive he did not feel the need to bother with the Rohypnol anymore, and saved it for the women he occasionally brought home from his nights out on the town.

Now she'd been drugged again: a different man and a different reason. "Why... Why did you—How could you do that to me?"

"I know you're stunned and angry. You have every right to be. I wanted to ensure that you would be safe and unharmed by the disease that is spreading through town like a wildfire. You must believe me when I say it's for the best. I need your help and can't have you falling sick and dying."

"What?" It was all she could think to say. A thousand

words, insults and questions strained to be let out at once. So many thoughts were racing around her head; she could hardly identify them as they whirled past. So instead, she simply said: "What?"

"They're spreading it through your town right now. It's all damage control. They need to make sure anyone I talk to won't live to talk to anyone else. I stole a few ampules of the vaccine and gave you one. The rest I intend to give to the world, so more can be made to counter this bug, if the army decides to use it in combat."

Shelly shook her head. "What I meant is, what's going to happen now? To me?"

"It's been about two hours since I gave you the dose. You'll start feeling queasy and nauseated soon. Then you'll come down with a slight fever and suffer some chills and achy joints. The whole episode should last no more than a day. Then you'll be right as rain. If you release me, I can care for you once the symptoms begin."

She felt like a caged mouse, being rattled around by a wicked eleven-year-old. Shelly couldn't sit any longer and got up to pace, but on the first circuit back from the kitchenette she found herself short of breath, light-headed and queasy. Her stomach lurched suddenly, and she bolted for the toilet to empty the crackers she had eaten after tying Fallon to the couch.

On her knees she sat back, resting on her ankles, she took a few deep breaths, wiped her mouth with a hand towel, drank a handful of water from the tap and wrestled to her feet again. The room tilted sideways on her and she nearly fell into the tub before catching herself on the toilet tank.

*Saved once again, by the porcelain god,* she thought and almost laughed.

She was sweating and freezing at the same time. Chills boiled just beneath the surface of her skin. When she emerged from the bathroom, she nearly walked into the back of the couch where Fallon was secured. She fought back against the overwhelming urge to vomit again. She felt her way around the couch, desperately clinging to it for support and fell into the cushions next to Fallon.

Her vision cleared for a moment and when she looked into Fallon's face, she could see the concern etched there.

"If you untie me, I can help you," he said, trying to make his voice as soothing and comforting as possible.

Shelly's stomach lurched again. "You... did this... to me!" She gulped hard.

Fallon nodded, sadly. "Yes. I did. But it was only to protect. You won't die from it and if you'll allow me, I can make you more comfortable until the symptoms pass."

Instead of responding, Shelly leaned her heavy head back, closed her eyes and faded away.

Cold. Burning. Sweating and shaking. Every joint on fire with pain. Hard to breathe. Hard to see. Hard to hear. Stomach cramped from vomiting. Muscles aching from spasms. Misery, misery, misery.

This was Harold's whole world now. The eggs and toast he had fixed for supper were lost shortly after he'd consumed them, heaved onto cold, white porcelain. Feeling nauseous, he decided to lie down, but that did not help matters one bit. The mild sweat he had developed while parking the rig and clocking out intensified. During the drive home, his vision doubled several times. He passed it off as exhaustion at the end of a long shift. Once he arrived home, he barely noticed the slight tingling in his toes and fingertips as he hugged and kissed his wife good morning. Every pore in his body seeped. His night clothes and bed sheets were quickly soaked through. With every passing minute, his agony grew worse. Then the coughing started: horrible, booming, retching explosions, which doubled him over, spasming pain through every nerve ending within him. It was almost too much. After each bout,

Harold could only lay in bed, as still as possible, whimpering and wishing he were dead. Burning tears streaked from his bloodshot eyes.

Harold's wife, Chrissanne, did her best to ease her husband's suffering. But she had never in her life seen anyone grow as sick as Harold as quickly as he had. After a particularly wretched coughing fit, she found a bloody pile of tissues in their bathroom garbage basket. The sight of those few red specks almost sent her into a blind panic. She didn't know what to do. She paced the hallway between the kitchen and the bedroom several times before managing to get herself under control. Taking deep breaths, she checked on Harold one more time, to make sure he was sleeping, then went to the phone in the kitchen and called nine-one-one.

A male voice answered after two rings. "Nine-one-one, what's the nature of the emergency?"

Her voice trembled as she spoke. "Hello, my name is Chrissanne Cunningham. My husband is very sick. I think he may need to be brought to the emergency room."

"Can you describe his symptoms for me please?" She did so. "Thank you. Yes, we've had a few cases similar to your husband's already today. If you give me your address, I'll have someone out quickly to bring you in."

"Our house is on Hogarth road, off Highway 95, number 2497. Hurry please. I'm so worried about him."

"We'll be out there as quickly as we can, ma'am. Try to remain calm and comfort him as best you can until we arrive."

"Thank you so much."

"You're welcome." Then the voice was gone, replaced by the dead air of an empty phone line. Chrissanne sagged in her chair and stared at the canary-yellow paisley wallpaper of her dining room. She felt relieved. Someone was coming to help Harold. She didn't have to worry anymore. She only hoped they would allow her to ride in the ambulance with him when they took him away. She wanted to be there to comfort him as long as she could. They had been married for a little over twenty years. Long enough to see their two children grow up and start lives of their own. If something were to happen to him, she didn't know what she would do.

Standing up, she went to the kitchen sink and wet a hand towel, to wipe away the sudden sweat from her forehead. Her stress and heart-wrenching worry that something was seriously wrong with Harold must have gotten her more worked up than she'd imagined. Her vision doubled as she went down the hall to hold her sleeping husband, to hold his hand and tend to him while waiting for the paramedics to arrive.

Twenty miles away, Specialist Drexler, who was manning the reactivated emergency phone lines, hung up with Mrs. Cunningham and informed his immediate superior about the new outbreak. Five minutes later, a platoon was speeding towards the Cunningham house, and another platoon was dispatched to his work.

Around nine o'clock in the morning, a mass text message was sent out to every active cell phone in town. Additionally, an auto-dial machine, like the ones cold call centers use to ring up potential victims, called every registered household number. The voice on the other end of the auto-dialer spoke the same pre-recorded message as the text, which was also broadcast on every major radio frequency in town. The resulting information blitz and overlap was to ensure that everyone got the message: tune in to their televisions at eleven o'clock for an important message from their mayor, concerning the crisis that had befallen Harper's Glen.

By nine-fifteen, the blackout resumed.

As far as Aldridge's electronic warfare shop was able to determine, no one had managed to get a call or text message out while the jamming was temporarily lifted. This was a relief. The last thing he needed was worried family members, or worse, the media, coming to town, snooping for answers. So far, he had been lucky, and the operation had been kept quiet. The government kept a tight reign over local and national news outlets at the moment. Once the crisis was over, a story would have to be concocted and disseminated. Something of this magnitude could not be kept under wraps forever.

By ten-thirty, Mayor Henderson and the town council, all of whom had been vaccinated, were assembled at town hall. A camera crew had been brought in as well, to record and broadcast the mayor's words throughout town. The mayor would have preferred to hold a public meeting, so he could personally allay any fears and answer any questions the townsfolk might have. But Aldridge would not allow it. They could not risk large gatherings of people. There was no way of knowing who might be a carrier. Transmission of the virus through a large group like that would only cause more unnecessary deaths and extend his mission more than was acceptable. He was there to capture Fallon and prevent the spread of the disease he carried. When weighing one decision or another, that was the thought that was first and foremost in his mind; if he happened to save these people along the way, so much the better.

The speech the mayor was going to deliver—written by Aldridge's staff—was carefully worded to provide information and hope, as well as dispel any rumors and prevent public panic. It asked them to trust the army and police, to come to the hospital if they were feeling at all ill, to avoid gathering in groups, or meeting with friends or family outside their immediate household. It had been written weeks ago. This was the third time the speech had been used; each time, it was customized to fit the town being addressed.

Major Panelli handed Henderson the speech only twenty minutes before he was supposed to stand before a camera and read it to his constituency.

"You want me to read it right off the page?"

"Of course," said Panelli. "It'll seem more genuine that way. Like you didn't have the time to prepare a speech as such and are instead reading facts and notes and speaking from the heart to your people. It makes the statement sound more genuine."

Henderson looked unhappy. But there was nothing he could do about it. Best to just go along and do what he could to make things better for everyone in this bad situation.

At exactly eleven in the morning, the mayor's statement was broadcast on every channel in town. TVs all over town were turned on, and a frightened city listened as their mayor spoke to them. Henderson read the entire statement in ten minutes. He didn't add anything or personalize it in any way. He merely read what he was given, clearly and mechanically. He finished it off, saying: "By working together and with the military, we will get through this crisis quickly and smoothly. Thank you all for your attention and God bless us all." Once the cameras were off, the blackout resumed.

Up at her cabin, sleeping fitfully, Shelly never received the messages to tune in to the mayor's address. She had left her phone at home on her beside nightstand. Instead, she dreamed disturbing dreams about Fallon and Brad chasing her through the halls of Saint John's.

While she slept, the virus and its antibodies multiplied in her body.

Huge drifts of new, white snow piled against buildings and over cars. The roads were slippery, but the residents of Harper's Glen were used to these wintery conditions and knew how to handle them. Chains had been purchased or retrieved from the garage and snow tires installed weeks ago. People were ready for whatever the season could throw at them.

What they were not prepared for was the presence of the army. The first to notice the occupation were the early-morning commuters, who drove out of town each day for work. They were turned back at the highway on-ramps. No explanation was given. They were simply told it was for their safety. After that, people noticed the lack of early-morning TV and talk radio. The friendly, comforting presence of the local disc jockeys and network talk show personalities was distressingly absent during their morning "getting ready" rituals. In some cases, their absence was as hard-hitting as the lack of that first cup of eye-opening coffee. When people called in to the TV and radio stations to complain, they were greeted with only silence on the line. Not even a dial tone. Some grew worried at this, but most just assumed it was due to the storm that blew through the night before.

Then came the mass calls and texts and the mayor's broadcast. This fanned the smoldering embers of fear and doubt in many people's hearts. That something like this was happening to them was unthinkable.

Second Lieutenant Philip Lopez stood outside the hospital watching the crowd gathering at the front entrance. People had realized by this point that they were cut off and under military control, and they were clearly unhappy about it. The mayor's broadcast had done little to assuage their fear. In fact, it seemed to have made things worse. Instead of staying home, people were out in droves and swarming in his direction.

Freshly graduated from West Point, this was his first duty station. He had been commissioned for less than eight months. Initially, he thought the post was a nice, cushy assignment. No field rotations to worry about, and everything happened on a schedule that was planned out weeks or months in advance. Lopez loved it. It reminded him of academy life. After his first week, he thought to himself, "If all my duty stations are like this, I can definitely put in another twenty-five or thirty years." All he had to do was put in the time and check the right boxes. His dream job was to work at the Pentagon, and eventually to become one of the Joint Chiefs of Staff.

That was before Fallon and the chase. Now, he wasn't so sure he liked the army much. Sleeping in his vehicle or on the cold ground wasn't his idea of a productive rest period. Constantly moving and rushing about made him terribly uncomfortable. The unpredictability of field life was not something he enjoyed. Not at all. He wished he were still back at the base, where things were unsurprising and simple. Just show up, spend as little time as possible in the office, work out at the gym, go home, repeat tomorrow. Out here, he had to make decisions. He had to plan for the unexpected. It was not something he was used to. The men he was placed in charge of were mostly combat veterans older than he was. They mistrusted him and treated him as though he were something distasteful that they had to deal with. The feeling was mutual. The way they looked at him, questions in their eyes, demanding to know what he expected them to do next—it irritated him to no end.

This occupation was another hassle he could do without. The people in this backwoods little town were testing the limits of his patience. They had only just gotten set up, but these hicks acted as though they had been imprisoned for months. Now they were surging at him, a great unruly mob of them. All these small-town people screaming their threats, making rude gestures, and crowding in closer than he liked; he hated them all and couldn't wait until this awful business was over. Then he could go home and things could return to normal.

Outside the quarantine zone around Harper's Glen, far away on the other side of the country, General Phillip Collins sat at his desk, scowling.

General Collins was not happy in the least by what he saw in Harper's Glen. The images in front of him were less than ten minutes old and showed a dozen soldiers attempting to control a large crowd of people swarming in front of the hospital. This was the first morning of the quarantine, and from the reports he was receiving, the situation was already volatile and threatening to tumble out of control.

*If even one of those people is sick,* he thought. *Then they're all sick. What the hell is Aldridge thinking, letting them gather in public like this? Is he even thinking at all?* Collins shook his head.

The security cordon around Harper's Glen was in place at least, and Collins' people were keeping a tight grip on the news media, so no word had been leaked to the public. Yet. The longer this farse went on, however, the greater the chance that could change. Aldridge had chased Fallon over hundreds of miles and through three small cities to apprehend him, without success. Now, it was make or break time. This was the third town they'd had to quarantine, and he was tired of cleaning up after Aldridge. The commitment of manpower and resources was staggering. Each time Aldridge pulled up, stakes and moved, he demanded more troops, more vehicles, more supplies, with nothing to show but a ghost town left in his wake. This travesty had gone on long enough, and Collins wanted to see it ended.

After listening to a recording of the mayor's statement, Collins thought he sounded cold and detached. In fact, the whole statement sounded coerced, which wasn't the way to ensure public cooperation and prevent a mass panic. If all the public services were as uncooperative as this mayor appeared to be, then obviously Aldridge had less control of the situation than he indicated in his reports.

He pulled the secure phone close and dialed the number for Aldridge's command post. The soldier who answered connected him the colonel's office.

"General Collins," Aldridge slurred into the phone. "What can I do for you?"

"Still on the drugs, I see," he said. A hint of a smile found its way to his lips.

The silence on the phone was heavy with things unsaid. Biting remarks and shouted insults, questions of competency and charges of insubordination. It was a tired, old game they played, and for once neither one of them wanted to play it.

"As you very well know, I'm still recovering. The doctors say they'll start weaning me off in a couple weeks." Aldridge paused for several long and insubordinate seconds before adding, "Sir."

"Where will you get your pills from then, Colonel? Once you're no longer prescribed them, it'll be illegal for you to keep taking them. You're in a position of authority here; it's a liability for you to be on drugs."

"There's only one liability here, sir, and it's not me. I'm in complete control of the situation."

"Is that so? Then how come I'm seeing images of crowds outside your command post? Why is it that you are moving so slowly to secure and seal off the city? Most important of all, how come Fallon is still at large?"

Aldridge said nothing and Collins smiled into the phone. He was enjoying making the smartass hero squirm. It served him right.

"I'm taking the steps I deem necessary to control this situation. Fallon's head start has allowed him to find a hideaway here. It's only a matter of time before I locate him. As to your concerns about the civilians, I am working to limit their exposure to the disease and facilitating treatment for those who have become infected."

"Seems like you're doing very little of either right now."

"I'm sorry it looks that way to you, sir. Maybe you just don't have the correct perspective on the situation. Come down here and see for yourself. Then you might understand the difficulties I'm having."

"Neither I, the chief of staff, nor the president care at all for your troubles, Colonel. You were given a mission, and you're failing to carry it out. Un-fuck yourself and your operation, or else I'll find someone who can."

"Did you have something useful you wanted to tell me, General? In case you hadn't noticed, I'm pretty busy here right now."

"Watch your tone, Colonel. I am calling for a progress report. It's been some time since we've heard from you, and we are growing worried that you might not be up to completing the mission."

"For the last time, I'm handling it. If you want a progress report, then read the daily emails and PowerPoint slides my staff sends up. They'll tell you all you need to know."

"Believe me, Colonel, I've been reading everything you've been sending up. I find it all lacking in pertinent details. So, you will answer my questions and consider it a privilege that I'm calling you on the phone instead of dragging your arrogant ass back here to Washington to explain your fuckups. Do you understand, Colonel? Colonel Aldridge?"

There was a long, silent moment before Collins realized he'd been hung up on. He replaced the receiver in its cradle. He stared at nothing for a few minutes. Then he stood and called for his assistant to gather his staff and his sergeant major. It was time to take matters in hand.

Lopez stood out front, trying to calm the crowd when the first hard-packed snowball struck him. He staggered back a step, hand to his face, and suddenly found himself on the ground when his foot found a particularly slick spot. A hesitant cheer erupted from the crowd. Behind him, Lopez could hear the muted chuckles of his soldiers.

Wet, cold, embarrassed, and now with a sore ass, Lopez struggled to his feet. Another snowball missed him by inches, accompanied by more jeering insults. He saw several more people bent over, packing several more snowballs. Enough was enough. These small people in their shitty little piss-ant town had the nerve to assault him. He was an officer in the United States Army. He deserved their respect, their reverence even. He whipped around to his men and bellowed, "Lock and load!" He had meant to sound stern and imposing. He wanted to strike fear into the hearts of these ignorant hicks. Instead, his voice sounded shrill and panicky, even to his own ears.

His soldiers stopped chuckling. He could see the worry in their eyes behind their protective masks. Uncertain, only a few of them chambered a round in their weapons.

Another missile passed his head; this time it was a chunk of brick. Then some burly, stupid-looking lump of a man stepped up to Lopez, slapped the bull horn from his hands and shoved him back down. The sore spot on his butt erupted with pain upon this second landing. Then the hick threw up his arms triumphantly, pounded the air once and returned to his spot in the mob.

The crowd was laughing and cheering.

Lopez got to his feet again. "I said, lock and load!" he snapped. This time they all complied. "Step forward!" One woman in the crowd was being particularly abusive, yelling insults over the rest. Calling Lopez and his men "Nazis" and "baby killers." Lopez thought she might have been the one who threw the brick. He hoped that she and the fucker who pushed him would get shot first.

"Get ready!" Lopez bellowed. His men hesitantly complied. One or two looked around in doubt.

"Aim!" They raised their carbines in unison, though several of them immediately lowered the muzzles so they weren't pointed at the crowd. Almost to a man, they wore looks of disbelief, as though they couldn't believe what was happening.

A leaden hush fell upon the mob. The cheering and chattering had ceased. Even the woman shouting insults had quieted. Everyone at the forefront of the crowd stared in disbelief at the wall of gray clad soldiers pointing their rifles at them. Some were frozen in place. Some tried pushing their way to the back. The raucous feeling in the air had been replaced with one of dread.

Sonny Dixon groaned and spat as he sat up in bed. His head was pounding, and his mouth tasted like a well-trod carpet. His morning routine after a night at the bar began with an aspirin and Gatorade, followed by a long hot shower and a heavy, greasy breakfast. Even when he wasn't hungover, he wasn't a cheerful person in the morning. He owned a local video store a few blocks from his house. So, while many of neighbors had to get started earlier than usual to make it to work on time through the snow, Sonny started his day and leisurely walked to work at the time he usually did. He liked to arrive early to prepare for the day's business.

Sonny wasn't a fan of bullshit morning radio or talk TV. He didn't own a cell phone and refused to answer the unknown numbers that showed up on his caller ID. Living so close to the video store, he didn't need traffic or weather reports beyond looking out his front window. So, his morning ritual was conducted in complete, blissful silence and he missed the broadcast, which was why he was headed into work on the first morning of the quarantine like nothing had changed. As far as he knew, everything was business as usual. Same uncomfortable cold, same hangover, same everything. He was sure he had a flask in his desk. The thought of an Irish Coffee perked him up. Dreading another day of dealing with people arguing over late fees and haranguing him about the availability of new releases, Sonny was already looking forward to meeting his friend Benny at the bar after work.

Sonny was forty-two and on the heavy side. He had no wife or children and lived alone in an eleven-hundred-square-foot condominium. The short distance to work, and his lack of interest in morning entertainment, left him completely unaware that anything was wrong until he arrived at the store. That was when he noticed the crowd gathering outside the hospital, which was two blocks farther up, on the opposite side of the street.

He paused before inserting his key into the lock and stood there for a minute watching the commotion, trying to figure out what was happening before he pocketed the key ring and joined the crowd outside Saint John's. He saw Craig, a frequent customer and bar buddy of his, and moved to talk to him. He had almost reached him when he finally noticed the soldiers standing in front of the entrance and stopped in his tracks.

*What are soldiers doing here?* he wondered and hurried over to his friend. He reached the other side just as a convoy of six Humvees sped past, snow spraying from their tires. He watched as they turned the corner at the next street and disappeared behind the hospital.

Sonny turned back to the crowd and started lumbering through to reach his friend. "Craig?" he said, tapping him on the shoulder.

His friend turned in surprise. Recognizing Sonny, he gave him a short, quick smile and said, "Sonny, man you startled me."

"Sorry. What's going on?"

"Beats the shit out of me, man. I just got here a minute ago."

Sonny winced. Craig was all but shouting to be heard over the noise of the crowd. Being in the middle of them was making his head hurt worse. "Me too. Why is everyone here, though? And what's up with the army keeping people out of the hospital?"

Craig shook his head and shrugged. "I haven't heard. I only found out about this all from my neighbor, Mrs. Carle. The nosy old bat came out to chat me up while I was scraping my car off for work. You know how much she loves to spy on the people who live around her. Anyways, she said some soldiers arrived at Doc Francis' house, hauled him and his family away. I've heard from a bunch of people here that they've been doing that all morning. Anyways, I got my car all warmed up, I started out for work, but got stopped at the highway. There's a bunch of soldiers there, too, keeping anyone from leaving."

"What? Are you serious? There's no way they can do that. They don't have the right."

"Whether they have the right or not, they're doing it."

"Was there anything on the news about this? Like an accident or something?"

"I forget sometimes, you hate TV. You know? That's a weird trait for a guy who owns a video store."

"I watch movies. They're fine, but most of what's on TV is crap. So, was there anything on the news or not?"

"Oh, yeah. After I got back home, I got a call to turn on the TV. Then the mayor came on and asked us all to play nice with the jarheads and do what they say. Other than that, there's nothing. TV and radio are completely blank."

"What do you mean, blank? All the radio and TV stations are having technical difficulties?"

"No. I mean they're just not on. Not broadcasting."

"Maybe it's just your set. It is a pretty old TV, after all."

"True. But I've talked to a couple other guys around here and they've all said the same thing. There's no TV, no radio. Phones don't work, either."

Sonny was about to ask Craig to repeat himself when he noticed movement out of the corner of his eye. Another soldier joined the twelve or so standing guard outside the hospital entrance. The newcomer spoke to the others for a moment before raising a bullhorn to his facemask. That was when Sonny noticed all the soldiers were wearing facemasks.

"You people are ordered to disperse immediately." Because he was standing close to the front of the crowd, the soldier's magnified voice hurt Sonny and Greg's ears. "We are in the middle of a medical emergency and you are blocking the entrance to the hospital. Return to your homes. You will receive further instructions soon."

"What instructions? What for?" someone a few feet to Sonny's left yelled.

"Why should we?" yelled another.

A woman to his right called out, "You don't have the right to order us around like this!" A grumble of agreement came from the crowd. Sonny felt people pressing against him, moving forward, inching closer to the officer with the megaphone.

"Leave now. Return to your homes, where you will receive instructions and information."

"Why don't you give us some information?" someone yelled.

"Why don't you fucking fascists give us a reason to leave?" screamed the woman to Sonny's right. The crowd edged still closer to the soldiers. The shouting and cursing blended unintelligibly. The crowd's aggression had nearly reached a breaking point.

The soldier raised the bullhorn to his mask again, presumably to repeat himself. But he didn't get the chance. A snowball flew from the crowd and hit him in the face causing him to fall.

*Oh shit*, was Sonny's first thought. *This sort of thing never works out well in the movies.* It didn't here, either. A couple more snowballs flew. Then somebody threw what looked like a rock.

By this point, the line of soldiers had been pressed almost to the hospital doors. A large man wearing work coveralls stepped out from the crowd and shoved the officer. The man lost his footing and fell again. The crowd laughed. The soldier on the ground scrambled up and started yelling at the soldiers standing behind him.

After a moment of indecision, they took aim and fired into the crowd. Blood sprayed into the air, lightly showering Sonny and Craig and those around them. Sonny heard a snap to his right and saw that the woman who'd been shouting the loudest, was now a heap in the melting, red snow. In an instant, the anger-filled mob degenerated into a fearful rout. The crowd scattered. Dismayed shouts, panicked cries and screams of agony echoed down the street. Everyone ran for their lives. Sonny ran with them. Sonny lost all track of Craig seconds after they turned to run. All he wanted to do was get away from the soldiers and their guns.

Someone battered into Sonny from behind, knocking him to the ground. His stomach heaved and he spat whiskey flavored bile on the rough, slushy street surface while people trampled past. Sonny tried to stand up, and got as far as his hands and knees, when a man in an old brown parka tripped over him and split his forehead open on the sidewalk curb. Sonny was knocked flat again, his cheek pressed to the freezing concrete. Looking sideways at the man who had tripped over him, he saw a huge amount of blood splattered on the curb and dripping from his head. Someone else trod on Sonny's outstretched hand. He cried out as he reflexively curled into a ball around his injured hand. After a moment, he tried again. This time, he made it to his feet. The crowd was thinner now. Most of them had already rushed by in their desperation to get away. Now that he was on his feet, Sonny started moving again.

He dashed to his store, unlocked it and hurried inside. Leaning against the door and panting heavily, he slid down until he was sitting. Fear-fueled adrenaline caused his hands to tremble.

He heaved again. His chest and belly now covered in more bourbon and stomach acid; warm, wet, reeking.

When he managed to calm down enough, Sonny stood, peered through the front window, and saw Craig crumpled in the street. The snow beneath him was red.

Sonny dropped to the floor, cupped his face in his hands

and sobbed.

Suddenly everything pieced together before him. No way to communicate with anyone outside town and no way to get out. They were trapped and at the mercy of the soldiers who'd trapped them. Sonny felt cold inside, which had nothing to do with the cold outside.

He desperately wanted a drink.

Randy Mills stared. He couldn't help it. He had never seen soldiers up close before. Especially not when they were covered head to foot in biological suits. The protective masks they wore over their faces looked like skulls to him.

He was quite intimidated by their presence in his store.

*They're like big, green storm troopers,* he thought.

Most of what he was seeing didn't register in his brain. He'd been awake for over twenty-four hours and remained conscious only through the massive amounts of coffee and stay awake pills he had ingested. Yesterday, Arline, the bitch who was supposed to work during the day, had been fired for skimming the till and fucking her boyfriend in the stockroom on the clock, so he was forced to work her shift during the day, as well as his normal night shift. The overtime was good, but he really wanted to sleep. By now his synapses simply weren't firing as rapidly as they should have been and his stomach churned uncomfortably, due to the various chemicals he'd ingested to keep awake and alert.

He felt like throwing up.

He'd been daydreaming about his bed and looking forward to his boss coming to take over in forty minutes when the group—squad, he reminded himself, thinking of the proper military lingo he'd learned from playing hours of first-person shooter video games—of soldiers burst into his store near the end of his shift, flashing pictures and demanding to see the security camera tapes. He stared wide-eyed at them. His only response was to say, "Sure." Then he led their boss—

commanding officer—to the manager's office in back where the security camera footage was saved.

The officer in charge of the group of soldiers surrounding him identified himself as Lieutenant Glover and handed Randy a few photos.

"Have you seen either of these people before?" Glover asked.

Randy looked at the pictures but could barely focus. Glover shook the pictures in front of his face a couple of times, indicating Randy should take them to get a better look.

He glanced briefly at the photos. "I don't know. Look man, I been on the clock since eight yesterday morning. Do you know how many people I see in here each day? I'm sorry, but I don't recognize them."

Glover sighed. It had been a long shot stopping here. This was the only twenty-four-hour store near Shelly Christianson's house. He didn't want to report back that he had lost Fallon's trail. The colonel would have his ass. It had been a long night. The sun was up, and the trail was cold, both figuratively and literally. This burn-out store clerk wasn't any help. Glover wanted to leave and start looking again, but he wanted to make sure Fallon had not stopped here.

Randy was seated in the back office and after twenty minutes of fast-forwarding through several dull hours of nothing, looking for anything odd, it dawned on Randy to ask Glover, "Why are you having me do this, man?"

Glover's answer was muffled slightly by the mask he wore. "You were on duty in one of the three all-night convenience stores last night. We need to make certain that the individuals we're looking for didn't come through here."

"What're they wanted for? Must be something bad if the whole army's after them. What'd the guy do? Steal the presidential underwear or something?" He chuckled nervously at his own joke. When Glover didn't laugh with him, he cleared his throat and returned his attention to the monitors.

Something clicked in his exhausted brain then. "Hey man, can I see those pictures again?" This time the photos sparked recognition in his caffeine-addled, sleep-deprived brain. "Yeah. Yeah, I seen these two. They came in here a few hours ago, like around dawn, bought a bunch of food and shit. The chick was a fox, but her boyfriend was creepy as hell. Kept leaning in close to me while I was ringing them up. I seriously thought about telling him that he was in my happy bubble and needed to back off."

Glover was about to press him for further details, but before Randy could answer, he doubled over coughing. The sudden fit went on and on. He tried to breathe and found it nearly impossible. His chest and stomach seemed to be spasming out of control and the coughing would not stop. The next thing he remembered was being rushed from the store into a waiting army truck and they drove him to the hospital.

# January 9th

General Collins hated flying, which was unfortunate, since his position at the Pentagon required him to do a lot of traveling. Driving took too long, and one could not get anywhere by train anymore—that left flying. His current flight, while uncomfortable, wasn't as bad as the flights he'd made to and from overseas deployments. Those were commercial passenger liners, packed to the brim with soldiers and gear for twenty-plus hours. This time Collins sat near the front of a small private jet, shared only by the flight crew, him and his sergeant major, his staff was seated in the back of the plane. Rank had its privileges. They would be landing in a couple of hours and then it was straight on to Harper's Glen. Collins tried to sleep but couldn't manage to get comfortable enough to do so. Thoughts of falling from the sky in a fireball kept him awake. Instead, he spent the three-hour flight thinking and planning how he was going to handle things once on the ground.

The situation was getting out of hand. Preston Aldridge had repeatedly failed to apprehend Fallon and it was time to take corrective action. Twenty-four hours after Aldridge hung up on him, Collins was heading for Harper's Glen. While in the air, he received a constant stream of updates about the situation on the ground. It had only been two days, and already Aldridge had managed to turn the entire town against him. Collins learned about the shooting minutes after it happened and used it to convince his superiors that he was much better suited to the task of cleaning up the mess in Harper's Glen than anyone else, especially Colonel Preston Fucking Aldridge. Collins relished the idea of embarrassing his rival yet again. He didn't quite hate Aldridge, but he disliked the man enough to sabotage his career whenever the opportunity arose.

In a different world, the two men might have been friends. They had both gotten business degrees with similar GPAs from esteemed colleges. They had both been appointed the Battalion Commander in their respective ROTCs. They were both athletic and intelligent, with a burning desire to win and be the best among their peers. They had first met attending the Leader's Decision-Making Assessment Course in Fort Lewis, Washington, between their sophomore and junior years in college. From the start, they competed for Honor Graduate, which Aldridge won, though only just. They met again after graduation, when they went to their Basic Officer Leader Course in Fort Benning, Georgia. For the next five months, they were at each other's throats, each trying to outmatch the other. This time, Collins took home the honors. Afterward, they were both sent to Fort Carson, Colorado for their first duty assignments and were even assigned to the same infantry battalion once they got there.

Instead of becoming friends through their mutual experiences, this fostered a passionate feud between the young officers.

When the War on Terror broke out in 2001 and their unit was deployed to Afghanistan, First Lieutenant Aldridge was handed a platoon and glory, while First Lieutenant Collins stayed behind on the Forward Operating Base to serve as the company executive officer. This was the first of many petty resentments against Aldridge that Collins nurtured and kept score of over the years.

After that deployment, both men went their separate ways, still in the same brigade, though in different battalions. They would run into each other occasionally at the Post Exchange or around Colorado Springs. Each meeting was civil, even jovial on the surface. Underneath, there was always an undercurrent of animosity between them.

Like a cruel joke, three years later, they were both selected to attend Captain's Career Course together, and since they were both infantry officers, this meant they'd once more be competing academically. The competition was savage, but Collins again came out on top, winning Honor Graduate over Aldridge.

So it went over the years. Their private war escalated during times of contact and cooled off once they were no longer around each other. Their careers took them on separate paths, with different units and on different deployments. But neither ever forgot the other. Every time Collins heard about Aldridge's exploits and the heroic things he was accomplishing, his blood boiled.

They were reunited one more time in 2012, during their last deployment together. At the last minute, Collins was assigned to be the deputy commander of the same brigade in which Aldridge commanded an infantry battalion. The professional army is a relatively small organization, especially as one accumulates rank and service time. Given enough time in service, old friends will meet and serve together time and again around the world. The same, unfortunately, is true of old enemies.

The action, which made Aldridge a hero, and destroyed his knee and his career, happened late in the Afghan war. After the US had finished the drawdown in Iraq, US forces were surged into Afghanistan in order to bring that conflict to a successful conclusion. Once again, Aldridge was given a line unit and Collins remained on the Forward Operating Base in an administrative job.

A platoon had been cut off in a mountain pass, far from any available support. Aldridge, whose FOB was only ten miles away, decided to mount a rescue mission. He personally led two companies from his battalion outside the wire, with the intention of extracting the embattled troops. Collins, who was on the brigade staff at the time, was trying to bring together a more organized rescue effort. When he learned that Aldridge had stolen the march on him and blundered ahead without authorization, he was livid.

Aldridge's companies engaged and fought off insurgent forces for three days, as they slogged their way closer to the beleaguered platoon. On the fourth day, they arrived and began putting the wounded and battered men on the helicopters Collins had sent in. For this effort, Aldridge's men were showered with awards and praise. Aldridge himself won his second Silver Star for valor. All of this, although he had disobeyed orders. Collins' orders. As the brigade's deputy commander, Collins had directed Aldridge to stay put, while other closer units could be coordinated to respond. In typical Preston Aldridge fashion, the young, hot-shot lieutenant colonel ignored those orders and charged ahead for the glory of it.

This was the final straw. Collins had a better record, but Aldridge was constantly given assignments where he could shine. Even though Collins played the political power game well, he was always left standing in Aldridge's shadow, always outdone by the brash officer. He couldn't stand it any longer. While Aldridge was recovering in the hospital from a shattered knee—because the brigade commander, Colonel Swan, had been in Germany receiving treatment for kidney stones—Collins had been acting as the commanding officer. Collins used his position and every ounce of political pull he had to silently reprimand his rival. The fact that Aldridge had disobeyed direct orders gave Collins the tools he needed to begin dismantling his reputation and career.

Immediately following their redeployment to the states, Collins was promoted to full colonel, whereupon he did everything he could to ensure Aldridge's questionable medical status blocked his own promotion. Then he instigated a review of Aldridge's actions during the deployment, which cast doubt upon him and his ability to lead. Finally, as Collins' star rose, he made sure Aldridge was given one backwater, dead-end assignment after another.

The dismal commands in backwater posts had apparently driven Aldridge into a deep depression. His career and his marriage suffered as a result. The effect this had on Aldridge's marriage was something Collins was unaware of until he heard through the grapevine that his wife had left him for another man. This news at first dismayed Collins. He had wanted to ruin Aldridge's career, not his life. He wanted to prove he was the better officer, and he had. After the news had some time to sink in, Collins found himself happy with the outcome. Aldridge deserved every unhappiness heaped upon him. It meant that Collins, whose wife was still faithfully by his side, was not only the better officer, but he was the better man and husband as well.

On the plane, General Collins smiled as he remembered how expertly he'd steered the arrogant bastard's career towards obscure ruin, while he'd continued on a meteoric rise. Collins' future was bright indeed. He had his sights on becoming the army chief of staff. But that was still a long way into the future. In the here and now, he had to deal with Preston Fucking Aldridge one final time. With him out of the way, Collins had no serious competitors.

So here he was, on his way to clean up a mess Aldridge couldn't handle. It almost seemed like divine providence. He'd dug the grave, led the man to the empty hole and allowed him to climb in. Now it was time to bury him.

Shelly awoke with a screaming headache and a raw throat. Squinting against the half-light shining through the part in the drawn curtains, she rolled over and pressed her head deeper into the pillows. Then she snapped awake. She was in bed. How had she gotten there? She threw off the covers and leaped to her feet. She was still dressed in the same clothes she'd passed out in, except for her boots, which had been neatly placed by the door. Cautiously, she crept to the door, opened it, and left the bedroom.

Sticking close to the walls, she tip-toed through the front room to the kitchenette, where she heard Fallon working and whistling. He was standing at the sink, with his back to her. On the counter behind him, she could see Uncle Rory's pistol. Fallon was so intent on rummaging through the boxes of food and stocking the small pantry, he hadn't yet noticed her.

Slowly, calmly, she stepped away from the wall and tip-toed towards the gun. She was just three short steps away when Fallon suddenly turned to her and smiled.

"Good afternoon," he said, resting his hands on the countertop on either side of the gun. He gave no sign he was surprised by her presence. "It's good to see you up and about. I'm just tidying up a little in here. How are you feeling? Better, I hope."

Shelly said nothing. Her whole body was tense. Her fight-or-flight instincts had shifted into high gear and she was about to bolt. He had the advantage now. Her only option was to run for it.

She was just about to dash for the door when Fallon picked up the pistol by the muzzle and held it out to her. "I guess you'll want the gun back. I've got no need for it."

Without even the slightest hesitation, she snatched the weapon from his hand, dropped the full magazine from the hand grip and checked the chamber. Then she slapped it back into place and jacked the slide. Instead of aiming the gun at Fallon, she held it down by her side, with the safety catch still engaged.

"You put me to bed," she said.

"Yes, I did. You were out of it. I managed to free myself and hauled you into the bedroom. I figured the bed was a much better place than the couch to recover. Let me tell you, that couch is not the most comfortable place to sleep." He placed a hand at the small of his back and grimaced.

"How long was I asleep?"

"About a day, give or take a few hours."

"And you didn't try to get away?" *Or hurt me?* "Why?"

"I've already told you, Nurse Christianson, I have absolutely no intention of hurting you in any way. And as for why I didn't attempt to escape... Without you, where could I go? You're my salvation. I'm safer here than anywhere else on. Why would I run from that? I hope that we can learn to trust each other."

She glared at him. "You drugged me," she said.

"I immunized you," he corrected.

"What proof do I have that whatever you gave me is what you say it is? It's possible you gave me a roofie and then fucked me while I was passed out. What proof can you give me that you're sincere?"

"I gave you back the gun."

Shelly couldn't think of a response to that. She still didn't trust Fallon. But he wouldn't willingly give away his only bit of power and protection unless he was telling the truth, about some things at least. Still, Shelly felt sure there was more Fallon wasn't telling her.

"Temporary illness is often a side effect of vaccination. As a nurse you know this. As an example, after a flu shot, many patients display mild, flu-like symptoms, which pass relatively quickly. It took me nearly twenty minutes to work my way free. By that time, you were nearly choking on your own vomit. I cleaned you up, removed your boots and carried you to the bed. I in no way molested you. I watched over you to make sure you remained on your side in case you vomited again. Once the fever broke, I left you to sleep in peace and came out here to the kitchen."

Shelly's head was spinning over the sudden turn of events. Not long ago, the man before her lay near death in a hospital bed, under her care. Now their roles had reversed, and he had cared for her in the same manner. Life could be odd sometimes. An unexpected twist could slink up when least expected and change everything, like it did when Brad found out about Timothy.

That one moment had changed her whole world forever.

Shelly met Timothy at the university library while she was studying to become a Registered Nurse. She had been a Licensed Practicing Nurse for a few years by then and felt that working in a hospital would be a better career path to take. It had taken months of pleading to convince Brad to let her out of his grip long enough to attend classes. Even then, he only allowed her to take a few credits at a time. This bothered Shelly less than it should have because, for a few hours each day, she was free. The library was one of the few places Brad would allow her to go unattended. He didn't care for books and had nothing but disdain for people who read for pleasure. Shelly had to convince him that there were very few works of fiction at the university library and the stacks were made up of mostly research materials before he allowed her to go on her own. This was only a half-lie. Most of the library was indeed dedicated to various non-fiction works to assist students in their research. However, there was also a treasure trove of fiction there as well. Mostly classical literature, again for students writing papers. Shelly couldn't get away with reading around Brad at home. He simply wouldn't tolerate someone wasting time sticking their nose in a book, when more useful things could be accomplished. So, in addition to her schoolwork, she used the library as an escape and read there. It was a place where she knew Brad wouldn't check up on her. A place she could be safe, if only for a little while.

Timothy was a graduate student. His degree work was in applied physics, and because of his passion for Shakespearian sonnets, he held a Bachelor's in English Literature. He approached her when he saw her sitting alone reading a biography on Ernest Hemmingway and told her he was writing a paper on the writer's life for a lit class. She knew right away he was probably using this clichéd happenstance as an excuse to talk to her. But she didn't mind. It was fun to have a man—other than Brad—pay attention to her. They spent nearly an hour discussing Hemmingway and other literary figures. Shelly lost track of the time and had to rush out of the library at a run in order to catch Brad in the parking lot. He fumed at her for being late, but nothing more.

She got off lucky that time.

Over the next couple of months, Shelly and Timothy became friends. They'd meet twice a week at the library to discuss school and what they were currently reading. Because Shelly couldn't read anything at home, she would talk about books she'd already read with him, the books she loved and the ones that had made the greatest impact on her. By the third meeting, she knew that Timothy was interested in her and was maneuvering to get her into bed with him. By their fifth, she was surprised to find she desired him as well.

This frightened and excited her. Brad kept her cloistered away from people. She was rarely allowed out of range of his control for long. There was hardly a moment when he left her alone, and he intimidated any other men away from talking to her. The thrill of knowing that another man wanted her almost overshadowed the fear of what would happen if Brad found out. Almost, but not quite.

Shelly took great pains to keep her relationship with

Timothy as secret and as chaste as possible. She knew she could never hide a clandestine affair from Brad, at least not for long. He had a way of nosing her secrets out from under her. She therefore kept Timothy at a distance. She never met him anywhere but the library and always coaxed their conversations towards academic topics.

After just a little over three months, Shelly knew Timothy was growing dissatisfied, that he wanted more from their relationship. His suggestions of going out elsewhere grew more frequent and insistent. Shelly found herself also wanting more. She was attracted to him and curious what the sex would be like. However, she was absolutely terrified of being discovered by Brad and what he would do to her, so she didn't dare allow it to go any further. Their covert meetings gave her a thrill, and she just couldn't bring herself to halt them. Whenever she looked into Timothy's face, with his bright eyes and well-manicured but rugged good looks, she felt warm inside. At night, while Brad slept, she indulged in dozens of fantasies about him. Her favorites involved him storming in some night to see Brad in the midst of disciplining her, fighting him off and whisking her away. She was scared and miserable all the time, and her dreams about Timothy made her feel happy, even if it was just for a moment, even if it wasn't real. He'd been the one who'd noticed and approached her; she could never have mustered the courage on her own. She'd begun to genuinely care for him, and thought he felt the same. She even began to imagine he would be able to help her escape her husband. That he could rescue her.

Because of this, she thought it was strange when she went to the library on their usual day at their usual time and Timothy wasn't there to meet her.

*He's probably tired of me,* she thought. She tried not to let it hurt but felt an ache in her chest anyhow. *He must think I'm just a tease, stringing him along for the fun of it.*

After waiting for ten minutes, just to be sure he wasn't

held up in traffic, she gave up and went home. She couldn't call him, nor could he call her. She insisted they never exchange numbers. That would be the easiest way for Brad to find out. The drive home was dreary. It was raining and Shelly felt more alone than she had in a long time. Brad was at work, or screwing his assistant, so he wouldn't be there to notice her returning earlier than usual. She didn't cry, but she felt like it. Several times during the drive, tears threatened to pour like the rain streaking down the windshield.

Shelly arrived home twenty minutes later to the shock of her life. Timothy was laying on their living room floor, unconscious and bleeding. Brad stood over him smirking, and for a moment he looked almost like the man she had fallen in love with, soft good looks, an easy smile, effortlessly funny, sincere in his complements. The way he made her glow inside. The way he treated her like there was no one else in the whole wide world but her. It was all so wonderful at first. Her own personal Prince Charming. He had his own medical practice and was well respected. Wealthy, witty and handsome, what more could a girl ask for?

Then she moved in with him and things gradually started to change. First came the backhanded compliments, followed by the critical eye attuned to her every action and word. She became leery of discussing work with him, because he would belittle the job she did, saying she was just a nurse—if she had any real interest in medicine, she would have become a doctor like him.

The physical abuse started slowly. Squeezed hands during conversations. Open handed slaps during arguments. Insults shouted at her in private, because of some perceived embarrassment in public. Shelly began making excuses to her friends for her absence. During the three years she lived with Brad, her life was spent at the hospital and at his home, living in fear of saying or doing anything that would upset him.

"Good afternoon, whore, here's your boyfriend," Brad

hissed. She tried backing away. Brad grabbed her before she could, and pulled her close.

"You've been fucking around behind my back for three months. Three fucking months! Did you think I wouldn't find out?" He hit her, breaking her nose. Usually, he had the presence of mind to only hit her on the body where the bruises could be easily covered. Today, he showed no such restraint and hit her again, splitting her bottom lip.

"Brad, we didn't do anything. We're just friends. He helps me with schoolwork—" Brad cut her off with a door-breaking kick to her chest, which sent her flying.

"I've given you everything." he screamed. "And this is how you repay me? Cheating on me. You fucking cunt!"

Brad charged at her, spitting, and howling and swinging his bloody fists. Shelly ran. She always ran, though it never did her any good. Brad caught her and slammed her against the wall. While she was dazed, he kneed her in the stomach. He brought his fist up and punched her in the nose again. Then he threw her into the main hallway, where she hit her head on the terra cotta floor tiles.

She spat blood. One of her teeth, a bloody incisor, lay on the floor before her, crimson on ivory.

Then Brad was hauling her up. He hit her in the stomach and shoved her. She pin-wheeled for a moment before catching her balance. Brad grabbed her ear and punched her in the nose again and she crumpled backwards.

Shelly had been beaten many times. Too many to recount. With his bare hands, or with whatever was nearby. His rages were sudden and terrifying and extinguished just as quickly as they ignited.

One look into his rage-twisted face and she knew. *He's not going to stop this time. He's going to kill me. Then he's going to kill Timothy. And he's going to get away with it because he always has. He has money and influence. No one will bat an eye that he's murdered us. They'll say it's a crime of passion and give him their condolences.*

Shelly felt strangely calm after realizing this. There was no panic. No sense of urgency. No fear. She looked over at Timothy, lying in a heap on the red-spattered mother of pearl carpet. She saw his blackened, swollen face, covered with cuts and abrasions. And just like that, she decided she wasn't going to let Brad win. Not this time. Not without a fight.

She lashed out. Years of cowering before him had conditioned Brad to believing her to be broken of spirit. So, when her foot connected with his groin, he was not only introduced to pain on an intimate level, but shock and surprise as well. He reeled away and doubled over, cupping himself.

Shelly aimed a kick to his face, which missed and by happy fortune, caught him in the throat. He sputtered, gagging, and clutching his larynx as he fell to his knees.

While he struggled to breathe, Shelly staggered into the kitchen. Initially, she was looking for a way out. An escape from him. But then she saw the butcher block. Shelly knew then what she had to do. Brad would never change, never let her go, never stop beating her, unless she forced him to.

She was reaching for the biggest knife in the butcher block when she felt a hand take hold of a fistful of her hair and tug back painfully. She whipped around, throwing up an elbow and caught Brad in the left eye. Again, he stumbled back. Her attacks had him off balance, but not for much longer. If she didn't act quickly, she'd never be able to get away. He was too big, too strong, too fast. Her sole advantage lay in surprise and that was already wearing off. She reached again for the block. Initially, she intended only to use one of the knives there to keep him back while she escaped. Her fingers curled around the contoured handle of a paring knife and drew it forth. She sensed Brad looming up behind her, ready to strike again. Shelly spun around and drove the little blade into his neck.

He blinked at her, as though suddenly realizing he may have gone too far this time. Then he reached for her again.

Shelly pulled the little knife from his neck and slammed it into his chest. His knees buckled and he landed on his butt. He looked up at her a moment in childlike wonder, tinged—for the first time ever—with fear before slumping backwards. His head gave a dull *thunk* when it hit the tile floor.

She would remember the look of confused terror on his face forever as she straddled him, pulled the knife out and stuck it in him again. And again. His attempts to ward her off were weak and in vain after the first strike. He started crying. Mewling in pain and fear. He heaved her off him and tried rolling over to crawl away. Shelly caught herself, slammed a knee into his stomach, forced him onto his back and stabbed him again.

And again.

And again.

And again, until his chest was completely torn open, his heart reduced to a shredded mess of bloody tissue and his life was emptied all over the pale ceramic floor. She left the knife embedded in his shattered chest and got up. Shelly glared into Brad's eyes. The crying and whimpering had stopped. Slowly, she saw his eyes dim and wink out entirely.

That was two years ago. Shelly didn't have to worry about Brad anymore. Her therapist believed she was repressing her feelings and her fears about him. Shelly knew better. She had looked into his lifeless, staring eyes for five minutes before calmly calling the police and an ambulance for Timothy. She knew he was dead and would never be able to harm her again. She wasn't going to let her past rule over her present and shape her future.

Standing there in the kitchenette of Uncle Rory's cabin, holding his gun in her hand, she took a deep breath and decided not to allow her fear of Brad control her any longer. She decided to give Fallon a chance.

She met his eyes. "Thank you," she said.

Fallon wasn't sure he had heard correctly. "Thank you," Shelly repeated a little louder, "for taking care of me. I'm sorry I hit you and threatened you. I didn't know what to do, and I panicked."

This was music to his ears. He had won her over. Nurse Christianson was on his side. She would help him after all. The Lord had tested him and found him worthy and provided for his safety. For the first time in nearly a month, Fallon felt sure of success.

"Your apology is not necessary. You saved me. In your position, I feel like I would have done the same as you. It is I who owe you an apology, for how I treated you in your home. I should have trusted you with the truth and explained everything." He sighed as though in regret over missteps. Then he picked up a can from the bag on the counter beside him. "You must be hungry. Would you like me to fix you something to eat?"

"I would like to not feel like shit any longer. And I think I should shoot you for giving that crap to me."

"That crap, as you call it, is going to keep you safe from the army's virus. Besides, if you feel well enough to complain, then you feel well enough to eat."

"Whatever." Shelly said petulantly. Feeling ill always made her that way. Brad used to say she was the biggest baby when she was sick. Always crying and whining and begging for someone to make her feel better. She learned very quickly not to bother him for anything when she was sick. He wouldn't help, and quite often she would get smacked for her trouble.

Later that night, as they were sitting down for dinner, Shelly pressed Fallon for more information. "Why is this colonel so hell-bent on chasing you down?"

Fallon smiled at her choice of words. *Hell-bent, indeed.* "As I told you before, Colonel Aldridge is trying to save his career."

"Everything you've told me and everything I've seen so far implies more than simple ass-covering. It sounds more like he's got a personal grudge against you."

Fallon frowned, trying to think of how to word his response. "In a way, I suppose he does. He's a war hero. He disobeyed orders to rescue a platoon of his men and in the process, destroyed an enemy stronghold and drastically weakened them in the region he was operating in."

"That sounds very commendable," she said.

Fallon gave her a weary smile. "It does, doesn't it? He was decorated for it. Silver Star. His second, I believe. But his superior, the one he made look foolish, made sure to punish him for his valor, which is how he came to be stuck commanding the post guarding the lab."

"No good deed goes unpunished."

"Exactly so," said Fallon. "This has made him jaded and bitter. An assignment like that, babysitting a bunch of brainiacs staring into microscopes all day, that's a career death sentence for a man like him. To a man of action, boredom is a fate worse than death."

"What happened next?"

"His wife left him. Rumor had it that, since returning from the war, he was impossible to live with. Then being handed one dead-end assignment after another, it was a strain their marriage couldn't handle. So, one night she packed up their daughter and left."

"Oh, no."

Fallon nodded in an understanding way. "He has nothing left now you see. Nothing but the chase. He views capturing me as not only a way to protect his career, but a way to save it. One more glorious mission to uplift him from obscurity. He'll stop at nothing to see me in chains and himself, once again, in high regard among his peers and superiors."

"A man like him... it sounds like he could be capable of anything."

Fallon nodded. "He is." *And so am I.*

# January 12th

The situation in Harper's Glen was deteriorating fast. Since the incident on the hospital steps three days ago, the townsfolk had stopped freely coming to the hospital. They weren't interacting with Aldridge's people. Even the hospital staff were leery. This forced Aldridge to send out patrols. That his people were already stretched thin only made matters worse. People weren't reacting well to the show of force. The patrols were meant to provide the townsfolk with a safe means of transport to the hospital, and to maintain the integrity of the quarantine. Immediately following the shooting, a squad of his men had been attacked. No serious injuries, just a few people throwing rocks from alleys and rooftops. But it was a bad sign.

General Collins had apprised his superiors in Washington D.C. of the situation. So, they knew all about his inability to detain Fallon, the attack on the crowd outside the hospital and his perceived sluggishness in establishing a quarantine zone around the town. General Collins made sure they heard his version of events first, and opinions were rapidly turning against Aldridge. If he had wanted to, he could wade through the quagmire of army political affairs and fight back against the general. He didn't. He was tired of it. He had realized some time ago that he simply didn't give a damn anymore. All that mattered was stopping Fallon in this little town. Everything else was a bullshit distraction.

Aldridge leaned back in his chair and rubbed his eyes. He sat that way for several brief minutes when he heard a knock.

"Enter!" he said, louder than he intended.

Major Panelli opened the door carrying a folder. "Sir, I have the latest reports here."

Still rubbing his eyes, Aldridge said, "Summarize them for me."

Panelli opened the folder. "We have a full cordon around town, and a security presence within it. There have been thirty..." he flipped back a few sheets, "thirty-six new cases of Martin's Disease reported. Those patients have been brought here and are currently receiving treatment in isolation. There have been no new incidents of people attacking our security patrols, but the men have reported feeling hostility from the townsfolk they encounter on the streets. Actually, sir, it appears as though the shooting may be working in our favor." Aldridge frowned at this. "People are staying off the streets and in their homes. In effect, they're quarantining themselves and slowing the spread."

"We can't count on that to last," Aldridge said. "We need to use this respite to tighten up our positions. If they're going to give us this time, then we need to take advantage of it. The priority is still locating and detaining Fallon."

"Yes, sir," Panelli said. "There's one more thing. Here's a list of the people we currently have in isolation. Most were from that first big group, as well as the snowplow driver we believe drove Fallon here to the hospital, his wife, and co-workers and their families." He pulled a stapled packet from the folder and handed it to Aldridge, then placed the rest in the colonel's inbox, then turned and left. The first page was a list of names, the next forty pages contained information about each person, attached to each name. For most of these people, it was already too late.

The refrigerator truck hauling the supply of vaccines arrived that morning along with the last stragglers. The hospital and his medics were setting up to receive patients and cure them. The only problem was that the supply had been drastically depleted by Aldridge's efforts in the previous towns where Fallon had hidden. With the medical staff inoculated and now the local police and fire department, there wasn't much left for the public. What they had would be quickly depleted.

*We must get more soon. I'll make sure West puts in the order and have him check on how long it will take for the delivery.*

Aldridge stared at the names on the list, trying to conjure faces to go with each one. He had only seen these people once as they were brought in. A blur in the shape of a face accompanied each name he read. By this point most of them were symptomatic and the disease was progressing rapidly. There was little chance they could be saved. His techs were working as fast as possible. It just wasn't going to be quick enough. All that could be done was to make them as comfortable as possible.

He caught a notation beside one of the names. He leafed through the packet till he found the page he wanted. He skimmed the report, then slapped the whole packet onto his desktop in frustration.

The patient in question was pregnant. Terrible things happened to pregnant women who contracted Martin's Disease. Aldridge clenched his fists in anger. This whole horrible ordeal was getting to him. He wasn't sure he could take anymore. He had survived two tours in Iraq and three in Afghanistan, during the period of heaviest fighting in both countries. He led men into combat and out again. Had faced death on the battlefield and survived. He could handle that kind of death. This death, though, was different. People, American citizens, not combatants, were dying indiscriminately and he was powerless to stop it. In war, casualties were expected, no matter what steps were taken to minimize them. It was the nature of the beast. This was different. This was no accidental shooting, or misplaced missile or artillery strike. This was murder, pure and simple and Colonel Aldridge felt just as responsible for it as the man who created the fucking virus.

To make matters worse, Collins was due to officially arrive sometime today. Aldridge greatly disliked having prying eyes over his shoulder in the best of times. Now, however, he wished he could make the troublesome prick disappear.

Aldridge put away the patient information without looking at the other reports and brushed away thoughts of the soon-to-be-dead people in the isolation ward. There was nothing he could do for them. His only concern was Fallon. Dead or alive, he had to be stopped. The longer Aldridge followed him, cleaning up after him, the more convinced he became that death was preferable to capture.

He checked his watch, it wasn't quite time for his pills yet, but he took them anyway. The constant presence of pain was held at bay by his pills, however, lately they had begun losing strength against it. No matter how many drugs he took, no matter what he did to distract himself, the pain never really went away. It was always there, waiting, ready to pounce. It was his constant companion. There to greet him in the morning and keep him company in the dark when sleep wouldn't come. Fear nagged at the back of his mind. Fear that soon the medications would lose their effectiveness altogether, and he would be left to deal with the pain unaided. That day seemed to be approaching faster than expected, filling Aldridge with dread.

Word of the shooting had spread fast and most citizens had retreated to their homes, afraid to go outside for fear they would be next in the army's crosshairs. Terrified eyes watched through covered windows as military vehicles patrolled the streets with impunity, afraid of what would happen next.

Everyone except Nathan Benedict. He wasn't afraid; he was angry. In fact, he was in a pissed-off rage.

Like most of the residents of Harper's Glen, Benedict learned of the military occupation from the broadcast blitz. He tuned in at the appropriate time to hear what their puppet mayor had to say. When the televised address was over, he knew just how well and truly screwed they all were. Benedict was a survivor. He figured the best way to do that, was to remain invisible. He'd been in the crowd when the soldiers opened fire. He was at the hospital for a checkup. During the cold months, his shoulder and leg ached like mad and he wanted to see his doctor about a refill on his pain pills. While he was there, he had planned on getting a flu shot as well. Just to be on the safe side. This winter was already shaping up to be a particularly harsh one. And besides, his VA disability benefits required him to get a yearly checkup if he wanted to continue receiving checks.

The crowd was already unruly when he arrived outside the hospital, and the soldiers twitchy. The air felt electric with the expectation of violence. He pushed his way to the front to see exactly what was happening.

Benedict saw exactly what incited the shooting: the jeering, the snowballs, the embarrassing spill the lieutenant took after being shoved. When the officer ordered his men to lock and load, that was when he decided to leave. The rifle reports cracked in the frosty morning air, silencing the angry shouts of the gathered mob. There was a second of stunned silence, as though people on both sides couldn't believe it had happened. Then the silence was broken again a half second later by the screams of the wounded and the fearful shouts of those running to escape the massacre. He didn't look back. He just ran as fast as his single leg could carry him. He heard the soldiers shoot twice more while he ran to safety. There was no way for him to know how many had been killed, how many were wounded, or how many had been trampled beneath the human stampede.

Two blocks from the hospital, safe beneath the overhang of a deli, Benedict paused to catch his breath. The crowd had scattered to the four winds, but there were several people on the streets around him. While running, he had seen at least two people fall with bullet wounds. Many others slipped and fell on the treacherously slick streets. They had seen what he had. They were as scared as he was. Listening to their puffing and sobbing, Benedict felt anger growing white hot inside him.

"Motherfuckers. How dare you?" he said aloud to no one. "This is America, goddamn it! How fucking dare you come here like this!" By the time he started walking again, Benedict was scowling. Ideas and plans were already forming in his brain, storming and turbulent. He was going to get them back for this. He wasn't sure how, yet. But he was determined to make them pay.

The more he thought about what had happened, the angrier he got, until he was a tightly-wound ball of rage. Somehow, he was going to make them pay for defiling his home like this. However, first things first, he needed a drink. With that determined, he went to the bar just up the street from his house, Lucy's Tavern, which is where he spent most of the day, contemplatively staring into each beer he drank.

The tavern had a simple layout. There was a main sitting area in front of the bar. Three of the four walls were hung with big-screen televisions, so no matter which way a patron was facing, he or she would be able to catch whatever game happened to be playing. Today, all three screens were dark. At the back of the bar, opposite the entrance, sat two aging pool tables in separate alcoves, along with all the cues, chalk and space needed to play. Benedict sat at the bar, his face illuminated only by dim lights and neon beer signs. He was far from alone. Though it was eight in the morning on a workday, the place was packed. From what he could overhear from the other patrons, the other two bars in town were just as busy. The bartender, Kaleb, had had to call in the night shift early to keep up with the crowd. Even Lucy herself had shown up to help.

The whole place was buzzing with news and rumors of what was happening.

"They've got both on-ramps to the highway blocked off. How am I supposed to feed my family if I can't get to work?"

"Did you see the barbed wire they put around the Sherriff's station? They're turning it into a fortress."

"They've got a helicopter parked on Cantrell's field. The thing's been in the air every second the weather's clear."

"No TV. No radio. No phones. They've got us completely cut off. Don't they know the Super Bowl's in a couple weeks? If this don't end soon, we're going to miss it."

"Murdering bastards. They didn't need to shoot at them people at the hospital. It was just a damn snowball."

"Somebody needs to do something about this. There's no way they can just come here and kidnap a whole town like this."

The door opened. In the bar mirror, Benedict saw his friend, Sonny Dixon, enter and raised a hand to catch his attention. There was an empty stool next to him, and he was tired of drinking alone.

Sonny saw him and started cutting through to the bar.

"How's it going, Benny?" Sonny asked taking the proffered seat. He ordered a locally brewed beer from Kaleb.

"Things were good," Benedict said. "Until I found out the army had us surrounded."

"I can't hardly believe it. Did you hear they shot a bunch of people at the hospital?"

"I heard. I was there."

"Me too. They killed Martha Wax. I think she was the one who threw the first snowball. She was yelling at them, too. She always did have a mouth on her."

"That's no reason for her to die," said Benedict. He downed the last half of his beer and ordered another. Then added a shot of whiskey.

"No, it's not," agreed Sonny.

For a while, the two men sat quietly, just listening to the unrest in the bar around them. Benedict and Sonny had been friends for a few years. Both men had served in the military—Sonny in the Air Force and Benedict in the Army—and both men had left the military disgruntled with the wasteful ways in which the armed forces and the government were run. It was one of the things they'd bonded over when they first met years ago, right there in Lucy's Tavern. Since then, they were constant companions. Hunting, fishing, camping, hiking, skiing, and drinking at Lucy's late into the night. They'd had long discussions about the problems with the country, the leadership, the economy, schools, welfare programs; and both men agreed that something needed to be done to fix it.

Sonny was the first to break the silence. "Somebody should stand up to them," he said.

Benedict nodded. "You're absolutely right." He turned to Sonny. "So why don't we?"

*If you're going to go against the Man,* Benedict thought. *It's better to have a friend with you. Just to be on the safe side.*

The hospital cafeteria was packed with soldiers lined up for breakfast. Because of the limited space in the serving lines and seating area, they were encouraged to eat quickly and leave to make room for the next soldiers in line, or else to grab their food to-go. Private Marie Jones hated being rushed through a meal. She felt it was bad for digestion. Besides, she wanted to sit and talk with her buddies about recent events.

The entire cafeteria was buzzing with talk of the shooting.

"They should be fucking court-marshaled," she said, loudly to her squad mates at the table around her. "And that retarded butter-bar should be tied to a fucking post and shot."

"A little harsh, don't you think?" said Kowalski. He was her best friend in the company. There were few people who could stand up to her in an argument, and he was one of them. Most people wilted beneath her verbal lashing, but he knew her well enough that he could take it and lash back. A long time ago they'd considered dating. Though the sex had been surprisingly good, they mutually decided they worked out better as just friends.

"Not in the least," she replied. "It's bad enough that My Lai-style massacres happen overseas when we're actually at war. But these dumb fucks shot Americans in their hometown."

Turner, sitting to Jones' right chimed in, "I heard the crowd was about to riot and was attacking them."

Jones gave him a look that said she thought he was an idiot. In fact, she *did* think he was an idiot, but tried not to tell him so every day. It was bad for the poor boy's fragile self-esteem.

"You are right, Turner, they were attacked. With snowballs, big, scary snowballs. Maybe when the rioting mob was done with the snowballs, they planned on giving them wedgies and making fun of their mothers. I can see why those dickheads were so afraid." She often used sarcasm as a weapon against anything she didn't like, and when it came to the army, she didn't like much. "I can see how you think they were totally justified in shooting civilians, dip-shit."

"You weren't there, Jonesy," Kowalski said. "You can't know what happened."

"I know that snowballs aren't bullets. A fucking snowball won't kill you and leave your wife a widow and your kid an orphan. Those brainless assholes need to be held accountable for what they did. In five minutes, they single handedly turned this nice little hick town into a fucking war zone. Whatever chance we had of these people cooperating with us has been shot to shit by those pricks."

When meeting her for the first time, a lot of people were put off by her nearly constant profanity. Here was this tall, blond girl, who looked like a model and cussed like a drunken sailor. Her squad mates were used to it, and being soldiers themselves, were normally just as vulgar. This morning however, Jones was in rare form and wouldn't let them even get a word in. As usually happened when she was angry about something, she spoke her mind loudly and colorfully. As a result, her chain of command didn't like her.

Even though most of the people sitting with her outranked her, she'd been in the army for six years, which was at least two years longer than all of them except Kowalski. She had been deployed to both Afghanistan and Iraq. Her biggest fault, other than her mouth, was the fact that she was a heavy sleeper. So, when she was late for two morning PT formations in a row, her squad leader, Sergeant Jackson—who hated her most of all—presented her with five back-dated negative counseling statements she had never seen before that day and informed her that she was going to be subjected to non-judicial punishment. At his recommendation, they threw the book at her. For forty-five days, Jones was restricted to post, her pay was reduced, and she was given extra work details after the workday was done. Additionally, they took her rank, knocking her from specialist all the way down to a nothing private. This effectively killed her hopes of going to the promotion board and becoming a non-commissioned officer. She figured they were making an example of her to increase discipline among the rest of the company's soldiers. This only added to the already large chip on her shoulder. Since then, her "ah, fuck it" attitude had only gotten worse. She had just under a year left on her contract and had made up her mind that she was definitely getting the hell out and going to school. In her view, the army wasn't worth the hassle she'd been put through. She'd lost a fiancé during her first deployment and a longtime boyfriend during her second. Jones felt that she'd freely given so much, only to be screwed over in the end.

She was about to continue her diatribe when someone behind her called out, "Jones, get over here."

She looked back to find Sergeant Jackson, her squad leader, glaring and waiting impatiently. He looked pissed, too. She rolled her eyes and got up to see what he was going to yell at her about this time.

"Yes, Sarn't," she said, assuming parade rest in front of him.

"Jones, I've been listening to your bitching for the last ten minutes. You need to knock that shit off."

"Roger, Sarn't." She kept her face and tone completely neutral and impassive. Even the slightest tick would set him off. When it came to dealing with her superiors, she mostly just wanted to do her job and be left the hell alone.

"Your negative attitude isn't helping matters here. We've all got a job to do. An investigation will determine whether those men were at fault for what happened. Not you screaming for a fucking witch hunt. You've been downrange; you know that shit happens during crisis situations like this."

She almost laughed in his face. She'd been overseas twice for a full year apiece, not counting her year in Korea; Jackson had been in seven and hadn't been downrange even once. Now he was lecturing her on what combat was like. It took every ounce of control she had to keep quiet.

"Do you understand what I'm telling you, Jones?"

"Roger, Sarn't."

"Good. Now you and the rest of the squad finish up and get down to the motor pool. We've got a patrol in an hour and a half and y'all have been sitting there jaw-jacking long enough."

"Roger, Sarn't." She returned to the table sullen and quiet. The lecture hadn't affected her so much as the implication that the shooting would be swept under the rug and the shooters would go unpunished. This deeply troubled her and made her sad.

Kowalski took one look at her and asked, "You okay?" Sometimes—most times, actually—it was better to leave her alone at times like this. But he was willing to risk her wrath to find out if she needed to talk. He was her closest friend and felt an obligation to provide help when the situation called for it. Sometimes she opened up to him and after talking it through, felt better. Other times she bit his head off and clammed up for the rest of the day.

He could tell already that she wasn't going to talk to him at all. She shook her head. "I'm fine. It's nothing. Everybody finish up and get down to the motor pool. We've got a patrol soon."

There was the usual grumbling upon hearing this, but everyone got up, cleared off their trays and filed out the door.

Jones was last. "I thought we were here to help and protect these people," she said under her breath.

Kowalski heard her, though he was sure she hadn't meant for him to. He nodded, silently agreeing with her.

It had been three days since Fallon slipped Shelly the vaccine. Though the worst of the aches and pains had subsided, she was still light-headed and nauseous. While Fallon muddled around in the kitchen to make them something to eat, she sat on the sofa, holding her head. She felt ill, but what made her feel worse was the predicament she found herself in. If what Fallon said was true, then in all likelihood the army knew he had come to her for help and were looking for her. She wanted to run and hide but knew that staying put was the safest option. Nobody knew about Uncle Rory's cabin. It was her private hideaway from the world. A place she could go when she felt life closing in on her. Now, against her will, she was sharing her special place with another.

Twice today she'd heard helicopters flying and hoped they weren't searching for them.

"Do you feel well enough for some soup?" Fallon called from the kitchen.

*Only if you don't poison me with something else,* she thought.

Aloud she said, "I think I can handle it."

"My mother used to make me soup when I was sick. I got pneumonia when I was little. I was home for three weeks, bundled up in blankets. She never left my side the whole time. Members from our church would bring by food and well-wishes. One night, I remember waking to her praying over me. I couldn't understand what she was saying, but for the 'amen' at the end of every sentence. Seeing her on her knees, rocking back and forth, praying for me to get better... It's all I really remember about her."

Fallon brought out a steaming bowl of chicken soup and placed it on the coffee table in front of her. She simply stared at it. After a moment, Fallon sighed and spooned some into his mouth. "It's safe," he said. "I vaccinated you once, so the disease the army's spreading won't make you sick. I don't need to do it again." He tried giving her a reassuring smile, but it didn't work well on her.

Reluctantly, Shelly dug in and quickly finished the bowl. She hadn't realized just how hungry she was. Fallon got her a second bowl.

"Why is the army spreading a virus?" she asked.

"I'm not sure, exactly. I think it's some kind of experiment. Either that, or they're using it to lock down the town while they search for me. It's probably not fatal, just something to incapacitate everyone and keep them more docile."

"That doesn't make any sense. If they wanted us to

cooperate, they could have asked us and kept us informed about their intentions. There is no reason to lock up an entire town just to search for one person."

"I'm afraid that's not the way the military operates. They believe in control for control's sake."

Shelly wasn't sure she believed him, but let the matter drop and finished her second bowl of soup. Already she was feeling better.

Fallon also felt a change of subject was needed, but couldn't think of anything else to say, so he let silence fill the space between them for the rest of the night.

# January 13th

Harper's Glen was a rustic little town. Not quite a "blink and you'll miss it" kind of place, but not a burgeoning metropolis either. At night, all the traffic lights but the six along Main Street, which connected the town to the highway, blinked yellow. The town council mandated that all buildings have an Old West feel to them. Main Street ran the length of the town and boasted most of their business franchises. There were three McDonald's and a Wendy's, two car lots, a Walmart, and a movie theater.

Main street still wore the remnants of last year's holiday season. Large plastic wreaths hung from lampposts, bunches of fake holly dangled between traffic lights, and the large pine in front of city hall still wore its Christmas dress—though the lights had been disconnected. The recent snow made it impractical to take it all down. The holiday atmosphere was marred by the concertina wire, armed patrols, and US Army helicopters circling above.

The largest building in Harper's Glen by far was the Catholic Church, Saint Michaels, located in the northwest corner of town, two miles from the highway. It was built in the style of a classic cathedral, though it was nowhere near as big as the more famous cathedrals it borrowed from. It remained a source of pride for the predominately Catholic citizenry.

The little town was chalk full of hard-working folks, who paid their taxes, mowed their lawns on Sundays during the warmer months and celebrated July the Fourth with great zeal. There was a war memorial across from city hall in the shape of an old muzzle-loading cannon on a plinth. Inscribed on a plaque were listed the names of all the Glen's sons who'd fought and died for their country, from World War One on through the more recent wars in Iraq and Afghanistan. It was in Iraq that the first woman was added to the list of the honored dead.

In all, Harper's Glen was a town of true-blue American patriots, which was why their captivity came as such a grievous shock. Cut off from the rest of the country, armed soldiers roaming the streets, and a deadly sickness burning its way through their population. How could their favorite uncle treat them in such a manner? These were people who wholeheartedly believed in what America stood for. Though few of them had ever even been to another, most residents truly felt they lived in the greatest country on the face of the earth. Yet here they were, prisoners in their own homes. Their immense feeling of betrayal fueled their outrage. So, after six days of occupation, when the attacks against the soldiers began, many silently applauded the men with the daring to do what they could not by striking back.

The presence patrols, soldiers in the trucks driving around picking up the sick and dying and ensuring people remained compliant with military rule until the crisis abated, were the easiest targets. Their task, keeping citizens away from the sensitive areas in and around the hospital, became harder by the day. Townsfolk were scared and the army's presence wasn't helping ease their minds. Ever since the shooting, people simply didn't trust soldiers and were afraid to approach them for help. This made rendering assistance difficult and hindered information gathering. The local cops—and a couple state troopers who called Harper's Glen home—assisted the army in these efforts, though their hearts just weren't in it. They felt the same sense of betrayal and heartbreak as everyone else. Besides, there were only twenty-three of them in total. So, there was little chance of them filling in where the army was thinnest.

Roadblocks and sandbag bunkers formed checkpoints throughout and around town. Since the harassment began, residents were regularly stopped and searched, heightening the already tense atmosphere. But the search teams had it the worst. They were tasked with going into people's homes and removing their sick to the hospital for care. Fear drove many people to violence when the gray-clad soldiers arrived on their doorsteps. Tears and hysterics met them as they tried to calmly take loved ones away.

Eddie Tate was there to record all of this. He was one of three staff reporters for the local weekly newspaper. Though he was currently unemployed due to the military lockdown of the newspaper office, he still had his notebook and pen. His plan was to catalog everything happening inside the quarantine: every atrocity, every abuse of power and negligent act inflicted upon his town. He and the rest of the staff, at his urging, had spent every day since the city was locked down observing and documenting.

Eddie had no idea how he was going to get his information to the outside world when – if – the quarantine was lifted. But he knew he had to try. Somebody had to tell their story. Somebody had to let the world know about the horrors they were enduring. That somebody, Eddie decided, should be him. And if somebody happened to win a Pulitzer along the way, well then somebody would accept the award with the utmost dignity and humility.

In reality, Eddie was thrilled to cover something big for a change. To catch some real news, not just the deals at the farmer's market on Sixth Street, or how the changing price of poultry affected the wage standards of the town's workforce.

No, this was big. Huger than huge, and he was right smack in the middle of it. At night, while he typed out and collated the daily notes gathered by himself and the others, he imagined that this was what it must feel like to be a war correspondent. There, in the thick of the action, with nothing more than a pen and a camera, telling the world how they should view the action as it unfolded. The Blitz of London, the Fall of Hanoi, the Battle of Fallujah: that was cutting-edge reporting, reporters in the right place at the right time. History documented for the masses by brave journalists selflessly risking life and limb for their stories.

Now it was his turn.

He wasn't blind to the horrors around him. He simply shuttered it away, filed it for later use. He was as outraged about what was happening as the next man. But he chose a more passive form of resistance. To channel his righteous anger. He would make them pay after the atrocities were over. Becoming a world-renowned and award-winning journalist would be merely a byproduct of delivering their comeuppance.

Every night, he saved what he had to disks and stored them in a safe place. The hard copies of notes and handwritten outlines were shredded, then burned in his backyard barbeque. If they discovered what he was doing and searched his home, there was nothing in his house to show he was documenting anything.

The one bit of data eluding him was the exact numbers of the sick and dead. He could estimate, based off the numbers of people being admitted to the hospital each day and the number of people being taken off the streets. From that number, he could assume that most of them were dead. Once they went into the hospital, they never came back out again.

There were disturbing rumors everywhere. He couldn't report rumors, but he listened to them to develop leads.

It was Tuesday; the army had barely been there six days and already the Glenn seemed empty and hollow.

He was finishing up and had just saved his work when he heard a knock at his door. According to his watch it was nearly eleven at night, well past curfew. Expecting trouble, he went to the door, hesitantly slipped on the chain, and cracked it open. "Can I help you?" he said to the man he didn't know, standing on his front step.

"You're Edward Tate, the reporter, right?"

He nodded. "That's right. Who are you?"

"I was wondering if you might allow me inside so that we can talk some business."

Eddie paused. He didn't want some stranger in his home, poking through his things. Besides, his work was still open and out on the desk in front of his computer. "Uh, I don't know if this is a good time. See, I was just about to clean up and go to bed."

"You might want to consider letting me in. There's a patrol headed this way right now and if they catch me out after curfew, standing on your porch, they'll sit us both down for questioning."

Eddie balked. After another moment of indecision, he slid the chain off and opened the door for the stranger. By the light of his front room lamp, Eddie thought he recognized his guest, but didn't think he'd ever actually met the man before. He was good with names, better with faces, and Harper's Glen was a small town.

Once the door was closed, the stranger stuck out his hand. "Hello, Mr. Tate. I'm Nate Benedict. Ha, that's kinda funny: Nate and Tate." Eddie shifted uncomfortably, stealing furtive glances at his open office door and the whirring computer inside.

"What can I do for you, Mr. Benedict?" He gave the

proffered hand a quick shake.

"Well, sir, I think we can help each other. The word around is that you've been keeping tabs on what the army is doing around town."

"Where'd you hear that?"

Benedict shrugged. "From people. But that's not the point. See, I'd like you to help me out with this thing I'm doing."

Eddie started to protest, but Benedict cut him off. "You won't have to do any more work than you're already doing. I would just like you to make special note of the times and routes the patrols take and if you see anything interesting, you pass the word along to me."

"Why should I? What's in it for me?"

Benedict nodded as if he expected this question. "Your reward, Mr. Tate, is expelling the army from our town. But if you need more than the pride of being a good Samaritan, I'll make sure to share anything interesting I find out with you, too. And I'll find the location of their jammers and shut them down so that you can transmit the story you're writing to the rest of the world. If you help me, that will speed up the process. Besides, you wouldn't want them snooping around here, would you? They might find your papers before you have a chance to burn them at night. Or they might catch you on the way to your locker in the bus station and find all the disks you're storing there."

"I don't... You... How do you know about that?"

Benedict shrugged again. "Do we have a deal?" Benedict stuck out his hand again.

Eddie swallowed hard. He was trapped and he knew it. On the plus side, if this man could do what he said, then Eddie's fame would be even greater. He'd be the reporter who gathered intelligence for the Harper's Glen resistance movement. Cast in that light, it seemed like a pretty good deal indeed. He shook Benedict's hand again.

"Great. Glad to have you aboard. A man needs friends in

this time of crisis. People he can trust. Just to be on the safe side." He clapped Eddie on the shoulder. "Now, what have you got for me tonight?"

Barney Goodwin sat at his workbench in his store, reloading powder, and projectiles into spent brass for a customer. Guns were his passion and had been ever since he received his first twenty-two rifle on his seventh birthday. He was good with people and provided inexpensive firearms supplies for the community. The services he provided included ammunition reloading, weapon maintenance and a three-lane firing range for handguns and rifles. Being the go-to guy in Harper's Glen for any firearms-related questions or issues, he also sold any hunting equipment, licenses and paraphernalia needed during any of the year-round hunting and fishing seasons. Most of the time, he dealt with shotguns, hunting rifles and some handguns, but for a few discerning customers, he could procure more exotic weaponry.

He'd owned and operated his own store in Harper's Glen for fifteen years and had been an under the counter dealer of illegal weapons for ten. Most of the people he dealt with were enthusiasts, like himself, who merely wanted to possess a fully automatic rifle or four. Some of his deals included "prepper" nut cases living in Montana, Idaho, or some other backwoods state, who thought that the government was out to get them and decided to build an arsenal to defend their private bunkers. He rarely dealt with people he didn't know, and most of his transactions were conducted through a third party. That way, there was less of a trail leading back to him if the authorities caught on. He never transacted any deals over the Internet. The World Wide Web scared the bejesus out of him. In his opinion, the more you did online, the better the government was able to track what you were doing, and for an arms dealer, that was not a good thing.

During his years in business, he'd been lucky enough to

avoid popping up on the radar of John Q. Law. His regular business and his side income had provided him and his wife, Cathy, with a comfortable lifestyle. It allowed him, in fact, to dote on his wife to his heart's desire. He never refused her any request. When she wanted to build an addition to the back of their house for a sewing room, he gladly wrote out the checks and the extension was built. When she decided she wanted to take college courses and then later photography and cooking lessons, once again he provided. He and Cathy had been high school sweethearts. Barney loved her with all his heart and believed she truly was the better half of his soul. The only thing he ever insisted upon was the location of their home and his business. He chose to live in Harper's Glen because it was a small, out of the way town, near major highways, but quiet and scenic and an unlikely place to look for a merchant of illicit weaponry. An added benefit to the locale was the trees and the clean mountain air, which were good for his wife, who had developed respiratory problems of late.

At his bench, Barney was sweating. He'd been working almost non-stop for six days, stopping only for short naps and brief meals. Six days ago, the love of his life had been taken from him and he was beside himself with anguish. He couldn't believe she was gone. There was seldom a day in the last eighteen years that they'd been apart. It was like he had lost half of himself.

On the night she disappeared, she'd complained about stomach pains and had gone to Walmart to get something for it. She never returned home. He found out later that she'd been taken to Saint John's when the army arrived. He went to the hospital after the shooting to find her and they informed him that she was a patient, but he was not allowed to see her under any circumstances. Barney felt sick inside. Casting about for someone to blame, he became convinced the army had killed her. He knew she was dead. He felt it down in the bottom of his soul and it tore him apart inside. In her absence, he wandered about their house, lost. He'd start work projects only to become distracted by tears after a few minutes. He would find himself staring at something of hers for hours at a time. Not moving, just quietly weeping. Barney truly didn't know what to do without her. But he knew all too well who was responsible, and he intended to make them pay for taking her from him.

Being the proprietor of the town's only gun store made him an instant target for the army. They dropped in on him the first morning after they had seized control and took full stock of his inventory. Afterward, the snot-nosed little officer in charge ordered him to close shop. He was forbidden to sell any guns or ammunition for the duration of the military quarantine. Barney smiled, nodded, and said, "Yes, sir," in all the correct places. Officially, he fully intended to comply. He didn't wish to draw undue attention to himself or his side business. Unofficially... now that was another matter entirely.

Barney was among the first to be recruited by Benedict, in Lucy's, right after he and Sonny decided to do something about the military presence. Being a part of Benedict's group let him in on lots of interesting information. It gave him a purpose he didn't feel when he was alone at home. Everything he learned told him that anyone who entered the hospital didn't leave again alive. Benedict sought him out and expressed grief for his loss, and together they started planning how best to get back at the army for what they'd done to him and his wife. He gave Benedict everything he asked for: firearms, ammo and even a couple of specialty items he'd been holding for a preferred customer. Nothing he gave to Benedict's revolution could be traced back to him. Barney was sure that if any man could avenge his wife, Benedict was that man.

It was freezing in the tower. Private Jones stamped her feet and shuffled back and forth in the small space to stay warm.

A small space heater had been set in the corner and if she stood right next to it with her hands on its sides, it kept her warm. The trouble was that the M240B machine gun was three feet away from the heater. The open gap where the machine gun poked out of the tower was too far for the hot air to reach. The cold and the wind poured through the opening and seeped through her thick outer layers and into her bones.

Sergeant Jackson had given her tower duty. Probably to quietly punish her for speaking her mind. He was an asshole like that.

The entire town on was edge. She'd heard that three separate patrols had been harassed today alone, while collecting sick people and bringing them to the hospital. She had personally witnessed at least a dozen people walk by giving her the evil eye. In Afghanistan she would never have let them within fifty meters of her tower. But Afghanistan this was not, and she couldn't go popping off rounds without a fuckin-A good reason for doing so.

Jones checked her watch and saw that only half of her eight-hour guard shift had passed. She sighed and returned to her spot, huddled by the heater, bored but watchful. This wasn't what she had signed up for. Though, to be completely honest, she wasn't sure why she'd signed up anymore. The recruiter filled her head with dreams of seeing glamorous sights around the world and had made the army sound like a glamorous and exciting adventure. Freshly graduated from high school, Jones had bought every lie and over-exaggeration without question. It wasn't till she'd gotten to her first unit after completing Basic and AIT that she realized just how boring and intrinsically idiotic the army really was. She'd hoped to be stationed in Germany, or someplace exotic. Instead, she got Camp Casey, in Dongducheon South Korea, and did basically nothing for her first two years except clean a locker room and motor pool.

Despite all of that, she had loved the army at the time. She found the structured chaos of daily army life exciting and challenging. Jones operated best during times of high stress, and little is as highly stressful as doing nothing all day long then being handed a laundry list of tasks ten minutes before close of business and told you would be staying until they were all completed. The long hours, the field rotations, the occasional stupid detail, she had enjoyed it all, thinking it was just a part of being a soldier. She had even studied for the promotion board so that she could advance and move her career forward. She had wanted to be a leader. She felt it was important to have goals in life. Right now, her biggest goal, the one thing that mattered most in the whole world, was to hug close to the space heater and down a pot of hot coffee the very second she left the tower.

After two years of tedium, she was transferred to Fort Lewis, Washington and immediately deployed to Afghanistan. The deployment wasn't bad. She liked it better than garrison life at Camp Casey, which was in her opinion, the armpit of the army. She had even reenlisted overseas, thinking she might be able to make a career out of the army after all.

The same tedium found her again upon returning stateside. She rallied against it and proactively worked to improve herself and her job performance. But after being passed over for the promotion board several times, Jones found her zeal for army life waning. Her next deployment in Iraq was much the same as Afghanistan, however Jones found herself dreaming of a life out of uniform. Now here she was, chasing some asshole from one shithole little town to the next, freezing her ass off, surrounded by idiots who hated her and wanted her to leave. The last month had been worse than the twenty-four she'd spent getting shot at in Afghanistan and Iraq.

Jones paused in her circuit of the tower when she noticed a man standing across the street staring at her. She couldn't tell much about him because he wore a thick winter parka with the hood up. From the size and the way he stood, Jones assumed it was a man.

*How long has this guy been standing there watching me?* she wondered.

Hairs on the back of her neck prickled up. Experience had taught her that it was never a good thing when somebody outside the wire paid that much attention to what was going on inside the wire. It meant she was being studied. A little voice in the back of her mind told her she was just being paranoid, her experiences overseas coloring her perceptions today. She hushed the voice and reached for the radio to call Base Defense Operation Control.

"B-DOC, this is Tower One, over."

"Tower One, this is B-DOC."

"B-DOC, I've got what appears to be a military-aged male, northeast of my position, about forty or so meters away, standing near the pet store. He hasn't moved for the last ten minutes and appears to be watching my tower closely; over."

"Roger, Tower One. Can you give me a description?"

"He's looks to be average height, average build, wearing blue ski pants and a heavy red and black winter coat with a hood. He doesn't appear to be armed."

"Can you see anything else distinctive about him?"

"Sorry. That's the best I can do at present. He's too far away for me to see anything else; over."

"Roger. Understand all. Stand by, we'll spin up a patrol to come out and look. For now, just keep eyes on and call us if he does anything else; over."

"Roger, B-DOC. Tower One, out."

Jones replaced the radio and looked back at the guy watching her. Three minutes later the patrol arrived, pulled the man aside, shooed him away. Jones watched all this with a small sense of satisfaction. She hoped the guy was just an innocent bystander with a legitimate reason for doing what he was doing. But at the same time, she didn't believe that was the case.

Jones had seen the first man, the obvious man. She never had a clue that there were three others watching her tower, carefully timing her reactions and those of the response team dispatched to deal with that first, obvious man.

# January 14th

Wednesday dawned with a break in the weather, during which the army tightened its grip on Harper's Glen. Under the cover of helicopters and drones, several checkpoints were established throughout the city. A desperately needed shipment of vaccine, food and other supplies was air-lifted in and immediately distributed. It was insufficient to deal with the growing number of cases appearing in the hospital. There were already over two hundred people afflicted, with more coming in every day. Caring for so many at one time was stretching the hospital's and the army's resources near to the breaking point. The gymnasium of the local high school was commandeered and filled with beds and isolation equipment, in preparation for an escalation in the numbers of sick and dying.

Collection points were set up in the town common and in the movie theater on Main Street. These sites were used to diagnose, triage, and prepare newly sick individuals for transport. EMTs and firefighters ran each station, with a squad of soldiers and some cops for protection.

Motorized patrols were out in force to head off trouble

before it could begin. Most people saw this to keep the town under the army's thumb and compliant. The soldiers, tired and on edge, could sense the rage and hostility simmering just below the surface, and were wary of the civilians. The daily patrols had already become a tedious routine. Everywhere they went, they were treated with disdain. Several patrols reported rocks and bricks thrown from alleys or dropped from rooftops. The hospital shooting had made both sides mistrustful of each other. Altercations occurred daily as they went about their business, and the jail was already full of troublemakers. It was only a matter of time before this state of affairs reached critical mass.

Jones expected the worst. When she mentioned her concern to Kowalski, he shrugged it off and joked that her PTSD was acting up again. This morning however, she wasn't in a joking mood. They were going on a raid, and any number of things could go wrong.

They surrounded the building on all sides and made sure the area was secure before dismounting. Not that there was much foot traffic. It was too early, too cold and most people were still at home, too scared to come out. Jones looked up and down the deserted street, her breath misting before her with each exhale. It was sunny and bright outside. She could hear a pair of helicopters in the air making a circuit overhead. Though the sky was clear, it was still miserably cold. The only people out there with her platoon were a pair of cops, there to put a local face on the operation, to legitimize it and hopefully to keep people calm, and a nurse.

"Now we're holding up pharmacies," she muttered in disgust. "I can't believe this shit." Jones shivered as she opened the back door of her truck. "Come with me, please, Nurse Littlewolf." She motioned for the nervous-looking woman wearing sky blue scrubs under her heavy topcoat to follow her and escorted their guest to the front door of the building her platoon had surrounded. Inside, Jones began immediately sweating. The little bit of exposed skin on her neck and wrists burned from the sudden temperature change.

Her platoon leader, Lieutenant Bowing, was at the front counter, arguing with the owner. At least Jones guessed he was the owner, by the fight he was putting up to keep them from taking his inventory.

"I don't give a shit who your orders come from!" the portly man in the white lab coat yelled. "You have no right to come in here and steal from me!"

He was directing his anger towards the officer in front of him, paying no heed to the fifteen armed soldiers arrayed around his counter watching the exchange. Jones spotted Kowalski standing directly across from her. His mask prevented her from seeing his face, but she could tell from his stance that he was smirking at the scene.

*He probably thinks it's just as ridiculous as I do,* she thought.

Jones looked forward to discussing this with him later. She glanced at the rest of the soldiers with her. They were alert and ready. She earnestly hoped this ordeal wouldn't end in violence. She didn't think it would. Ell-tee Bowing was pretty smart, for an officer. He wouldn't fuck up the way that idiot Lopez had. Regardless, she had decided that unless someone was pointing a gun at her or someone in her squad, she wasn't going to shoot anyone, no matter who gave the order. She was a soldier, sure; but she was a person too and refused to kill unless it was in self-defense. Besides, these people were not her enemy; they were Americans, just like her, and there was no way she was going to kill one of her countrymen in cold blood. Especially when they were supposed to be there to assist and protect them.

In a calm voice, Lieutenant Bowing explained his position: "Sir, we aren't stealing anything from you. We are procuring the pharmaceuticals in your store for use at the hospital."

"Listen here, you commie punk. I know what you're trying

to do. You and that pussy in the white house are trying to turn this whole damn country into a pinko state. Well, I won't stand for it! I won't, goddamn it! I fought in 'Nam to stop this kind of shit and I'll be damned if I'll let you just up and take whatever you please. I have rights."

Jones almost laughed. *Really? He thinks we're still fighting the communists. Someone needs to check into the twenty-first century.*

Lieutenant Bowing was unfazed by the old man's diatribe. "Sir, we are going to keep an accurate accounting of what we take. We have a representative from the hospital here and you're more than welcome to watch us work and check our documentation before we leave, to ensure that everything is on the up and up. Once this situation has abated, the government will reimburse you for your losses today."

"I've already told you—"

"Sir! You're acting as if you have a choice in the matter. You don't. All you can do is accept it, stand back, and let us do our job. You will be compensated after this is all over, I assure you. Now please stand aside and let my people do their jobs."

The owner closed his mouth with a snap. Then he looked around, as though noticing for the first time that he was surrounded. His gaze stopped at the nurse standing next to Jones.

He visibly deflated. "Follow me," he said, leading her into the back where he kept his stock. Jones and several others followed along. They were there to do the heavy lifting.

Under normal circumstances, Jones would have agreed and argued on the side of the pharmacy owner that they were stealing from him. But this was hardly an ordinary situation and the hospital needed the drugs if they were going to be able to keep helping the people of this little town. Feeling torn over the issue, she decided not to think about it any further. There was no point. They were going to take the drugs whether she agreed with it or not.

"This sucks," she muttered, while bringing a bulk package of pain killers to the nurse to be recorded, checked off and stacked on a pallet. She caught Kowalski's eye and made a masturbation gesture at him, indicating what she thought of this detail. Kowalski visibly chuckled and nodded his agreement.

They spent another three hours moving and stacking and double-checking lists. When they were done, they packed up and returned to the hospital, and the pharmacy owner was given a copy of what they had taken and instructed to take it to his nearest IRS office for reimbursement.

Later that afternoon, Jones' platoon was on the other side of town in a small, upscale strip mall conducting a supply raid of the local branch of a national chain pharmacy. The manager there didn't have a personal stake in the inventory he was signing away. He was only concerned about keeping his job and ensuring that everything was properly documented in triplicate for his home office. It was all very calm and orderly, for which Jones was glad. The last thing she wanted was to be a part of another shooting incident.

When one of her squad mates started grumbling, Sergeant Jackson quickly cut the man off. "We're doing this so that the hospital can continue to provide care for this community, Wagner. The weather's making air drops unpredictable and these supplies will go a long way towards helping the people who need it. Besides, the owners are going to be compensated. The only one losing anything here is you, because you can't spend the day sitting on your lazy ass in front of your laptop. So, quit bitching and let's get this shit done as quickly as we can so that we can get back to the hospital. Okay?"

Wagner nodded. But as he stalked off to get more boxes, Jones heard him mutter, "Douche-bag," under his breath. Jones completely agreed but was happy that Jackson wasn't yelling at her for once.

# January 15th - 16th

The stark, bright fluorescents cast harsh shadows everywhere. Even the transparent glass beakers were outlined by the shadows they cast. The air was sterile and flavorless, scrubbed clean of particles and contaminants. Every surface was clean, cold, and hard stainless steel. The medical tools and equipment filled available space. On the slab table in the center of the room lay Mr. Jensen. He was naked and exposed under the harsh, sterile light. His sightless eyes stared upward into nothing. Mr. Jensen wasn't alone. His companion was dressed in a fully enclosed biological segregation suit. Tear resistant fibers separated Mr. Jensen's companion from everything else in the room.

Mr. Bio-Suit stepped over to the table where Mr. Jensen lay, then lifted a scalpel and began making incisions. His fluids pooled near the table drains and were collected in tanks beneath for later study and incineration. With the torso open, Mr. Bio-Suit began removing Mr. Jenson's organs one at a time and placing them on a scale next to the table. As he was cutting out the heart, Mr. Jenson's eyes suddenly opened, and he started screaming.

Fallon snapped awake. It was only a dream. The memories that made up the dream haunted him, drove him on. He felt more tired than when he'd shut his eyes. His watch said it was just after midnight.

He'd slept for six hours.

Fallon closed his eyes in the darkness. He was on the couch in the front room. The fire in the hearth had burnt to embers. He made no move to rekindle them. Nurse Christianson was asleep in her bedroom, with the door locked. He'd proven himself worthy of her trust time and again, and even though she was willing to put up with his presence, it was plain she didn't completely trust him.

While he lay there, seeking sleep, his thoughts returned to Jensen, the man in his dream. He hadn't thought about him in several weeks. Not since well before his escape. The man had been a nonentity in the world. Born to an alcoholic mother, he had been abandoned by the age of six. He was mentally retarded, due to fetal alcohol syndrome, and had been forced to repeat two years of school before dropping out in the ninth grade. Jensen had drifted through life without purpose. By the time he was seventeen, he was addicted to heroin. By age twenty, he was making and selling meth to support his own dependence. At twenty-five he fell in love with one of his clients. She would regularly sleep with him to feed her own addiction. One night, in a fit of rage, he beat her to death with a work boot. He was discovered trying to dispose of her body in an alley trash bin, which in turn brought to light his other activities. After a lengthy trial, he was found guilty and sentenced to die by lethal injection. He was put to sleep at twelve noon, August the fifth. Three days later, he awoke at the institute with Fallon. From then until the end of his life, Jensen was in the clutches of the Director.

The two men had many long conversations during their weeks of seclusion there. Fallon learned about the simple hopes and dreams and desires of Jensen's former life:

obtaining his next fix, finding a hot meal and someday, hopefully and with God's help, getting clean. Two weeks after waking at the institute, he was injected with the virus. The Director wanted to study the effects of the disease on a drug addict. Twenty-four hours after the initial infection, Jensen became symptomatic. Three days later, he was dead. His body, weakened by years of abuse, withstood the virus' onslaught less than half the time of a normal healthy person.

The Director got his data. After the death of his beloved Elaine, Fallon was lost and indolent. Life held no meaning or purpose anymore. He even seriously considered taking his own life to end his pain. That was when the revelation occurred. The Lord spoke to him and showed him the error of his ways and how to proceed to find redemption so that he could meet his wife again in heaven. That was when he'd decided to turn away from evil and repent. To do that and to win his way into God's loving embrace, he first had to make sure the others paid for their evil ways as well. There was nothing left for him at the institute. He was surrounded by death on all sides and felt it closing in on him. Jensen's death was the catalyst that made Fallon realize he needed to escape and atone for his sins. The best way saw to do that was to expose the atrocities being committed.

Once Fallon had held the Director in high esteem. Had thought the Director could do no wrong, in fact. Jensen's bad death and the way he had been used by the Director and his project had disabused him of that idea. Fallon had realized then that he was on the side of wickedness. He wanted to make the world a better place, a safer place. But he had come to realize that following the Director's path was not the way to accomplish that. So, he struck out on his own, after sabotaging the project, and putting an end to the evil entity—he couldn't bring himself to think of the Director as a man—who ran it. Fallon would never in a million years allow himself to become like that again. He was on the side of the angels now, spreading the word of God and striking down those sinners who had the temerity to stand in his way.

In the eyes of that dead addict, Fallon rediscovered God.

Fallon was tired of sitting and revisiting the past. There was no use in it. What was done was done and couldn't be changed. All that mattered was how he dealt with the present and the plans he made for the future. Nurse Christianson was destined to play a prominent role in those plans, he was sure of it. Even if he failed, she would be able to carry on his work. Even if she was unaware, she was doing so. Thinking happier thoughts, Fallon closed his eyes and drifted back to sleep.

This time he dreamt the dreams of the righteous and thought nothing of Mr. Jensen. The man was dead and could neither help nor harm him. Shelly Christianson was alive and was the key to escaping Aldridge's clutches again.

Shelly and Fallon were enjoying a quiet dinner. While most of their meals were quiet, this one seemed especially calm to her. She thought it was because the weather outside wasn't blustering and blowing against the cabin, making the silence inside the cabin seem more ominous. Neither were in the mood for small talk during this rare respite from the constant clatter outside. Shelly didn't want to discuss herself with Fallon, and he didn't show any interest in asking. Besides, apart from the situation they found themselves trapped in, there wasn't much to talk about. They spent their time together as two polite strangers, occupying the same space in silence.

Out of the blue, between bites of chili con carne, Fallon said, "This is a nice cabin." Shelly paused, a forkful of canned chili hovering in front of her mouth. Small talk was so rare between them, that she was thrown off a bit by his comment.

She placed the uneaten bite back into her bowl. "Thanks. It was my uncle's. He recently passed away and left it to me."

"I'm sorry to hear that," Fallon said and seemed to mean

it. "He must have loved you very much to give you such a beautiful place."

Shelly nodded. Despite this new-found chattiness, she didn't feel like sharing the personal details of her life with him.

"My wife would have loved it here. I never told you I was married, did I?"

"No. This is the first time you've mentioned her."

Fallon gave her a little smile. "Elaine. We met in college. She was the most beautiful woman I had ever laid eyes on. It took me nearly a month to work up the courage to ask her out. I was so nervous. When she said yes, I nearly fainted. Then when I proposed and she said yes, I wanted to hop up and down, I was so happy."

Shelly found herself smiling. She remembered the early days with Brad and what it felt like to feel that happy in another person's company. Truth be told, she missed that feeling. "Does she live nearby? Is that where you're trying to get to?"

"She's dead."

Shelly was caught off guard by this, and it took her a moment to respond. "Oh. I'm sorry."

Fallon's face screwed up with emotion bubbling to the surface from deep within him. He let out a sigh. "It was a few months ago. You never think it can happen to you. You never think that you can wake up after eight years and the person you love most in the world is gone."

"What happened?"

"I was working late. I was always working late. She was driving home from a movie with some of the other project wives, when she was hit by a drunk driver named Felix Stanhope."

"Oh, God."

Tears welled up in his eyes and he wiped them away with the paper towel from his lap. His voice had a quiver when he spoke again.

"The collision itself wasn't that bad. He lived, though now he's serving a sentence for vehicular manslaughter. She probably would have survived it too, but the brakes on our car were bad. They were on my to-do list, which constantly got put off for work. When he hit, she lost control and they failed completely. She rolled six times and skidded to a stop upside down in a creek. She was pinned in place and drowned in ten inches of water."

Shelly almost got up to go around the table and put an arm around him. It was a knee-jerk empathy response to hearing Fallon's sad story. She held herself back and remained seated across from him. She had heard hundreds of tales like this before. As a nurse, she encountered them almost daily. She repressed her sympathy and just listened.

"I didn't find out she was dead until eight hours later. I was in the lab, working and couldn't be reached. I was never there for her when she needed me. Now she's gone, and for the life of me, I don't know what to do next. Once this is all over with... I just don't know. If I hadn't put off fixing the car, or if I'd taken her to the movies myself, if I'd been a better husband to her, maybe she would still be alive today." Fallon pushed his bowl away and placed his head in his hands to cry. He stayed that way for a few minutes before Shelly helped him to the couch. Then she cleared the table and went to bed herself.

A few hours later, things had returned to normal, as though he hadn't shared his terrible story with her. Shelly could tell he blamed himself for her death. That he felt agony over not being there to hold his wife's hand during her final moments.

The idea that a man could be reduced to tears for the woman he loved was strange to her. She'd seen it on TV, of course, but had rarely ever experienced it firsthand. She wondered if that was what was driving him. Her death might have been the thing that galvanized him to such a desperate act. Running away, trying to expose what he knew to be wrong. To prove that despite his failures, he was in fact a good man, even though he had been employed by monsters to create horrific weapons. She couldn't be sure of this, of course, but it felt right to her.

Shelly debated a moment about telling Fallon about her own past, then thought better of it and shook the idea away. The moment for confessions had passed, the silent status quo had returned. Besides, she hadn't even told her friends and coworkers at the hospital about her ordeal with Brad. Why should she open herself up to a stranger about him?

Fallon's story had put her in a funk. To feel better, she went to the bookshelf and took down one of Uncle Rory's books. It was one of his Miles Freemantle adventures. The wealthy amateur detective had been making her uncle money for over fifteen years.

With a few exceptions, most of Uncle Rory's books were mysteries or thrillers. He had written a biography of Ulysses S. Grant and a book about the nature of familial love and devotion and even a collection of poems, all under a pen name. They didn't sell nearly as well as his Freemantle works. Shelly had read and loved everything her uncle wrote. Though most critics called him a Patterson knock off, she thought he was a much better writer. She would also be the first to admit that she was hardly objective about the subject.

Uncle Rory, never a vain man, didn't keep copies of his own books out for display in his homes. He felt that was what bookstores and libraries were for. When she inherited the cabin, she'd had to stock the shelves with his works herself. Book in hand, she sat in the rocker with *Casting Shadows* and began reading. Halfway through the fourth page, she was crying. She missed him. More than anything else on earth, she wished she could have her uncle back.

Suddenly resolved, Shelly wiped her eyes, got up from the rocker and walked over to Fallon sitting on the couch. She was tired of being cooped up. Though it had only been a few days, she wanted to get out. The aftereffects of the vaccine were gone, and Fallon was no longer weak from his bout with hypothermia. She wanted to be rid of him and get back to her life.

"We can't stay here much longer," she said. "We are almost out of food. And besides, we have no idea what's happening in town. It's time to look before we start going hungry."

Fallon had also been reading, Rory's Grant biography. He closed the book, marking his spot with a finger.

"We shouldn't leave yet," he said. The food situation couldn't be ignored. They were down to a single package of saltines, two cans of condensed soup and one can of chili. There were a couple MRE's left over from when Rory owned the place. Those were old, and Shelly wasn't prepared to trust them.

"There are a ton of backroads. We can stick to the outskirts of town, make our way to the highway... There's no way that the army can be watching them all."

*They most certainly can,* Fallon thought.

"We can look around, get some food, and find a way out for you."

Fallon could sense he wasn't going to talk her out of it this time. There was no use in arguing. Much as he would have liked to, they couldn't stay at the cabin. The longer they remained there, the greater the odds that Aldridge's men would find them.

"How about tomorrow, first thing?"

Shelly smiled in triumph. "Deal."

The sky began clouding over again and the army meteorologist section predicted that another line of storms was heading their way. In the isolation ward, the patients brought in that first night began to succumb. Unable to leave bed, eat, or even bathe unassisted, they were already too far gone for the vaccine to be of any use. There was little the doctors and nurses could do, except watch their patients die painfully. What little vaccine had been delivered had already been used up inoculating the hospital staff and treating the most recent cases. Cathy Goodwin was the most recent to die. She was a small, pretty woman in her early forties, who had been brought in with the group from Walmart. Her body was already weakened by undiagnosed ulcers and a bad case of chronic bronchitis, began shutting down early that morning. Blood seeped from her eyes, ears, mouth, and anus. Her internal organs, which had been practically liquified by the infection, could no longer function without the aid of medical equipment.

Doctor Francis was making rounds. This was slightly unusual; as the chief of medicine, his duties were mainly of an administrative nature. Ever since the quarantine began, however, he'd felt a need to be a real, full-time doctor again. He wanted to do his part to combat the plague inflicted upon his home. He'd assured Colonel Aldridge that all hands would be on deck to fight it. The situation was bleak. Each patient had to be given three doses of the serum and the number of patients had long ago surpassed the supply of vaccine the army had brought. Though the weather above Harper's Glen was clear for now, it was bad to the south, where the next expected shipments came from. This delayed the arrival of new vaccine. The hospital was nearly out of beds for everyone being cared for. All they could do was attempt to make the sick and dying as comfortable as they could. This cut deeply into their on-hand supplies of pain killers. Doctor Francis didn't know what they would do once they ran out. It wasn't something he wanted to picture. But he knew he'd have to bring it up to Aldridge's flunkies soon.

He paused at one of the isolation rooms. They were running out of room too fast. Sooner than they had expected, people were going to have to be sent to the ward set up in the high school gym. He sighed; something else to bring up to the flunkies. Like the rest of the hospital staff, he had been inoculated. Despite that and the barrier suit he was about to don in the air lock separating the ward from the outside world, he still felt slightly uneasy being near any contagious patients.

The room he was scrubbing to enter housed eight people. The last holdouts from the first group. Among them was a nineteen-year-old girl. Though he tried to remain detached and dispassionate, this case had affected him the most. She'd been pregnant when she was admitted. When the infection began turning her body against her, it attacked the barely formed fetus first, before moving on to consume the rest of her. She'd been granted a few more days of life, at the expense of her unborn child. She was beyond saving now. Even if she got the vaccine in the next ten minutes, the disease had advanced too far to do her any good.

Or so the army doctors claimed.

Doctor Francis looked at her pain-lined face and decided he would insist—no, he would demand—that she be given a dose.

Miracles could happen. He'd seen many unexpected and inexplicable things during his twenty-three years practicing medicine.

He sighed, replaced her chart, checked on the other seven occupants of the ward and left, making sure to snuggly close and seal the air lock door before removing his barrier suit to scrub out.

While he washed, Doctor Francis prayed for a miracle. He prayed hard. Then he left to try and find some vaccine for his patient.

In the night, clouds rolled in low, and a flurry of fat snowflakes fell, obscuring the entire town from satellite view; but not before they were able to take a few interesting photos. Aldridge's airpower was also grounded and useless, unable to assist him in the search for Fallon. To make matters worse, General Collins arrived to personally oversee the operation. He didn't take command away from Aldridge. Not yet. But it was only a matter of time. By midnight it was snowing full gale again. They were back to transporting everything by ground, and even that was becoming more difficult by the hour as the snow piled up on the streets. The storm wouldn't let up for another nine days.

"So, tell me what happened next, sir," said Private First Class Bailey, who was conducting the debriefing. Open in his lap was a large green notebook. He'd already filled three pages with notes, and First Lieutenant Michaels sitting across from him wasn't anywhere close to being done with his account. Later, Bailey would type up a full report to be delivered up the chain, probably all the way to Colonel Aldridge himself.

Lieutenant Michaels rubbed his eyes. It was nearly two in the morning and he had been up and moving since before dawn. "After dismounting, I had first and second squads cordon off the area and provide overwatch, while my third squad moved into the alley behind the house. The intel we received said that the septic individuals there refused to come out and had to be forcibly removed. The snow was falling thick by this point and once we were ten feet from the vehicles, we couldn't even see them anymore."

"What happened when you reached the target house?"

"About what you'd expect: a lot of yelling, threats, cursing. The usual. It took us about ten minutes or so to get them calmed and moving. I had one fire team remain outside, while the other came in with me to clear out the septic locals. It wasn't till we got back to the trucks that we noticed Sergeant Haynes and Private Torres were missing."

"What happened when you found out?"

"We searched the whole area. The wind had picked up and the temperature was dropping fast, so I didn't want to keep my platoon out there any longer than necessary, but I couldn't leave them behind."

"Were you able to find them, sir?"

Michaels sighed. "We found Haynes three houses away, in a backyard. His throat was cut. The snow was falling so thick we could barely make out any tracks. I woke and questioned the people who owned the house and their neighbors, but no one had seen or heard a thing. We wrapped his body and loaded him in the back of my truck. We looked for another twenty minutes, but never found Torres. By that point, it was too cold, and the snow was blowing too hard to do anything more, so we mounted up and returned to the hospital."

The look of exhausted anguish on Michaels' face was hard to look at. Bailey knew that this wasn't the first man Michaels had lost, but he also knew from recent experience that it never got easier losing someone.

"Do you think this was an isolated incident, sir, or could this attack be a part of something bigger?"

Lieutenant Michaels rubbed his red eyes again. "I think this is just the start. Right now, these people hate and fear us. The longer this goes on, the bolder and more desperate they're going to get."

Bailey looked down at his notes. "I think that'll be enough, sir. Thank you for your time." Then he turned away and opened his computer to begin typing up the debriefing summary. Outside, he could hear the wind howl as the snowstorm intensified.

*What a shitstorm,* he thought. *In more ways than one.*

Shelly couldn't sleep. She'd been tossing and turning all night long. Even though she still had the gun and Fallon hadn't made any crude suggestions about sharing the bed with her, she was uneasy and had been since she'd brought Fallon to the cabin. In fact, he'd been chaste to the extreme towards her. In a way, this almost made her more uneasy. She expected most men would try to take advantage the situation and get a little action. But he hadn't so much as looked at her in a lecherous way since their arrival. She wasn't sure what to think about that. It wasn't normal male behavior.

Then there were the surreal events of the last week. Everything was catching up with her and she couldn't believe it was all actually happening. This was the stuff of bad fiction and cheesy action movies, not real life. Yet, there she was, an innocent, caught up in a storybook nightmare, and she hadn't a single clue how to get out of it. When she thought about it, her whole life had been little more than a chapter in a storybook nightmare. The four years she'd been with Brad had been magical and terrible. He gave her the princess life every little girl dreamed of and took a toll of her flesh in repayment.

Their last night together could be counted as the worst and best night of her life, when she gained her freedom and became a killer. Shelly was surprised to find she was crying. The memories of that night were still fresh and horrible, even after two years. Now her life was out of her control again and that terrified her.

She wiped away the last of her tears and stifled her sobs.

"I survived Brad Duncan. I can survive this!"

Thinking about him made her anxious and jumpy. Recent events brought back the memories often these days. Knowing that she would work herself into a panic attack if she didn't stop, Shelly forced herself to think of something else. Instead of Brad, she thought about Uncle Rory and remembered the day he first showed her the cabin.

It was just after the conclusion of her trial. They were driving up the highway towards Harper's Glen, a place she hadn't seen since leaving her drunken father's house at seventeen. They spent most of the seven-hour drive silent. Uncle Rory focused on the road ahead and Shelly was lost in her own world, barely even noticing the lush green summertime forests they were travelling through. The ordeal of killing her husband and the trial had completely drained her. The judge had felt she was a flight risk and so for the past six months she'd been living in the L.A. County lockup while her trial proceeded. The prosecution's case, which had never been particularly solid, was torn apart by Uncle Rory's team of lawyers. Key evidence in their arsenal was the medical records from several hospitals and emergency clinics, which painted a clear picture of her abuse.

Because she was a nurse, Brad didn't like her going to her work to get patched up after he beat her, so she was forced to go to emergency care clinics, a different one each time. He also insisted she use a false name to further insulate him from any accusations. Uncle Rory's lawyers hunted down every single bit information they could find. Photographs and tissue samples and records were gathered from these numerous clinics to prove that Shelly was a severely abused woman. The records were even used to provide a timeline which showed that the violence Bradley Duncan dealt out to her had been escalating. Her defense team was even able to locate two of Brad's former girlfriends, who testified that he was a controlling, manipulative, abusive man.

What clinched the ruling in her favor, though, was Timothy's testimony. She hadn't spoken to him since that day. They'd both been taken to the same hospital. But she was under arrest and the guard outside her room wouldn't let her leave or receive visitors. She had no idea how Timothy felt, or what he had been doing the months since she'd last seen him. She felt sure that he would hate her for what she had put him through. His testimony on her behalf, however, was clear and descriptive. Uncle Rory's lawyers had obviously coached him, and he withstood the barrage of questions and verbal traps the prosecution threw at him. He recounted for the jury being lured to her house by false text messages Brad had sent him from her phone. How he was immediately assaulted at the front door by the now-deceased, Bradley Duncan. His telling of her confrontation with Brad was a little less specific. He had been unconscious for much of it. But he did recall hearing Brad screaming and violently beating Shelly.

He never once looked at her the entire time they were in the courtroom together. When he was dismissed, he left the witness stand and the courtroom and that was the last time she saw him.

In the end, the court ruled in her favor, that killing Brad was an act of justifiable homicide in self-defense.

When she was processed out of jail, Uncle Rory was there to pick her up. Cameras and news crews swarmed the building's entrance, so he draped his coat over her head and rushed her to his Bronco. The media circus surrounding her ordeal had been tremendous, and Rory wanted to spare her. She'd been exposed to it enough for the last one hundred and eighty-seven days. He knew she needed peace and quiet, away from L.A. and anything even remotely resembling a major city.

To that end, he had promised her the use of his cabin.

"How are you doing, kiddo?" Rory asked, while they were driving up the lonely road to Harper's Glen.

"I'm fine," Shelly said, without turning away from the window. But she wasn't. Not even close. Her husband was dead by her hand. The world had turned against her during the trial. Even though she had been exonerated, she could feel their suspicion when they looked at her. Now here she was, going back to her childhood home. When she left, she promised she would never, under any circumstances, come back. Just another broken promise in a long line of them.

"Don't worry, hon, we're almost there. We just got to make a stop off for some supplies first."

"Okay."

"I think you'll love the place. It's completely secluded. Not a soul for miles and miles around. Hell, you can't even get to it without four-wheel drive."

"I know, Uncle Rory. You've told me that already."

He frowned, still watching the road. "I know, kiddo. I guess I'm just trying to perk you up a bit. I know how hard these last few months have been for you. Hell, these last few years! I wish I had known what was going on a long time ago. I'd have killed that son of a bitch the second he laid a finger on you."

"I know, Uncle Rory." It was all she could say.

"It's just that, well, with your dad gone, you're the only family I have left. I want to take care of you. To make sure nothing like this happens to you ever again. I've been kind of a piss-poor uncle. Wasn't there when you needed me. I'm so, so deeply sorry about that. But I'm here now and you'd better believe that I'm not going to abandon you."

Tears blurred Shelly's vision. "You're not a piss-poor uncle," she said. "You have your own life."

She didn't tell him that even if she had wanted to, Brad wouldn't have allowed him in her life while they were together. He controlled where she went, what time she was gone and who she talked to. Thinking back on it, she was amazed he had even allowed her to keep her job at the hospital. She wanted to tell him. She wanted to tell him everything. But the words kept on catching in her throat.

Forty-five minutes after getting gas and groceries, Uncle Rory parked the Bronco on the concrete pad beside the cabin. Shelly was awestruck. The beauty of the place left her mesmerized. Uncle Rory took her around and then they unloaded the food. She didn't know it then, but she was falling in love with her uncle's cabin. By the end of the week, she had made her decision to move to Harper's Glen.

The warmth of this memory calmed Shelly enough to go to sleep.

The pain had returned. It was never really gone. It was always there in the background, waiting, creeping up on him. Aldridge could no longer imagine life without the pain. He barely remembered life before the pain. The pills helped him get through each day, allowed him to function, but they couldn't restore him to a time before the pain. General Collins knew of his addiction. Aldridge knew he was biding his time, waiting for the perfect chance to use his knowledge against Aldridge.

Collins' arrival was a thorn in his side. Aldridge believed the man was an insufferable idiot, who'd only gotten as far as he had in the army by kissing the appropriate number of asses and stabbing the appropriate number of backs. All morning long, he had been dogging Aldridge's movements like an uncomfortable shadow. He questioned every report and second-guessed every decision Aldridge made. Aldridge tasked a lieutenant to walk Collins around, answer his stupid questions and keep him occupied so Aldridge could get some work done. He knew why Collins was there: to see to it that he failed, or to take credit for success. He had made it completely plain the moment he arrived that he was just looking for an excuse to take over.

Aldridge set aside the patient reports and picked up the operational reports. Everything had gone clockwork smooth. With the most recent delivery of vaccine - which had arrived just ahead of another storm - they were even starting to get ahead of the virus. With a little luck they would be able to stay ahead. Aldridge mentally crossed his fingers and prayed that would be the case. A few missteps aside, the operation was going well this time. His patrols had been able to catch the flair up outside the town, and quarantine a snowplow driver, his wife, and coworkers, and had even managed to round up almost all the hospital staff who were on duty when Fallon was admitted. The quarantine was established, and he was in complete control of the town. That his people had been unable to locate Shelly Christianson, was a dark spot on an otherwise successful operation. She, like Fallon, was still at large. It was almost certain that she had come into contact with the infection during her shift. By now she was extremely sick, dying and beyond their help. God only knew how far she had spread it. It annoyed him to know that despite everyone's best efforts, there was still a high likelihood of failure.

Everything was quiet now, so Aldridge redirected his patrols to begin sweeping the outskirts of town. According to the most recent land survey, there were dozens of abandoned farms and old hunting cabins in the wooded hills around town. Fallon could be hiding in any one of them, just waiting for his chance to make a break for it.

He turned his mind to a matter he'd been putting off until he could give it his full attention: reading the after-action reports from the shooting. He had considered having the lieutenant arrested and court-marshaled for what happened. Out of thirteen soldiers, only four—including Lieutenant Lopez—had actually fired into the crowd. Lopez had to stand at attention for thirty long and horrible minutes while Aldridge screamed at him, cursing, and calling him every kind of fool imaginable. Aldridge was hoarse by the time the ass-chewing was done. There would be a time later for a court-marshal, for now Lieutenant Lopez and the other four soldiers were disarmed and locked up.

The pain was very real now, almost unbearable. The itch of his addiction seemed to amplify it. Each day he tried to hold out as long as possible before succumbing and taking the pills. Every minute he delayed was a test of his willpower. Pure agony.

Finally, it was time for sweet relief. Twitching and breathing heavily, he shook the pills into his palm and dry-swallowed them.

No Modafinil. Not this time. He wanted to sleep. Needed to in fact.

His leg hurt to the point there were tears in his eyes. The itch he felt was maddening and had crumbled his willpower completely away. He shook out a second dose and downed it with a tall glass of water, then laid back and let sleep take him. He wasn't doing anyone any good by staying awake all the time, so he figured he might as well get some rest while it was calm. Maybe the search teams would have better luck tomorrow.

He could only hope.

The howling coming from the corner of her room drove a rail spike through her skull. Mary Brickenbaur's head hurt all the time now, no matter how many aspirin she took. It had all started three days ago, when she'd called into work sick. At the time she'd thought it was a mild case of the sniffles but hadn't wanted to get anyone else at the pharmacy sick. She regretted not getting flu shots for herself and her little boy months ago when she had the chance. Quicker than she would have believed, she had developed a hacking cough, couldn't keep food or fluids down, and suffered a grinding headache. Worse still, her ten-month-old son, Robby, had caught what she had.

She wouldn't be in this situation now if she had called in sick. The problem was one of money. She would have had to pull double shifts to pay the bills, and most of the extra cash would go to Tammy Macintyre, the extortionist who watched Robby when Mary was at work. Between keeping the lights on and food on the table, there wasn't enough left for medicine. Her insurance wouldn't cover the shots because she'd already used her coverage when Robby came down with bad case of chicken pox last summer.

Mary knew she should take herself and Robby to Saint John's but couldn't find the energy to do so. The effort of getting out of bed that morning to change Robby and make his breakfast had completely drained her.

Besides, she'd heard all about the soldiers murdering anyone who tried to get in. She had no desire to leave Robby without a mother. Robby's father, at least the man Mary suspected was his father, was a deadbeat without a job, who wanted nothing to do with his son. He refused to even submit to a paternity test to determine if he was indeed Robby's sire. Mary couldn't leave Robby with a man like that. Her mother had effectively disowned her when she became pregnant, so she couldn't turn to her. With few options, she decided she and her son would wait it out and get better on their own.

That had been her thinking three days ago, before the headache-that-never-went-away, before Robby's unceasing cries, before the cold sweats and before she saw blood in her puke the last time she threw up. The sight of it in the pot she kept bedside this morning made her rethink her choice to tough it out. She decided to take a short nap and then she would wrap Robby up in his favorite blanket and drive to Saint John's to get them both some help.

But the pounding in her head and Robby's screaming wouldn't let her sleep. From his crib the corner of her bedroom, Robby suddenly hiccupped. His crying stopped and she heard a slow gurgle. Alarmed and in pain, Mary got up and shuffled to the crib side. She looked inside and immediately started screaming. The small mattress, security blanket and several stuffed animals were all soaked with blood.

Mary's stomach lurched and she threw up again and toppled over. Blood streamed from her nose and mouth. She hadn't eaten anything in the last three days. The chunks of half-chewed meat splattered on the carpeted floor in the pool of blood she'd just vomited were pieces of her stomach.

Seth was parked just past the intersection of Willow and A Streets. The heater of his 2002 Honda was blowing hot, but his fingers and toes were still freezing. This was going to be the night; he just knew it. Weeks of courting and playing hard to get and nervously making out were about to culminate tonight in him finally getting laid. The seventeen-year-old boy couldn't keep himself still. He tapped out rhythms on the steering wheel and dash, while his feet moved in sync. He played drums in the school marching band, but his real passion was jazz. After he graduated high school, he was going to move to L.A. and become a drummer in a big famous band. He'd told this to neither of his parents; they'd only discourage him. He was meant for something great; he could feel it in his soul and wasn't about to let them get in his way.

Lately, his passion for music had been overtaken by another passion, which occupied his thoughts almost constantly and was the reason he was parked on the street, past curfew, in the freezing cold: Tracy Johnson. She played the clarinet, and for the past month they'd been secretly seeing each other. Her parents, Seth was sure, would kill him if they knew what their daughter intended to do with him tonight. His parents would be none too thrilled about it, either. But he really didn't give a damn. He loved her and she loved him back. Besides, it was her idea, after all. He hadn't pressured or coerced her at all to go all the way with him. Not that he was in any way against it. Sex is pretty much the most important mystery for a teenage boy, and he was more than ready to solve it.

Their relationship had started slowly and awkwardly. During the fall, when the band had made a road trip to support the football team at an away game, they'd sat next to each other near the back of the bus. It was a three-hour trip, and they spent the whole time talking, while everyone was laughing and joking. The team won and that night, during the trip back, Tracy intentionally sat beside him again. Nearly every seat was filled with a boy-girl pair. In stark contrast to the riotous noise during the drive up, the bus, darkened and quiet, was subdued, as several new couples explored each other's mouths and bodies in the dark. This happened a lot on away games. New couples would form, only to break it off a week later. But Tracy was different; she was his first real girlfriend. A week later, she still ate with him at lunch. After two weeks, they were going to the movies together. Here they were, four months into their relationship and were still completely ass over tea kettle for each other. During a New Year's party, he had confided with her about his dreams in L.A. and asked her if she would go with him. Breathlessly, Tracy accepted. They were both graduating this year and there would be nothing left to hold them back.

The arrival of the army had skewed his plans slightly. School was closed for the foreseeable future, which meant that classes would most likely have to be made up during the summer and graduation delayed. The shooting, the curfew, people being taken from their homes and the crackdown on travel had both of their parents terrified. It had been a week since he had last seen Tracy. He craved her, the way an addict craves the needle. Being unable to see or touch her was driving him mad.

Then yesterday, the note arrived. Written in her precise, looping hand, was a proposal that they should meet. She wanted him to take her to their make-out spot at the edge of Morgan's Farm. Seth's hormone-drenched teenage mind leapt to the conclusion that they were going to finally have sex. The prospect filled him with anxious joy.

Now here he was, illegally parked after hours, awaiting the arrival of his beloved, eagerly anticipating the life-altering event that would take place tonight. A shadow flitting through the night caught his eye. Sitting up straighter, he craned his neck to see if it was her. He was only a block away from her house, so it shouldn't take her long to reach his car.

Suddenly she was there, outside his window, looking like an angel in the snow-bright night. He disengaged the power locks and she slid into the passenger seat.

"T-t-thank God you've got the heater going! It is f-f-freezing out there." They leaned towards each other for a long embrace. He drank her in. The taste of her breath, the soft feel of her lips pressed to his, the warmth of her tongue as it danced playfully in his mouth. He pulled her closer and kissed her even harder and listened to the quiet moans coming from her throat. He was in heaven. This was the girl he wanted to spend forever with. He was sure of it.

When they parted, he gently ran a hand down her cheek, still gazing into her eyes. “I love you,” he said.

“I love you too,” she answered. “I’ve missed you so much. My parents are freaking out so much. You wouldn’t believe what I went through to get away tonight.”

“I know what you mean. I’m practically a prisoner in my house. I can’t wait till we can get out of here.”

“It’s you and me forever, babe.” She smiled at him and he touched her cheek.

He smiled, high on the sight of her. He was about to lean in for another kiss when she turned away suddenly and violently coughed into her gloved hand.

“Oh! Excuse me,” she said. “I’m sorry. My mom and dad have both got colds and they gave it to me.”

# January 17th

Benedict didn't mind the cold. In fact, he loved it, thrived in it. Before his injuries, he'd been an avid skier. The frost in the air, the tremble in his fingers, his breath a mist before him. It reminded him he was alive. He needed all the reminders he could get these days. After all he'd been through, they were the only ways in which he could prove to himself that he could still feel anything at all.

A light flurry of snow fell, which was a change from this morning when he and his people had set out. The snow may not have been as heavy as he would have liked, but anything was better than nothing. This snowfall wouldn't cover his tracks, but it might obscure them enough to misdirect any pursuit.

He waited in a sniper's roost atop a three-story building on D Street, three blocks from the town center. Across the street, Sonny Dixon waited. Two buildings down the street, five more men had taken positions on the second floors of buildings on both sides of D Street. In ten minutes—if their patterns held true—a four Humvee convoy would turn onto D Street from 11th Avenue and pass into their midst. Benedict had marked out a kill box with pairs of red streamers tied to a lamp posts on either side of the street, so his people would know when to fire. When the second truck passed the markers, Sonny and he would take out the gunners standing in the hatches of the first and last trucks. Then they would shoot the gunners in the middle two trucks. Once the convoy stopped and the soldiers were dismounted to engage Benedict and Sonny, his other five men—one of them was a woman, but he couldn't help thinking of them collectively as his men—would spring the trap. The plan was to kill or incapacitate as many soldiers as they could, to make them pay for every inch of his town. Benedict knew that even the very best-laid plans were often the first casualty of contact with the enemy. His experiences in the army and overseas taught him that.

Years before, he'd enlisted. He wanted to serve his country and do something he could be proud of with his life. He quickly made sergeant and led a squad. Over the next six years, he'd been deployed four times. Each time he came home was like returning to someone else's life. He didn't know how to act around his own wife. His son was a stranger to him, his house a foreign land. They had made a life and seemed content to carry on without him. He had become little more than an inconvenient guest in their home.

During his last Iraq tour, a roadside IED vaporized the truck in front of his. While he and the rest of his patrol moved to secure the area and take care of their fallen comrades, a secondary device was triggered, resulting in more casualties, including him. Nine hours of surgery later, the doctors were left with no choice but to amputate his right leg just below the knee. There followed many long, painful, humiliating months of physical therapy and prosthesis fittings. Typical of army assembly line medicine, as soon as his allotted hours with the doctors and therapists—both physical and mental—were finished, he was cut loose and turned over to an unsympathetic and overworked Veteran's Administration.

Unable to work and with bills piling up, which his disability checks barely covered, he started drinking. Then he and his wife started fighting. During one particularly bad row, she admitted to having an affair while he'd been deployed. Three months, one paternity test and a costly divorce later, and Benedict was free from an unfaithful wife and a son that wasn't his. Then the VA decided to audit his benefits. They determined he was fit to return to work and cut his disability checks in half. It wasn't enough to keep him in groceries, let alone pay his bills each month. With no other choice in the matter, he built a greenhouse in his basement and started growing marijuana.

"I just need enough to live," he told himself. "No one else is going to help me, so I'll help myself."

Within a few months of his first harvest, Benedict was pulling in eight thousand dollars a month. The world and the country had turned its back on him, so he had to make a living however he could.

Once again, the military was screwing him over. The occupation of Harper's Glen was the final straw. He'd had enough of taking shit from the army. He was ready to start dishing some back. After all they'd done to him, ruining his life a little more every time he turned around, now they were here to compound the insult to his injuries. Hadn't they stolen enough from him already? When would it be finished?

Gathering a group of people, just as unhappy as he, hadn't been difficult. Neither was securing the weapons and munitions to strike back. Barney Goodwin, whose wife had disappeared into the hospital the first night, provided the weaponry. Benedict had barely even hinted at what he had in mind before Barney enthusiastically signed up. Though Barney wasn't in the field personally, and never would be, he was one of the most important people in Benedict's group. Without him, they wouldn't have the means to fight back. Benedict also had people, like Eddie Tate, all over town noting the times and routes of the army patrols.

Today's operation was vitally important. It was a test of everything Benedict had spent the last few days setting up: the observers, the weapons, the planned escape routes, the hideouts. If everything worked today, he knew they were clear to continue to fight back against the bastards who had invaded their home. It was important for another reason as well. Benedict wanted to send a message to the army that they weren't wanted here, that people were willing to take a stand against the tyranny foisted upon them and that the army would lose people from now on until they packed up and left.

The lookout on a roof at the nearest the intersection waved a red flag, signaling that the convoy was approaching. "Right on time," Benedict said, before waving to the others to let them know it was almost time.

Benedict's observers were on the ball and the army was cooperating with their punctuality. They couldn't use radios, due to the army jamming equipment blacking out the town, so the claymores they'd set in place were command-wired, ready and waiting for him to trigger them.

The convoy was just about in the kill box. Just a few more yards. They were lined up perfectly.

The second truck passed the red streamers.

Benedict raised his rifle, got a good sight picture on the soldier standing the gunner's hatch of the lead truck and squeezed the trigger.

Private Whittier was driving for his platoon leader on what was quickly becoming a routine mission. They were the second vehicle in the convoy. It wasn't snowing as heavily as it had been, but the roads were still slick and visibility was short, so he drove cautiously and slowly. Their mission was threefold: maintain a visible presence in town, gather any possible leads on Fallon's whereabouts, ensure sick people got to the hospital.

Whittier thought the last was a waste of time. The people here didn't trust them.

"Sir," he said to his lieutenant. "This whole setup is really stupid. These people won't talk to us, and they damn sure don't want to go to the hospital after Lieutenant Lopez shot a bunch of them."

"That's not the only reason we're out here. We're here to find the fucker spreading this shit, so we can pack up and go home."

"That's exactly my point, sir. How are we supposed to find this Fallon guy, if nobody in town will talk to us? The only way these people will overcome their fear and hesitation and bring themselves to us for help is when there's no other choice and they know they are definitely sick. Only by then it's too late and we can't help them. So, if they won't come to us, what makes anyone think they'll talk to us at all about him? Basically, we're shit out of luck, sir, and just wasting our time."

"All we can do is drive on and do what we're told."

"Gotcha, sir," he said. Then after a moment's pause, "It's still fucking stupid though."

They rounded a corner. Whittier liked driving for the ell-tee. It was a hell of a lot better than working on the burn detail. That shit was gruesome. The infected people who finally made their way to the hospital were issued protective masks and then they were separated from each other by at least six feet, by order of Doctor Francis. This helped, but not enough. The virus was still spreading. The number of infected people had surpassed the vaccine supply again. The last delivery hadn't been enough, and the next shipments were delayed. As a result, people were dying, quickly and painfully. Bodies were stacked chest-high in the morgue. Seventy-two hours after death, their remains could be incinerated without risk of further spreading the disease. By then the virus inside the corpse was just as dead as its host.

He had been on the burn detail twice. Just thinking about

it made him shiver. He would much rather be on patrol. It was riskier, sure, but this close to the hospital, the risk was minimal. Which was fine by him. Excitement was best left to the movies. He liked his army life nice and boring.

They were heading through a business district. The place looked deserted. Up ahead he saw a red ribbon tied around a telephone pole and almost stomped on the breaks. He had spent two tours driving in Iraq, and this rang alarm bells in his head. But he quickly quieted them. This was hometown America, after all. There's no IED risk here. Besides, even if there were IEDs out here, there was little use in worrying about them. The vehicles they were driving wouldn't provide any kind of protection against them. The convoy was made up of canvas or aluminum-skinned Humvees, which were terrible, because the heaters didn't work in half of them. The chemical hand-warmers in his gloves were the only things warding off frostbite. He dreaded to think of what he would do when they ran out of them.

He had passed the phone pole with a ribbon when he heard a pair of pops, followed immediately by two more pairs. Behind him Blackwell, their gunner, crumpled to the floor. He looked to his right and saw ell-tee clutching his throat, while blood spurted through his fingers. For a second, he just stared, unable to comprehend what had happened. Whittier wanted nothing more than to floor the gas and get out of the kill box. But the truck in front of his stopped, blocking the road. He couldn't see their gunner either and realized he must have been shot too.

He grabbed the radio hand-mic and called out on the platoon frequency, "Contact, contact; ell-tee's been hit. I say again, ell-tee is down." The line was buzzing chatter, there was no direct response. Outside, Whittier heard gunfire, a lot of it. A second later Sergeant McVrey, commander of the truck behind his, appeared crouched next to his window.

"Ell-tee's hit, Sarn't," Whittier told him.

"No shit. We're being ambushed. They've got snipers on the roofs. Call it up and get us some support."

"Roger." Whittier turned back to the radio, turned to a second preset frequency, reported what was happening and he sent up a medevac request for the wounded.

Outside the truck, Sergeant McVrey was instructing his men to move into the building next to them. Half of them provided covering fire, while the other half bounded away from the stricken convoy. Each team leap-frogged the other, moving in five-second rushes. The snow covered a layer of ice, and every few steps someone would slip and nearly fall.

Over the radio net, Whittier was told to hold his position. More troops were on the way. Outside his truck the shooting had stopped, and twenty heads were swiveling in all directions, looking for threats.

The world erupted in smoke, noise, and pain. Three IED's composed of PVC plumbing pipes packed with homemade explosives, nails, nuts, bolts, and other small bits of metal exploded, shredding the vehicles and soldiers of the convoy.

On the north side of town, while assisting a middle-aged couple and their four kids into the civilian van that would take them to the hospital, Jones heard the distinct staccato tattoo of gunfire. Instantly, she turned towards the sound. Kowalski was standing next to her and also stopped to listen. "Is that someone shooting?" he asked.

Jones glanced at him, about to make a biting remark, before she remembered that he'd never been deployed before, and the closest he had ever been to a firefight was the qualification range. She nodded. "Yeah, it is," she said. The intensity of the shooting steadily increased until it was cut off by a loud boom that vibrated the ground under her feet. "Oh, shit. That's not good."

Shelly was too far away to hear the small arms fire, but

she heard the explosion clearly and when she stepped out the front door and looked towards town, she saw a thick plume of smoke curling into the air.

"It's started." Shelly hadn't heard Fallon come up behind her and almost jumped out of her skin when he spoke.

"See?" he continued. "The army has begun using force on your little town to flush me out. They'll stop at nothing to see me in shackles, or dead. You were right. We can't stay here. The sooner we leave, the better."

The column of smoke was dissipating, so she went back inside to pack up their meager supplies and work on the problem of their escape with Fallon.

Paula Freeman went to her shop every day without fail at four in the morning, and she was open for business every day without fail by eight. A hard-working, no-nonsense woman of fifty-six, she'd owned and operated her own bakery and deli in Harper's Glen for nearly twenty years. She and her shop had weathered recessions, burglaries, two bad husbands, daycare for three children and the loss of one of those children in Iraq. But she wasn't sure they could survive this. The quarantine had cut the town off from all the supplies it needed to carry on daily life and the effects were starting to show.

In the land of plenty, her city was going hungry.

More and more people were turning to the army for food and care, like hostages thanking their captors for bread rinds and water.

It sickened her to see her friends and neighbors relying on the welfare of the people who had imprisoned them. On the fourth day of the quarantine, she opened her doors and offered her wares, free of charge, to any and all who came calling.

Things were going good until the soldiers came and shut her down. The snotty little officer in charge, who looked barely a day over fifteen, explained about disease vectors and contagion hotspots and the need for public safety.

It all sounded like a load of bullshit to her, but not wanting to be a target for more bullying, she closed her doors again, this time for the duration.

Though she didn't keep the hours she used to when she was in business, she still went to work every day. What else did she have to do, after all? Staying at home sounded boring enough to make her skin crawl. Her shop was her home; her house was just where she slept and bathed and kept a few of the things she'd bought.

She stepped around the corner at 9$^{th}$ Avenue and D Street and stopped in her tracks by the sounds of gunfire. Lots of gunfire.

One hundred feet from where she stood, a battle raged. She stared in dismayed interest at a line of army trucks stopped in the middle of the street and under fire. Soldiers scrambled around their trucks, vainly searching for a safe place from which to return fire. Their attackers picked them off from above with impunity. She could see a couple soldiers on the ground, still and bleeding.

Something sizzled past her head and it occurred to her that she was standing in the open, watching a gun battle like it was pay-per-view. Prudently, she ducked back around the corner. She could still hear the rapid pop-pop-pop of the shooting, the cries of the wounded and orders being shouted back and forth.

Then the shooting was cut off by a massive explosion. The roar hit her in the chest like a fist. After that, there were no more shots, no more cries and no more shouting. Just nothing. As suddenly as it had started, the battle was over.

Ears ringing, Paula peeked around the corner and gasped. The smoke was slowly clearing, revealing the carnage that remained. The second truck had been flipped onto its side, the two trucks in the rear were largely undamaged, but the first had been turned inside out by the blast. Two or three soldiers wandered about in a daze. Most simply lay on the ground, unconscious or dead.

Without a thought for her own safety, Paula ran to them. As a summertime lifeguard and a part-time EMT with the fire department, she knew what she had to do. She started first aid on the first trooper she came to. In the distance she heard sirens, but that was another world. All that concerned her now was the injured boy in front of her. The soldier was unconscious and had a few scrapes and cuts, but nothing serious. He was starting to come around, even as she checked him for bleeding. Paula moved on. The next soldier had a bullet wound in his shoulder. She was in the process of controlling the bleeding with a bandage from his first aid kit when more soldiers, firefighters, cops, and paramedics arrived.

She bandaged and splinted four more soldiers before they were carted off to the hospital. The ground around the lead truck was littered with the more gruesome remains; she avoided that altogether. When the last of the wreckage, gore and wounded were cleared off the street, it was almost half past ten in the morning.

As she was finishing up a bandage for a female soldier with a severely burned arm, Paula was approached by another baby-faced officer. "Ma'am, I'd like to thank you for what you did for these men," he said, holding out his hand for her to shake. "Here's a card with my name and contact information on it. We're expecting more vaccine in a few days. When it comes in, I'd like you and your loved ones to be at the front of the line."

"I was just doing what any good citizen would do, young man," she said.

"I wish that were the case, ma'am," he said. "I truly do. We need more citizens like you these days. Still, you have my thanks. Please come and bring your loved ones when we get the medicine."

She looked at the name on the card, "I did what I could, Captain West. I only wish something like this hadn't happened in my town. I've lived here my whole life, and I can't believe somebody here would do such a thing."

"Some people will go to great lengths for their ideals. Would you like us to send a truck to pick you up when the time comes, ma'am?"

She thought about it for a second. "No, I think we'll be fine coming in on our own."

"Very well. Good day, ma'am."

Paula looked at her soot and blood-stained hands and clothes and decided to go back home. This was more excitement than she needed for one day. It was time for a shower and a nap.

Benedict and his people fled the scene long before more soldiers arrived. The plan had gone off without a hitch. The enemy had acted and reacted exactly as he knew they would. Now an entire platoon was dead or incapacitated. Running down the flight of stairs, careful not to trip and knock off his leg, he couldn't help but smile. Today he'd sent a clear message to the army, that the price of their continued presence promised to be high. More than that, he had proven he could stand up to the enemy and spit in their eye.

*Next time won't be so easy,* he warned himself. He knew he'd caught them with their britches down. From now on, they would be expecting him. He had to keep on his toes to keep them on theirs.

Ideas for the next attack were already percolating in his mind as he exited the building to the back alley and started down his preplanned escape route. He wanted to hit them again and soon. But for now, he had to get away and lay low for a bit. This was only just beginning.

Aldridge blinked at the report before him. It was unbelievable. Six dead, twelve injured and two vehicles severely damaged, one destroyed. To make matters worse, the perpetrators had gotten away clean. His worst fear had been realized. Up till now, he'd been able to maintain control. It was hard enough to pacify a civilian population while searching for one man without retaliatory violence. Now his job and the jobs of the people under his command had been made immensely more difficult. More people were falling ill every day and they still weren't getting enough vaccine to treat them. The facilities manufacturing the serum were running full tilt, but the supply just wasn't reaching him.

*Collins is going to have a field day with this,* he thought.

There was no avoiding it. Since the general had arrived, he'd been poking his nose in everywhere, looking for dirt on Aldridge. And now these home-grown terrorists had handed him what he needed on a silver platter.

Aldridge had his staff and subordinate commanders immediately institute maximum force protection procedures. No one went anywhere in groups smaller than four, body armor was to be worn at all times when outside secured areas and escalation of force measures were now in effect. If his people felt threatened in any way, they were authorized to use deadly force to protect themselves, their unit or any civilians who might be in harm's way.

He hated that it had come to this. He had envisioned capturing Fallon quickly so as to avoid exactly this situation. As the days went by, a quick resolution seemed less and less likely.

*What if he's already gone? What if he's already escaped?* Aldridge didn't want to acknowledge that dark thought. That they would have to pack up and resume the chase all over again was something he didn't want to think about. *Not another chase. Not another city. I don't know if my men can take any more. I don't know if I can take any more.*

He picked up the phone on his desk and dialed his operations officer.

"Captain West," the voice on the other end answered.

"West, this is Colonel Aldridge. What's the likelihood that Fallon has already slipped our nets and gotten away?"

There was a pause on the other end while West considered the question. "Sir, I think it's unlikely, but not impossible. He could have gotten away that first night while we were still emplacing. The cordon wasn't complete yet, and he could have slipped through."

"Has there been word of any new outbreaks outside of town?"

"No, sir. We're still monitoring all local, state, and federal channels for anything that might indicate another outbreak. Aside from the small group of snowplow drivers and their families, there have been no indications of any further spread."

"Then your official analysis is that Fallon is still here in Harper's Glen?"

"Yes, sir. He has most likely gone to ground. He probably contacted that nurse we couldn't find, Shelly Christianson, and used her help to hide. Given the time between then and now, she is most likely dead or dying by now." West paused. He'd seen this before. Aldridge already knew everything West had just told him. Whenever Aldridge had a particularly difficult decision to make, he liked to review any pertinent information with his subordinates. "Is everything okay, sir?" West didn't even bother trying to keep the concern from his voice. He was aware of the attack and what it implied, but Collins' presence altered the situation for the worse.

"Everything is as good as it can be under the circumstances, Captain. I'm just worried that we're becoming too entrenched here. As a contingency, I want you to begin putting together plans to pull out in case Fallon makes it past us and escapes. We need to be able to un-ass this town quickly to pursue him."

"Right away, sir."

Aldridge replaced the receiver and picked up the report to

read it again. He couldn't bring back the six soldiers he'd lost, but he could make sure the rest didn't become careless again.

*Goddamn it. And goddamn you, Fallon. I'm going to find you and make you pay for this.*

The world was a haze around Peter McVrey. All he could see was white. Occasionally he heard people talking at his bedside in hushed tones. He knew he was hurt, but in a distant way. The pain was far removed, as though calling in to him from a long distance. It was still there, but it didn't affect him.

When the explosives went off, he was crouched beside his truck on the outer edge of the blast funnel. The vehicle and hard plates in his vest absorbed most of the killing blast and shrapnel. When he was brought into surgery, his right shoulder was barely attached by sinew, there were large chunks gouged out of his right side and buttocks and several pieces of shrapnel had punched through his neck and throat, narrowly missing his carotid artery. His helmet protected his head from the worst. He was alive, but in bad shape. After six hours on the operating table and five blood transfusions, McVrey had been stabilized. Doctor Francis did his best, but there was no chance they could save his arm. The weather was still too bad for helicopters to conduct an airlift, and the roads were even worse. So McVrey was stuck with them for the foreseeable future.

Francis was shocked when he heard about the attack, shocked again when he saw the casualties as they were brought in. Outwardly, he was sympathetic and outraged, as a doctor should be. Inwardly though, he was glad to hear that someone out there was fighting back. This didn't change his job, however. He took his oath as a doctor seriously and intended to treat every patient under his care with equal attention and compassion. He couldn't banish these dark thoughts though, no matter how hard he tried. Earlier that same day, even though he'd administered a double dose of the vaccine, Emily Dollard died. Consequently, he secretly hoped he would see more soldiers like McVrey on the operating table. Then the army would be forced to leave, and things could return to normal and nobody else would have to die. He hated thinking that way. It made him feel ill. It was not how a doctor, a healer, should think. But he couldn't help it. He wanted the army gone and his neighbors free. He would continue to do his job and patch them up as they came in, but he wouldn't be happy until there were none left in Harper's Glen.

Private Jones was doing her best to keep the vehicle on the road while being buffeted by the wind in the predawn dark. It was snowing, making it impossible to see more than a few yards ahead in the whiteout. Her platoon had had a busy morning. During the night, strong winds began blowing, snapping numerous electrical lines, cutting power in several blocks on the northeast end of town. Jones' platoon had been tasked with helping the town engineers with restoring the power.

*As if they even need our help,* she thought, shaking her head. *What the hell do they expect us to do? It not like anyone here has a fucking electrical engineering degree or anything. More army dumbshit. Just a few more months and I'm a free woman. Gonna go to college, drink my ass off, smoke some weed and get fucking laid! To hell with the army. I'm going to get me a real fucking job. Get rich and forget I was ever stupid enough to be a soldier.*

At the edge of her field of view, just where her headlights stopped, Jones saw movement. She squinted, then tapped Sergeant Jackson on the knee and pointed, "Do you see that Sarn't?"

Jackson squinted into the haze. "Not a clue, Jonesy." She hated being called that and figured he did it on purpose to annoy her. She hated driving for her squad leader. He always made sure she was on his crew so he could, "Keep an eye on her." Like she would go streaking down the street naked or forget to clip her toenails and wash her socks if he weren't there to remind her. Dumb asshole.

A few feet further and the figure became a woman in a house coat and slippers, frantically waving them down. "Stop here," Jackson said. The woman rushed up to Jones' door and started rapping on the window. Her face was wild with fear and panic. Jones opened her window to see what she wanted.

"Help me," she screamed. "Please! You have to help me. My son's trapped."

"Ma'am," Jones spoke evenly to the hyperventilating woman. "Please, calm down, take a deep breath and tell us what's going on."

She took a breath, but it didn't help much. "The tree. Please help me. It's fallen and trapped my son. Please!" She was panicked, hysterical and clearly freezing.

"Hop in back," Jones said, without checking with Jackson.

"Ma'am, I need to you show us where you live," said Jackson, then he radioed the Tactical Operations Center that they were moving to take care of an emergency. The woman sat behind Jones in the truck and directed them to her house, half a block further up the street.

When they arrived, Jones saw what the woman was talking about. A massive old elm tree had fallen over into her house. Most of the front was caved in.

"He's in there. He's right in there." She pointed to the far corner of the house, where the tree had fallen through. When Jones got close, she could hear the boy crying above the wind. She didn't wait to be told what to do but went straight to the back hatch of her Humvee to get the axe and saw from the pioneer kit. By the time Jackson was organizing the rest of the squad to follow, Jones was already attacking the tree to free the trapped child.

It took them the better part of an hour to cut their way through to reach the little boy. Then, while under the care of the patrol medic, the mother and son were escorted to the emergency room. En route, the medic examined the boy for injuries, hypothermia, and infection. He appeared to be fine. Jackson wanted to make sure though and insisted they be taken to the hospital.

After dropping them off, Jones stood outside the ER entrance, sheltered next to a wall to keep out of the wind, smoking a cigarette, when Jackson clapped a hand on her shoulder. "Good job, Jonesy."

Jones took a drag before responding. "Thanks, Sarn't." She didn't like Jackson. She felt that he was a piss-poor leader who followed the maxim, "Do as I say, not as I do," when it came to leading. So, she ignored his compliment and continued smoking her cigarette.

"I'm going to put you in for an award when we get back."

Jones shrugged. She had been disappointed too many times in the past and so knew better than to put faith in anything she was told by a superior, especially Jackson. He was great at making himself look good but didn't do shit when it came to taking care of the soldiers beneath him. Jones fully expected that Jackson was just making an empty promise, something he thought he was supposed to do as a squad leader.

"You know," he said, before she could get away from him. "You're not a half-bad soldier, Jones. But your attitude sucks."

"Roger, Sarn't."

"If you weren't such an opinionated smartass and loudmouth, you probably would've been sent to the promotion board and gotten some stripes on your chest a long time ago."

"Roger, Sarn't."

Jackson shook his head. He seemed to realize she was placating him and that he wasn't going to get anything more out of her. "Anyway, good job, Jonesy." Then he walked away to check on the rest of the squad.

Jones turned away, flicked the cherry off the end of her

cigarette, pitched the butt into a nearby trash bin and went back to her truck. Once everyone was done smoking, they mounted back up and resumed their patrol.

# January 18th

The staff meeting dragged on longer than he wanted, and Aldridge ground his teeth in frustration. Everything was breaking down. Despite the smooth start-up, everything that could go wrong, had gone wrong. Bad weather, bad luck and bad timing were all taking their toll on the operation. They'd almost had him that first night, but Fallon had slipped away. To make matters worse, now they had a minor insurgency working against them.

Almost. Almost was the word that Aldridge most identified with his career.

Major Panelli was the loudest voice of dissention. The other officers had been mostly silent during the meeting, watching the two of them butt heads. Aldridge hated the back-biting little prick. But since he had no legitimate reason to fire him, he was stuck with him. He glanced around at the officers in the room with him, happy he'd been able to call the meeting without Collins knowing. The less the general interfered, the better things would be.

"I don't care how thin our supplies are, Major. I want a field kitchen set up in the movie theater. I want to ensure that everyone inside is fed. The kitchen will serve a hot meal at lunch and provide one MRE for dinner, each day to any civilian who wants one."

They already had plans in place for how the kitchen should be set up. The queue would have traffic cones set at six-foot intervals and armed soldiers would watch and make sure people didn't cluster up. Additionally, a temporary shelter was set up in a church in the blacked-out area where another team of soldiers handed out rations, blankets, coffee, and cocoa to people waiting to eat.

"Sir, I understand what you want, but I'm telling you we don't have the manpower or food supplies to support it."

"Apparently you don't understand shit, Major. These people see us as nothing but thugs and murderers who are holding them prisoner. The only contact they have with us is through our presence patrols and when we round up the sick for transport to the hospital. We need to show them we're not monsters, that we have their best interests at heart. This is the way to do it."

Panelli spread his hands and said, "I don't see how we can, sir." He was an unimaginative and—in Aldridge's opinion—dim-witted officer. If it wasn't in a manual or typed in a memo, he was lost and completely useless.

"Put the troops on half-rations." Panelli started to protest again, but Aldridge rode roughshod over him. "We're due for resupply soon, provided the trucks can make it through. These efforts may seriously tax my already strained manpower and resources, but they need to be given top priority. We must show these people that everything that's been done, a few mistakes notwithstanding, has been done to protect them. Hopefully, handing out food will prevent more riots and quell the rash of attacks we've been seeing. We must do something to regain the goodwill of these people. We need their help if we're going to catch Fallon. I want soldiers circulating his picture around, so if anyone recognizes him, they'll trust us enough to come forward."

The frown on Panelli's face told Aldridge what he thought of the idea. He didn't care. The hospital shooting had done more damage to their operation than a hundred roadside bombs could. Nobody came to them for help, or came to help them, for that matter. That needed to change. The chances of finding Fallon without assistance from the community were slim. The longer they stayed in place, the harder it would become and the more these people would suffer.

"Sir, I just don't know."

"You don't have to know, Major. I'm in command here. All you have to do is say 'Yes, sir.' Then move to carry out my orders with maximum speed and motivation. Understood?"

Panelli pouted from the rebuke, but said, "Yes, sir."

"Good. Now get out of here." To the rest of the staff officers present, he said, "Make sure that everything goes smoothly here and make sure my company commanders understand what's expected of them." There was a chorus of "Yes, sir's" as they filed out of the hospital conference room.

Aldridge looked out the window. The dawn air was clear, bright and cold. The storm of the night before had blown away the clouds that had been lingering overhead. There were two flights inbound, carrying some much-needed vaccine and other supplies. They were hurrying to make it in before the next storm front moved in. If they timed it exactly right, they would arrive just in the nick of time. He wished the Chinooks could continue making supply runs all day, but the weather to the south was deteriorating and they would only be able to make this one drop for him. The ground convoy was less than twenty miles away, but they were still being held up by the road conditions. More people were getting sick every day. If he were going to contain this outbreak, Aldridge needed all the vaccine he could lay his hands on. More importantly, he needed to find and stop Fallon.

"Did you hear the way that condescending prick was talking to me?" Panelli said to a couple of staff officers after they left the conference room. "All I was trying to do was show him the reality of the situation and he treats me like I'm a fucking child."

"You were pretty condescending yourself there, sir," said a voice behind him.

Panelli spun and saw Aldridge's pet, Captain West, standing there. "What the fuck do you know about it, kiss-ass?"

West shrugged. "I know, sir, that we've all been given direct orders, with clear guidance for how those orders are carried out and our commander's intent for the outcome of those orders. So, there's very little anyone can do to drag their feet or misinterpret our instructions. Not without repercussions, that is."

Panelli's eyes narrowed. "And that's supposed to mean what, Captain?"

"It doesn't mean a thing, sir. But several of the NCOs and officers I've spoken with in the convoy you lead here think you dithered and wasted too much time waiting on the side of the road instead of making your way here, like you were ordered to."

Panelli looked from West to the other officers standing around them and back again. "You shouldn't listen to idle gossip, Captain. It might get you into trouble if you don't watch yourself."

"Yes, sir." West shouldered past him and went to work.

Panelli turned to the others, "Get to work," he snapped, then stormed to his own little office, fuming at the impertinence West showed him. He paced the room in a fury, pondering what he could do to take care of the little ass kisser. It wouldn't be easy. No, West was Aldridge's favorite. He'd have to find a way to deal with them both at the same time.

It was snowing again. There was no wind, but fat flakes were falling hard and fast. "This will keep the army's helicopters and UAVs grounded," Fallon said. "There are probably satellites stationed directly overhead, but there's no sense in worrying about them." Fallon was standing in the little kitchen area of the cabin, contemplating what to eat for breakfast, their last can chili con carne, or their last can of chicken soup.

"What's the likelihood that they'll find us here with the satellites?" Shelly asked.

"That depends on what else is happening around town to keep the army occupied. Hopefully, they will be too busy looking for us there, to think to check out here, for a little while longer. That explosion we heard indicates they've got their hands full. So, I think we've got a good chance of staying hidden a while longer. Maybe even slipping through their fingers while they are dealing with this other problem." He held up the cans. "Hungry?"

Shelly made a face. "Just thinking about chili makes me want to puke again."

"Chicken soup it is then," he said and started opening the can.

She thanked Fallon when he handed her the bowl of broth. After eating, they were going to get moving, she grabbed her coat and went outside.

The air was thick with falling snow. The clearing around the cabin was white and unblemished. The trees looked like the kind of frosted plastic trees available from a department store for Christmas. It was lovely and peaceful.

Shelly heard footsteps crunching through the snow behind her. "Safe as we probably are here, we really can't stay much longer," Fallon said. "The more time we spend in one place, the more likely it is that they will catch us."

*Maybe I want them to catch us. Maybe I want this whole thing done and behind me. If the army finds you, then I can go back to my life.* She knew that wasn't fair. Given the atrocities that the government was instigating, Shelly wasn't sure that life could ever go back to normal.

"They're still after me and by now they have to know you're helping me, so you're in danger, too." The look he gave her implied all the horrible things the army would do to them if they were caught.

"What can we do? I mean, they followed you here and cut off a whole town just to trap you."

"The Lord provides," he said. He was watching the clouds and did not notice the odd look she gave him. "You're right, of course. The town is cut off. But there will be a way out. There always is. Something they will have missed that we can exploit."

"Won't that be risky?"

"No riskier than staying here. But you are right, we need to be on the move. You're sure you don't know of any back roads that lead away from here, any kind of back trail or something that would allow us to get away?"

Shelly thought for a moment. They'd been examining the maps they bought on the way to the cabin and hadn't been able to find an easy route out. "I think so. It's been a while since I've been four-wheeling out here. But I think there's a trail that will take us north through the woods and then back to the highway, maybe twenty miles down the road from the last exit. But I'm not promising anything. We need to get some food first."

Fallon was visibly relieved at this and smiled as they walked back inside. That smile disappeared after about an hour of looking over their maps with her.

"Most of the ground between here and the highway will be impassable right now," Shelly said. "Even with a serious four by four, we'd have a tough time getting through. We could easily get stuck out there."

"You're sure there's no way through?"

"Not in my truck, no. If we had snowmobiles, it would be a cinch."

Fallon sighed in frustration. It seemed that their hideaway had become a box canyon. They were safe for now, but there was no other way out. Sooner or later, Aldridge's soldiers would start looking beyond the city limits for them.

"Since we have to get food anyway," she said. "Let's look at the other side of town. There aren't as many trees, and the ground should be easier to drive through."

"That means it will be easier for the army to watch and follow us if we're caught."

"We might not have any other choice."

He continued poring over the maps, while Shelly went back outside. Once again, Fallon joined her. She suspected he was afraid of being alone, or more likely he was afraid she would run off and abandon him. The snow wasn't falling as hard as it had been, but it was going to be dark soon and the temperature was dropping. She patted her arms to warm them up.

"We'll keep looking for a way out," she said, in her most reassuring tone of voice.

"Good." He gave her a tired smile. "Pretty soon we'll be gone, and Aldridge will be left chasing his tail here."

Shelly frowned. She didn't like the idea of leaving Harper's Glen while it was still being occupied. It felt too much like running away. But she couldn't see any other choice. Even though she wasn't particularly close to many people here, she had a few friends, and her neighbors were nice enough.

"I'd like to be alone for a minute, if you don't mind," she said.

"Of course. I'll be back in the cabin." He turned away and carefully crunched back the way he came.

Shelly concentrated on the ground in front of her to keep from slipping and falling. She didn't want to think right now. The trail was invisible beneath the layers of ice and snow and she was forced to navigate by memory. They were only a few miles outside of town, but they could have been deep in the wilderness for lack of civilization around them.

Her uncle had taken her on many hikes and drives through the hills and woods around Harper's Glen, so she knew the area well enough to take them safely through the snowy countryside and thought she could get them away safely. It was true that the drive would be dangerous in her SUV. She was secretly sure she could make it. She just didn't know if she wanted to.

Scared and feeling completely lost and out of her depth, because of Fallon—he had made her a fugitive, like him—she still wasn't completely sure she trusted him. But everything seemed to support his story. She had a chance to help him expose this great evil being perpetuated by the military. If she could do this, if she could help Fallon do this, then maybe she could forget her own past.

She turned towards the woods and pictured herself driving down a narrow cut through the hills and making her way slowly through deep snow. There was a creek bed that would be frozen over that they could follow for half a mile before coming upon a paved road leading from the residential northeast area of town. If Fallon was right about the army's cordon being stationed close to town, once they were a few miles away they should be in the clear.

Shelly paused then, sorely tempted to turn away, just leave him there and head back to town, to the comfortable life she'd made for herself there. It was three miles of exposed travel, stop signs, alleyways, and intersections. Not to mention the icy roads and snow drifts and soldiers. It was the last that worried her the most. Undoubtedly the army had a description of her vehicle by now and would be searching for it. Once spotted, they could pounce on her from anywhere; roadblocks and machine guns ready to stop and put an end to her.

She waited a second longer before she turned her back to

Harper's Glen and walked back to the cabin.

Benedict awoke in the dark, covered in sweat. It was always the same dream; struggling in suffocating smoke, lost and helpless. With crystal clarity he relived the attack that cost him his leg over and over again every night.

The IED strike had obliterated the front end of the truck in front of his and flipped it onto its roof. He was the first one to make it out to the dead vehicle. Inside, none of the others had even stirred. Without pausing for thought, he dove inside to get the crew out. Smoke had filled the cabin, making it hard to see and harder to breathe. Benedict had just managed to free the driver and maneuver him to where he could pull him out when the second IED went off.

They'd shipped him back home after he spent nearly two months in a hospital in Germany, then medically discharged him. During his final few months in the army, he had been treated for post-traumatic stress disorder, but it hadn't helped. This was early in the Iraq war and the army's medical professionals didn't have much knowledge or experience about treating his internal wounds. Though he was a patchwork of burn scars and skin grafts, they'd knitted his body back together fine, and given him a top-of-the-line replacement leg. It was the wounds that weren't visible that they'd dismissed, that were still giving him trouble.

Nearly ten years had passed, and that day still haunted him. Every day his mind travelled back there. The back-to-back missions, constant firefights, ambushes; not knowing if the guy on the street was an innocent bystander or an insurgent about to blow him up. There was no relief.

Throwing back the covers, he pulled on his foot and got up to get some water. His house was small, but neat. Being somewhat paranoid, he'd intentionally purchased a place located near the edge of town, so there were plenty of escape avenues. The walls were bare of any kind of décor. Everything was kept clean and orderly. It was the only way he could keep the chaos at bay. On his way back from the kitchen, he stopped in front of the full-length mirror hanging from his closet door. Standing naked before it, he carefully examined his many scars for the thousandth time. The army had chewed him up and spat him out—like so many thousands of others—without a second thought for the lives of the soldiers they spent. Once they were finished, they washed their hands of the mess that remained.

Though he didn't feel like it, Benedict was a lucky man. By some twist of fate, he had escaped the secondary explosion with only the loss of his leg, a concussion, and some burns. The only other soldier in the truck to survive with him was a triple amputee, with only three usable fingers on his left hand, who drank his food through a straw.

His recent attacks on the patrols in town made him feel guilty for visiting harm upon the poor troopers. He'd been just like them once upon a time: blindly naïve and stupid. Killing and hurting them made him even angrier at the people who'd caused this. He wanted to lash out and kill every authority figure he could find. But he knew that such an act would do no good. Anyone he killed would just be replaced. If there was one thing the army had in abundance, it was replacement soldiers. The only thing he could do was keep pressure on them. Make them realize his town was not expendable. Maybe he would let the world know what was happening here. Show them all what the monsters in charge of his country were doing to their own people. That reporter, Eddie Tate, could help with that. He had already collected one hell of a story. No matter what happened, Tate would let them all know what happened here and how a few brave citizens had resisted. At first Tate had been hesitant to join Benedict's group, but once he saw the information Benedict had and realized there was much more where that came from, his hesitation went away and committed himself totally to the cause.

Benedict was careful to keep Tate away from the command post, though, in case he was discovered during his snooping around. That way he couldn't bring down the rest of the organization, such as it was. The army was very effective at ferreting out insurgent cells. They'd had more than ten years and two wars worth of practice. Benedict had only met with Tate twice more after the initial agreement. Their communications were mostly through dead drops. Benedict had read all about them in Tom Clancy novels and thought they were the coolest thing ever. So, he used them as often as possible when communicating with his people.

Thinking about the reporter brought another thought to mind. His group was too centralized. They needed to split up the organization if they were going to be successful. Keeping all their eggs in one basket was just asking for the army to wipe them all out.

He quickly dressed and then left for Sonny Dixon's place. He had to travel by alleyway and backstreets to avoid being spotted by any roving patrols, which made the trip ten minutes longer than it would normally be. When he finally reached his destination, he stole into the backyard and rapped on the back door.

"Who the hell is it?" Sonny demanded, after Benedict had been knocking for a few minutes.

"Sonny, it's me. Listen, we need to talk, man."

The door opened and a very sleepy—likely hungover—Sonny peered out and shivered as the cold air blew through the door at him. "Right now? Man, it's three in the morning. Can't this wait till I get up in four hours?"

"Hey man, sorry I woke you, but it was urgent we meet. I have some things we need to discuss."

"All right. Come on in. I'll put on some coffee." Sonny sighed loudly and let the door open wider. Benedict saw he was wearing a white tank top and an old pair of boxer shorts that refused to close completely in the front. He was immediately thankful it was dark in Sonny's house.

Benedict and Sonny spent the next three hours deciding how they would divide up their existing forces and any people they might recruit in the immediate future. They made arrangements for meeting places and times, as well as locations for more dead drops, should they need to contact each other without arousing suspicion. They also brainstormed ideas for their next strike. Both men wanted it to be soon. They knew they had to keep the pressure on to make the army give up and pull out.

With everything sorted and arranged, Benedict left, taking a different route home. They would put everything in place tomorrow and then work on dividing into two separate cells. Once home, he undressed and popped two Zoloft and an Ambien before crawling back into bed. Leading a clandestine organization was tiring work, but the prospect of more action to come had him amped up and unable to sleep.

Ten minutes after taking the pills, Benedict was snoring loudly into his pillow.

Captain West sat his desk looking over reports from the afternoon patrols. Happily, nothing extraordinary had occurred today. The people of Harper's Glen were still afraid of the army and therefore avoided soldiers as much as they could. In fact, most chose to stay off the streets and indoors. This fact didn't hamper the virus, which was still spreading rapidly through the civic population. That morning, Colonel Aldridge had ordered three field clinics erected around town to deal with the growing number of sick. Their purpose was triage. They would determine whether an individual was infected and refer them to the hospital. It was hoped this step would free up the staff and allow quicker, more efficient treatment. All too soon, it wouldn't matter. As quickly as new vaccine supplies arrived, they were administered. Everything that could be done to arrest the spread of the infection was being done. Now Colonel Aldridge wanted to refocus their efforts towards finding Patient Zero. He was still at large somewhere within the town population. Finding him was the surest way to prevent further spread.

West thought Aldridge was feeling pressure from General Collins. But he wasn't about to question or judge his superior's actions. He'd been with Aldridge since Afghanistan, leading one of the platoons Aldridge had taken on his rescue mission. And being an officer firmly in Aldridge's corner, he was also relegated to the same career vacuum.

The door of his closet-sized office opened, and General Collins entered without knocking. West snapped to attention. "Good morning, sir. What can I do for you?"

At first Collins said nothing. He just walked over to West's desk and began leafing through the papers in his inbox. Though he didn't show it outwardly, this infuriated West. He didn't trust Collins and felt the general was only here to make trouble, all he had done since arriving was undermine Aldridge.

"Can I help you, sir?" he asked again.

The general looked up, as though noticing West for the first time. "What's your opinion about this operation, Captain? How it's being conducted? Chances of success and so forth?"

"I think we've handled this operation as well as possible, given the circumstances, sir. Mistakes and setbacks notwithstanding, of course, the soldiers have done an outstanding job here. Once the supplies of vaccine, food and other necessities start arriving more regularly, I think we stand an excellent chance of beating this thing and capturing Patient Zero."

Collins dropped the memo he wasn't reading, sat on the edge of West's desk, and leaned towards him. "And what do you think about failings of your leadership?"

West blinked, wary of the question. "I'm not sure what you mean, sir. As far as I'm aware there haven't been any failings."

Collins was fishing for dirt on Aldridge, and West would be damned if he was going to give him anything.

"What I'm asking, Captain, is what do you think of Colonel Aldridge's handling of this operation to date? Specifically, your appraisal of his missed steps, errors of judgment and so on. I'm trying to get a feel for his competency. Have you ever noticed him acting erratically, indecisive or unable to focus, like he is under the influence?"

"Sir, I think Colonel Aldridge's conduct of this operation has been exemplary. He has contained and eradicated the spread of this disease in three towns so far and pursued Patient Zero across the state. I believe we're closer now to apprehending him than we've ever been. I've never noticed any signs of the behavior you're referring to. Quite frankly, I'm uncomfortable discussing the matter with you, sir."

General Collins pursed his lips, obviously unhappy with West's answer. "That's rather disappointing, Captain." He was a man who was used to those around him telling him what he wanted to hear. Anything else was a frustration and so far, Aldridge's entire staff had been frustrating him. "It's sad to see a promising young officer like yourself tied to a man like Colonel Aldridge, whose career is winding down, moving from one dead-end assignment to another. I'm sure an intelligent and capable man like you can see a way out, a way to save your career. You shouldn't go down with him, as though you're tied to the mast of his sinking ship. Let me help you, son. If you just talk to me, we can help each other."

West was silent for a long moment. Then he said, "Sir, I've answered your questions as honestly as I am able. If you have nothing further, I'm swamped and need to get back to work."

Collins frowned and got up. "That will be all for you, I guess." He turned and left.

After the door closed, West smiled to himself. If Collins wanted a turncoat, he would have to look elsewhere. He wanted to inform Aldridge about this encounter, but not just yet. The colonel had lain down only a few minutes ago. West knew how little sleep he'd been getting lately and fully intended to let him sleep four more hours before waking him.

West busied himself for the next couple of hours by preparing the colonel's afternoon briefing. He issued movement orders for the patrols in the north side of town tonight. Also, on his plate was the supply problem. The vaccine they needed wasn't getting through. The outbreak among the county snowplow drivers left the roads around Harper's Glen largely undrivable. The neighboring counties were taking up the slack, but they could only do so much, and more snow fell every day. The convoys hauling supplies were forced to clear the roads ahead of them as they went. This was a time-consuming chore, which left the troops on this end stretched thin on resources and supplies.

The command post radio operator knocked and delivered a new report. West read it, eyes widening, then dashed from the office. His earlier intention to let the colonel sleep forgotten, West had to wake Aldridge right away.

Aldridge was finally having a pleasant dream, the first in a long time, when he awoke to someone knocking furiously on his office door. In the dream, he was having a picnic with his wife in a green park. They were on their third date, and he was falling for her. The way the sunlight shone upon her skin and in her hair gave her a crystalline hue. He leaned in for a kiss. Her lips were full and soft against his. He caressed her jaw, ran his fingers through her hair and along the curve of her neck. The sharp rapping of knuckles on wood thundered in, shattering the illusion.

One moment he was holding the woman he would later marry and build a home with; the next, cold reality was slapping him awake like a bucket of water.

He had only just dozed off and felt wretched when he pried his eyes open. The insistent knocking came again. "Sir, are you awake?" came an urgent voice from the other side.

"It's open," Aldridge croaked, and Captain West entered.

"Sir, we've just had a big break I think you should take a look at." He was having trouble containing his excitement.

"What have you got for me, Captain?" Aldridge looked like hell. His eyes were swollen and bloodshot. He was pale and the lines etched into his face had become deepened furrows. He was listless and couldn't seem to focus on any one thing for more than a few seconds.

"Sir, I have a field report here, taken the first day of our operations in this city. It's from a gas station attendant. According to his statement, he saw Fallon and a woman, whom we've identified as the missing nurse, Shelly Christianson. The patrol leader, Lieutenant Glover, confirmed this with the store's security camera footage. The attendant also says in his statement that they drove north after leaving his store."

Upon hearing this, Aldridge's eyes cleared, and he sat up a little straighter. When he spoke, however, his words were still slightly slurred. "Why am I just now seeing this? We've been here for two weeks."

"Sir, the report was lost in the initial shuffle. The attendant fell ill during the interview and had to be removed to the hospital. We figure he may have encountered as many as thirty people during his shift, which leads us to believe that he may have been the reason our initial containment efforts when we first put boots on the ground here were ineffective."

"Goddamnit! We've been here for weeks and this information only just now surfaces!"

"Sir, there's more."

"More? Jesus Christ, what the hell else have we missed?"

"Nothing was missed, sir, it's just taken time to sort through." West pulled a detailed glossy photograph from a manila folder. The picture was taken from a high angle, so Aldridge figured it came from either a satellite or a drone, during the few days of good weather they'd been able to fly the damn drones. "Sir, here is an image from a satellite pass taken just as we were getting in place."

The photo showed a blanket of trees, dotted with a few small clearings and a logging trail or two.

"Okay," Aldridge said, passing the picture back to West.

"This photo shows the same area, taken yesterday when the storm broke. Look at this clearing right here." West indicated a small clearing near the edge of the picture with his finger. Then he passed back the first picture. "Now compare the two."

Aldridge instantly saw what West was talking about. There was a white vehicle parked next to a cabin in the second photo, but not in the first.

"The analysts think the vehicle is large enough to be an SUV, just like what Shelly Christianson drives."

Aldridge's heart was beating fast now. He stood up and peered more closely at the photos. They'd found him. At last, they'd found Fallon. He had taken Christianson's vehicle and was hiding out in that cabin. They would have to move quickly. There wasn't a moment to lose.

Ten minutes later, Aldridge was dressed and issuing orders to his staff. He wanted to send his entire force in to grab Fallon but knew he couldn't. He settled for sending a single platoon. With tensions in town growing by the day, it was all he could spare.

He allowed himself a little smile as his staff hurried to carry out his orders. By dawn tomorrow, this long, and terrible nightmare would finally be over.

Back in his office, Aldridge read and reread Glover's investigation of the gas station where Fallon had stopped during the night. Then he watched the footage from two security cameras, which had been brought to him. One feed showed the inside of the store and the other showed the lane of gas pumps. Both were synced so they ran at the exact same time. A third feed showed a satellite view of the town, zoomed in to show the gas station at the exact time of the other videos. At just past one in the morning, an SUV stopped at the pumps and two figures got out. The driver stayed and began fueling the vehicle and the other figure entered the store.

Aldridge turned his attention to the inside feed. The camera was placed behind the register, looking down at the cashier. It was probably more to prevent employees from skimming from the till. Therefore, it didn't have a view of the front door. Aldridge could see that someone had entered, but not their face. He would have to wait till the customer approached the counter to pay. Two minutes went by and the front door opened again. Aldridge looked at the parking lot feed; the driver was no longer at the pump.

Five more minutes of the clerk dithering about behind the counter before his two customers finally stepped up to the counter. Here Aldridge paused the tape. It was Fallon all right. Aldridge's pulse quickened at the sight of him. He didn't immediately recognize the woman with him but knew he was looking at Shelly Christianson. She was helping Fallon. Or she was his hostage. Either way, she was infected and most likely dead.

On screen they paid and left. The parking lot camera image showed them returning to the vehicle and departing to the north. The cabin from the satellite stills was north of town. It made sense. Still, he wanted to be sure and called West back into his office.

"I want my image analysts to go over all the satellite footage we've got from this date and track this vehicle from the gas station to its destination. I want to be sure that the vehicle we are seeing in the picture is the same one Fallon and Christianson left in."

"Right away, sir."

A nurse was brought in to view the tape and confirmed that the woman was indeed Christianson. "I just can't imagine why she would be with a stranger like that," said the heavyset nurse in her early fifties. "We invite her out all the time and she rarely agrees to come. She's just so shy and reserved."

*If I'd been through what she had,* Aldridge thought. *I'd be quiet and reserved too.* Aldridge figured she was protecting herself by keeping everyone at a safe distance. She couldn't know how her coworkers would react to learning she'd been accused of murder and acquitted.

The nurse was still speaking, but Aldridge had stopped listening. He was instead mentally reviewing everything he knew about Shelly Christianson. Her dossier was thick, especially when it got to the part about her ex-husband, Bradley Duncan and his death. Aldridge had her life at his fingertips. Her parents died in a drunken crash caused by her father when she was in her late teens. Her moderately famous writer uncle, Rory Christianson, was recently deceased and had left her nearly everything when he passed away, including the house she now lived in. She had no credit cards. Her checking account held less than seven thousand dollars, but her savings account contained nearly one hundred and fifty thousand, as well as other assets totaling over a million dollars, thanks to the inheritance from her uncle. She led a simple, anonymous life. If it weren't for the murder trial, she wouldn't have much of a file at all. As complete as it was, the file gave him no new clues or insights that would help him.

He looked back at the computer screen. "I'm close to you now, Fallon," he said. "Closer than ever before. I'll find you this time and God help you when I do!"

In the minutes before dawn, Aldridge stood at a window watching one of his platoons gearing up and preparing to depart. He hoped they would bring an end to this nightmare. Their mission was to capture or kill Fallon. Once that was accomplished, they could concentrate on healing the sick, saving those that could be saved and then departing. This long and terrible ordeal was nearly over. He could feel it. Soon he could finally rest. There would be consequences, of course. There always were in a situation as high-profile as this one was. A committee of uninterested civilians would go over every single move he and his men had made ever since Fallon's escape, nit-picking, and second guessing his every decision. His ordeal was far from over, but he was willing to deal with everything that was coming with glad expectation, if it meant he had put an end to Fallon.

# January 19th

After his people had successfully ambushed and destroyed one army patrol, Benedict stood in the cold, watching. He wanted to hit another one.

*Keep them off balance. Show them the cost of staying here,* he thought.

He wanted to make it impossible for the army leaders to maintain their occupation. He wanted to make them suffer for all they'd done, to him and to his home. They'd taken everything he had. Chipped away at his life, piece by piece, until all that was left was a seething ball of anger, boiling inside him. Retribution, though often slow in delivery, was sweet.

It took a lot of planning to execute each attack. He needed to strike at his enemy, but he couldn't endanger the few people he had on risky jobs. So, instead of attacking the hospital, wherein lay the heart of his enemy, he made a choice to attack the presence patrols which were dispatched into town every day.

"And there it is," he said softly to the people gathered around him, as a line of military vehicles exited the hospital parking lot.

This time wasn't going to be as easy as the last ambush. They had already adapted their tactics to counter his. Remembering the lessons taught overseas—lessons they never expected to use on American soil—the drivers of each truck in the convoy spread farther apart, driving slowly. The gunners were pivoting more and controlling their sectors more attentively. Drivers and truck commanders were watchful for telltales of ambushes in their path. Radio chatter between the trucks was likely constant as they called out warnings to each other. Patrol paranoia had set in.

Benedict remembered such actions had helped keep him alive downrange. But now they made his current job much harder. He turned to Sonny, standing in the shadows behind him.

"Let's move."

They piled into the waiting Suburban. The back of the truck was loaded with their rifles and ammunition, as well as a surprise for the soldiers when they caught up to the convoy.

Colonel Aldridge had stressed to Lieutenant Glover the importance of this mission, who in turn stressed its importance and the need for security to the NCOs and soldiers in his platoon.

"We don't have the time to fuck around today," Glover told the soldiers gathered around. Many of them had friends wounded in the ambush a few days ago. None of them wanted a repeat of that, and all of them wanted to kick somebody's ass in retribution. "You've all been briefed on the routes we're taking. Gunners, keep your eyes open for anything suspicious. Drivers, if you see anything in front of you that looks like it could be an IED or a targeting marker for an IED, you call it out. Most of you have been downrange before, so you know what to do. Once we reach the target area, we're going to cordon it off with standard four corners. Everything goes smooth and clean. We apprehend the targets, exfil back to the trucks and return to the hospital. Questions?" There were none. "Good. Let's go bag a bad guy!"

"Hoo-ah!" nineteen soldiers shouted in reply. Then they separated to their trucks and mounted up.

Glover's stomach was in knots. Their route took them through the shopping district and neighborhoods near the hospital. They would be travelling through the heart of Harper's Glen. A few blocks away from their route was where that platoon was ambushed. Burnt-out cars and pockmarked walls and shattered glass storefronts were like an open wound in the middle of town. Glover was painfully aware of its proximity as they drove by. But there was nothing they could do about it. This was the colonel's game, and they were all just pieces on the board. All they could do was keep vigilant and prevent mistakes like that from happening again.

There had been several smaller attacks since the shooting on the hospital steps, mostly harassment and a few fights. The IED attack that killed six was the most serious so far. According to PNN—the Private News Network, where some of the most reliable gossip and rumors were passed around like candy—some ex-Special Forces guy had started up a resistance group in town and masterminded the attack. Ridiculous rumors like that spread like wildfire in the army, but this one was almost too much for Glover to swallow. All the same, due to these attacks, everyone was on their guard and their convoy was arrayed in a protective column. The veterans inside each truck drew upon their experiences overseas, keeping their eyes open and their heads on a swivel, looking everywhere at once for threats. They were told to keep an aggressive mindset during the long, slow drive through town. Each vehicle was separated from the truck before it by at least twenty yards to prevent a roadside bomb from hitting two at once. The gunners on each truck watched their sectors, vigilantly searching for threats. None of them wanted to be caught off guard; their lives and the lives of everyone in their convoy depended upon each of them doing the job they'd been trained to do.

The radios chattered constantly, as gunners and drivers called out anything and everything that looked out of place or worrisome. They had to traverse two miles of city streets, tightly packed houses and buildings, where snipers could lay waiting. Alleys and blind corners made perfect ambush sites and IED strike points. Then they would finally clear the town and start into the backwoods. Glover, in the lead truck, wouldn't breathe easy until then. Just a few blocks and they were out of the city and into the trees.

Once they cleared that last row of houses, they closed their formation to ten yards between vehicles. The trail they followed would have been rough even during ideal conditions. Covered with snow, however, it was treacherous to the extreme. Away from the plowed roads, the top-heavy military trucks slipped and fishtailed, fighting for traction on the slick muddy surface. Slowly, they plodded along towards the objective. The sun was just creeping over the horizon and rays of light cut shafts through the trees. Through the window, he could see that the sky was completely clear of clouds. This break in the weather meant there would be a drone overhead monitoring their progress. Lieutenant Glover impatiently watched the terrain around them crawl by. The snow was hampering their movements to such a degree that they were already behind schedule. According to the operation order, they were supposed to be on the objective before dawn, with Fallon in custody thirty minutes later. Here they were, fighting through drifts taller than their vehicles, nearly twenty minutes late and the sun was already creeping into the morning sky. Glover hoped they'd still be able to achieve surprise when they arrived.

The rear end of his truck slew to the left and his driver, Private First Class Brown, spun the wheel to compensate.

"They should've outfitted our trucks with snow tires, sir," he said. The man was an eloquent complainer. No matter the subject, he could find some fault. Whether with the actions of his superiors, the intelligence of his NCOs or things that nobody could control, like the weather, he could find something to bitch about, loudly and with a good vocabulary.

Oftentimes, Glover found himself agreeing completely; but his position as the platoon leader prevented him from admitting so. Other times he had to fight hard to keep from laughing at Brown's often hilarious remarks. Today however, he was in no mood to listen to the enlisted man's griping. He had more important things to worry about. They'd been handed what was surely the most important mission of the operation. He needed to focus on the mission ahead, rather than the entertaining and humorous bitching of his driver.

"We don't have any snow tires, Private Brown. We were in such a rush to get here there was no way to bring any."

"That just shows a lack of planning and foresight, sir. If they knew winter was coming, they should've had some fucking snow tires delivered." He said it as though it were the most obvious thing in the world and that the dunderheads in charge should have foreseen the weather and known to bring the right tires. "Just another example of those on top screwing us over with idiocy."

Lieutenant Glover frowned. Normally, he would joke back with Brown, but this morning he'd had enough. "I'm not in the mood for your usual diatribe this morning, Brown, so please just shut the fuck up and drive."

Brown gave him a slightly wounded, slightly scathing look. Then he closed his mouth and continued wrestling with the truck in silence.

They crested a small ridge and before them lay the clearing and their objective. Glover ordered a halt to allow the last truck to catch up with them. While sitting there, he quickly went over what he wanted everyone to do, even though everyone in the convoy already knew with crystal clarity what to do. Once the convoy was together again, they started rolling for the cabin. Glancing at his watch, Glover decided they couldn't risk the time it would take to get into position to encircle the cabin. He relayed over the radio that he wanted the dismount soldiers from the first two trucks immediately to move on the cabin, while the remaining trucks and personnel continued into position surrounding the cabin.

When the first two trucks cleared the tree line fifty yards from the cabin, the convoy halted. Six soldiers, including Lieutenant Glover, got out. The second and fourth trucks split right, and the first and third went left. The plan was to have all four trucks take up positions surrounding the cabin at each outside corner. Once in place, the remaining soldiers inside would dismount and provide security for Lieutenant Glover and his men moving to the front door.

"Oh shit," Shelly said, upon seeing the soldiers through the window. The sun was just peeking over the trees, casting heavy shadows beneath them, and she'd had to squint hard to make sure of what she was seeing.

Beside her, Fallon was squinting too. The frown he wore gave voice to what he was thinking. "Soldiers," he said. "We'll have to find a way around them."

Earlier that morning, before the sun had even considered waking up and getting out of bed, they had gathered up their meager supplies, loaded them into the back of the Bronco and left Uncle Rory's cabin behind. It had been snowing lightly but constantly all day, forcing Shelly to drive slowly, carefully navigating the terrain between the cabin and town. Three times, Fallon had to get out and use a small shovel to dig out the tires because they had gotten stuck. Two hours after they started, they came to a farm road leading into Harper's Glen. Rather than follow it, they cut through the adjacent field, skirting around an old farmhouse. Shelly worried that the owner, or someone inside would come out and shout at them for trespassing, or worse call the authorities.

"The place looks deserted," Fallon said, when she voiced her concerns. "If someone were home, there would be smoke coming from the chimney."

Shelly looked and saw he was right. "That's the Varney place. I wonder what happened to him." Varney was a widower turned recluse since his wife passed away six months prior. Once upon a time, his farm produced prize winning squash and tomatoes. Now the only thing growing on his land were weeds. "I hope he's alright."

"He's most likely taken by the army. Either he's sick, or they relocated him to a cell in town."

Shelly hoped it was the latter. Another hour and half of driving through fields and backroads, they came across their first roadblock. They were stopped behind a clump of bushes. Fallon warned her to go slow once they came within sight of a greater number of houses and buildings. She kept that in mind at each hill, intersection, or bend in the road. So, she crept up to the tee intersection where Chicken Run road ended when it met Hillside boulevard. They were concealed by a thick stand of overgrowth. Once stopped, they could clearly see the roadblock, without being spotted themselves. Or so she hoped.

"I think I see three of them," Shelly said.

"That means there could be as many as five more out of sight," Fallon said. The soldiers had strung a double coil of concertina wire across both lanes and put up a little prefabricated shed off to the side with a small generator. Undoubtedly, there was a heater inside, and probably a few more soldiers. "What can we do now? Do you know another way?"

Shelly thought for a moment. Upon returning to Harper's Glenn, she spent many sleepless nights driving around, getting lost in the back roads around town and finding her way home again. Driving was one of the few distractions that worked to clear her mind and calm her down enough to sleep.

"I think I know a way," she said. "But I want to look at the map before we go."

"Why don't we go back to that abandoned farmhouse," Fallon said. "We can make something to eat while we plan our route."

Shelly nodded and put the truck in reverse.

At the roadblock, the soldier manning the roadblock noted their movements and called the command post.

Fallon knocked on Varney's front door, before breaking a window on the side of the house and climbing through. Moments later, the garage door began rolling up and Shelly pulled in. They had decided that the old man's farm was worth checking out as a place to stop and plan a new route out of town. The power was off, and after checking to make sure they were alone inside, they decided to risk a small fire. Fallon found a few gallon jugs of water in the pantry as well as some canned stew. They opened one to cook and packed the rest into the back of the Bronco.

Shelly unfolded the road atlas beside the hearth. "Here's an old dirt road we might be able to take. If the army hasn't blocked it off, it should take us up to Sand's Hollow road, and from there we can reach the highway."

Fallon followed her fingers as she traced the route. "That road runs pretty close to the garbage dump," he said. "There will likely be soldiers patrolling there. It might be too risky to go that way."

Shelly frowned. "It's the only way that takes us away from town and avoids any major roads and intersections. This is our best chance of getting away."

After a moment of looking at the map and mulling it over, Fallon nodded and turned his attention to the pot bubbling over the fire.

Satisfied that they had a plan, Shelly closed the atlas and

returned it to the Bronco. When she came back into the house, she paused in the kitchen. Standing there, in the dim chill, Shelly suddenly felt like she had stepped into an old photograph. All the colors were muted and washed out in the faint morning light tickling in through the curtained windows. It felt to her as though it had been a hundred years since the house had been lived in. There were no dirty dishes in the sink. No dirty clothes in the bedroom hamper. The refrigerator was practically barren. The vacant house was as still and hushed as a mausoleum.

Shelly hadn't known Roger Varney well. He rarely came into town and rarely spoke to anyone. She had gotten to know his wife Delila very well, however, during the three months she had spent in the hospital for her cancer treatments. She and Varney had been high school sweethearts. They had grown up and grown old together. According to Anne Littlewolf, Roger Varney stopped living the day his wife died.

Shelly shivered and decided she didn't want to stay there any longer. They would get back on the road the moment they were done eating. Passing the front windows, she saw movement outside from the corner of her eye. She parted the thin curtains and gasped at the sight of twenty or so soldiers in the field in front of Varney's house exiting their vehicles and forming up to surround the house.

"Fallon!" she called from the front window. Strangely, she felt calm, as though the army's presence at this time was inevitable. "They're here. They've found us."

Fallon leaped to her side, and immediately pulled her to the ground. She had never seen a man look as desperate and scared as he looked right then. His wild eyes darted around in terror, searching for a way out.

She could hear him muttering, "Please God, no. Please God, no. Please God, no."

She wasn't afraid. If anything, she was excited that something new was happening. Being cooped up with Fallon had started to wear on her nerves. It wasn't until she heard the first pops of rifle fire close by that she became scared.

Lieutenant Glover stood in the middle of the cottage, grinding his teeth in frustration. They had arrived too late. The targets had slipped away. There was clear evidence that the cabin had been occupied recently. But it was empty now.

"I'm going to catch hell for this," he muttered. This was the kind of screw up that could set his career back for a long time. It was all he could do not to smash something, anything. To be alone, he ordered his people to search the structure and the clearing outside for any indication of where the targets may have gone.

"Sir?" came a voice from the open door behind him. Glover turned and found Private Brown. "I've got the TOC on the line. They have an update for you, sir."

"Thanks, Brown," Glover said, then he put his helmet back on and returned to his vehicle. He closed the door and keyed the hand mic. "Strike X-ray, this is Phantom 2-6, over."

The reply from the Tactical Operations Center was immediate. "Phantom 2-6, Strike X-ray. Prepare to copy new orders, over."

Glover's heart started beating a little faster. He sat up straighter in his seat as he retrieved his notebook. "Strike X-ray, send it."

"Phantom 2-6, we have a new location for Target Alpha. The white SUV was spotted at a farm ten klicks from your present location. Prepare to copy grid coordinates, over."

Glover wiped his sweat-damp forehead. He had a second chance. "Strike X-ray, Phantom 2-6, standing by to copy grid coordinates."

The voice on the other end rattled off a long string of numbers and Glover read them back to ensure he had gotten them correct. "Phantom 2-6, be advised that Target Alpha is not alone. We have confirmation that he has a civilian with him. All care must be taken to ensure that both individuals are taken alive, over."

"Strike X-ray, that's a solid copy. We will bring them in alive, over."

"Strike X-ray, out."

With that, Glover leapt out of his truck and gathered his people around to inform them of the mission change. "Listen up, we are going mount up and drive ten klicks to another shack. Command says that's where our target is. Same deal as before, you know your fire teams and your assignments. We'll just consider this a rehearsal run. We are to make every effort to bring these people in alive. Questions?" There were none. "Good. Now let's bag this silly son of a bitch and go home! Hoo-ah?"

"Hoo-ah!" the platoon shouted in unison.

A minute later they were back on the road. Ten minutes after that they pulled into the fields around Varney's house, dismounted again and began moving onto their target.

*What will we do? What will we do?*

The thought shrieked through his mind over and over. There was no answer. No help coming. After every near miss and close call God had helped him through, this time Fallon knew he was done for. The enemy had arrived and caught them completely unaware. If they tried to run, he knew the soldiers wouldn't hesitate to cut him and Nurse Christianson in half.

They were almost on the front porch now, every step bringing them closer to him.

*Be patient.*

With that thought, Fallon felt a serene calm settle over him.

*Take cover.*

He rose to a crouch and pulled Shelly away from the window to the rear of the cabin. Then he turned to her and asked, “Where’s the gun?”

A rapid tattoo of gunfire came from outside. Fallon threw himself and Shelly flat, as the front window exploded inward, showering the floor where they’d been huddled only a moment ago with shards of glass.

Lieutenant Glover had almost reached the front door. The men with him were stacking, getting ready move to the door, breach, enter and subdue anyone inside.

From small clump of trees off to his right, he heard a distant voice yell.

The tree line erupted with gunfire and two of the men with him immediately went down. Screams filled the air, as the wounded called for help, and the able-bodied returned fire. Glover himself dropped into a crouch. Behind him came the throaty belch of an M-240B machinegun, as his people returned fire. Someone was shouting near the last truck in line.

Glover scanned the field. There was movement in the clump of trees to the right of the vehicles, more movement in an irrigation ditch running perpendicular to the dirt road they’d come down. His platoon was caught in a perfect intersection of fire. If they didn’t get out, if he didn’t get them out, they were as good as dead.

More popping from his right and the rest of his breach team was down. He turned away from the cabin. He needed to maintain control of the situation, to call for reinforcements and air support. He needed to find some cover. He needed to get control of the situation while he still could. Standing in the open while people were shooting all around was a health hazard. He needed to get back to his truck. Moving in a crouch, he ran back in the direction of the convoy. He could only hear one machine gun still firing.

A high-pitched shriek cut the air. Glover briefly saw a line of smoke lance across the field from the clump of trees and into one of his trucks, where it exploded upon contact. The shock wave from the blast knocked him back.

*That was my truck,* Glover thought. Brown was still inside, monitoring the radio and keeping the TOC apprised of the situation. In slow motion, he watched flames consume the vehicle. Neither Brown, nor his gunner got out. Two people, his people, instantly dead.

Before he could react, a second missile, this time from the irrigation ditch, streaked into another truck as the soldiers inside were getting out. Five more of his people were engulfed in a ball of fire. In an instant, over half of his platoon was gone.

Of the five men who left the vehicles with him, only he was still standing. One was dragging a wounded man to one of the surviving trucks; another was bleeding from a chest wound where a bullet had punched through the soft armor on the side of his vest and screaming for his mother. The other three lay still and silent in the red-soaked snow.

Glover tried to run. The world had slowed down, and his every movement felt like he was standing still. Bullets snapped around him, kicking up gouts of snow. The explosions left his ears ringing. He thought he could hear shouting, but it sounded as though it were coming from a long way away.

Something hit Glover in the side of the head. His helmet was suddenly jerked to the left. Everything went blurry and he toppled to the snow. *This isn't how it's supposed to happen,* was his last thought before darkness claimed him.

When it was over, Benedict and the rest of his little band of patriots entered the clearing and approached the farmhouse.

Benedict barked out orders. "Phillip, Sonny, grab their guns and any ammo they have left. Petra and John, bring the trucks around. The rest of you, keep an eye on the road and shout out if you see any company coming. I'm going to see who's home."

The front window was shattered, and the breeze was gently rustling the curtains hanging inside. Several holes had been punched through the walls by stray bullets. The door flew open when he stepped onto the porch. Before him stood a scrawny, wild-eyed man, holding a pistol at his side.

They stared at each other for a minute before speaking. "Sorry about the ruckus," Benedict said finally, with a smirk.

"Did you kill them all?" the man with the gun asked.

Benedict nodded. "That we did."

"Great." He clapped his hands. "God be praised, that's wonderful."

"Are you in some kind of trouble? I've seen them when they take people into custody and they don't usually employ the kind of firepower they have here for that."

"Yes, we're in trouble. Can you please help us? We need to escape before they come back."

Benedict thought for a second. Then he smiled. "Sure, we can help. Come with us, just to be on the safe side." He liked the idea of coming to the rescue just fine. It made him feel like a hero.

"You'll have to ride with us," Benedict said when they opened the garage. "It looks like your little truck took a bullet or three." Its windows were shot out and so were three of its tires and it was leaking copiously from the engine.

"I see. Well, if it's no trouble, we would love to accept a ride with you. Thank the Lord you've come! Just give me a minute to get my friend and some things."

"Don't take too long now. We knocked them back, but they won't take long to recover. They'll be back soon, pissed off and with a lot more guys."

"We'll hurry." Then the man was gone, back inside the cabin.

Benedict strode back to the waiting truck. His men had already picked the corpses clean and loaded the goods into the back. He wanted the weapons so that he wouldn't have to rely completely on Barney. He was already deep in debt to the gunrunner for the ammo they'd already used, not to mention the two old LAW rockets they'd shot off today. When this was over, he was sure going to have a huge bill to pay. He was simply happy Barney had given him the rockets. Without them, he wasn't sure they'd have been able to take out the platoon as easily as they had. So far, he'd led his people on two completely successful attacks and hadn't lost a single person. He knew that this kind of lucky streak wouldn't last much longer. He intended to enjoy it while he could.

Petra was leaning against the open tailgate looking downcast.

"What's up, Petra?" Benedict asked.

Without a word, she nodded in the direction of the trees. Benedict turned in that direction and stopped after a few steps. The others were all standing over Sonny Dixon, where he lay dead.

Benedict felt as if someone socked him in the chest. *No. Not Sonny!* It took a moment, but with some difficulty, he managed to tear his eyes away from his friend's corpse and get the others moving.

"We have to move on," he told them. "We'll honor him later. But we can't stay here any longer. Petra, make some room in the back of your truck. We just rescued some folks. They're grabbing their things and coming with us."

The others got moving. Benedict took one last look at his friend. Sonny was a good man and a great friend. He quickly wiped the tears from his eyes and got behind the wheel of his SUV.

Three minutes later, the man stepped outside again. Following close behind him was a woman Benedict was sure he recognized. Both were bundled up, and each carried a paper sack of what he figured were clothes or food or some such.

When they reached the Suburban, the man stuck out his hand, "I'm Martin, by the way."

Benedict took his hand. "Nate. It's good to meet you, Martin. That's Phillip and John bringing the bags in, and the chick behind the wheel of the other truck is Petra."

"It's great to meet you all. Thank you again. All of you."

"It's no problem. We're here to protect our home and the people in it." Benedict got a better look at the woman. "You work at the hospital, don't you?" She nodded. "I thought so! I never forget a pretty face." Behind the wheel, Petra snorted and shook her head.

"I'm Shelly," the woman said. "Thank you for rescuing us."

"No problem, honey. No problem at all."

Shelly and Fallon got into their truck and they drove away from the smoking carnage of Varney's Farm.

The feed displayed on the forty-six-inch TV monitor showed two trucks or vans, one black and one red, pulling away from the farmyard. The pilot rotated the camera to track the vehicles. The room was occupied by a dozen officers. They'd witnessed everything live, unable to do anything about it. Dumbstruck by the slaughter, no one spoke. Apprehensive silence filled the space between each of them, so thick it was hard to breathe. No one could speak. Watching the live ambush and murder of a whole platoon was too devastating for words.

"Tell the pilot to stay with them," Aldridge said to his RTO, who relayed the instructions to the pilot of the Unmanned Aerial Vehicle. He turned to a captain standing behind him by the name of Driscoll. His voice was a harsh croak and there were tears in his eyes. "Get the rest of your company ready to move. I want them on the road in ten minutes."

Driscoll composed himself. His face a stoic, blank mask. "Yes, sir," he said. He had just watched one of his platoons get murdered. Aldridge figured it was only right that he and the rest of his company be allowed to get some pay back.

Once Driscoll was gone, the room again sank into

oppressive silence. Aldridge accessed the previous minutes of the drone feed on the computer in front of him. He skipped past the footage of the attack; he couldn't watch it again so soon and paused it just as two figures emerged from the farmhouse. With a little manipulation of the high-resolution footage, their faces were revealed. The first one was Fallon; of that he had no doubt. The other person looked like the nurse they had been looking for and assumed to be dead, Shelly Christianson. But there was no way that could be her. She had been exposed the first night, weeks ago. She should be dead.

He picked up the phone and called down to the motor pool. When Captain Driscoll came on the line, Aldridge gave him new orders. "Captain, when you get there, you'll find a woman with them. Take her into custody and bring her directly to me. I'm extremely interested in her."

Collins stormed into Aldridge's operations center, yelling the minute he learned of the ambush, startling one young private nearly out of his skin. It took several minutes, but Aldridge managed to convince the general to continue the discussion in his office.

Once the door closed, the yelling resumed. "You arrogant, stupid, incompetent son of a bitch! How could you send a single platoon out there without support for a mission of this magnitude?"

"The situation was unfolding rapidly. I was counting on surprise to cover my men," Aldridge said calmly. "I don't have the extra manpower to mount a proper assault, while still keeping the town pacified. I've had to make do with what I have available."

Collins waved a hand dismissively. "Another excuse. That's all I get from you. Shitty little excuses. You've botched this operation since day one. All you had to do was catch one man and you've failed repeatedly."

"With all due respect, sir, it hasn't been that easy."

"Of course, it was that easy. He's one man! And you've let him outsmart and outmaneuver you three times."

"Fallon is smart, and he is desperate. He's managed to slip away every time we get close. The problem hasn't been merely catching Fallon, I've had the difficult task of cleaning up after him, as well as tracking his movements. Every time he reaches a new city, we've had to fully support the local population, in addition to the manhunt. It hasn't been easy. My people are tired."

"More excuses. It's always something with you, isn't it, Colonel? Can't you stand up and take responsibility for your fuckups just once? Now what about these attacks? Do you have even the slightest idea, any idea at all, who's behind them?"

Aldridge folded his arms across his chest. "Actually, we do."

Collins waited for Aldridge to continue. "Well?" he demanded when Aldridge didn't.

"I have people handling the situation as we speak."

"Give me the details."

Aldridge grinned and shook his head. "I have no reason to tell you. My orders give me full autonomy here. I don't answer to you... Sir."

"Watch yourself, Colonel. You've got the rope in your hands now. Don't mistakenly hang yourself with it."

"And make your life easier? I wouldn't dream of giving a prick like you the satisfaction."

Face red, Collins turned on a heel and slammed the door behind him. He'd had enough. He'd spent too many years being snubbed by that insufferable man. It was time to take care of Aldridge for good. He'd crossed the line way too far this time. All it would take is a phone call. But first things first, he crossed the hall and knocked on another door, then entered without waiting for permission.

Major Panelli looked up, then snapped to attention. "Sir,

how can I help you, sir?"

"Relax, Major. Sit down." Collins put on his best lying-at-a-congressional-hearing smile. "I'd like to discuss some things with you."

"Like what kind of things, sir?"

"Like, Colonel Aldridge's mishandling of this whole operation, his disregard for the safety of the people under his command, and how his drug use and other bad personal choices have been jeopardizing this mission from the get-go. A task this important needs to be handled by someone better suited. Someone who's not a burned-out addict. He has many of the more junior officers in his pocket, and they'll back him up if I try to relieve him. It would complicate matters. But I think I know of one officer who is willing to do his duty, without letting personal feelings interfere."

"Sir?" Major Panelli looked up at Collins like a child lost in a supermarket; worried, confused, afraid of what was happening around him.

*What an idiot,* Collins thought. "Major, we need to ensure that the success of this operation is the number one priority here. We need to bring Fallon in and rid this town of the disease afflicting it. Up to this point, Colonel Aldridge has been unable to accomplish either of these tasks. But as I said, I think I know of an officer who can."

Panelli's eyes narrowed. "I don't quite follow, sir."

Collins rolled his eyes. *Do I really have to spell it out for you, moron?* "Yes, I think you do. I'm talking about a change in leadership here. But I need to know if I can count on you, Major. Your assistance in the matter will be greatly appreciated and generously rewarded."

Collins could almost hear the click as everything suddenly made sense to him. Panelli smiled. "Have a seat, sir."

The house was a two-story cube, with a wraparound porch, sitting on two acres of open land, backed up to the largest municipal park. A scattering of trees lined the edges of the property like a natural fence. Behind the house was a barn, converted into a garage. In which sat two sport utility vehicles. The place was modestly furnished. Almost spartan. There was a big TV and a shelf of movies in the front room, but no other decorations. Except for the coffee maker, the kitchen seemed unused, save for the counter lined with bottles of Old Crow whiskey. Three of the four bedrooms in the house were completely unfurnished, and the master bedroom only contained a queen sized bed, a dresser, and a hamper for dirty clothes. Like a blank canvas, the interior of the house was almost completely devoid of decoration and personality.

The basement, on the other hand, was set up in stark contrast. Where the rest of the house was a blank slate, the walls of the basement were covered with maps and photos, charts, and diagrams. There were street maps of Harper's Glen and topographical maps of the surrounding countryside. Each of these was marked to show patrol routes and times. There were spread sheets listing unit names and strengths. An incomplete roster of military personnel. Each picture portrayed a different individual in uniform, many of them taken from quite a distance away. Beneath each photo was a brief biography of the individual pictured. The whole space was organized and divided by function, for the purpose of waging war against the soldiers occupying the town.

To Shelly, it was like stepping into the war room of a military command post.

Benedict had been busy since the army came to town. Thanks to Eddie Tate and his network, he'd put together a nearly complete picture of the military operation in Harper's Glen.

"Welcome to my Command Post," he said, with a smile and a welcoming wave of his hand. "It's not much. I try to keep it light and mobile in case they find out my location and come to take me out. If that happens, I can pop smoke and relocate through this bolt hole here in as little as ten minutes." He indicated a passage on the far wall, partially hidden behind a bookcase. The first thing he'd done after he started growing pot in his basement, was to dig out a narrow tunnel leading past the edge of his property in case he needed to make a getaway. At the time, he hadn't imagined that he would ever use it, but it made him feel safer knowing it was there. And his VA therapist had always impressed upon him the need to feel safe in his surroundings.

"Impressive," Fallon said. He was looking around the room with guarded awe.

Shelly didn't know what to say. She was grateful for Benedict's help escaping, but felt she was being drawn deeper and deeper into a nightmare.

"I'm working on decentralizing our operation. That way if some of us are taken out, the rest of us will be able to continue the fight." Benedict seemed almost gleeful as he talked with them about his operation, like a child showing off his brand-new bike to a stranger outside the supermarket. "We'll keep on fighting until they're completely gone, driven away from our homes."

Fallon had moved to the wall of photos. "That's their commander, Colonel Aldridge, right there," he said, pointing to a fuzzy picture in the middle of the wall.

Shelly peered over his shoulder, trying to get a good look at the monster who had started the terrible nightmare her life had become. In her estimation, Aldridge didn't look at all like she'd envisioned. He was average height and had a slight build. His hair was dark brown, turning to gray. It was a bad picture, but she could see he was athletic and kind of handsome in a tired way. The picture was taken from a distance, so she couldn't see any more details. Seeing him, however, dredged up a deep anger in her.

*What right does he have taking over my town and cutting us off from the rest of the country? Hunting Fallon and me like animals and attacking us?*

Suddenly, she very much wanted to see him in pain. Writhing in agony for what he'd done to her life. She wanted to destroy him.

Fallon put names to the photos of several other officers.

"This is good to know," Benedict said. "Seems to me, rescuing you was the best thing I could have done. Thank you." He glanced at Shelly, saw her shivering slightly and mistook her rage for a chill. "I'm so sorry. You must still be cold; how rude of me not to offer you anything to warm you up." He gestured to a thermos and offered her coffee. Taking a sip, she smiled at how good it tasted. "I got tired of caffeinated brown piss-water in the army. Now I only buy expensive, good coffee."

"Thanks," Shelly murmured. The surreal feeling when she'd first agreed to help Fallon had returned full force, overwhelming her. Everything she saw and heard had a dream-like quality. She wandered away from the coffee pot and over by the doorway. There she stood and watched the others, dislocated, as if in a faraway dream.

Benedict and Fallon had moved to the large town map and were discussing how best to escape the army's barricade. The two were talking like old friends. Fallon made a joke and Benedict leaned back, laughing. Shelly had trouble reconciling the violence that occurred not even an hour ago with the warm cheeriness around her. Now that the slaughter was behind them, everyone seemed to have forgotten all about it.

Fallon was giving them a little bit of background on the officers he'd previously named, who oversaw which patrols and what trucks they were driving, using the pictures pinned next to the street map.

"How is it you know so much about their operation?" Benedict asked. "It's taken us weeks just to identify their line officers."

"I know what I know, because I'm the man they're

hunting."

Benedict stopped cold. Friendly smile immediately erased and replaced with a suspicious glare.

"You? You brought them here?"

Fallon saw the change in Benedict's demeanor and quickly tried to calm him. "Hold on. Let me explain—"

But Benedict didn't hold on. "Yes! Please explain to me just exactly why you brought the United States Army here to infringe upon my personal liberties. Dozens have disappeared already into that damned hospital, never to be seen again! They're snatching people off the streets in broad daylight. Please explain how this happened. I would love to hear it!" He turned his head to cough violently into the crook of his elbow. Then he straightened up and fixed Fallon with a death glare. The rest of his people had entered the room, summoned by their leader's raised voice, armed, and glaring.

Fallon looked at each of them and backed away, hands raised. "Please, you don't understand. I'm not your enemy. I can help you." His desperate eyes gleamed with real fear as he backed away into the far corner.

Shelly was completely forgotten as they pressed closer to Fallon, passing her by as though she weren't even there. Her heart beat faster as she watched her life take another nightmare dive.

Jones' squad went in. They had driven to within one hundred yards of the objective, where she, Sergeant Jackson, Kowalski and Turner, joined by the dismounts from the truck behind them, hiked the remaining distance. The rest of the platoon circled around the target area, securing it to ensure there was no ambush awaiting them. Another platoon from her company was clearing the roads even farther out. Once the security cordon was in place, it was time to clear out the insurgents that had been making so much trouble. With the rest of her squad, Jones scanned the area for threats, until

Sergeant Jackson motioned them in.

With their weapons ready, they quickly crossed the open distance between the trucks and the building. With smooth, well-practiced motions, they stacked up outside the front door, Kowalski in front, then her, then Jackson, with Turner bringing up the rear. Jones felt a tap on her shoulder from Sargent Jackson, the signal to go, and tapped Kowalski. He gave a slight nod and tapped her back to show he understood, and she passed that signal back along to Jackson. A moment later, Kowalski kicked in the door, and as one they moved through the door and into the enemy house.

Once through the fatal funnel, each of them peeled off to clear a corner of the first room. When they were all set and deemed the room was secure, a second team entered the house and immediately moved to the stairway leading to the second floor. A third team followed behind them and started clearing the rest of the ground floor as Jones' team stacked up again to clear the kitchen and the backside of the house.

Her heart raced. The fear and anticipation of what lay in the next room never dampened or went away. No matter how many times she did it, room clearing, in training and in real life, it was still terrifying for her... In training, she had been to a shoot house numerous times and cleared dozens of rooms. She herself had been "killed" more times than she could count. Even with blanks and plywood enemies, room clearing was stressful and nerve wracking. But the training paid off. Although women were technically barred from combat roles, in Iraq she had to conduct missions that involved clearing houses of suspected terrorists and had been forced to engage in close quarters combat three times. Each time, she counted herself lucky that she had come through alive.

This house was perfect. The lack of furniture and decoration limited the number of blind spots for someone to hide in and attack from. It almost felt like she was just going through another training session in a shoot house. The adage,

"Train like you fight, and fight like you train," occurred to her as her fire team stacked to clear the kitchen.

In the kitchen they could hear muffled shouting from behind the door leading to the basement. She signaled Jackson and pointed to the door. He listened for a moment, nodded, and signaled the rest of them. They stacked up for the third time, ready to open the door and descend into the basement.

It had been twenty seconds since the initial breach. Twenty seconds without contact. Jones knew this would be it. She could hear the other two teams shuffling around in other parts of the house. They hadn't found anything either. Jones suspected that when she and her team went down those stairs, they would find the fuckers responsible for the slaughter at the farm. Then they would kill them. Her breath through the protective mask's regulator was loud and heavy in her ears. She couldn't see the faces of any of the rest of her team, but she knew they were feeling the same things as she. Kowalski quietly opened the door, and then they were moving.

From her place by the door, Shelly heard a thump followed by a muffled crash and the sounds of shuffling feet upstairs. Everyone else was distracted by Benedict shouting at Fallon and wasn't aware that someone had entered the house.

"Excuse me," she said, "I think something's happening upstairs."

No one heard her. Benedict was standing close and pointing a finger in Fallon's face. To his credit, Fallon didn't flinch or back down.

She heard footsteps on the stairs. Without thinking, Shelly dropped her coffee cup and crouched down against the wall. Seconds later, the first of four gasmask and camouflage-clad figures burst into the room.

The sounds of shouting and gunfire was deafening in the small space. The first soldier through the door shot Petra twice in the chest. The second soldier shot Philip, who was standing just a couple steps away from Benedict and Fallon. John was the third to fall, bleeding from the chest and stomach. One by one, as the soldiers filled the room, Benedict's little army fell dead. Most of them never even had a chance to raise their weapons. The soldiers, moving with robotic precision, cut each of them down before they could get a shot off.

Benedict was the last to die. He managed to get a hold of a rifle and squeezed a three-round burst from the M-4 carbine he'd taken off a dead soldier that morning into the leading attacker. Two bullets struck the lead soldier in his hard frontal chest armor. He would have survived with some bruising, maybe a broken rib or two, if it hadn't been for the third shot that punched through his throat. He fell, sputtering and gurgling. The two soldiers behind him pumped a dozen rounds into Benedict. Knocking him around like a rag doll before he crumpled to the floor in a limp heap.

It wasn't as dramatic as the gun shots on TV were. No lingering echo. No slow-motion heroics. Once started, the action ended with startling suddenness. Leaving Shelly hiding in the corner. The smell of spent gunpowder lingered in the air, almost causing her to gag. The sharp ringing in her ears made her head hurt. Shelly thought she heard someone talking to her. She didn't care. She wouldn't acknowledge these men who'd just shot and killed more of her neighbors. Then she was hauled to her feet, flex-cuffed and rushed from the charnel room. Before she was through the door, she risked a last backward glance. She'd known these people. They weren't close, but she'd lived here long enough to have treated several of them at work. Also, being a new, young, and attractive woman in a small town garnered a lot of attention from the opposite sex. Men like these. Now they were dead, and she acutely felt the loss.

Outside she was placed in an idling Humvee and it sped away. Shelly knew exactly where they were taking her.

The hospital.

Jones couldn't believe how smoothly it went. They'd stacked up outside, kicked the door and entered, just like the hundreds of repetitions they'd completed in the live-fire range. As the second soldier in the room, she even personally dropped two of the murderers herself: a fat man and an ugly bitch. The last fucker in the room was the only one who got a shot off at them, hitting Kowalski and dropping him. But Jackson and Kowalski shot him up, turning him into a stain on the floor.

Now that it was over and she was coming down from the adrenaline high, she felt drained. Her heart was still pumping hard and she was breathing heavy through her mask. The threats in the room had been neutralized, Jones turned to find Kowalski bleeding and gasping for breath and rushed to her friend's side. His body heaved in pain. She tried to staunch the bleeding from his neck by pressing her left hand over the wound. With her right, she tore off her mask and dug into Kowalski's medical kit for his quick clot gauze. The material was impregnated with a substance that clotted upon contact with blood and was effective at sealing combat wounds.

"Medic!" Jones screamed, before tearing open the packet with her teeth.

As she pressed the gauze against Kowalski's neck, she could already see it was too late. His eyes had glassed over, and he was staring up into the great nothing beyond her. Her heart lurched and tears welled up in her eyes. Her only friend in the unit—the only real friend she'd made since coming back from Afghanistan—was gone. Another, in a long line of empty places in her heart. She slumped back, almost fell over. It wasn't fair. Kowalski was the only one in the unit that she could talk to. The only one who understood her.

Numb, she looked around and saw Sergeant Jackson trying to talk to an unarmed woman hiding in the corner.

"Ma'am, are you okay? Have you been injured?" he asked.

Jones could tell he was trying to remain calm, but his blood was up and full of adrenaline, so the moron was yelling right in her face.

The woman didn't reply. She only stared at the dead bodies crumpled around the room.

He shook her shoulder. "Ma'am, are you hurt?"

Still nothing.

Shaking her head, Jones stepped up beside him and touched his arm. He turned aside so she could handle the woman on the floor.

She didn't resist when Jones pulled her to her feet, or when she flex-cuffed her and escorted her out of the house to a waiting vehicle. Their orders were to capture two individuals, this woman and Fallon. Jones recognized her from the circulated photos, but there was no sign of the guy they were looking for. Still, orders were orders, and Jones sent her on her way to the hospital. At least they'd gotten the bastards who had shot up the other platoon. Word was that these were the guys responsible for the IED ambush earlier that week, too.

Jones felt good about that. The idea of killing people ran contrary to her nature, but she knew these people were murderers. If she and her team hadn't stopped them, then in all likelihood they would have continued planting bombs and killing people. Eliminating people like them and protecting people who couldn't protect themselves was the reason she'd joined the army in the first place. But all the grief she endured had soured the experience for her. She was tired of the bullshit. Tired of the institutional hypocrisy, of idiots being promoted over her, of all the useless crap she had to deal with on a daily basis. Mostly though, she was tired of the people she cared about being taken from her. She was done with it. Her term was almost up. Just as soon as they returned to base, once this nightmare was over, she was going to start the long process of getting out of the army.

The army had taken enough from her. She was done. It

was time to move on and start fresh.

The drive was uneventful. Even though they'd taken out the insurgent cell, the soldiers were still on full alert as they drove through the narrow, snow covered streets. Nobody spoke to her. The only break in the silence was the occasional crackle from the radio.

When they arrived, Shelly was removed from the vehicle and escorted through the EMT entrance into the ER triage area. The familiar beige halls and rooms with their pastel floral prints felt strange to her now. Like a different world. The whole staff appeared to be at work today and Saint John's was crowded and bustling and frantic. The waiting area had been converted into a triage zone, divided by clear plastic isolation curtains. People wearing surgical masks were everywhere, sitting, laying down, or pacing around sick. A cacophony of coughs and painful moaning greeted her inside. Behind the emergency room doors, Shelly heard the frenzied sounds of her coworkers struggling to treat and save more sick patients. She caught sight of more than a few familiar faces as she was led, still flex-cuffed, to an observation room. There she was seated and made to wait until another nurse, Anne Littlewolf, came in and gave a small, surprised gasp. She glanced from Shelly to the armed soldiers in the exam room and back again before she composed herself and silently went to work examining Shelly and checking her into the hospital.

Blood was drawn, mouth swabs collected, and a urine sample taken. The process was over in twenty minutes. Then Shelly was led out of the frenetic ER and through the busy hospital to a consultation room, which had been converted into a makeshift office. She was seated and locked inside with one of her escorts.

There she waited.

According to the clock on the wall, it was nearly three o'clock. An hour had passed in silence since the guard wasn't talking to her, and she felt no inclination to try speaking to him. She just sat there, staring at the wall until she had started to doze off. She was thinking about laying down on the cot in the corner when the door opened, and two new soldiers entered. Unlike the others she'd seen, they wore no protective masks, suits, or gloves. One of them was leafing through a thin manila folder as he circled the room and sat down behind the desk, where he continued reading, while the other remained standing. After a few minutes, she realized she recognized the soldier sitting before her. She remembered his picture from Benedict's lair. She was looking at Preston Aldridge, the man responsible for everything she'd been through for the last two weeks.

Aldridge signed one of the pages in the file and handed it to the officer standing next to the desk. "That will be all for now, Captain."

"Yes, sir." Captain West accepted the folder and paused to look at Shelly for a moment before departing.

Aldridge then motioned to the guard standing behind her. "Cut off her cuffs and wait outside." A minute later her hands were free, and she was alone with the man responsible for this whole shitty situation.

Aldridge watched her for a moment, then removed another folder from his desk and started reading. He leafed through the file for another five minutes before he closed it and looked up. "We'll, you'll be happy to know that you're in good health. You've been vaccinated against the virus. The worrying part, however, is now you're a carrier. The doctors are working on isolating the specific virus genes to come up with a new version of the vaccine, which should completely cure you. This may take a little bit of time and they may need to get more tissue samples from you. This way you won't transmit the virus to anyone you meet."

Shelly hadn't the faintest notion what he was talking

about. Rather than incriminate herself, she held her peace, with her hands folded in her lap.

Aldridge and Shelly faced each other across the desk. He impassively watched her glare back at him. He had no doubt at all that she hated him. It was written all over her face. Aldridge almost smiled. Fallon had changed tactics on him. Now the bastard was enlisting help among the people he was killing. This woman had no idea what she was doing. Fallon, like all good con artists, had completely duped her using the truth, which was more convincing than any lie.

"Nurse Christianson," he began again. "We need your help finding Fallon. Thousands of lives are in danger, millions maybe. The longer he's at large, the more dangerous he becomes."

"Why is he dangerous?" she demanded. "Because he's a threat to you and your project? Because he's going to expose your entire monstrous operation, the horrible experiments you've been subjecting people to?"

"He's dangerous to everyone—"

"I'm not convinced he's a danger to anyone. It is men like you, Colonel, who operate outside the law and conduct illegal biological experiments in weapons development labs, who create these nightmares. *You're* the one who's out of control. *You're* the one who's dangerous."

"If you'll let me explain—"

"There's nothing you need to explain," she interrupted for the second time. "I know everything. You were the leader of the project that spread this disease here. You created this plague. I've seen what's been happening in town. Innocent people dying in the streets, either killed by your virus or shot by your soldiers. Even children are trapped and unable to protect themselves from this hell you've created. All to protect yourself. I know all about you, Colonel Aldridge."

Shelly knew she should stop. Knew that this man held her life in his hands. That he could make her disappear with the slightest gesture. If imprisoning an entire town was easy for a man like him, then it would take almost no effort at all for him to dispose of her. She knew she should feel afraid of him. But she wasn't. Instead, all she felt was anger. White hot rage at everything Colonel Aldridge had done, to her, to her neighbors, to her home. She seethed with it. Let it spew forth. A torrent of rancor that she was powerless to stop.

"You're a monster," she continued. "Now you've cut us off and you're killing us, to protect your ass and cover up the truth. You'll wipe us all out without a second thought. Fallon said he'd already killed the project director; it's a shame he couldn't have managed to get you, too.

Aldridge suddenly snapped and slammed his fist onto the desk. "Would you shut up and listen for a minute!"

"Or what?" she demanded. "You'll silence me too, just like you want to silence Fallon? Get rid of all evidence and witnesses to cover up your crimes. If I'm going to die anyway, I don't see any reason to keep silent."

Aldridge trembled with indignation, but also felt embarrassed by his tantrum. The stress, the deaths, the lack of sleep, the pain, it was all gaining on him. He closed his eyes and took several slow, deep breaths. When he opened them again, he reached into the bottom drawer of his desk and removed a thick folder. "Read this," he said, sliding it across the desk to her.

"I don't want to read any of your lies. I—"

"Please, just read it."

Maybe it was the pleading sincerity in his voice. Maybe it was the changeover from screaming at her to asking politely. Maybe it was just plain old curiosity. Shelly took the folder.

"You think you have the truth, Ms. Christianson. But you don't. Not the whole truth. Fallon fed you what he thought would convince you to help him. The whole truth is much more frightening." Before Aldridge had seemed like a man struggling to maintain control and not doing a good job of it.

Now he just looked tired. "Look at those pictures on the top. What do you see?"

She couldn't speak. The gruesome scenes in front of her were unspeakable. Full color photos of corpses. There were documentary-style photos which showed the progression of the illness in the patients. Life stills of sick people in glass cages surrounded by blood and filth, or strapped to beds and bleeding from their eyes, nose and mouths, their faces frozen in time as they wailed in agony. Finally, autopsy shots showing the victims mid vivisection open and being examined from the inside out.

"Look at the back. Flip the photo over." Aldridge was back at his desk and had removed a pill bottle. He shook out several pills and dry-swallowed them.

Shelly did as she was bidden. On the back were handwritten notes, descriptions of the images in the picture, terribly detailed and clinically detached. Also listed were the names and vital statistics of each person pictured.

"Look at the signature at the bottom. Whose name is that?"

She couldn't believe what she was seeing. Once again, her world, everything she knew, had been turned upside down.

The notes on the back of the photo were signed: Martin Fallon, Project Director.

The emergency patient ward in the high school gym was a dismal affair. Rows of beds lined up beneath harsh florescent lights. Each one sealed off from the outside air by a clear plastic curtain. Inside was the standard ICU equipment: EKG and heart monitors and breathing machines. The beds themselves emptied almost as quickly as they were filled. Scurrying up and down the rows and between the beds, the hospital staff and army medical personnel fought a losing battle against the disease. The next shipment of vaccine was delayed again due to the weather. Helicopters couldn't fly, and ground convoys got stuck as the area was attacked by yet another round of storms. Without the medicine, there was little the doctors could do except make each victim comfortable until they succumbed.

Anne Littlewolf was the most experienced nurse on staff, and even she was starting to feel the strain of watching her friends and neighbors fall ill, then die. After the first hellish eighty-four-hour shift, her mask of professionalism had started to crack. At night, after she went home, she lay awake in tears, unable to sleep till it was nearly morning and time to rise to do it all over again. She, like the rest of the staff, had been inoculated and was therefore immune and safe. But her immunity only made it harder to see her patients suffer. No matter what she did, she couldn't save them.

The most difficult patient she had was David Wessex. He was going to die, he knew it, she knew it, and they both knew there was nothing that could be done to stop it. He'd been one of the early cases, having contracted the virus while shopping at Walmart. That he'd held on this long was something of a miracle. He wasn't a difficult patient because he made life hard on Anne or the rest of the staff. Nor was his case particularly different from the other dozens of cases currently being treated. He merely lay in his bed, quiet, watching the world around him through the transparent barrier. He was difficult only to Anne, and only because she loved him. Seeing him in the isolation tent day after day, laying in agony on the mobile hospital bed, broke her heart.

They'd known each other since they were kids. They went to school together from kindergarten to high school, but never really ran in the same circles. After graduation, they went on to lead separate and unrelated lives. If it weren't for a chance meeting at a mutual friend's New Year's party last year, they might never have noticed each other at all. They met near the punch bowl, then spent the rest of night together talking and laughing. After the ball dropped, he suggested they go to his place. Slightly drunk and willing to take an uninhibited risk, Anne agreed. When she left in the morning, David promised he'd call her, and she was surprised when he did the next day. She was even more surprised that she answered. A coffee date was arranged to see if they could tolerate each other without alcoholic assistance. It turned out they could. She found him just as charming and funny as he had been at the party, more so because they were both sober and coherent.

A few dates later and they went to bed together again. Their affair burned like passionate fire and she thought he might be considering popping the question to her. They clicked in every way that mattered. In their short time together, they had grown to quickly desire and even need each other. They'd started planning a future.

When the army rolled into town twelve days ago, she had been shocked to see David's name on the patient list along with the other people hauled in. Shocked and scared. The nightmare was still early enough for her to be hopeful. The disease was still new, and she thought the army would supply them with the necessary medicine to save David and the others. But that hadn't happened. Anne grew more depressed each day that passed without the promised cure.

She often found herself at David's bedside while she made her rounds. Checking and rechecking his chart, making sure he was comfortable. At first, she was chatty and flirty with him, even optimistic about his chances. She was a naturally upbeat person, which David claimed was part of what made him fall for her. She wanted to make sure his every need was met, but she also missed him: his voice, his eyes, the touch of his hand on the back of her neck. So, she made every excuse to go by his bed as often as possible.

As the days passed, she felt more and more drained. Anne didn't smile or laugh anymore. She didn't chat or joke with her patients anymore. The easy smile she always wore was nowhere to be seen. Her eyes were hollow, ringed by deep, dark bags and constantly bloodshot from the crying and lack of sleep. Worry lines had etched her cheeks from frowning. Her shoulders were slumped, and her head hung low.

She looked defeated.

She was defeated.

So it was, on the day Shelly Christianson was brought into the hospital under guard, Anne left the ER to be at David's bedside at the end when he took his final, ragged breath. After taking tissue samples from Shelly for testing, she forgot all about her coworker, she didn't know or care what had happened to Shelly during the last two weeks. She only wanted to be with David. Even in his sorry state, the sight of him filled a need in her heart. She stood at the foot of his bed, desperately not looking at him. It broke her heart watching him deteriorate before her eyes. Dozens of new cases had come and gone, too many deaths, with too many more on the way. Still her David clung to life. Above and beyond what the army doctors had said was possible. She even held out the hope that he might recover on his own. That he was special and would survive his ordeal and rejoin her and the life they wanted to build.

His condition took a turn the previous night at 0438. David was circling the drain.

Anne arrived just in time. His eyes were clouded from pain medication. The dosage was so high, she doubted he even knew where or who he was anymore. Sensing his end was near, Anne broke quarantine protocol and opened his isolation curtain to hold his hand. If any of the other nurses or doctors noticed her kneeling beside him with her head bowed, holding his hand, they didn't say anything.

She stayed by his side that way for several minutes. Her gaze drifted from the flat lines on the monitor, to the stillness of his chest, to his vacant, staring eyes. She didn't cry. This surprised her. The love of her life was dead before her, but she had no more tears to shed. They had all dried up. She felt empty. Hollow.

After a few minutes of watching David, she let go of his hand, signed off on his chart, added a notation for Mortuary Affairs to come and dispose of his body. Before leaving his bedside, she leaned over, gave him one final kiss, and said goodbye before leaving the hospital for good.

When she got home, she lay down in her bed and calmly inserted the syringe containing three hundred milligrams of morphine she'd smuggled from the hospital into her arm and went to sleep forever.

Fallon had to keep moving. The more time he spent stationary, the greater the chance of Aldridge finding him. He cursed his own foul luck. Despite his every effort, here he was, back at square one. Worse than square one. Before, he'd had a car and the means to escape. Then he'd had Nurse Christianson to help him. Now, he was trapped in this small shit hole town on foot and on his own. The colonel was closer than ever before. Fallon could feel him breathing down his neck. He'd almost trapped Fallon twice today.

The chase would go on and on. Forever. Until one or the other of them grew too tired to carry on. Then there would be blood and retribution. Fallon knew this from the start. He knew in his heart he'd never be able to outrun Aldridge forever. The man was possessed with a maniacal fury and would never stop till he ran Fallon into the ground. Fallon was tired and scared and alone. It seemed like every step he took brought him two steps closer to capture. Close to despair, he wanted to just sit down and give up. But he knew he couldn't. His was a holy mission, and he had to see it through. He didn't have to evade Aldridge forever. Just long enough to spread the word of God far enough to be unstoppable. He wasn't even sure he would be able to do that now. He was out of ideas and out of hope. His one ally was in the enemy's clutches.

Fallon didn't like the idea of abandoning Shelly

Christianson without discovering what had happened to her.

*You can't save her.*

"I have to try. She's the only other person who can continue my work, once I'm gone."

*Forget about her. She's lost in the enemy camp. Your only option is to run.*

"I'm tired of running."

*The work is before you. You've barely begun.*

"I know. Believe me, I know. I need to go someplace to think."

*Go to her house. You will be safe there for a time.*

"All right."

Fallon started in what he thought was the direction of Shelly's home. After a block or two, he pulled the phone book map he'd torn that first night to set himself on the correct path. Her home was just a little over a mile away. With army patrols out in force looking for him, the journey would be perilous. They knew approximately where he was and were scouring the streets for him. Still, he was confident he could make it. The Lord had gotten him this far; he wouldn't be abandoned this time, either.

The more she read, the more horrified she became. The file in her hands was written in clinical terms, but the experiments described within turned her stomach. Even though the details were sanitized, and the victims just nameless numbers, reduced to facts and figures on dispassionate data charts, Shelly could picture each one; their pasts, dreams and stolen lives. She could feel the pain they had been forced to endure. Brad had always mocked her overdeveloped sense of empathy. The discomfort or failure of others wasn't something that concerned him. If it didn't contribute directly to his success and his life, then it wasn't real. Shelly wasn't built that way. She gave personal attention to every patient she attended. She shared in their troubles and pain. While in her care, they became hers. This was why she couldn't imagine how a highly educated man like Fallon, could commit the outrages described in the bland paperwork before her.

For five years, Fallon was project director, developing and weaponizing the virus that had been unleashed upon her town—that he had unleashed. Nearly all the notes and analysis were his, as well as the recommendations for future lines of research. Ostensibly, the project was begun in response to reports of a similar project underway in North Korea. They had been originally tasked with developing a vaccine, not the virus itself. In the early stages, the defense of the American public was the driving concern. It was Fallon who made the case that to better understand what they were dealing with and to develop more effective defenses, they needed to cultivate the actual live virus. Even after that, the work done was still benign and defensive in nature. Somewhere in the middle of the second year, however, their focus began to change, as Fallon began steering their work in more sinister directions.

"What happened during the second year?" she asked.

"Success and tragedy." Aldridge was seated back behind his desk, rubbing his leg. Even though he seemed calm, he was still agitated and with every step his limp, which was barely noticeable before, became more pronounced. "His research was moving at an extraordinary rate. Everything was falling into place. Doctor Fallon pushed hard to move the project to early human trials. When Phase II was approved, the success rate continued unabated. Thirty test subjects were gathered, from the dregs of society: homeless, drug addicts, criminals on death row and such. They were officially disappeared and brought to us. I think this put a great deal of strain on him, which caused him to snap when he suffered a personal tragedy later that year. I think this was what pushed him over the edge."

"You're talking about his wife's death?"

"He told you about that, huh? Yes, that's just what I'm referring to. After she died, he began to withdraw from his colleagues. He became more secretive and suspicious of others.

"In the back of that folder are Doctor Fallon's personal notes on the project. They read like the official notes in the report. After her death, his notes on the human trials began to take on an apocalyptic tone. Several times he mentions God and what He would think of the work they were doing. You see, he was raised in an extremely religious household. His mother was domineering and abusive. He was taken into foster care at the age of nine. According to the psychological reports I was given access to after he ran away from us, he had blocked away most of what she'd done to him. But the loss of his wife seems to have brought it all back. He was a genius and excelled at school. He was working for a pharmaceutical company when the government asked him to head up this project. After reading his notes and interviewing his colleagues, the head shrinkers think he snapped. He became a recluse, worked all the time, spending fifteen to eighteen hours a day in his labs. His loss, plus the stress of the human trials, convinced him that humanity didn't deserve to continue. In his later entries, he talks about finding God in his work and carrying the 'holy vessel,' as he called it, to the ignorant masses, in order to wipe the earth clean and start anew."

Shelly shook her head, unable to believe that the man she knew could think like that. "I've spent the last two weeks with him. He didn't seem crazy or talk about God or wiping out the human race. Not once. Just under great strain from being hunted."

"What did he talk about with you?"

Shelly hesitated. "Not much, actually. Mostly he talked about you and the army. We discussed plans for getting away.

He said more than once that you specifically were the cause of everything that was happening. He claimed you were chasing him because of what he knew. He claimed he wanted to show the world exactly what you were doing."

"He wasn't lying there. But he wasn't telling you the whole truth, either. Nearly a month ago, he'd become erratic and hostile at work. He was abusive and secretive. A few of the doctors working under him began to suspect he was working on something on the side. Something he wasn't telling anyone else about. When they brought their suspicions to me, I ordered his room, office, computers, and labs thoroughly searched. We acted too late. Turns out he had already completed the work alone and he was working on a mutant strain, one that would infect, but not kill, allowing the person carrying it to freely spread the disease without succumbing. In his room and on his computer, we found literature about a woman named Mary Mallon."

Shelly recognized the name but couldn't place it. "Who's that?"

"Mary Mallon is commonly known as Typhoid Mary."

It clicked and her jaw dropped, as the implications of what he was telling her settled in.

"You mean to tell me he's infected himself and he's trying to spread it as far and wide as he can?"

Aldridge nodded. "What I'm telling you, is that he's infected himself and now you, to spread this virus as far and wide as he can. We've been chasing him for over a month now, cleaning up after him. This is the third town he's taken refuge in and attacked with his virus. Ever since he ran, we've been manufacturing the vaccine around the clock. We just can't get it here because of the damn weather."

She thought about when she became mysteriously ill. Fallon had admitted to giving her something that had made her sick. "He said he'd given me the cure to the virus you were spreading."

"He did. He also made you like him. Now you're a carrier, immune to the effects of the disease. You'll spread it without growing sick yourself. Now that we have a sample of your blood, we can begin manufacturing a more refined version of our vaccine."

Her mind was reeling. So much had changed, and she simply wasn't prepared to deal with it. She felt like a ping pong ball being knocked back and forth. Part of her wanted to believe what she was being told, but part of her still didn't trust Aldridge, and still another part of her refused to believe either of them. Her mind was at war with her heart and her instincts were taking pot shots at both sides. She was completely at a loss for what to do and how to feel.

She couldn't understand how someone could be so evil. Even Brad hadn't been the monster Fallon had turned out to be. He beat her, cheated on her, and dominated every facet of her life, but he wasn't out to harm total strangers. He just had a fetish for control and pain. To everyone else he was a great guy: handsome, charming and witty. It was only towards her that he showed his true nature. The only people Brad harmed, other than her of course, were those he felt were in the way of his goals, or had wronged him in some way. Fallon, on the other hand, was indiscriminate in how he caused harm to others. Slowly she came to grips with what Fallon was. Though they were completely different, both men were similar in their appetite for anguish. Brad hid himself from the world behind a dazzling smile and only she saw the monster beneath. Fallon had hidden his true nature from her and intended to use her to further his monstrous schemes. She felt like crying. She had been made a fool of twice, even though she should have known better. She should have listened to her instincts that first night and turned Fallon in.

"You're speaking as though you know his mind. What he's thinking," she said.

"I've spent the last three months studying him. We didn't

let him know we were on to him initially. I made the decision to allow him to continue working. I wanted to find out what he was up to, if he was going to sell his discoveries to the North Koreans, or some other rogue state. I wanted to gather as much information as possible before acting. But he had us figured out from the start. Like I said, he's a genius."

"What did he do when he found out?"

"He released the virus in the compound and set fire to the onsite apartment block, where he and all the senior personnel lived, killing thirteen people." He halted there. The memories were like fresh wounds exposed to salt by an uncaring hand. After a moment he gathered himself and continued. "I ordered the lab to begin manufacturing vaccines immediately, and then I gathered the soldiers under my command and took off in pursuit. I've been playing hide and seek with him ever since. He's killed over a thousand people in three different towns by this point. I'm tired, Ms. Christianson. Very tired. I want this whole ordeal ended. So, I'll ask you again to help me find him. Please, help me end this."

She was about to answer. To tell him she would help him, when his door opened admitting a trio of armed soldiers, who immediately encircled Aldridge.

"Colonel Aldridge, I have orders to place you under arrest, sir," the MP sergeant said.

Aldridge could only blink. In the doorway behind them, Aldridge saw General Collins, wearing an insufferable smirk.

Shelly sat where she was, frozen in shock. One moment she was convinced Colonel Aldridge was the greatest monster in history, the next he was delivering shocking revelations about Martin Fallon, and now he was being arrested by his own men. Though it was hardly funny, she felt like laughing at the insanity of it all.

When Aldridge didn't say anything, the MP sergeant repeated himself, somewhat annoyed. "Sir, by order of General Collins, you are under arrest, pending investigation into your actions here and your handling of this operation."

"General Collins has issued an order for my arrest?" Aldridge's exhausted mind was slow to grasp the magnitude of what was happening. How had he lost control, just as he was beginning to take matters in hand? Just when he'd found his best chance at capturing Fallon. How had this happened? It was all so close to ending; the chase, the stress, the waking nightmare his life had become. It was all taken away from him. General Collins had seen to that. Politics had finally caught up with him. One thing Fallon had told Christianson was absolutely true, the army would string Aldridge up as a scapegoat.

The MP sergeant tensed as though Aldridge would suddenly leap at him and attempt to escape. But he didn't. Calmly, Aldridge stood and allowed the MPs to flex cuff him and lead him away. They tensed again when he stopped before the general, who was standing in the hall, watching. The two men stared daggers at each other for a few seconds, before Aldridge was nudged to continue moving.

Victory at last. Collins couldn't help but smile as Aldridge was taken away. The son of a bitch had been a thorn in his side for years and now he was going to pay for it. Seeing the pompous war hero in shackles was immensely satisfying.

*What goes around, comes around, Aldridge,* he thought, *and you've had this coming for a long time. Now to business.*

He rubbed his hands together as he turned towards the operations center. He had already sent word to the officer handling the supply runs. A convoy carrying a huge load of vaccine, as well as a thousand more soldiers, was holding position five miles from the outer quarantine ring, awaiting his signal to complete their journey into Harper's Glen. Collins had ordered them to hold up there until he gave the go ahead. At his word, they were now moving into town. Collins intended to systematically round up every single man, woman and child in town and have them vaccinated. This way there would be nowhere left for the disease to spread. While that was going on, his extra manpower would tear the town apart looking for Fallon, their little lost birdy. There was no place left for Fallon to run and hide. Not anymore.

Collins hated to admit that Aldridge had done a decent job of quickly sealing the town off. There had been little in the way of spillage this time. No small fires to put out. Just the inferno in Harper's Glen. Fallon had escaped him often enough for Aldridge to have gotten good practice containing the outbreaks. With the outer cordon in place and reinforced, Collins could systematically root the monster out, no matter where he hid. Then he'd be arrested, put on trial, and likely condemned to death, which would most likely commute to a lifetime prison sentence. The best part was that Collins himself would get all the credit for the capture and Aldridge would go down for being a failure.

In the command center, he gathered Aldridge's former staff together to lay out exactly what he had in mind.

"Listen up, people. Colonel Aldridge has been relieved of his command and I have taken charge here. We are going to flood this town with vaccines. Block by block, we are going to go through and vaccinate everyone. At the same time, we are going to search every house and structure in town for the target. We've been fucking around long enough, people; it's time to get some results and save some lives."

The officers nodded their understanding. Most of them weren't happy to be taking orders from Collins. In fact, more than a few of them thought he was a shady and underhanded son of a bitch who'd usurped Aldridge's command, but they went along because they were soldiers, he was their superior and that was how things were done.

"What's the ETA on the convoy's arrival?" he asked the sergeant in charge of the shift.

"Sir, they should be here in less than an hour. A second

convoy, carrying more vaccine, as well as MREs and ammo, is also en route and should be here later today or early tomorrow."

"Very good." He turned back to the assembled officers. "Now, does anyone have anything to add? No? Then please see Major Panelli for the details on the new phase of this operation. You know my intentions; I expect you to carry out my orders with greater proficiency than you displayed under Colonel Aldridge. Now get to work."

Fallon was shivering and miserable. Somehow, he had misread his phonebook map, gotten turned around and walked four blocks in the wrong direction before realizing the error. By now he couldn't feel his nose and his fingers were aching and his eyes were burning. The wind had picked up, cutting through his jacket to his bones. Snow fluttered down in lazy sheets, as the sun sank towards the western horizon.

Three times he had seen patrols moving down cross streets and managed to duck out of sight in time, avoiding certain capture. The ground was slick with slush and icy patches, forcing him to gingerly pick his way down the street. He was concentrating so hard on his footing, he didn't register the sound of another patrol until it was almost on top of him. They slowly pulled through the intersection ahead of him. The top gunner in the second truck leveled his machine gun directly at him, the muzzle looked like a dark and evil eye, staring into his soul, and for several paralyzing seconds Fallon thought he was going to shoot. He couldn't dodge out of sight. That would look suspicious and surely cause them to stop and investigate him. All he could do was put one foot carefully in front of the other and keep moving.

The gunner, apparently deciding he wasn't a threat, reoriented and started scanning the buildings on his side of the street. Then the truck was through the intersection and out of view. The patrol was past, the danger was gone. Fallon nearly collapsed with relief.

*Don't panic. You will be all right. If you keep moving, they won't take any more notice of you.*

"Easier said than done," he muttered.

*He is just ensuring that you mean his vehicle no harm.*

"I'm scared."

*Don't be. You will make it through this. I will provide.*

He would have been a strange sight to see, if anyone had been on the street to see him. He was shuffling down the street, wild eyes flitting everywhere, holding an animated conversation with someone only he could see. He looked like a crazy homeless man, wandering in search of a warm place to stay and wait out the storm.

"Don't give me that load of crap. You can't provide anything. You're dead. I killed you weeks ago."

*I'm dead, but I'm still here with you. I'll always be with you.*

"Shut up!"

*You think just because you decided to change your ways and repent the sins of your life that you can call me dead? That's a cop-out if ever I've heard one, my friend.*

"I don't have to listen to this. You're not real."

*I'm as real as you want me to be. Face it; you feel guilty over what you've created. That's why you're doing this.*

"I'm doing this to make a better world. Once mankind has a clean slate, we can start again. Like the flood cleansing the world and washing away its wickedness. I am the Noah. I am the ark."

*You don't really believe that. You are a man of reason. You can't really believe that one man can change the world.*

"I do. One man can change the world, if he's the only one left in it. I'm going to get free of this place. I'm going to finish my mission, and I don't need you to do it."

*You need me more than you know.*

"No. I don't. You are a terrible person. You're a scientist

with no heart and no scruples, who ignored or cast aside everything important to you. You lost what little humanity you had and sold your soul for some government esteem and pat on the head. You ran away from life when it became too complicated for you to handle and hid in your lab, unable to face the world. Even when your assistant told you about the accident, you just had to continue working. To hell with everybody else, your own wife included. I'm glad you're dead and I'm glad I killed you."

*But you didn't kill me. Not yet. We're in this together, you and me. I'm the one who's gotten you this far. You would be lost without me.*

The conversation so distracted Fallon, that he stamped into a slushy hole, instantly soaking his foot with freezing water. He swore and kicked his foot in a vain attempt to shake off the slush.

"I am finished with the past. I'm finished with your science, and I'm finished with you, Director. Because of you, the one thing I loved is gone, and I can never get her back. Leave me alone. Please. For the love of God, leave."

Nothing. No response. The Director had been with him, helping him, during the month of his exodus. Maybe longer. Fallon felt a terrible moment of doubt. It was strange to be without the reassuring voice telling him what to do next. He hated it but had always been strangely comforted by the Director in the past. He couldn't remember a time when he didn't feel like there was someone watching over his shoulder, guiding and critiquing his every action. To be free of it now made him feel truly alone for the first time.

Gathering himself, he pressed onward. Shelly Christianson's house wasn't far. Just a few more blocks. Then he'd be warm and safe, if only temporarily, and he could plan his next move.

Shelly felt out of place. The hospital she knew so well had

become foreign and hostile. Familiar faces were strangers. Everywhere she turned, she was confronted by soldiers hustling about. The sounds of the sick and dying filled the air. It was the first time she witnessed the unhappy work Fallon had committed himself to, and she hated herself for being so blindly naïve. She'd trusted a man she hadn't known. It wasn't like her. Ever since Brad, she'd held people at a distance, never let them close. Somehow, Fallon had worked his way past her defenses and convinced her he was righteous. Now that she could see what was really happening, she cursed herself.

Her only toehold on reality, Aldridge, was gone. Arrested and taken away, just as he'd started showing her how wrong she'd been. She was left alone in his office after the MPs had taken him. They didn't know who she was and so hadn't given her a second thought. It was nearly fifteen minutes before she worked up the courage to leave. Clutching the folder on Fallon Aldridge had given her to her chest like a Bible, she wandered the hospital in a daze.

She followed her feet into an emergency triage ward when someone grabbed her arm and spun her around. She instantly swung an elbow up at her assailant's face. The man holding her arm ducked under the blow and grabbed her other arm. Facing her was the young captain who had been with Aldridge when she'd been brought in.

"Don't struggle. I need you to come with me," West said.

"What do you want?"

"You're going to help Colonel Aldridge find and capture Fallon."

"Why do you think I can help him?" She was instantly suspicious. "Why *should* I help him?"

"You can help him because you've been closest to Fallon while he's been here. You are going to help me because you prolonged our mission here by assisting Fallon. Hundreds of people are dead and hundreds more are dying. If you don't want that on your conscience, you'll help." His face was a mask of determination, but his eyes betrayed the despair he felt. "Please, help us," he said. "And help yourself."

Unable to find any words, she nodded and followed him.

She could feel a palpable change in the atmosphere of the hospital. Word had spread of Aldridge's arrest and Collins' takeover. She could hear whispers of the new orders. Instead of surgical employment of force, the general wanted to swamp the little town with soldiers and firepower. He had more troops on the road to Harper's Glen that very minute, forcing their way through the drifts and unplowed roads to reach them. Any means necessary to reach the end state he desired: Fallon's capture and the end of the outbreak. Everything else was just collateral damage.

West hurried her through the crowded halls and down the central stairwell, to the parking lot. She was afraid that at any moment someone would stop them. But no one noticed. They were all too busy to see her and Captain West leaving.

After a few twists and turns, he pushed open a fire door and started down a flight of stairs, with her trailing close behind. They weren't running when they exited the door into the parking lot, but they weren't taking their time either. With no hesitation, he walked straight towards one of a dozen parked Humvees, unlocked the pad-locked driver's side door and climbed inside. Then he reached over and unlatched the passenger side for Shelly.

"They've taken him to the local jail," West said, after they left the motor pool. "We should be able to get there before they get him into lockup. Show me the quickest way from here."

Shelly almost felt like laughing. Here she was, guiding another unwelcome visitor around town. She again thought of just how insane the last week had been and how uncertain her future was. Not only was she a fugitive for aiding and abetting Fallon, but now she was going to accomplice herself in Aldridge's jail break.

*What do I have to do to have some peace and quiet?* she

thought. *I just want to be left alone.*

"Turn right up here," she said aloud.

Harper's Glen was normally a quiet, peaceful little town. Nothing out of the ordinary ever happened there. Thursday night Bingo at the church, monthly town hall meetings on the second Tuesday of every month, bake sales during the spring and summer months, a summer country music festival and harvest parade in the fall. Most teenagers thought nothing ever happened there and that the town was totally boring, and they were right. It was a boring place to live, and that was how the locals liked it. Life was simple and predictable.

It certainly made Sheriff Andy Landon's job easier. The most dangerous things he had to deal with were typically weekend drunks, speeding teenagers and hunting accidents. The predictability of small-town life suited him fine.

This morning, however, he wasn't exactly sure what to make of the situation developing in his station. Everything that had happened since the army rolled into town had been strange and far out of the ordinary, but this was pushing it. It brought to mind that ancient curse: May you live in interesting times. Landon couldn't remember if it was from China or India, but he was sure he'd had enough interesting times to last him the rest of his life.

Landon was exhausted. Ever since the army arrived, he'd been pulled in six different directions. There just weren't enough hours in the day to deal with everything that had been heaped on him. Landon worked for the county and didn't like taking orders from the soldiers that held his home hostage. He was the law in these parts, and that was the way he preferred it. He wasn't a bad sheriff, prone to abusing his authority or anything like that. He just liked the respect that came with the badge and the occasional free cup of coffee or slice of pie at Freddie's Diner. Being controlled by the military, he was no longer the only rooster in the hen house, and it grated on his nerves. So, when the switchboard operator, Lilly, called him on the radio a few minutes ago, telling him that they needed him, he returned to his station as quickly as he could.

Landon entered by the back door, barely had time to drop his coat in his chair before one of his deputies immediately found him. "You'd better hurry, Sherriff. Some bad shit's going down here." He followed his deputy, a twenty-three-year-old kid named Byron Millby, down the hall to the front desk. There he paused in mild shock.

Standing in his booking area, flex-cuffed, between two mean-looking MPs, was Colonel Aldridge, the very same man who had shut the town off from the outside world and started giving him orders.

"Well don't this beat all?" he said.

Deputy Millby nodded. "What are we going to do, Sheriff?"

Landon looked over at his deputy. *Poor kid,* he thought. *This whole ordeal has been rough on him. Almost too much to handle.* "We're gonna find out what the esteemed colonel is being charged with, and then we're gonna process him like any other perp. Just 'cause he's a big wig soldier, don't mean he's above the law."

"Yes Sheriff, but that's only part of the problem." He pointed at the two soldiers flanking Aldridge.

Landon pursed his lips. A second look at what was happening in his reception area told him that Colonel Aldridge's arrest wasn't the reason he had been called back. Millby told him that the MPs had barged into his station and immediately started ordering his people around without giving a single reason why. He could see them haranguing Lilly, and this pissed him off to no end. Due process was due process, after all, and Sheriff Landon would be damned if he let some trumped-up baby-killing soldier-boys lock a man up in his jail without giving him a reason. Furthermore, he was not about to sit by and listen to them berate and insult the people working for him.

He sauntered into the booking area where the bigger of the two MPs was giving Lilly Anderson, a forty-year-old single mother of two, a hard time. She had been putting in as much overtime as the rest of his department because of the occupation, hadn't been home to be with her kids hardly at all during the last week and didn't need to be bullied by some ignorant jarhead.

"Listen to that I'm saying, Grandma, okay? I'm not here to fill out any paperwork," the MP said. The man was tall and broad and carried himself like he was used to bossing people around. His partner was bean-pole skinny; Landon could see that even through the thick winter suit he was wearing. Too Tall continued, "I'm here to drop off a prisoner. You're going to take my prisoner off my hands so I can go back to work. I don't have time for this shit. In case you didn't know it, I have a city full of hicks to watch."

Landon kept a grip on his temper as he stepped up and asked, "What's going on, Lilly?"

"These gentlemen want us to take their prisoner into custody, Sheriff, but they're refusing to fill out the proper booking paperwork."

Landon looked up at Too Tall. "You have to fill out this paperwork, son. We can't hold him without knowing what he's charged with. This is still America. No matter what he done, he still got rights. I'm not going to imprison a man on the word of some brown shirt, without knowing why. It'll just take a few minutes so have a seat and get started. While you're doing that, I'll have Deputy Millby here take your prisoner down to the cells."

Too Tall was already shaking his head. The "brown shirt" comment hadn't upset him, so Landon figured it either went over his head, or he was just too stupid to know he'd just been called a Nazi. "Negative. I'm not filling anything out. You're going to fill out anything that needs to be filled out."

Behind him, Bean-pole was starting to shift from foot to

foot nervously. "Come on, Price. Let's just fill out the forms and go."

Too Tall swung around and stabbed a finger at his companion. "Shut the fuck up, O'Neal. I'm handling this." He turned back to Landon. "Sheriff, you don't seem to realize what's going. We're in charge here. You don't have any room to tell us shit. We tell *you* shit. Got it? This is the third pissant burg I've been through this month and I'm sick and fucking tired of you yokels trying to order me around. Now, you're going to have Deputy Fuck-Stick back there take my prisoner to your cells, Grandma Stretch Pants here is going to do the paperwork for it, and then me and my partner are going to leave and do some real work, or there's going to be some real fucking trouble. Got it?"

Landon's temper was slipping. "Son, I already told you. I will not take a prisoner into custody without due process. It's the law, you arrogant little shit. Now, if you're not going to fill out my paperwork, then your prisoner is not going to stay in my jail, and you can find somewhere else to put him."

Landon could easily have taken the prisoner and sorted the forms out later. He could have avoided the whole altercation and things could have gone smoothly. But he was tired of seeing these tin soldiers strutting around his town like they were ten feet tall and their shit didn't stink. In Landon's opinion, they were nothing more than little kids with big guns and no brains. He and his people had been disrespected by the thug in front of him and he wasn't willing to take it anymore. It was time to teach the little punk some manners.

Two more deputies had entered the booking area, standing behind and on either side of the MPs. The Bean-Pole, O'Neal, glanced nervously at them. "Price, I think we should just—"

"I said, shut the fuck up, O'Neal! You think you can boss me around, old man? Is that it? You think I'm afraid of an old piece of shit like you?"

Aldridge had held his peace up till then but saw that the situation was spiraling out of control fast and turned to Too-Tall. “Specialist Price, you’re out of line. You need to stand down.”

Too-Tall glared at him. He had his chest out and working himself up for a fight.

But Aldridge was not intimidated in the least. “I said, stand down, soldier! You need to do the right thing and let these people do their jobs.”

Too-Tall snorted. “Who the fuck are you? You’re my prisoner. You can’t give me orders anymore. You ain’t shit. I’ve got you in cuffs and you think you can still boss me around? Fuck you.” Price glanced around, noticing for the first time the other deputies in the room. A quick look of panic fluttered over his face before he turned back to Aldridge. “Bullshit!”

Lilly gave a short scream and dropped to the ground behind her desk as Price raised his weapon, flipped the selector switch from safe to semi and aimed at Aldridge. Landon, who’d had his hand on his pistol since the colonel spoke, drew first and fired in one fluid, well-practiced motion. The report was deafening. The three-fifty-seven magnum bullet stuck Too-Tall in the center of his armor vest, knocking him back and throwing off his aim. His shot went wide, missing Aldridge, even as the colonel threw himself to the floor.

Landon saw O’Neal raising his carbine to fire at him. He was about to squeeze the trigger when Millby shot him. The impact staggered him for a moment, then he refocused on the young deputy, swung his rifle around and fired wild. After shooting O’Neal, Landon watched Millby dive behind the reception desk next to Lilly, as he himself ducked back into the hallway behind him. Price fired a controlled pair in his direction. One bullet threw splinters into his face. The second bullet had torn through his Kevlar and into his stomach. His bulletproof vest wasn't rated to withstand the rifle rounds. He leaned against the wall feeling like he had been punched in the gut. Looking down, Landon saw his belly soaked in crimson.

Another one of his deputies, Morris, came running out of his office, weapon drawn, and began firing at the soldiers. A nine-millimeter round struck Price in the back armor plate, and another struck his right shoulder, knocking him forward.

O'Neal had dropped to a crouched firing position and returned fire upon Morris; all the while screaming, "Let's get the fuck out of here, Price! Let's get the fuck out of here!" He pulled the trigger again and again, and the top of Morris's head disintegrated as he was ducking for cover in another office doorway.

Both Millby and Landon popped up at the same time and pumped a dozen rounds each into O'Neal. The hard ceramic front plate of his armor shattered from multiple impacts. One bullet caught him in the neck and the other went through his armpit, between his armor plates and punched sideways through his chest cavity. O'Neal slumped to the floor with a sigh.

All the while, Aldridge was curled into a ball, forgotten at Price's feet. Hot spent brass littered the floor around him. Upon seeing O'Neal fall, Price charged the reception desk, firing as he ran. Millby was riddled with bullets when he tried to fire at Price again. He fell, sprawled over Lilly, who had been screaming in terror the whole time.

Landon took careful aim. the agony radiating outward from the bullet hole in his stomach made that difficult. His last shot punched through Price's temple. Then he slid to the floor, leaving a thick red streak down the wall behind him.

The sounds of the firefight were clear and loud outside as West entered the station, pistol in hand. Moving slowly, he crept down the hall to the booking desk. He paused at each doorway, mindful that anyone could be inside, waiting to ambush them. The scent of spent gunpowder and blood made his nose wrinkle.

He rounded a corner and drew up short at the sight of the carnage before him, just as the wounded Sheriff Landon looked up and fired. By reflex, West aimed and fired twice. Landon dropped and didn't get back up. A woman jumped up from behind the reception desk and ran out of the reception area screaming, as West crumpled against the wall, clutching his left side. He could feel hot blood pumping through his fingers as he slid down to rest on the floor. Suddenly, Aldridge and the nurse were both there, kneeling in front of him. Aldridge was looking into his eyes, telling him everything was going to be okay, while the nurse had her hands pressed into his ribs, trying to staunch the bleeding.

"Everything will be okay, West. Just hang on." Aldridge turned to Nurse Christianson. "What the hell are you two doing here?"

Shelly Christianson grunted, but was too busy working on West's wound to answer. West blinked, trying to remember. He was having trouble catching his breath and just wanted to rest a bit. He coughed once and blood sputtered from his mouth. "Brought the nurse," he managed. Aldridge looked back at him and leaned in close to hear. "A truck. Outside. Go." He pushed his pistol into Aldridge's hand. "Find him. Stop him."

Shelly had stopped working. West slid onto his side, dead. Aldridge closed his friend's eyes. He knelt there beside West's still warm corpse, with his head bowed. He didn't cry. He was too numb for that. But the loss he felt sat like a weight in his chest, preventing him from breathing. West was gone. Taken away like everything else. Heaving a deep breath, Aldridge cut away his wrist bindings, and got up. There was too much still to be done before he could properly mourn. Behind him, he could hear Sheriff Landon moaning in pain and the desk clerk in another room on the radio screaming for help. He still had a mission to complete.

He hated himself for running away, but there wasn't a moment to lose.

Outside, they jumped into the idling Humvee, Aldridge behind the wheel and Shelly in the passenger seat.

Aldridge didn't say anything for several blocks. He just wanted to get as far away as he could. After taking several twists and turns, he stopped in an alley, to make sure they weren't being followed.

Suddenly he started trembling uncontrollably. His breath came in short, shuddered gasps. Try as he might to hold them back, tears filled his eyes and spilled out. He covered his face with his hands. West was dead. It was hard to believe that was even possible. The man was tough and well-trained. He had survived three extremely difficult tours in Iraq without a scratch and was even decorated for heroism on his last one. He had been Aldridge's closest ally and most loyal officer ever since this nightmare began. Now he was gone. Dead. Everything he knew and loved and fought for was just a broken memory for other people.

"What am I going to do now?" he whispered into his hands. "What am I going to tell his wife? God help me, I don't think I can take anymore. I can't do this anymore."

They sat in the alleyway, idling, for a few more minutes. Shelly was uncomfortably trying to ignore Aldridge's sobs.

Finally, he sat up and wiped his eyes. "We should be safe for a bit," he said, as though there had been no breakdown. It was past and all he could do now was drive on and finish the job. "Now we just need to find Fallon. Nurse Christianson, where do you think he is?"

Shelly was astonished by the question. She bit her bottom lip in frustration. "I don't know."

Instead of safe and comforted, Fallon felt trapped in Shelly's house. However, there was nowhere else for him to go. Everything he tried, all his plans, had failed one by one. To make matters worse, his only supporter had fallen into the clutches of his great enemy. The Almighty alone knew what Aldridge was doing to her right this minute. The ruthless son of a bitch was probably having her water boarded to get information about him. A twinge of guilt gnawed at him over abandoning her. But there was nothing he could do. It was clear to him now if he managed to escape again, he would have to distribute his few remaining blessings at random. It took too much time and effort to befriend and convert someone, only to have them taken away by Aldridge.

He patted the case in his pocket for comfort, reassuring himself that he still had them. Three little vials remained. Three more disciples to help him do God's work, even if they didn't know they were doing it.

"I'll get away. I always have before," he said aloud to the empty house. There was no response from the Director. The walk to Shelly's had been blessedly and eerily quiet. Fallon didn't think the Director was gone for good, just sulking because he'd been insulted.

"It's just a matter of finding a way." Nothing. "I'll steal a car. A truck that can deal with the back roads and snow." Still nothing. "First, I'll warm up here, then I'll leave." He glanced at her cupboards. "Got to eat something first."

Fallon started going through Shelly's cupboards, growing more disappointed with each bare space he found. He had forgotten that there hadn't been any food during his first visit. Even her fridge was empty. An orange juice carton with a sliver remaining at the bottom and a piece of stale cherry pie were the only offerings. Without enjoyment, he feasted on this meager banquet.

With his stomach growling angrily, Fallon realized he was tired. It had been a long and eventful day.

"A short nap. Yes. Then I'll be on my way. Not too long, though. Of course, not. The Lord's work awaits. And Aldridge never sleeps." Then he wandered to the back of the house where Shelly's bedroom was.

"What do you mean you don't know?" Aldridge demanded.

Shelly shook her head and shrank back from him slightly. "I mean exactly that. I don't know where he is. We didn't exactly hit it off. We never discussed any backup plans or meeting places in case we got separated, or one of us got captured. All we talked about was how to get away from the cabin and break through the quarantine."

All the deaths, his broken marriage, the demise of his career, his arrest, the chase, and all the sleepless nights caught up with him. He felt suddenly like screaming and giving up.

*What's the use?* he thought, *Everything that matters has been taken from me.*

The game was over, and he had lost.

Out of that despair, an image of Fallon laughing at him in victory arose. Resolute, Aldridge pushed his concerns aside and focused on the only thing he had left: finding Fallon. He was the only person left in the world Aldridge cared about. He had to find him. He had to kill him.

Staring out the windshield, his eyes began drifting closed on their own. It was well past time for his pills, which were in his desk at the hospital, where they were no help at all. Struggling for control, he unclenched his hands, forced his eyes open, and in a calm and measured voice asked, "When you first met, how did Fallon find you? Why did he pick you?"

"I don't know why he picked me," she said. Seeing him on the verge of losing it frightened her. She mentally prepared herself to escape the vehicle and run if he made even one violent gesture in her direction. "He just showed up at my house after I got home from work. As for the first time I met him, that was in the hospital. He was the last patient I checked on before my shift was over. He woke briefly and we talked. I saw him for a minute. Barely even that. I don't know why he thought I was so special, or why he thought I would help him."

Aldridge frowned. "He came to your house?"

"Yeah. He broke in, scared the living shit out of me and begged for my help."

Aldridge thought for a moment. "He must have remembered your name and gotten your address from a phone book."

Shelly frowned. "I guess that's possible. When I moved back here, I meant to have my name unlisted. But by that time, the reporters had stopped calling and hounding me, so I didn't see the point."

Aldridge was lost in thought and didn't seem to be listening. He knew all about the trouble she'd had with the press. Killing her abusive husband had caused a short media circus. But he wasn't thinking about that.

"Take me to your house," he said at last. "It's one of the few places he knows. He will go there."

"How can you be sure?"

"I'm not. But he'll want someplace safe to hole up while he figures out his next move. It's the only other place in town he knows." Shelly wasn't convinced, and it must have showed. "It's as good a place to start as any. We can't sit here any longer. By now Collins has learned of my escape and will have people out looking for me."

She almost laughed. For a moment he sounded just like Fallon. Shelly pointed. "Turn right at the next street."

Aldridge put the truck in drive, and they got rolling.

Ten minutes later, they pulled into the alley behind her house. Not wanting to advertise his arrival, he cut the engine and coasted till they came abreast of her backyard.

"He broke a pane in my back door. I haven't been back since we left, so it should still be open." She briefly worried about people breaking into her home during her absence and making off with her stuff, then discarded it as a petty concern.

Aldridge checked that there was a round in the chamber

of West's pistol. "Wait here. I'll go and check it out. If I need you, I'll signal."

"You want me to wait here?" she said. "What if he's inside? You might need my help."

"Fallon is dangerous. I don't want you to risk your life any more than you already have. I have to take care of this on my own." The look in his eyes told her he wouldn't hear any further arguments on the matter. This was personal for him, and he was going to finish his mission alone. Shelly nodded. "Okay. I'll stay here."

He got out of the truck, but Shelly stopped him before he could close the door. "Be careful. I think he has my uncle's forty-five with him."

"Thanks for the heads up." Aldridge paused. "My name is Preston, by the way."

"Shelly." She tried a smile, but it felt strange, so she let it drop.

"I'm sorry this happened to you, Shelly. After everything you've been through, I'm sorry it was you he picked."

She didn't know what to say in response, so she simply said, "Good luck, Preston."

He nodded his thanks. "The way things have been going lately, I'm going to need it." He closed the door and crossed the yard to the back of her house, visibly limping as he went.

The back door was indeed open, and he could see signs that someone had been in the kitchen recently. There were footprints in the built-up frost on the floor. Inside it was cold. Colder, it seemed, than it was outside. Though the broken windowpane was small, the storms had blown a lot of snow in through it. Snow flurries and frost, coming in through the broken window, had dusted every surface.

Fallon was here. Every instinct he possessed said so. He took a slow step forward, into the kitchen. His steps crunching in the frost. His heart pounding. After all this time, Fallon was his. Pistol ready before him, Aldridge stepped further into the dark, chilly house. He wished he'd been able to get his hands on a carbine. He would have felt much better if he had superior firepower. But there was no helping it. It was time to end this long, deadly, stupid game. Both he and Fallon were out of moves; all that was left was to finish it and pack up.

He put his back against the refrigerator. During the drive, Shelly had described the basic layout of her house. He was comparing that with what he saw before him, trying to decide where would be the best place to look for Fallon. Stepping as lightly as he could, he made his way to the living room.

*What was that?* The Director's voice boomed, waking him from his doze. *Wake up!*

Fallon wasn't sure, but he thought he'd heard a noise from the front of the house. He couldn't tell if his mind playing tricks, or if there'd really been something. It wasn't a loud noise, just a slight crunch. A whisper of someone trying to be quiet in the snow.

It came again.

This time he was sure he'd heard it. *You're not alone. Get up.*

Cautiously, Fallon drew Shelly's forty-five from the back of his waistband and crept to the bedroom door, slowly opening it. His pulse pounded in his temples and cheeks. Though it was freezing in the house, his whole body was burning and a bead of sweat trickled down his spine, tickling him as it rolled.

The hall was empty.

"Am I just being paranoid, Lord?" Fallon whispered, as he sidled into the hall.

*No. Someone is here.*

"It might just have been the wind coming through the broken glass in the kitchen?" he said hopefully.

*You know who it is. You know what you must do.*

With his back against one wall, he inched towards the

main part of the house. Trying to expose as little of himself as possible, he peered into the kitchen. The back door was open. "Probably just the wind blew it open. That's what I heard."

Feeling suddenly very silly, he went to close the door. The Director was far from convinced and remained uneasy. *I'm not so sure. It didn't sound like a door swinging open, it sounded like a foot crunching snow.*

Fallon quelled him, "It couldn't have been Aldridge," he whispered. "Aldridge wouldn't sneak in. He would surround the place with a thousand troops, then firebomb it from space." The noise must have been the wind pushing open the door, magnified by his worried over tired imagination.

Stepping around the center island, he froze. A fresh set of footprints, trampling over the top of his own, led from the open door and into the living room.

*Oh, but it is Preston Aldridge.* The Director immediately started shouting. *He's found you again. He's here. He's in here with you. Now, you'll have to deal with him once and for all. If you don't, you'll never get away.*

Fallon was briefly annoyed by the sudden return of the Director. He had harbored the simple hope that the voice was gone for good. No such luck. In any case, the Director was right. It was high time that he dealt with the murderous bastard hounding him. Enough was enough.

He followed the trail of footprints into the front room. He moved as quietly as he was able, silently cursing every crunch his boots made in the snow. His eyes darted everywhere, frantically searching for the intruder. He glanced down the main hallway, just as Aldridge stepped out of the shadows by the front door foyer. Fallon didn't waste any time.

In one jerky motion, he spun and raised the gun to fire, but slipped on the frosty linoleum and fell back instead.

Shelly was shivering. The heater in the Humvee wasn't particularly good. It wheezed and rattled and blew for all it was worth, producing remarkably little heat. To distract herself from the cold while she waited, she leafed through the file on Fallon. It was incredible. The man was literally a genius, holding a doctorate in three different medical and scientific disciplines. She couldn't help but be impressed, even though she knew that he was quite possibly the most deluded and evil man she'd ever met.

She wished she had refused to listen to him and his wild story. She wished she had driven away from the gas station, leaving him inside and gone to the authorities. She wished she had shot him with Uncle Rory's gun and then reported it. She didn't know for sure how many people were dead. But she knew they were dead because she had been too cowardly to act. Because she fell for the lies and half-truths Fallon spoon-fed her. She was nearly overcome with self-loathing. She hated herself and all the choices of her life. She hated her weakness and willingness to be led around by the nose. Most of all, however, she hated Fallon for heaping this misery onto her.

She snapped the file closed, cursing herself for being duped by another man. She didn't want to think of herself as particularly naïve, but here she was again, following the bidding of another man. First Brad, then Fallon and now Aldridge. When would she learn? When would it stop?

Three loud bangs woke her from her self-pity. Sharp cracks that broke the silence of the evening.

*Gunshots,* she thought, instantly alert.

Fallon was there, inside her house. Now he and Aldridge were shooting at each other. She couldn't hear any cries of pain or shouting, and there were no more gunshots. The quiet that followed seemed just as loud to her ears. A glance at her neighbors to either side told her no one was coming to investigate the disturbance. No curtains fluttered in windows. No doors opened and no one peeked out to see what was happening. Either they were too scared of the army and the disease ripping through town to check on her, or else her neighbors had already been claimed by it and been whisked away to the hospital to die.

Thinking of her safety, Aldridge had told her to wait in the truck for him to return. Every instinct she had, reinforced by years of training and work as a nurse, urged her to investigate.

Without a second thought, she popped open the door and ran for the back door of her house.

Crouched in the living room, Aldridge heard a door down the hall open and crouched behind the sofa. It was the perfect spot. He had a view of the hall and of the kitchen back door, while remaining out of sight.

The sounds of shuffling feet told him Fallon was creeping down the hall and had entered the kitchen through the hallway entrance. A second later, a man-shaped shadow appeared and stopped by the open back door. Slowly and quietly, Aldridge stood and took aim. Suddenly, the figure spun towards him, lost its footing, and crashed to the icy floor, just as he pulled the trigger.

Fallon's ass hurt.

Everything happened in a blur. One moment he was on his feet and turning to shoot. The person in the living room was backlit by the fading light coming in from the front picture windows. He could line up a perfect shot. Then he was falling. With the sudden pivot and shift of his weight on the frosty floor, his feet lost traction and flew out from under him. Fallon landed hard on his backside, biting his tongue in the process. He heard and felt Aldridge's bullet snap above his head, barely missing him.

On his back, he quickly aimed and squeezed off two shots. He heard a grunt and saw the silhouette—Aldridge—stumble back and topple.

He was having trouble drawing breath. Felt like a horse had kicked him in the chest. How could he have missed? His target was less than ten feet from him and stationary. He had always qualified expert on the pistol range and should have been able to hit a target like that with no trouble at all. If the guys at his gun club learned of this, they'd never let him live it down. What kind of bad luck allowed Fallon to trip and fall the very instant he fired?

He coughed, spattering blood into his hand and down the front of his uniform. The droplets from his mouth joined the blood pouring from his wound. He was tired. So very tired. Should have taken his pills. Would have been more alert. Wouldn't have missed. Maybe he could take one now. No, they were back at the hospital. Can't go there. Collins will arrest him again. Can't sleep. Not yet. Too much to do. Too much to do. Fallon was right there in front of him. So close. Don't lie down. Can't afford to lie down. No strength. So tired. Time to let go. Maybe just for a minute. Eyes closed for a minute. That wasn't too much to ask. Was it? Just a rest.

Someone knelt before him. Fallon. Aldridge tried to raise the pistol, but it wasn't in his hand anymore. So instead, he raised an arm to ward Fallon off. He felt hands reaching for him. Grappling with him. Tearing at his clothes. Aldridge struggled harder. He had to get away. Where was the gun? This close there was no way he could possibly miss. Where was the gun? He had to get it so he could shoot again.

"Stop fighting me, Preston, goddamn it!"

That wasn't Fallon's voice. He'd sat through many weekly meetings, listened to all his voice notes, and followed his decline into madness, to know his voice intimately. It wasn't Fallon.

Entering her home for the first time in weeks was a surreal experience for Shelly. At first, she was shocked by how little everything had changed. To her, it seemed as though the entire world had been upended and turned inside out, but her house was the same as she had left it. She found that curiously discomfiting.

Fallon was sprawled on the floor, wide-eyed, in her kitchen. Farther into the gloom she saw Colonel Aldridge slumped over where he'd fallen in her living room. She could hear his labored breathing and rushed forward, ignoring Fallon altogether. She dropped to her knees in front of him and began removing his parka to see his wounds. Almost immediately, Aldridge began struggling against her, slapping her hands away and doing his best to keep her from helping him.

"Stop fighting me, Preston, goddamn it!" she snapped. He heard her, or at least seemed to, because he stopped struggling and calmed down enough for her to work.

She unfastened his parka and unzipped his camouflage tunic, revealing a blood-soaked tan undershirt beneath. There was a single small bullet hole in the center of his chest on the right side.

Moving quickly, she tore his shirt, examined the hole, and then rolled him towards her and found a larger exit wound on his back. Working in a calm and well-practiced rush, Shelly laid him left side, then retrieved her first aid kit from above her fridge. She cut strips of medical tape and grabbed two five-inch squares of tough plastic to seal up both wounds to stop the bleeding. If she could get him to the ER quickly, he had a chance. All she had to do was control his bleeding and shock.

"Stay with me, Preston," she said, roughly patting him on the cheek to keep him awake. "We're almost done. We've got to get you to the hospital to fix you up. Just stay with me until then, and we'll get through this."

"So tired," he whispered. "Tired. Can't sleep. Not yet. He's right here. Behind you."

Aldridge was fading. His breathing was shallow. His skin was cool and clammy. Shelly thought his right lung might be filling with blood but didn't have any way to stop it. They needed to get him to the ER right away if he was going to make it. She thought about calling an ambulance, but her phone was still in her Bronco back at the Varney farm. She stood, looking around for something to help her carry him out to the truck. There was a throw blanket over the back of the couch. If she could roll him onto it, she thought she might be able to drag him to the truck.

The report from the gunshot startled a scream from her. Before her eyes, the top of Aldridge's head disintegrated and splattered across her far wall and front door.

"I was waiting for you to move," Fallon said, the forty-five smoking in his hand. She couldn't speak. At her feet Aldridge lay dead, a bloody hole in the center of his forehead.

Shelly just stared in disbelief. "You killed him," she said. "I could've saved him. I had already controlled the worst of his bleeding. I just needed to get him back to the hospital."

Fallon had been staring at Aldridge's corpse and he looked up at her. "I know. That's why I killed him. He never would have stopped. He would have hunted us forever. Don't you see? By saving him, your good intentions would have condemned us both. Now we're free."

She felt for a pulse. Checked his breathing. Pupil dilation. He was dead.

"This is fortunate for us," Fallon continued. "With his death, the rest of them will be momentarily confused. We can get away. We can continue our holy war. I'm so glad you brought him here. I don't know how you managed it or what you said to lead him here alone, but well done. Well done! You came back to me. Do you see what this means? It means that we are truly on the side of the angels. The lord has blessed us both, and He will see us through to the end."

*What is he saying?* Shelly thought. *Does he really think I'll go with him? Does he believe that I'll trust him?*

"You and I will cleanse the earth. Using God's own body,

we will rinse the land clean of sin, like the great flood. We will recruit others to our cause and start humanity anew."

On and on he went, sounding more insane with every word uttered. Though Shelly had stopped listening, that didn't stop him from sermonizing. It was almost as though he were trying to reaffirm his own conviction in what he was doing. *He's talking more to hear himself,* she figured, *than to convince me.* Shelly simply sat on her knees in front of Aldridge's lifeless body, letting him prattle on without responding. Her arms and chest were speckled with Aldridge's blood and bits of brain. Tears flooded her eyes, blurring her vision. She'd fallen in with another insane, manipulative asshole. Why did this keep happening to her? She looked up. Fallon had stopped talking and was looking at her.

She cleared her throat. "I'm sorry," she said. "What were you saying?"

Fallon smiled, as though he were speaking to a dear, but slow-witted child. "I was saying we need to leave now. Your neighbors will have heard those gunshots. Doubtless the authorities will be on their way by now."

"Of course, you're right. We should be going." He wouldn't let her go this time. She would not be free of him. She had no choice but to go with him, to help him with his scheme. Thousands would die now. Maybe even millions.

Fallon held out a hand to help her up. Shelly ignored it and stood up on her own. He turned from her and started for the back door. "We'll take the colonel's truck. We might even be able to sneak through the quarantine cordon with it. This is our chance to get away clean."

As Shelly gathered herself up to leave, Fallon was already heading through the door. If there was a way out this time, she couldn't see it. Fallon had won and she had helped. The world's best chance to stop him lay dead before her. It was hopeless. Tears of regret streaked her cheeks. She felt ashamed that she had allowed herself to be duped by such a monster.

That's when she saw it.

Her eyes went wide, and a small, sudden smile spread across her lips. Clear as day, Shelly saw her way out.

It was so simple. She could do it. She'd done it before.

She had no other choice. It would just take a moment, then she would be free again. With no hesitation, she took the solution in hand and went outside. Fallon was waiting by the open driver's door of Aldridge's Humvee, arms at his sides, face upturned to the sky heavy with black snow laden clouds, a look of serenity on his face.

*Rapture,* she thought. *That must be what rapture looks like.*

Resolute, she went around to the passenger side of the truck and got in. Uncle Rory's forty-five sat on the radio mount between the front seats, within Fallon's easy reach.

She closed her door and buckled her seat belt.

Once Fallon was inside, he turned to her. "Together we will be unstoppable. You're doing the right thing, Shelly Christianson," he said, smiling again. Victory had made him smug.

Shelly smiled back, "I know."

She raised Aldridge's pistol and shot him point blank, twice in the chest and once in the face. He tumbled out the open door and onto the ground beside the truck.

Her ears rang as she got out and circled around to him. She reached down to check for a pulse. Finding none, she left both handguns behind in the truck and went back inside her house.

No matter what else happened, at least she had stopped him. Fallon was dead. Her nightmare was over. She could get back to picking up the pieces of her life. In the distance she could hear sirens approaching.

It started snowing again as she went back inside her house and closed the door.

# About Atmosphere Press

Atmosphere Press is an independent, full-service publisher for excellent books in all genres and for all audiences. Learn more about what we do at atmospherepress.com.

We encourage you to check out some of Atmosphere's latest releases, which are available at Amazon.com and via order from your local bookstore:

*Saints and Martyrs*, a novel by Aaron Roe

*The Recoleta Stories*, by Bryon Esmond Butler

*Voodoo Hideaway*, a novel by Vance Cariaga

*The Weed Lady*, a novel by Shea R. Embry

*A Book of Life*, a novel by David Ellis

It Was Called Home, a novel by Brian Nisun

Grace, a novel by Nancy Allen

*Shifted*, a novel by KristaLyn A. Vetovich

*Because the Sky is a Thousand Soft Hurts*, prose by Elizabeth Kirschner

*Stronghold*, a novel by Kesha Bakunin

*Unwinding the Serpent*, a novel by Robert Paul Blumenstein

*All or Nothing*, a novel by Miriam Malach

*Eyes Shut and Other Stories*, by Danielle Epting

*The Heroic Adventures of Madame X*, a novel by A. R. Gross

# About the Author

Bryan McBee lives in Boise, Idaho, with his wife and daughter. After serving in the US Army, Bryan attended Boise State University, where he graduated in 2018.

CPSIA information can be obtained
at www.ICGtesting.com
Printed in the USA
LVHW050113080422
715626LV00006B/1031

9 781637 528822